AMERICAN

A Novel

BLUES

Polly Hamilton Hilsabeck

SHE WRITES PRESS

Published 2022
Printed in the United States of America
Print ISBN: 978-1-64742-077-2
E-ISBN: 978-1-64742-400-8
Library of Congress Control Number: 2021915646

For information, address:
She Writes Press
1569 Solano Ave #546
Berkeley, CA 94707

She Writes Press is a division of SparkPoint Studio, LLC.

All company and/or product names may be trade names, logos, trademarks, and/or registered trademarks and are the property of their respective owners.

This is a work of fiction. Names, characters, places, and incidents either are the product of the author's imagination or are used fictitiously. Any resemblance to actual persons, living or dead, is entirely coincidental.

As a form, the blues is an autobiographical chronicle of personal catastrophe.

—FROM RALPH ELLISON'S REVIEW
of Richard Wright's *Black Boy*

BOOK 1

Almighty God created the races white, black, yellow, malay, and red, and he placed them on separate continents. And but for the interference with his arrangement there would be no cause for such marriages. The fact that he separated the races shows that he did not intend for the races to mix.

—Virginia trial judge Leon M. Basile from his 1959 opinion on Richard and Mildred Loving's violation of the state ban on interracial marriages

He took a hundred pounds of clay,
And then He said
Hey listen
I'm gonna fix this-a world today,
Because I know what's missin'
Then He rolled his big sleeves up and a brand-new world began
He created a woman and-a, lots of lovin' for a man.
Whoa-oh-oh, yes, He did.

THE SUMMER OF 1961 SOUNDED the sentimental notes of Gene McDaniel's hit song and drummed the urgent beats of Freedom Riders' chant, as twelve-year-old Lily dipped her fries in ketchup, looked up at the Pepsi clock, and wondered where she'd be ten years from now. At the Lone Oak in Greenville, Texas, still listening to the men talk about their projects and work for the day, throwing out wisdom like café philosophers as they chewed on cheeseburgers and fries?

Maybe these were honest men doing an honest day's work, but she didn't like them. They were loud and took up the whole space wherever they were. They presumed their place.

It was hot here. Always hot. The red-faced men with beard stubble had rings of sweat under their arms where the salty toil of their bodies met the cotton of their T-shirts.

They were frightening with their mansmell and talk of agency. What they would and wouldn't do. And if *they* ever caught one of them boys lookin' at their little girl, they'd cut his balls off and feed 'em to the hogs.

They talked like that and all agreed. Heads nodding. A race club. Charter members renewed their credo over cheeseburgers and fries and a twenty-five-cent cup of black coffee poured into heavy pink mugs.

Their own skin was burnt and browned by the same sun as those straying-eyed boys they talked about, while sucking and poking around with toothpicks. She had no doubt they would pursue anyone who broke their rules with the same intensity they used to pick bits of cheeseburger out of their teeth.

What if it weren't their own little girl? It wouldn't matter; they'd go after whoever looked at anybody's little girl wrong. Especially if Black.

Lily presupposed safety with her own father. She was real little when the foreman showed up at her house to report her father's forklift accident. Her mother was just taking down a pair of her dad's overalls when the man with the mirrored glasses slowly strode up the bits of cement that was the Wallaces' front walk. No shade tree to hide under. No place to hide, period.

The only shade was in the living room with its World War II surplus couch, a rocking chair that her gramma had rocked her mama in, and fake flowers stuck in a dusty glass vase with peeling paint.

The curtains keeping out the hot afternoon sun were too heavy to be hanging in the house. Drawn, the house felt like a prison. Lily preferred to be outdoors; indoors was only tolerable at school, where she could observe others.

Other than her mom's cooking, which filled the house every Sunday and lingered for the rest of the week, Lily hated the house.

Lily was curious about what was inside other houses that made her mother so fearful. "Don't go there, Lily. Stay away from there. Keep away from those people, Lily. They're trash.

Don't be associating with trash. You're better than that. No Wallace has ever been trash, and we're not starting now."

There must be "trash" at school. Lily pondered her class and the contradictions of being a Wallace living in Greenville. Her teacher Miss Petty was fat, but not ugly. The smell of her face made Lily curious about womanhood.

WHEN THE AVON LADY CAME around, she spent a couple of hours, even though her mother only ordered a lipstick or a bottle of cologne every now and then. It didn't seem to matter to Claudi's mother. She was a businesswoman second, a neighbor first. If she made a little bit of change, that was extra. Her husband, like Lily's dad, made enough for the whole family and didn't count on what his wife Flo might bring into the Stamp family kitty.

More or less, selling Avon gave Flo something to do during the day, which gained her entry into the lives of the other women of Greenville, Texas. She got to see how the other wives did with what they had, and she prided herself on her subtlety in finding this out.

A recipe exchanged might reveal the existence of a social life. News about a family's health was always a rich source of information, especially if it included whether another baby was on the way, and if not, the why or how come of it.

The women shared their encyclopedic knowledge of the world as they knew it, and the world expanded with each encounter so that the size of the house didn't matter, so much as the temperament of the meeting over coffee and cinnamon twists.

There were shades of brown and maroon in Mrs. Stamp's demonstration kit not found on any female faces that Lily saw on the glossy sample panels.

"This is a nice shade, Lucille. Yeah, this is your color, honey," Flo would say to her mom as she applied some to the backside of Lucille's wrist.

"You get some nice foundation now, and then some powder—you'll be lookin' so pretty," Flo oozed. "You keep that man wonderin' beyond the grits in his stomach, 'Who is this fine lady I married?'" Flo would tease and cajole, thinking herself more of a love life consultant than a cosmetics peddler. "He'll be figurin' he got a good deal marryin' y'all, Lucille Wallace."

Taking the bold step of applying some of her wares to one side of her neighbor's face and handing her a mirror, Flo would ask, "So whaddya think?"

Lily's mom would grin like she'd been caught doing something grown up and scary and was now asked to justify herself. "Well, I don't know," she would say. But it wasn't the applied color she didn't know about.

Lucille Wallace considered whether or not she should spend money on what was neither food nor cleaning agent. She came to her senses, as if she had stepped out of a movie theater into the squinting light of day, weighing what she should do. It wasn't really right to spend Frank's money on something she might only use for special occasions, but even more telling, would it make him suspicious, fixing herself up like that? Was she fixin' to leave him? Frank would want to know.

Color on her face could invite an unwanted scrutiny of her everyday life, with Frank studying her and every repairman, grocery clerk, butcher, and Sunday School superintendent with whom she came in contact to see if there might be something going on behind his back.

At the other end of the spectrum was Lucille's fear that making up her face could lead to unwieldy attention from a husband who was way past being her boyfriend. Frank first noticed Lucille when she was sixteen but had to wait another year before he was allowed to take her on a date. To be asked out was a thrill then, even if it was only to church and back. Seventeen years gone, she wasn't sure she welcomed or could accommodate the thrill of ardor now.

Lucille wondered where those worldly women whose faces peopled Flo Stamp's laminated foldouts came from, and how they had the courage to be an Avon model seen by hundreds of women everywhere. Lucille shuddered, glad that she would never have to be in the public eye as an ideal of feminine looks.

"Well, I don't know," Lucille continued, now ruminating about who her daughter might grow up to be and if she were the right mother for her.

Maybe Lily needed her to buy what the Avon lady was selling, something more than a pack of wieners. It would last a long time. It could last her whole lifetime. Besides, the bottle was pretty, and she'd like to put something pretty and distinguishable as hers on the Formica countertop in the bathroom, more intimate than the Formica countertop in a kitchen that belonged to everyone. One day Lily would need something of her own, reasoned Lucille as she came to a decision, relieved that her purchase at this point had a maternal, and, therefore, loftier purpose.

"Well, why not," Lily remembered her mother to say, breezily laughing and tossing her hair, mocking her prior ambivalence as if it were a lapse rather than the constant state of her being.

"I think you'll be pleased." The words gushed through the space between Flo's front teeth. "Real pleased."

Lily would wait until the session's conclusion before asking if Mrs. Stamp could spare one of the stubby testers of pale pink lipstick.

Flo Stamp had been proud of her accomplishments as an entrepreneur. Moreover, she had a sense of calling, as she incorporated strategies from *The Avon Lady's Visit* picked up from the district supervisor. Get them talking. Get them dreaming. Get them pretending they're backstage about to go on to play the role of their lives.

Flo Stamp believed in her soul that she brought something extra to the lives of her customers; talking neighbor women into buying her wares of lotion and shampoo, rouge and powder came after first talking their dreams into being. Flyaway talk between the conjurors was a sweet potion in the middle of the day when women were shelling peas or hanging out the wash or repairing a hem on a dress that wasn't yet ready for the ragbag.

Flo's own juices would run when she located herself at a kitchen table, opened the flaps of her faux leather case, and began the summoning of dreams. The colored contents of bottles and tubes of lipstick had a smell all their own, recalling the stuff of adolescent fantasy, where most of the dreaming had ended for Flo and her coconspirators.

Whether or not they bought anything, Flo could get neighbor women to pilot their own planes. Whose life would change today? Flo did not know but could only hope to be the catalyst, as she arose each morning to wash and put color on her face before reviewing the contents of her case and setting off for another neighborhood of stay-at-homes who read articles in *Ladies Home Journal* and ordered items for their household from the Sears catalogue.

The Avon lady's stopping by was a matter of utility for wives as well as husbands, though with one important difference: the wife thought it an event to be reported; the husband, as uninteresting a mention as a trip to the market or kids getting their booster shots.

IT COULD HAVE BEEN A BAR. Two men with too much to drink start throwing punches and one pulls out a knife. One is left standing. Another bleeds to death on the floor, while the bartender calls an ambulance. Everyone knows or thinks they know how it went down.

The fight is over a woman. One man with no business even being there looks at another man's woman wrong, like he wanted to do her. Doesn't think about anything else but his swaggering self—all packaged in the look which he put on the woman with sparkly eye shadow and greasy red lips.

If not a bar, it could have been a bedroom. Same two men, one not the husband of the wide-hipped, greasy-mouthed woman. Rage pulls the trigger, killing the man on top of the other man's wife just after he whispers *Baby, oh sweet baby* in her gold dangled ear and leaves his sweat on the sheets of the bed that is not his.

If not a woman, it could have been something else taken. Caught in the act of stealing, his brother pops him and puts him in his grave saying, "You won't never do that to me again. Never again, you goddamn hear?" But the man can't hear because he's dead, and he won't ever take what doesn't belong to him again, either.

But it was not another man's woman or another man's goods that got Sam Jefferson killed. Not exactly. It wasn't a smoky drop-by-for-a-drink place or another man's trespassed bedroom that Sam's eyes saw last.

Sam was caught like prey and removed from his own bedroom in his own house. In a wilder, overgrown place, venom and dirty insults accompanied accusations of crimes he didn't commit. A rope was slung, and Sam's head was stuffed through a noose.

The frenzied hands that last touched Sam's head smelled of raw fish, and piss sprayed over his naked body by those who exploited the cover of night to take a Black man out to die.

AFTERWARD THE YOUNG KILLERS OF the American dream mistook despair for jubilation, surrounding the lynching with cheap talk and warm beer. Hunting rifles cradled at their sides, they fired occasional shots into the night sky, exploding bits of branch and spring leaves that fell back on their sad, laughing heads.

They would not be subject to current civil rights legislation from a bunch of goddamn hypocrites who knew, just as their uncles and fathers before them, that the only way to keep the Black man in check was to hang him.

Policing the boundaries of race was a matter of rightful heritage and racial superiority. The success they experienced in keeping those boundaries in place seemed a confirmation of their entitlement, only recently called into question by fools sowing tares in fields of southern tradition.

THE REVEREND WILLIAM KNOLL FINCH III was not a pleasant man. He was a righteous man. He grew up breathing privilege by way of breeding and economic status.

His father, William Knoll Finch Jr., owned land worked by Black families who, after the Emancipation Proclamation, declared their freedom but came to know sharecropping as just another of the slavery medusa's ugly heads.

As soon as it could be loosed from her curled hands, W. K. Finch Sr. inherited the land from his mother, who died when he made the age of majority.

A place of conception and birth for prior generations of Randolphs, the land became the securing base of Finch family ambition, which expanded to manufacturing with William Sr.'s quest for new sources of capital. From field to factory, Finch Sr. had control of both raw material and finished product.

The demand for cordage on farms as well as ships made the senior Finch a wealthy man. Where his fellows were tentative, Finch was robust. He spurned notions of prudent investment in hard times and instead poured money into the system he helped create.

Finch Jr. inherited both his father's genius and his recklessness, but in different proportions. Having the right investments in the midst of the stock market crash, he experienced no Great Depression in the thirties.

Life continued in affluence, such that his son would be in a position to maintain, or even increase, the family's prosperity.

It was not to be, however, as the father wished. William Finch III would not carry on the family social order of land ownership and venture capital with new enterprises.

Billy went to war, and when he returned, repacked his bags for the seminary. His eyes had seen something of America no opportunity had before afforded him.

In the dark of a bunker with all manner of men, Billy saw in the flashes of light produced by crossfire, an America at war with itself. It was a terrible light that found young Billy Finch that night. As he lay hiding from the enemy on another continent, he saw, revealed, the enmity of brothers at home.

———

THE RECTOR OF ST. LUKE'S Episcopal Church did not know how long the dirty scrap had been on the altar. He did not know what hand had torn the piece of brown bag and taken up pencil to scrawl over the paper fragment like a snake on its belly, nor the acolyte that carried and placed the declaration of hateful triumph on the altar as an oblation of white supremacy. He suspected some who might act as tutors, those practitioners of racial segregation who deemed murder an ultimate test of loyalty, though unwilling to do the deed themselves.

The Reverend William Knoll Finch III's head felt like a bell tower with tones pounding tones, clanging overlapping clanging, urgently summoning generations of white mothers and fathers to gather and be judged. On their knees, now, he saw them encircling the altar, hands raised, wailing and crying out for forgiveness from another realm.

In the darkest watch of the night when he felt most alone, their torment was like a visitation of grace. His mouth as dry as the psalmist, his bones as broken and scattered as the prophet, Finch was in the company of church members and clergy who had gone on before, smugly certain of their place in heaven as on earth, whose eyes could now see what would not be seen before.

The Reverend Finch assumed that the smudged, grinning note on the altar was for him to find in the stunned silence of the church after doing what he could to help Cyrl Jefferson and her children take their shock and a few clothes to the home of her sister after the police were too late to keep the peace just outside Greenville that night.

The minister of the church of St. Luke the Physician was, indeed, the first one to see the dung of the cowardly beast that howled in the shadows. The note and deed, however, were addressed to a larger audience. The filth that lay on the altar signaled alarm to the entire congregation: the segregating beast stalked them as well, tearing human flesh from their flesh, and human bone from their bone.

CYRL COULD NOT MAKE SENSE of what had just happened. Her sister Pearline and husband Lester each took an arm to hold her up, as they dug her out of the chair at a neighbor's and led her to their idling station wagon.

In the middle of the night, it was the end of the world. Cyrl could not go back and sleep in the imprint and smell of Sam. Their bed now had a loathsome odor, a lingering repugnance invading floorboards and walls that would not yield to cleansing and time.

Looking back at what was no longer her house, the teeth clattering and shaking began again. Cyrl's body contorted and moved in ways that could not be quieted, ever since the police came, siren announcing their approach from miles away, red light flashing, headlights piercing the next-door neighbor's living room, heavy boots on the doorstep.

The police tried to question her, but Cyrl could not speak. Terror seized and spun her insides, wringing life from her clenched body and her mind careened brakeless into every memory of her beloved, leaving its jumbled wreckage inside her tortured head.

Cyrl could only form images with no words to describe the pointed white heads which grunted shameful things about her good Sam and rooted in the house that used to belong to them.

Even if she survived the next minute, Cyrl did not think she would survive the next hour. She felt the rough hands that shoved her and grabbed her husband. She heard the crack of the baseball bat meeting Sam's shins, saw him trying to stand, saw the cords of his neck constrict in pain, his eyes searching the faces of his wife and each of his children before he was dragged out the door, holding in his cries of pain for the sake of the children.

Cyrl heard her own voice repeating, "Daddy'll be okay. Look away to God. Look away now. Look away."

But Cyrl's last look would not be away. If God were anywhere, better be in the face of her Sam.

Why did the wind blow like it did, leaving its deposit of horror at their house? Why did it not pass over their family, their generation who dared to dream and know their dreams in the daylight?

Pearline, who could not sleep either, entered the bedroom quietly to check on her baby sister. She found Cyrl curled in on herself and shivering, even though she was covered in blankets. Pearline asked if she could get her anything, but Cyrl did not know what to ask for.

"Oh, my poor girls," she moaned. "Oh, my poor Sam. They never could've gotten him out of the house if they hadn've broken his legs. Pearline, they took a bat to Sam's legs like an ax to a tree. They would've had to shoot him. He would not go. He would not go and leave us."

"That's right, baby girl," cooed Pearline as she stroked Cyrl's head and cheek.

"They tried to bring him low," said Cyrl, "but they can't. They don't have him. They won't ever have him."

The following day, officers came to her sister's home to notify Cyrl that her husband had been found dead. Apparently, they said, from strangulation.

LILY HAD PLANNED TO SPEND all day at Riverside Church in a consortium meeting, hashing out plans for an interfaith service for Yom Hashoah—the day of remembrance of the Holocaust—when the pastor of First Lutheran came in late with news of the lynching.

"Black man in his thirties with a wife and kids was hauled out of bed by the Klan and strung up in the woods just outside of town. Happened about 10 p.m. Wife's shrieking woke up a neighbor who finally called the cops, but by the time they got to the house and wrote up a report, the deed was done."

Silence. Eyes passed a shock wave from one to another around the table. A collective breath was sucked in and then discharged in an eruption of questions and expletives.

"Jerry, where did it happen?"

"It was, I think, South Carolina. Yeah, yeah, it had to be South Carolina just outside of Mapes, a tiny town somewhere in South Carolina. I don't know. I've never heard of it. Anybody here from that part of the country?"

"North Carolina, but I don't know South."

"Oh my God! This is 1973! What the hell is going on there?"

"Who is he?"

One of Riverside's support staff stuck her head in the door, "Lily, phone's for you."

"Excuse me. I'll be right back." Lily guessed it was her boss Hugh Lovelle, the current Executive Officer serving with the Presiding Bishop (PB).

"Lily? Me, Hugh. I have some terrible news. A lynching reported to have happened last night in South Carolina. . . ."

"Jerry Slocumb was just telling us. My God. How did you hear?"

"Gray Temple, bishop there, called. He's one of ours."

"What do you mean 'one of ours'?"

"Man by the name of Sam Jefferson was the sexton at St. Luke's, Greenville. Midsized parish. Sam and his family live in a little town on the outskirts. Klan took him from his home. Parishioners are all being informed now by phone tree. There's a meeting set up at the church tonight. I think you and I ought to be there. The PB isn't due back from Jerusalem till Tuesday."

"Right, right. He left yesterday." A sensation of breeze and hot summer gardenia smell and southern dirt started swirling around Lily's head. "When can we leave?"

"It's two now. Deidra is checking flights. I'll call you back as soon as she finds something. Oh, and Lily, how's it going there—the planning, I mean?"

"Fine. It's just such a curious juxtaposition of genocide. I'm wondering what it even means to be an American or a Christian in America . . . I can't imagine. I can't even imagine. I'm trying to picture the wife. Any kids?"

"Three girls."

"God have mercy." The next moment stood still, not making a sound.

"Lily?" Hugh had to go looking for where it was hiding.

"Anyway," she muttered, "get back to me and I'll start winding up here."

The words "one of ours" kept crashing around in Lily's head, as she left messages for the next day's appointments. Simultaneously, she roughed out a revised schedule for the pool secretary in the office of the PB and her boss.

"YOU MADE IT." **HUGH CONSULTED** the digital clock above the counter.

"Yeah, the traffic wasn't all that bad and the cabby jammed. Thank God. He heard the story and wanted to do what he could to help. Whew. Yeah, I made it."

"Catch your breath."

"Sorry about the earlier flight. There was just no way I could get my stuff together by then."

"No problem. Good hustle. The important thing is that you made it. I got us booked on a flight into Atlanta and from there we'll take a jumper to Greenville. Ever been to South Carolina?"

"No. I grew up in Texas but didn't really see much of the rest of the country till I went off to college. What time is the meeting at St. Luke's?"

"The rector, Bill Finch, was aiming for a service at seven. People have been in and out of the church all day. They set up a prayer vigil, both at the church and at the Jeffersons' home."

"Sounds like they've had some experience."

"Unfortunately. St. Luke's gave a lot of support to civil rights workers in the sixties."

"They mixed?"

"Still mostly white, but they've come a long way, mostly due to Finch. He's been there a long time."

"Are Sam Jefferson and his family members?"

"Technically, no. Practically, yes."

"You said they have three girls?"

"Age seven and under."

"My God. What would your kids do if they saw you taken away?"

"Same as you, I imagine, if the Klan came for your daddy in the middle of the night."

"This whole history of violence. It's like exploding shrapnel. The pain has to be lodged in every American whether they realize it or not. How can life just go on when something like this happens?"

"People, Black and white, have mouths to feed, family to care for—and, yet, some do become martyrs."

"I feel like an outsider coming to pay respects."

"We're both outsiders."

"But I'm the white one who flung her southern roots out the window on the way to the Big Apple."

"Texas 'southern' may not be the same as South Carolina 'southern.'"

"So I heard growing up—and why I avoided anything in the South outside of Texas."

"And do you find New York the hallmark of social revision and Constitutional justice for all?"

"New York has its share of drug babies and unemployment, or maybe it's *dis*employment, but to date, I haven't read about any lynchings in *The Times*."

"When James Baldwin named 'another country,' he wasn't talking South Carolina-South or even Texas-South. He lived in Europe as a refugee from New York City."

Lily wished for some disguise to throw over her ignorance, but then admitted simply, "Perhaps, I have a lot to learn."

Her mentor caught the words like they were precious and fragile, and in a gentle voice said, "You and I have more in common than meets the eye."

THE BLACK MAN ACCOMPANYING A younger white woman had, indeed, caught the eye of the waiting area. Some stared hard like judges presiding over criminal proceedings; others imagined a Harlequin romance and hoped to be seated near the couple to continue their page-turning.

"It looks like we're boarding," said Hugh, as the counter attendant flipped the flight numbers. "Do you just have the one carry-on?"

"Lots of baggage," joked Lily, "but, yeah, only one that goes in the overhead."

Then suddenly, the purpose of the trip reasserted itself and threatened to cut off her breath. Lily gasped to Hugh, "I don't know what we can say to Mrs. Jefferson and her girls and the people at St. Luke's."

"We won't, Lily," coached the gray-haired man in clericals. "We're there to listen to what *they* have to say. And to pray with them for the peace that passes understanding."

———

THE SPEAKER VOICE ANNOUNCING THE departure made their mission official. While attending to the practical matters of transportation to the airport and delegation of tasks to others for the days she would be gone, Lily could easily force the reality of the trip back down in her gut.

Now, waiting for her row to be called, the strangeness of the formal request for *pastoral accompaniment* by the national office from a bishop of the Church limned a threshold.

Before the evening was over, Lily would be in the land of strange fruit. She felt unequipped for what lay ahead, as if she had been asked to pilot the plane herself.

Reviewing the afternoon rush of putting a plan in motion for life to proceed in her absence, Lily found that life wanting. A new measure of what was important had just extended its hand to Lily, and hers went limp.

Despite the attendant calling out rows, people crowded as if the gate were the only exit from a burning building. *And it's only Tuesday*, Lily thought, her work week a blur.

Halfway down the ramp, the physicality of bodies and briefcases bumping into one another brought the week back into focus, and Lily realized that it was Friday and the end of the week, after all. The last bit of fresh air sneaked in at the seam between the accordion-pleated tube and the jet door, which could have been the hatch of a manned space module for all Lily knew about what lay ahead.

"What seat, please?" Even though assigned, passengers stampeded to secure their seat and overhead compartment space first, marking their territory with grips and satchels and whatever else they deemed essential for travel between one speck on the earth and another.

GOING TO THE SOUTH FELT to Lily like a foreign junket, but with no passport required. She wondered how many on board made the South their home and were returning from business in New York or to see family get married or buried, and how many were expatriates on their way back to the Old Country for just a visit, hoping it was evident how much they had changed from when they first knocked the southern dirt from their shoes and headed North.

These émigrés, careful to maintain the mystique of the North lest friends and family belittle their move above the Mason–Dixon line as nothing more than a shift from one rabbit hole to another, would not let on that the same old dog of segregation hounded them, just less officially.

Unhappy about staying, but too afraid to leave, relations still in the South were in good company occupying the same pews that their mothers and grandmothers had sat in as they fanned the preacher's words away to the next person, lest the Almighty's word land on them. Not now; not at this time. Don't want to get right with the Lord just yet.

The Holy Spirit knows where it wants to land and which tongues need to be loosed. The bodies that are folded up and packed in boxes of "yes ma'am" and "no sir" the other six days of the week are invited to dance and stumble with nobody bothered by somebody studying their business.

He saves the good wine till last. Yes, He does. The good wine for the people that harvested the grapes, neither trampling nor tasting, prematurely, the fruit of the vine.

Good people trusted that the Hand they looked to for strength today was the same Hand that held back the waters of destruction in Moses's time and more recently Martin's, when fire hoses turned on dark skin.

NIGHT DREW ITS SHADE OVER the day, and the corporate lives of scheduled ministry that Lily and Hugh knew in Manhattan were left behind to minister to an old wound freshly opened. Once more, American civility ruptured, exposing raw edges of humanity with seemingly little prospect of ever finding a suture strong enough to join what might be healed and fed by new arteries of common blood.

———

LILY WAS NOT EXPECTING TO hear Jesse Colin Young and the Youngbloods crackle over the sound system at an airport in South Carolina:

> *Come on people now, smile on your brother*
> *Everybody get together*
> *Try to love one another right now . . . right now . . .*
> *right NOW.*

She was also unprepared for the weather coming down in sheets, as she and Hugh dashed to the rental car parked two rows over from the protective covering of the Avis building.

In speech peppered with "y'all" and "hon," the woman at the counter asked if they would like an upgrade. The man ahead, whom she suspected of cheating on his wife said, "No thanks. The compact will do fine."

The woman savored the mystery of a Yankee couple coming to her counter, making her a part of their business in Greenville, South Carolina, whatever that business might be. She wondered if it had anything to do with the man they found hanging in a tree earlier that morning.

WHEN THEY FINALLY ARRIVED at St. Luke's, the Evening Prayer service was already underway. The wind kept the door open after they entered, and all heads turned to see what had blown in. The Episcopal congregation looked like a slightly wealthier cousin to the one in Texas where Lily had grown up.

Both Easter and the funereal occasion dictated church furnishings to be draped in white. The vestments did their best to dress up the harshness of the night and the heinous crime that called parishioners of St. Luke's to prayer, but, to Lily, the altar had never looked more like a sarcophagus.

Beneath its drape of embroidered brocade, Lily imagined Sam Jefferson lying inside and pronounced these parishioners, in some way, guilty. Then, looking around the nave at faces familiar as a family reunion, Lily panicked, as disjunction gave way to kinship, and disengagement to complicity.

LILY REMEMBERED BEING CALLED "NIGGER-LOVER" by kids on the playground, only the way they said it was like she loved dirt or feces. It was because of her friend, Delicia, who would come by with her daddy.

Maybe it would be a Saturday morning, and Delicia's daddy had some extra firewood to drop off. Or maybe he had a special kind of drill that Lily's father needed for a project.

Delicia always had a doll with her, so Lily would get hers. The dolls talked like their caretakers, as they went play-shopping together and to the beauty shop. They bought mostly the same grocery items, but at the salon Delicia's doll put Vaseline in her hair.

"Why does LaTonya use that?" Lily wrinkled her nose in disgust. "My grammie uses that, but she's old."

"I 'on't know," said Delicia. "Just 'cause."

Imagining what it would be like to have thick braids like her friend, Lily always asked if she could comb and rebraid the ropy hair; Delicia always said yes.

Other children in the neighborhood noticed the brown truck on the Saturday morning visits and started name-calling. Lily thought they were jealous, but, also, correct in that she did love Delicia, although *nigger* was not a word used in the Wallace house; Lily's family called them *darkies*.

Considering the different shades of people and how some were about as dark-skinned as a white person with a Texas tan, Lily thought the term flawed. She did see a real difference, though, in the way a naturally pecan-colored girl was treated versus one whose color came from sitting in the sun with a timer.

WHEN HUGH AND LILY STEPPED through the red doors of St. Luke's, Greenville, the priest was leading the recital of the *Song of Simeon*:

Lord, now lettest thou thy servant depart in peace, according to thy word . . .

But unlike the ancient who kept vigil in the temple until he saw the infant Jesus, Sam Jefferson did not die in peace.

For mine eyes have seen thy salvation which thou
prepared before the face of all people . . .

What did Sam see when men in white sheets broke into his house and tromped their nastiness to the upstairs bedroom like they were hunting down an escaped convict? Like they were the law-abiding ones doing their duty to keep the peace and ensure safety?

Maybe Sam Jefferson saw salvation; less certain, perhaps, were those left behind—Sam's wife and children.

There was no peace in Lily's breast, as she looked at Hugh and herself in business dress, poking their northern noses into southern business. She feared a reception as chilly as carpetbaggers got a century before and marchers and bus riders encountered in more recent decades.

Though no longer in residence and bound by Southern codes of unctuous decency, Lily had a visceral reaction to being back in the smarmy environment where night's congress drew back day's partition. The color line was bogus, else where did all those shades of brown come from? She remembered Baldwin quoting "a very light Negro": "Integration has always worked very well in the South after the sun goes down." And, though it was Easter season for this orderly, white congregation, Lily felt more like Holy Week with its absence of color and unresurrected light in an America whose soul was still cleaved by hateful convention.

Sent from headquarters up north, Lily knew she fooled no one and began to wonder just who exactly this ministry of *accompanying presence* was for. Did it include Sam Jefferson's murderers, who had done something no different than thousands of kinfolk before them?

All of a sudden, Lily saw those gathered to find peace, now covered in segregation's sticky blood sacrifice. She felt herself suffocating in Sam Jefferson's blood—thick and flowing over everyone, disgorging rows of pews parishioner by parishioner, rising up the neck of the priest and gagging his speech.

The flickering candles and monotone quiet of the liturgical event seemed an abomination. Lily wanted the priest to shout out for forgiveness, rend his clothes, and smear himself and everyone else in ashes.

AFTER THE FINAL AMEN, THE priest introduced the visitors: "Lily Wallace and the Reverend Hugh Lovell are with us from the Presiding Bishop's office." Then, looking at them directly, he said, "Thank you for being with us in our hour of need."

Right after the invitation was extended for everyone to continue their communing in the parish hall, a large woman on her right took Lily's hand and began reciting a checkered history with the parish. She seemed to be seeking some kind of absolution, which Lily could not give, even if she were wearing a collar.

As Lily looked around, she saw no children. Hugh busied himself with the rector who had come from the chancel to their pew, extending his hand in welcome. Everyone else filed past and into the parish hall.

Women in veiled hats and men with hats in hand juggled sandwiches and coffee, talking about children and business deals, respectively, trying to find the normalcy temporarily misplaced by the death of someone they knew or thought they knew.

The lynching itself prosecuted the victim's character, as if Sam Jefferson might not have been worthy of their trust after all and had brought on his own demise by some sinful disposition, heretofore unknown by those who paid his salary.

Those who didn't buy into such suspicion attested to Sam's good qualities and work habits: "Worked hard as any man. . . . Always kept this place looking sharp. . . . Never brought any complaints far's I know. . . . Yeah, nothing uppity about the man. . . . Just did his work and stuck to his people. . . . Never gave us any trouble."

LILY WENT UP TO ONE of the low-talking men in suits and introduced herself. Harold Farnsworth, though a fellow Episcopalian, tensed and responded as though to say anything would be disclosing too much. When Lily asked the group how well they knew Sam Jefferson and how they were doing with his murder, she got clipped answers.

Lily wondered how different the demeanor would be if this happened in New York and if what she had to offer was anything close to what the bishop or rector intended as *accompaniment*.

Everyone seemed to be humming the same tune: "It's not us. We're hospitable and polite. We're no marauding murderers." Lily believed them, and, yet, who or what was to blame?

A verse got added here and there around the room: "I hear Ms. Hammond's boy's involved. Mighty suspicious she's not here tonight."

"That boy never has been any good. I tried him out in the shop and he never was on time."

"Didn't smell right nor look right neither. I tried to help him and his mama out, but I couldn't afford him scaring away customers."

"That boy was no better than a . . . well, you know what I'm talkin' about."

Lily asked the woman pouring coffee if there was any hot water available.

"You mean tea, honey?" she interpreted.

"No, just the hot water." Lily explained that she was sensitive to caffeine, even in tea.

"Well, I'd have to go start boilin' some, Miss, Miss . . . I didn't quite get your name. You're with the minister over there, aren't you dear?"

"Yes, I'm Lily Wallace from the Presiding Bishop's office along with our national church Executive Officer, Hugh Lovelle," replied Lily, tipping her head in his direction. "We were asked by your bishop to come and support you all and Sam Jefferson's family."

Before Lily could inquire, the woman doing coffee service volunteered, "I really didn't know him too well. He seemed very nice." Then, to avoid any further probing of the Black man's lynching, she asked, "Do you take your tea light or dark?"

Lily felt as if she were standing in the wrong line with everyone knowing, but nobody saying. *Who was she anyway? Some young woman accompanying a man her senior, all the way from New York City where they don't know one thing about us* here *in Greenville, South Carolina.* They were right.

The print dress, the brown suit, the polished shoes, the slender calf of the organist, the thick neck of the father of five—they wanted what was usual and, in that way, for that moment, Lily was not much different. They wanted the orderliness of a bed made and things straightened after a night of passion.

———

HUGH WAS ACROSS THE ROOM speaking with the rector of St. Luke's. Hoping to catch his eye to motion him toward the door, but failing, exhaustion told Lily to do the next best thing: find the nearest chair and wait by the door.

The gathering had begun to thin out; only some of the faithful who had come out on a stormy night to ask God's forgiveness remained. They hesitated to venture back to their individual homes in white middle- and upper-middle-class neighborhoods for fear the decency on which they depended would no longer be there for them, not after the phone call about Sam Jefferson, the man who looked after their church.

"Why are you here?"

Lucius thought he had the woman's attention when he asked the first time. He deepened his voice and submitted his question to the blue-suited visitor again, this time introduced with an insistent, "Excuse me, miss—"

Lily turned to face the man seeking her immediate attention. "Sorry. I didn't realize you were speaking to me."

"I'm Lucius Clay with *The Sentinel*," he said, extending his hand now as a gesture of peace more than as a challenge to duel.

Meeting a grasp more sanely urgent than any yet encountered, she said, "Hi. I'm Lily Wallace. Sorry, again . . . you were asking me something?"

"My apologies for being so abrupt. I work and live by deadlines, which sometimes makes me less than gracious with those I'm trying to pump for information."

"Doubt you'll get anything from me. I just got here."

"That's what interests me. What brings you and the Reverend Lovelle here tonight?"

Lily wondered how she missed this shiny obsidian against the dull white marble.

"Why am I here?" Lily searched for something recently lost. "Ostensibly for accompaniment."

"Don't know the term."

"I work in the national office of the Episcopal Church which got a call from the bishop here in South Carolina, requesting a presence of the larger church . . . and there it is," she said, glancing in Hugh's direction.

"So, are you the accompaniment to the accompaniment?"

"Something like that."

"You do this often?"

"No, first lynching," Lily popped back. Then, suddenly horrified by her unthinking response, she quickly followed up with, "Oh, God. I can't believe I just said that. Please don't put that in your morning edition."

"I like the honesty." Lucius smiled. "But, no. I won't print that."

"I should have my tongue cut out," Lily said. "I really am sorry for that."

"Relax, Lily." Lucius wanted to see where she might go next. "Conversations like this don't happen too often with you, I take it?"

Feeling under siege by her own ignorance, Lily didn't know if "like this" referred to race or lynching or if it meant conversation with a stranger who didn't seem all that unfamiliar, but who was absolutely, as confirmed by the conversation, unfamiliar.

Before her mind could drift further, she threw a buoy to its nearest response. "No, I would have to say this is an exceptional conversation and an exceptional day for me."

"So, do I call you Reverend?"

"Not until the Church ordains women or I get a sex change."

"For your sake, I hope it's not the latter."

"No. I'm a lady-in-waiting for now. Seminary part-time and working in the Presiding Bishop's office in New York City."

"Under the watchful eye of the big white woman in the harbor."

Lily laughed and retorted, "I assume conversations like this don't happen too often for you?"

"Oh, hell yeah. Hotshot journalist like myself."

"So where is *The Sentinel* and where are you from and why are you here?"

"Los Angeles, D.C., and because I want the story to be told right. God gave you accompaniment—me, the ability to write."

"How common is lynching these days?"

"Certainly not as socially acceptable as other times. Depends on how it's reported or if it's reported. In my neighborhood, lynching covers a lot of ground—not just the specific act of stringin' up some poor Black man in a tree."

Just then, Hugh walked up, introduced himself, and while still shaking Lucius's hand, excused himself and Lily with a proprietary look. "It's been a long day."

Lucius met his look with one of his own but decided it wasn't worth the male muster. "For me too."

"Sorry?"

"It's been a long day for me, too, *Reverend*."

Lily asked an impatient Hugh to wait for her outside the double doors and turned to finish up her conversation with Lucius. "Will you be at Mt. Sinai Church of Deliverance tomorrow?"

"Yeah, I have an appointment with the pastor after lunch. How 'bout you?"

"We were told the service starts at three, so Hugh and I will probably be over there around two."

"Perhaps we can talk more tomorrow?"

"I look forward to it," said Lily.

They shook on the next day's appointment and said good night.

VERNON HAMMOND WAS A BOY who had tried, without success, to find his place in the community of Greenville, South Carolina. Feeling destined for failure, the only way Vernon resisted the temptation to shoot himself was to blame the Black man for leaving slave work in the field for paid work in factories and filling stations.

Sam Jefferson figured into the teen's stick figure mentality, because he worked in the church where Vernon's mother was a longtime member, and, in his mind, Sam's sooty black hands dirtied everything they touched. Worse, yet, some of his mama's pledge money paid his wages.

Vernon's thoughts shifted from doing away with himself to doing away with Sam Jefferson, the devil that kept him from having a job, which also meant no woman to love him and have his kids.

Hell, Vernon thought. *He bought a car with my mama's money and I don't have shit.* He began plotting Sam's end the first day he saw him on church property, cleaning bird nests and leaves out of the gutters.

Vernon wanted to knock the ladder out from under his ass right then and there. He wanted to see him fall and break his head on the concrete walk below and send him straight to hell.

Finding it increasingly hard to wait for a more judicious time when his own evil could be concealed by the greater, and more anonymous, brotherhood of evil, Vernon was sure that his buddies would be help enough in carrying out his plan to kidnap Sam Jefferson and take him deep into the woods where wild animals would be their only witness.

The sooner Vernon got rid of Sam Jefferson, the sooner he could claim the respect he had coming from the community. Unlike his fellows who had second thoughts and were already setting alibis in place so as to put the blame on him, Vernon was eager to execute his plan and broadcast its success, all the while looking forward to the tribute it would bring.

In that plan, Vernon saw his note to the Black-lovin' minister as a declaration of love and proof of loyalty to white supremacy and honor, the kind of attestation understood by real whites who knew what their survival depended upon. He would do anything to protect his sheep like the good shepherd of the Bible; and, like Jesus, he was a savior and didn't need a job or a car to prove his worth to his mama or the men in town who smoked fat cigars and played cards and felt women's behinds.

NORMA HAMMOND HAD NOT BEEN awake when her boy Vernon finally made it home—not that she ever did stay up waiting for him anymore. It had grown easier on her conscience to avoid seeing, hearing, and smelling the child whose inheritance was half hers and half that of a wicked husband who beat Vernon and her up until the day he slammed the broken screen door for the last time and drove away in the only thing of value the family had ever owned.

Norma cried about two seconds before rearranging herself at her husband's place at the table and treating herself to a sit-down meal her own hands had prepared. Since then, Norma relished the freedom of having no one to worry about but herself.

The day after the lynching started out for Norma as it usually did, with a piece of toast and a cup of coffee. She ate the end piece of the loaf and cut her coffee with two packets of the nondairy creamer she picked up at May's Diner just off the highway whenever she could get her neighbor to stop on their way into town for weekly errands.

The house was peaceful, and Norma's mind was busy with what she would do that morning after breakfast. It was spring and that meant getting the season's garden planted. The harvest would be pooled with her neighbor's, some of which would be eaten fresh-picked. The rest would be canned, a ritual that made Norma delight as much in the garden's close as in its seeding. A simple and profound satisfaction for a woman who could grow beans better than raise a son.

Norma saw her son's boots and was happy that he respected her and the house enough to remove them in the mudroom, even though sock prints trailed along the linoleum, growing fainter as they reached the bottom stair.

After his father left, Vernon moved into the upstairs bedroom, while Norma happily set up a bed in the dining room, which was already furnished with sewing machine, thread basket, fabric odds and ends, and a small metal cabinet with plastic trays for snaps, hooks and eyes, buttons, needles and whatever else she needed for sewing and mending and, occasionally, creating a whole new something out of nothing.

Vernon pushed open the screen door, scratched himself, and squinted at the sun showing its last rays before rain clouds covered its light. "Hey Mama—what's doin'?"

"Nothin' you cain't be helpin' your mother with." Placing the small carrots she had started indoors just so, Norma felt bold out in her garden. The rest of the time she feared her son fast becoming a grown-up in his body but not in his head. In his head, Vernon was still a boy needing her to do this or that, needing her attention, and as impatient as his old man had been. His words with her were rough, especially as Vernon started drinking with his friends and the day swaggered into night—another reason Norma didn't wait up for her son. And if she were awake, she pretended to be asleep and to be someplace else and someone else besides Vernon's mother.

"Mama, I brought you a present." Vernon had never been so sure of himself.

"What's all this nonsense?" Norma began stacking sandbags in defense. "You say a present, Vernon? You ain't never got me a present since you brung home pictures you drawed at school."

"Well, Mama, I ain't no little boy no more, and I sure ain't no school geek." He laughed, and Norma felt depleted.

"What I brung you is to show you and your friends at that church what they've needed to be showed for a long time."

"And what is that, son?"

"The Black man's place."

Norma's heart was racing like someone was chasing and catching up to her, even though her feet stayed planted in the soil of her spring garden.

"I got me a hunk of hair from that devil y'all have cuttin' the grass at St. Luke's."

The boy terrified his mother. "What are you saying, Vernon?"

"I'm saying he won't be around to mow nobody's lawn no more 'cause he's hangin' in a tree."

"Vernon, boy, what have you done—you Hammond son of a no-good pa? Boy! What have you been up to?" Norma came at Vernon with the trowel in her right hand. Vernon held her wrist and smirked.

"What I done, Mama, is put that thief where he belong. Where he belong all this time, which ain't cuttin' no white grass at no church. He belong in that tree, hangin' by his neck."

Norma dropped in front of Vernon. "Oh, my boy, my poor boy." Laboring her whole body, panting sobs brought grief from deep down inside where her baby once grew, nurtured by her mother blood. "Oh no. Oh no. Oh no, Vernon—not you, son! Tell me you makin' this up. Some terrible dream you jus' dreamed. Tell me you're not in your right mind yet. This ain't your right mind."

"What're you sayin', Mama? You not proud of your boy? You the one—you and those crazies at that church—*you* not in *your* right mind. You haven't been since you let that man on all y'all's property. Let him put his hands all over y'all's shrubs and walls. Let him touch everything and payin' him to dirty y'all's church."

Norma was on her way into the house, wanting to get away from this stranger ranting about her church and the Black man who kept the place looking presentable.

"Where you goin', Mama?" Vernon followed Norma inside the screen door, into the kitchen. "You not goin' t'make me some breakfast? I deserve a victory breakfast this mornin', Mama. Your son just returned from battle and he's hungry."

"You better run—you better get some clothes and what chump change you have and get out of this house," Norma growled. "You are not my son. You woke up as someone I do not know, cain't be knowin'—not this morning, not any morning the good Lord leaves me stand on his earth." Norma threatened her son with the knife used for butchering chickens and chopping onions.

"I'm not your son? Then you're not my mama. Your Black-lovin' ass don't deserve to be anybody's mama. You never *was* my mama—the right kind of mama. You best believe I'm leavin'. Just like my papa you chased out. You dried up, never-done-nothin'-in-your-life 'cept havin' a bastard son like me, old woman." Vernon took the mayonnaise jar of coins Norma hid in the cupboard, poured it all into a grocery bag, ran upstairs, then reappeared with clothes hanging out of a duffel bag. In the mud room, he pulled on his boots after lighting up a cigarette and flicking the still-lit match in Norma's direction, before sending the back screen door flying off its hinges and heading down to the road on the gravel driveway in a righteous strut, as the sky began to open up its content of dark clouds and drop rain like angry pelting stones.

Norma dialed the number of St. Luke's Church and asked for Mr. Finch, as soon as she heard the secretary's voice come on the line.

"I'm sorry. He's in a meeting right now—"

"I have somethin' I gotta tell him—I mean now! I gotta talk to the minister."

"Well, Norma . . . this *is* Norma Hammónd—"

"Yes, it's me, Norma—either I got t'talk to Mr. Finch now or start myself comin' down to the church. You tell me what's fastes'—this cain't wait!"

"Excuse me just a minute, Norma. I'll see what I can do."

There were a few minutes of dead silence before Norma heard a click and the voice of the minister. "Norma, what can I do for you?"

LILY DID NOT KNOW HOW many minutes she had slept. She only remembered the images that appeared when she closed her eyes. Women, as well as men, hanging like clothes on a line. Like they were resting in a state of suspended animation, eyes closed, heads only slightly slumped. It was only when the faces of those who did the lynching emerged as if shielded behind a pane of glass that Lily wakened, her heart beating out the terror of her dreams.

Around half past three she flipped through channels on the television in her room, but the only thing on the screen besides snowy dartboards bleeping station identifications was a John Wayne movie. In a show of frontier civility, the Duke tipped his hat to a corseted lady of means who shifted from haughty to panicked, signaling the entrance of a *savage*, played by a painted white man wearing a garish wig.

Disgusted, Lily clicked off the picture. After the last twelve hours, what she could have dismissed as laughable before had become sickening. Lily tried to fit her immediate experience of lynching with another idea of lynching that, according to any American history text she had read, was confined to a sentence on a page in a chapter on the post-Civil War years.

WHAT WAS SHE DOING HERE? Lucius's question nagged at her through a fitful night. In the morning, Lily was no closer to having an answer. So unprepared for this magnitude of hideousness. So unprepared to be among "her own"—people not giving the appearance of monsters, who, nevertheless, germinated seeds that sprouted monstrous brutality . . . people who cultivated social definitions as sharply as their divisioned rows of peas and okra.

In dawn's early light, Lily's life reeled like film through her mind, projecting the evidence and consequence of her unawareness of the subtle segregation of her childhood.

They arrived in a bus and became at once, a spectacle. It was football season and every year at this time the Hamilton Park High School marching band borrowed the Eagles' stadium field to practice complicated patterns prior to performing at the upcoming weekend game.

The stadium in the small Texas town was built on the same property as Greenville Elementary School. A smaller, original schoolhouse was home to developmentally disabled students of all ages.

The mother of Lily's friend taught the special ed kids. Lily was both curious and terrified of them, like the day she lined up to make a savings deposit in the lobby of the school's auditorium.

Two bank tellers came to the school every Wednesday at lunchtime. Maybe all the students would, like Lily, go to college on the nickels and dimes deposited with First National.

Big Paul spied Lily while she waited in line, then, picking her up like a pole and transporting her to the auditorium stage, said, "Dance," as he set her down and observed from the floodlights.

Feeling she was endangered, Lily thought she should run away.

"Dance," he repeated. Big Paul was grinning like

a proud parent at his kid's recital. Lily did a couple of steps just learned in tap class from her teacher, Miss Nancy, who, in a full golden pageboy, could have been a Breck girl.

Lily remembered waking up one morning, disappointed that baby-fine natural curls, cropped short by her mother's attentive home barbering, still capped her head. She yearned for the thick and long-enough-to-braid hair of her dreams.

Some of the girls marching in the Hamilton Park band had braids—lots of braids—that were exposed when they removed the brown grocery bags shielding them from sunburn during breaks.

The musicians were a spectacle, because of the makeshift shakos protecting them from the hot Texas sun, and because they were not from the community. They were a spectacle, most of all, because their faces were black.

These teens did not hang out of cars at Jack's drive-in, eating hamburgers or fries from a parchment-lined basket. They did not go to matinees and have popcorn fights at the Ritz when they were younger or buy popsicles at Robbie's Drugs. And Lily never saw any nutmeg-colored parents pushing their toddlers strapped into grocery carts at the Safeway.

Even though Hamilton Park was a new community just down the expressway, it might as well have been in another state. Lily remembered driving with her mother into Dallas, peering out the window of their station wagon at the neat rows of houses. Only scanned, never visited, Hamilton Park looked to her like a Ken and Barbie village—orderly and bordered by boundaries that didn't merge with another municipality.

Lily didn't get the race thing. But she had a sense from hearing others' epithets about the tidy bedroom community, that it would be better to be poor and white and live in Greenville than to be "one of them" in Hamilton Park. From the road, the only feature she saw missing was trees.

Lily's mind viewed the freshness of the new town outweighing the absence of trees. Much as she liked climbing trees, Lily liked riding horses even better.

Friends picked her up to ride double on their horses after school and on weekends. One pal, Jimmie Ray, would come right up Lily's front walkway atop her big, hard-mouthed palomino, gathering up her saddle partner to first explore the strip of horse properties separated from town by a field and, then, the netherworld of farming that lay beyond.

In the green of late spring and early summer, there was cotton and alfalfa; toward autumn, the fields became honey colored. If they rode far enough, Lily and her friends reached where the farmers were colored. Not root beer or licorice or coffee or tan. Just colored.

As she tanned in the summer sun, Lily's father referred to her as "a little brown berry." Other than that, Lily didn't consider herself to have color. Neither did her friends. They were either fair or redheaded, and, therefore, prone to sunburn; or they were olive-skinned and could get "really black" from hours on a towel in the backyard, at the community plunge, or poolside at the country club. Texas in summer was one big tanning salon. Whites only.

Lily swam with whites only; rode bikes on whites-only streets, borrowed books from whites-only libraries, and ate at whites-only restaurants with whites-only restrooms. So it was with much curiosity that Lily rode with her horseback friends to see Black sharecropper families who waved hello from unpainted porches and unsprinklered, mostly dirt yards.

Turf care, especially keeping lawns green during the scorching summer months, was a matter of pride for Greenville homeowners, and, therefore, a primary occupation. Saint Augustine with its thick, dense runners was preferred to Bermuda grass, which attracted chiggers and invaded flower beds.

Lily sang in the junior choir of Epiphany Episcopal Church and attended Sunday school in cubicles created by bulletin board partitions. On the Sundays she didn't have to sing in the service, Lily babysat in the nursery.

Sermons preached at Epiphany touched on areas of family concern, but race and gender never made it onto the minister's list. Hawai'i with its slurry of Asian-Pacific ethnicity had just become the fiftieth state; Civil Rights, per se, had not yet stirred the households of Greenville.

There were "situations," but Lily could recall none ever standing out enough to be investigated. "Incidents" that Lily could remember happened at the two places where races were together in numbers: the arena or stadium of sporting events or the grounds of the Dallas County Fair.

School let out for Fair Day. Students bought tickets at a discount to ride rides like "The Wild Mouse," a cylinder which spun them around on its axis while progressively changing its tilt, pressing them to the metal sides like sausages lining the inside of a can.

Trusted to the charge of older siblings, Lily and her friends would return to the Fair's Midway on the weekend for more thrill rides and to hear barkers announce the next show of human anomalies. On the weekend, there were not only Black workers, there were Black families who, to the curious and fearful collective eye of the white fairgoers, formed another sideshow, being human in ways incongruous with greater Dallas "society."

Lily had wondered, during such encounters, how she might be seen by "them." Now, for the first time, she wondered about seeing herself.

———

THE CASKET NESTING SAM JEFFERSON in its satiny folds rested in the back of a long black hearse parked to the rear of the raised platform. A cadre of pallbearers stood witness to the history they lived. The same muted, low-slung saxophone played the classic blues notes across time, seeping into the dark places, picking up sediment and carrying it forward into present time.

This should not happen. Since the assassinations of the last decade, people were never to have to gather in mourning like this again; Black arms linked with white, fortifying a human chain never again to be broken. But keeping the human body, with its range of color intact, is the delight or failure of each, not just one, generation.

The country knows itself in mourning. Other days— going through the contests of business, academia, and politics reporting bits of information decent enough to print—other days are the usual. The nastiness just under the skin, like acid ready to eat its way through the thin membrane of civility, may be contained for a while, but then it corrodes and etches the usual day into history.

LILY WAS AT ONCE RELIEVED and made edgy during the open public mourning of the lynching murder. It broke the news of racial unrest in a time of relative peace. Singing started somewhere in the crowd of nearly equal numbers of whites and Blacks. The sound expanded in volume, as more and more witnesses pressed into the cement promenade linking Greenville's city hall with its courthouse. Police in riot gear stood shoulder to shoulder along the line of sawhorse barricades stenciled "G.P.D."

The Reverend Bill Finch floated in a pond of people, some in black shirt and white collar, some in street dress. Spotting Lily and Hugh, he relaxed at seeing them apparently in one piece. He motioned for them to join him.

"What time did you have to start out to get here?" Bill asked.

"In thought—last night. In body—at the crack of dawn." Hugh spoke for both of the Northern out-of-towners. "Took a cab to just where the police were already setting up their fences. Lucky for us there were coffee vendors setting up too."

"Welcome to Greenville and its citizenry, which is not all tarnish—despite its lingering caricature, there's still a visible sheen." Bill paired palms, as he introduced Lily and Hugh to the group of Episcopal Church members from neighboring parishes and missions in the Greenville area.

After resettling in the new assemblage, Lily's eyes searched the crowd, returning to the corner where Lucius last stood. His sapphire black skin, brilliant in the rays of a tentative sun, caught and held Lily's attention. By now, he had moved front and center along with the rest of the press, to await the appearance of Greenville's mayor and council, followed by clergy representing local Protestant, Catholic, and Jewish congregations. Once they assumed their positions, the rhetoric of American ideals sallied forth.

Lily took it all in, her mind wandering back and forth between what was immediately happening and another time in history. Instead of decrying the hanging of a Black man, some whites back then might have celebrated with picnic lunches and time off from work. Blacks, sickened by the exhibition intended as a deterrence to further race code violation, would have firmed their resolve to escape to the land of milk and honey. If caught, well then—the sooner came their deliverance from earth's rebuff and their entrée to Heaven's welcome.

SAM JEFFERSON'S GLORY TRAIN STEAMED on into late morning, making its next stop at Mt. Sinai Church of Deliverance, where his memorial service had begun the night before in another sanctuary of the church with Mt. Sinai's choir of cooks glorifying God. Worshippers baked pies, fried chicken, assembled potato salad, and put greens to soak until early morning when Aunt Evie would resume preparations for a banquet on earth which prefigured its counterpart in heaven. Sam's church family met his train with foil-lined boxes of iced devil's food cake, canisters of molasses cookies, tins of homemade candies, and jars of homegrown peppers, corn, beans, and tomatoes.

It was not that Sam was a notable in the community; the members of Mt. Sinai Church of Deliverance simply did for Brother Jefferson what the rest would do for them. No scale of worth was hauled out to calculate the doing, because it was one and the same. For this community, deeds done by as well as for folded one into the other to make one solid loaf.

Whether it was a despicable death at the hands of evildoers or a stroke that took one of their congregation, the people of Deliverance kept their eyes on the One receiving—not on the who or what that caused the departure.

Their eyes beheld a future which made the present less sorrowful, believing that a God who created each and every life would surely be there to make the last days the first. The first of what, exactly, remained a mystery, but the promise was enough, and its renewal on the occasion of Samuel Jefferson's crossing over to the next realm of God's splendor secured that promise for the present generation and for each generation to come.

BY TWELVE NOON, CHILDREN OLD enough to be about the ritual with certain decorum were allowed by Aunt Evie to set tables unfolded by the more athletic men. Each was placed according to a plan that varied with each event, depending on what tables were actually available. Some of the tables with chewed-up ends and names carved into the tops had been donated after their rescue from a back alley or the local landfill.

Unless it was completely broken down, everything that could, would be used. Clever hands extended the life of appliances and furniture cast off by those bored with the old and wanting the new. Items tossed out as unfixable and put out for the junk man or whoever else might happen along with a wagon or the back of a truck were reclaimed to higher purpose.

Not only tables, but chairs, fans, lamps, rugs—even refrigerators and stoves could be picked up on a lucky day made even luckier if the castoff needed little repair or cleaning. To those a step away from the make-do and can-do of country life, recycling was not a new concept. After every reasonable bit of use was squeezed out of a factory-produced something, there was always someone down the line whose ingenuity pressed a little more, extracting further usefulness. Even decaying material was good for mulching a garden bed and protecting tender shoots poking up from wintered ground.

Weather permitting, a few of the tables, dressed in floral bedsheets held at the corners with clothespins, went outside where those who smoked could indulge their habit without disturbing the customary of the congregation. There were no declared smokers among the membership of Deliverance—the occasional tobacco stuffed in the bowl of a pipe or snuffed being too small a matter for discussion.

After the tables were covered, forks, spoons and, as far as they would go, knives, were set at each place. People would fill their own paper cups with sweet tea or lemonade poured from glass pitchers over ice chipped from larger blocks by older boys used to wielding the hatchet and hammer at Church of Deliverance functions.

The buffet started taking form with plates stacked on either side of the first of five tables. The dishes, in unmatched sets, were acquired by mailing in coupons combined with money for postage or by being fished out of giant boxes of laundry detergent; cups and bowls were retrieved from regular size boxes. In the rare event that the death of its last member meant a church family of means broke up house-keeping, Mt. Sinai Church of Deliverance found itself the happy heir to continue using items with the gracious dignity and proud freedom they symbolized.

The last table, designated for desserts, was expected to do its usual spilling over, crowding the fried chicken, ham, sweet potatoes, collards, rice, and gravy on the table before, because no time was in need of more sweetening than Brother Sam's send-off.

———

LILY AND HUGH STEPPED OUT of the car and onto the paved parking lot of Mt. Sinai Church of Deliverance, an impressive structure of hewn stone and stained glass. Even from the outside, the windows communicated light penetrating darkness; the massive walls and doors, permanence and solidity.

Hugh excused himself to go look for the pastor, Otis McGhee, while Lily wandered in the direction of the meeting hall and its adjoining kitchen. Broad smiles on broad-faced women greeted Lily, who felt like the dead among the living. There was an abundance of everything: food, flesh, laughter, "honey"-this, "sweetness"-that; every now and then the women dabbing the perspiration on their foreheads and necks with flour sack towels, which otherwise rested on their soft shoulders. Lily admired the practiced roles and ease with which they moved around each other in the relatively small space of the kitchen. One woman pulled a pan of rolls from the oven, turning them out on the counter on an old oven shelf used as a cooling rack which sat beside another, mounded with biscuits already baked and cooled. A second woman stirred the contents of a kettle and asked Lily if she wanted a taste. A third handed Lily a biscuit, because she "better have a thing or two to catch the 'taste'" which Lily found to mean the taste of gravy made from chicken brownings thickened with flour. All of this preceded a formal introduction with names.

"Where you from, Lily?"

"Currently New York City. But if you mean, where did I grow up?—it's Texas. A small town in the Dallas area."

"I have family 'bout there, but I don't s'pose you ever met any of my folk." And then to cover any awkwardness her comment might have raised, she qualified what she said with, "Yeah, last time I knowed them, I knowed them to be a bunch of uncivilized loudmouths. Everybody wants tuh tawk at once! That don't seem like you, Lily."

"Well, don't be too sure." Lily maintained the shared ruse. "I have an uncle who could out-talk and out-interrupt anyone! If you don't believe me, just ask his four wives. He talked his way in and out of each marriage." What Lily threw out was caught in agreement.

"I know that, honey. I know the kina man you be tellin'. He no better than lil ol' beetlebug get squashed 'neath th'heel of my old shoe!" Everyone laughed.

"How you know that kin' man, Tildie. Your man Ace is one sweet thing."

"I got ears don' I? And I got women friends wantin' to fill 'em with stories of their no-good men."

"Oh yeah," "Thassright," and other knowing sounds clickety-clacked through the air steeped in aromas of just-done rolls and baking ham and greens simmering with hogback fat—"always need a little fat to fight," the pursy woman, stirring, explained.

Looking for her reaction as she sampled a fried chicken wing and a biscuit dipped in gravy, the women clucked over Lily: "You jes' a li'l thing."

A trim woman who hadn't spoken before said, "You gon' faint, you not put somethin' in that stomach of yours, li'l Lily."

"On a day like t'day, you need a li'l somethin' delicious to praise the Lawd 'bout, 'cause He sho' hear 'nough our tears over Brother Sam and that mother's son who did his mess," testified another, who had been punctuating the words of the other women with "uh-huh" and "amen" and "don' I know."

"We been prayin' since we heard th'news that po' boy and his family. But today, we put away our tears—give 'em all to the Lawd. No tears in these biscuits. They salty 'nough. Today, we seein' on yondah, where the good Lawd take care ev'yone of us. One day we all goin' where Sam be now—but, today, He appoint us cook and baker to help Him take care those hongry souls still walkin' this earth."

Lily looked at her watch and asked if the women would be able to make it to the service on time.

"Honey, our ministry begin and en' in this heah kitchen," said Aunt Evie.

"We the first ones put on the apron and the last to take it off after the last chunka pie get wrapped in wax paper and sent home."

"An' don't forget the latecomers," said a woman who went by the name of Puddin'. "They not late arrivals—they jes' late peoples, and we here to tell 'em what's what regardin' the service."

AS CONTENT AS SHE WAS to linger in their company, Lily was, also, eager to find and continue her conversation with the journalist Lucius Clay. Thanking the women for their hospitality and promising to do better on the meal after the funeral than the little bit of nibbling she had done just then, Lily left the kitchen and walked back through the meeting hall where casserole dishes and dessert platters hinted at the full spread yet to be laid out before the final amen.

Outside, Lily saw cars lined up at the entrance to the parking lot. Nearing the church steps, she found Lucius standing off to one side, looking at a small tablet which he replaced in his coat pocket as Lily approached.

"Good afternoon, Ms. Wallace—how was your morning?"

"Moving . . . surreal. I saw you up front—how was it from your seat?"

"A clash of words and symbols."

Lily looked puzzled.

"O say, does that Confederate banner yet wave."

"No—where?"

"The obscene rag they still fly in this state."

"I didn't notice," said Lily. "I just listened to the words coming out of their mouths."

"Hell—could've been a ceremony recognizing another cultural genetics success: new crop of moron bigots."

Lily welcomed the silence entering as a third party in the conversation just then. Though she wanted Lucius to continue, Lily wondered if she had the stamina to persist without some sign that her ignorance was forgiven.

"I'm usually too busy reeling in details to *feel* an event. Only when I'm writing copy. Whole thing comes together, and I have to be careful about emotion getting in the way of what I keep to myself and what I throw back in. I try to remind myself that if I say what is, it's provocative enough. But what the hell was happenin' on that dais today? Violence might have been going on in South Carolina forever—but today? . . . Today, it comes as a big fuckin' surprise."

"The city hall guys on the platform this morning sure made it sound that way—"

"Fuckers have had a lot of practice."

"I've never been this close before . . . I mean, it's 1973— why did they do it?"

"Because we're still reconstructing how to live together? . . . Because the Supreme Court's decision on busing never sat well in South Carolina? . . . Because in this country, it's never taken more than a drop of black blood to convict and execute?"

"But why is it worth spending the rest of their life in prison?"

"Because it's likely they won't, unless they've pissed off the crackers who sit on the bench. Conviction tends to be the exception."

"Oh." Silence padded around the two again, having its say and granting Lily time to absorb both the message and the firsthand intensity of its messenger.

"Where were you before New York, Lily?"

"In a dot outside Dallas."

"Almost neighbors—" said Lucius, glad for a convenient way to resume the conversation on a lighter note. "I was born and raised in Galveston, but I'm more from an event than a place—both my father's people and my mother's people claim to be descended from Juneteenth slaves."

When he saw Lily's eyes narrow and her lips purse in confusion, Lucius gave Lily a brief tutorial about Juneteenth before following up with his next question, "Which dot outside Dallas?"

"Sorry . . . I'm still on Juneteenth," Lily reflected. "I don't think I can go back that far in my family history . . . and the people I grew up with—their memory doesn't go much beyond last Friday night's football game."

"High school?"

"Greenville Lions."

"Damn good ball—for a bunch of white boys."

"Better be—it's the lifeblood of the community. That and keepin' ever'one in thur place. Anybody in Greenville can tell you w'ar the ne-gras live and w'ar the whi-yetts live."

"There's the accent."

"Oh, I can still talk Texan."

"When did you leave?"

"Around the same time Black teenagers ripped down 'The

Blackest Land, The Whitest People'—Greenville's welcome sign on the main drag for almost six decades. Brown offered me a full ride in '67, and I was smart enough to take it. You?"

"Left for Duke and from there, Columbia. Never looked back."

"You've never been back?"

"Never wanted to—what did you study at Brown?"

"I intended graduating with a double major in American lit and biology before going to med school—probably staying on the East Coast. But by my junior year and biology lab, I knew that it would be impossible to doctor living people if I couldn't stand dissecting dead animals."

"So, how did you make the leap from medicine to theology?"

"It didn't use to be a leap," said Lily as she fingered the hoop of her earring. "For the last four to five centuries theology was actually the core of all disciplines."

"Ah—the academic soul," said Lucius. "And the place of theology for you?"

"Maybe I have an intellectual approach to God."

"No freaky shit—no bells goin' off, lights goin' on?"

"Might have, but you heard what I missed today."

"I think you caught enough."

"You can't be that interested."

"Do you see anyone else standing here?" Lucius looked around. "Yeah I am that interested. What pushed you, moved you, led you in that direction?"

"Theology started out a purely pragmatic choice. I wanted to go to grad school and do some more with the religious strand in American literature, but with a broader stroke in terms of ethnic groups." Lily checked Lucius's expression before going on. "At the same time, I had a conversation with this priest at coffee hour one Sunday. He asked if I'd ever considered ordained ministry. I said, 'Why would I?' He pretty much threw the question back at me, and I've been living with it ever since. Oh, and he assured me that the Holy Spirit is capable of course correction." Then, not wanting to get into any doubts she was experiencing at that moment, Lily deflected Lucius's gaze and said, "Your turn."

"Well, with considerably less thought than you've obviously put into it," began Lucius, as he shrugged his shoulders and sunk his hands into the pockets of his coat jacket, "writing was what remained after other notions of what I might do with my life revealed themselves as imposters.

"Writing is, simply, the first thing I think about in the morning and the last thing at night," he continued. Before Lily could comment on what Lucius had just disclosed, he asked, "So when do they lay hands on you?"

Lily snorted. "No hands have been laid on any female yet, except to tie her up and burn her for being a witch, which is what I think some would like to do now that women's ordination is getting serious play. But," she added with more bravado than belief, "too bad for the naysayers—it's only a matter of time."

"Take it from me—'only a matter of' can be a *long* time." Lily smiled at Lucius's understanding. "What about the *mean*time?"

"Continue taking classes at Union and not holding my breath that General—the Episcopal seminary—is gonna open its doors more widely. Continue with this job, which I got after Brown, as an aide to the Executive Officer, Hugh, whom you met last night and who is around here somewhere." Lily realized it was the first time she thought about her boss and her denominational affiliation since she stood with the St. Luke's contingent at the rally that morning. She looked around for Hugh.

"You're a freedom rider," said Lucius.

Lily's head went back and her eyebrows up as she said, "I think you're stretching the metaphor. Believe me—I don't have that kind of courage."

"So, where'd you board the bus?"

"Well, assuming there's even a shred of evidence that I have—" Lily answered. "That's a good question—I can't point to any dramatic reversal or awakening. I think I've always—maybe from a precognitive, sensory time even—felt rooted in this ground, on this earth. . . . Yourself?"

"That's a pretty solid statement. It could be that my collective unconscious is more unconscious than yours—or is covered in more layers of shit," said Lucius. "But I'm not sure I could stake the same claim. . . . You've never doubted?"

"Oh, yeah. You can't grow up female in Texas—maybe, anywhere—and not question, but it never takes absolute hold. I see this claim—as you refer to it—as an inheritance to which I am both entitled and responsible—but not in a singular sense. Of course, could be just Christian conditioning talking here—nevertheless, I do believe this—inheritance, and its obligation, is what binds you and me in common."

"Church tradition, Christianity—a two-edged sword: both the heart of Black community and what's torn its heart out. How do you reconcile the two?"

"I can't. I don't think it's possible," said Lily. "How would you answer your own question?"

"With another 'nevertheless.' Nevertheless, you and I stand here talking as just two people," said Lucius. "Which doesn't reconcile the past, but based on the past—proposes new questions, which is what I'm more interested in. Both formulating the questions and living into them.

"I was a grunt reporter first," Lucius continued. "Worked my way into investigative journalism. In the future, I want to do more in-depth writing. I want the credibility and respect that will allow me to cover—or uncover—stories that need to be told if Americans are going to be grown-up. I want to be in the midst of news as it's happening. I want to be known as a journalist with a declared perspective so that what I write bears my signature. I want to cast my byline into every pool of American culture, deal with the internationalism in these sometimes–united states. I don't need to go to a foreign country to be shot at—I can be a war correspondent right here in the so-called land of the free and home of the brave."

WHILE LUCIUS AND LILY TALKED, the women of the Mothers Union, in their distinctive white dress and gloves, had been greeting people at the door and ushering them to pews. The organ had gone from one end of the service to the other, as it accompanied the prefuneral rehearsal of the choir whose members in cherry red robes now formed a procession on the walk in front of the church steps. Twelve deacons in dark suits took their places in line behind the choir. Finally, the Reverend Dr. Otis McGhee, in black preaching robe with white shirt and red silk tie displayed in the vee of the neck, moved into place after bobbing and shaking hands and "how-you-doing?" all along the route from his office to those already queued up and awaiting their pastor before filing up the steps, into the church, and down the center aisle singing: "Holy, holy, holy—Lord God Almighty . . ."

VEILED AND IN BLACK, CYRL JEFFERSON sat stiffly beside her seven-year-old daughter, whose younger sisters pillowed in the laps of their grandmother and an aunt in the same first pew left of the center aisle. Great care had been taken in every detail of this coming together: from the undertaker's artistry of peace on her husband's last seen tortured face to the floral displays with ribbons on which messages were printed in gold letters. Still numb, Cyrl was unavailable to these or other acts of kindness.

Mt. Sinai Church of Deliverance, swollen with grief, remained a study in faithfulness. Faithfulness demonstrated one to another and to the God who brought them in safety to this one day—never mind the next. Each person hauled their heavy selves past the open casket, paying final respects to their violated brother, then moved to their business of tearful embrace and kisses of peace to the living in the front pew. After the first few mourners, big-handed uncles took the girls to play in the churchyard, leaving Cyrl and other family to receive both the strong and the frail press of condolence.

Men, as well as women, cried and blew their sorrow into ample handkerchiefs after laying a hand on top of Sam Jefferson's folded hands or forehead, assuring that their newly departed brother continued on his way not alone, but in the embrace of believers in life after death. It was this proclamation of life in the midst of death that the young and, especially, the old, came seeking that day.

Sam Jefferson's funeral was an unexpected second Easter following the official one, still in evidence, now, less than a week later, in the colorful dress of the children. The adults, who could not remember the rising of their Lord just six days past, put on solemn browns and somber blacks.

Each received love from the dead man now lying in humble mystery, his mortality in plain view. Love that could not be returned or recompensed was what Sam Jefferson offered to each person who came into his stilled presence; an intimacy not wished for but conferred, nonetheless, by death. And this love— would it also pass between the late Mr. Jefferson and Lily?

FINDING SEATING IN A BACK PEW, Lucius touched Lily's elbow as a signal to proceed. The church held something of the morning chill, so Lily kept her coat on as armor against stabs of coolness from the air, as well as from the look of the disapproving matron seated next to her. She pulled the front panels of her coat around her more securely and slumped slightly as she thought, again, about Lucius's question from the night before: What was she doing here?

Lucius had questions of his own to push around inside his head now that he was seated in a space familiar to him as a boy who grew up on the weekly staple of Wednesday night prayer services, Sunday morning testifying and amen-ing, and Sunday evening prayer and praise that followed in too-quick succession with the midday potluck served directly after the long stretch of worship and Sunday School.

Though he spent as much time on the basketball court as he did in church, Lucius—contrary to predictions of those who thought they knew him—aspired neither to the ether above the rim nor to that of the pulpit above the congregation; writing is what lifted Lucius to where he wanted to go.

He was nicknamed *Sin* after the great Lou Alcindor, but

basketball wasn't Lucius's sport. The game had served its purpose in earlier years of besting white competitors with every hoop he made, elbow thrown, female heart captured. He savored write-ups of his athletic prowess as confirmation from the white man's pen of his superiority, until he figured out the spin and started writing up life as he saw it—from the perspective of a Black man.

While the Board of Deacons led the opening devotion, the story of the last several days took shape in the journalist's mind: Sam Jefferson might have been safer as a ground troop grunt in Vietnam than he was as a Black civilian in America. As with generations of Black soldiers before, the contradiction of fighting for your country when your country didn't fight for you was made obvious to Sam's friends and family in the wake of his murder. The *Gazette* put out a special edition to cover the news and reactions of the Black community, while the white-owned *Greenville Record* sandwiched Sam's execution between reports of a burglary and a car theft, both crimes allegedly committed by Black males.

Forgive us our trespasses . . . Lily mouthed the familiar words to the Lord's Prayer being led by the associate pastor, but her mind played over her father's words pronounced at the threshold of her puberty: it was one thing to play dolls with her Negro friend, Delicia, but there would be dire consequences if she were ever to think about dating a Negro boy. She wondered if her father were just stating a fact of southern life—or was he saying that he personally would carry out the threat should his daughter consider crossing the color line? His point seemed moot at the time, as there were no opportunities for interracial dating in Greenville, Texas. In fact, after Delicia quit coming around with her dad, there were no opportunities for interracial anything.

The thought that her interest in a boy could cost him his life, if he were Black, at first terrified Lily into believing that her father didn't actually mean what he said, that he was just being as overprotective as her friends' fathers. At some later time, though, she found her father's warning so repugnant that she struck it from her mental record of growing up. Until today—in a church filled with Black people.

All of a sudden Lily felt surrounded by a cloud of witnesses—all there to observe, with dignity, a life taken, not because of anything to do with interracial love, but because of racial hate—and her emotions suddenly shifted. She feared being found out. Panic urged her to leave immediately; reason told her to wait and leave gracefully. She longed to be nestled in her life back in New York, which, confined by the physical structure of the office in which she worked and tamed by the social structure of traditional religion, was not as dangerous or, in fact, as interracial.

Lily grabbed her purse and whispered hurriedly to Lucius: "Please excuse me." Lucius looked puzzled, but, sensing her agitation, honored her request by standing up to let her pass more easily in front of him into the center aisle and out the church doors. He remained standing as the first to respond to the organ's cueing of the congregation with prefatory bars of "Lift Every Voice and Sing."

The Black National Anthem got everyone on their feet: Some were clapping, others were clapping and marching in place. *The Church agitant*, thought Lucius. *Lily would like this.* After the first verse, Lucius thumbed through the hymnal in the rack in front of him to find the words to the other verses he didn't know by heart. ". . . may we forever stand, True to our God, true to our native land." At the close of the third verse, Lucius looked at his watch and grew concerned about Lily.

Like an eyelash in his eye, Lily had Lucius's attention, despite knowing so little about her. Knowing so little about his subject was an uncomfortable, though intriguing, predicament for a journalist. As concerned as Lucius was about Lily's quick departure and length of time gone, he was, nevertheless, relieved to have a moment to examine the time spent with her, to inventory their exchange of statements, questions, responses, and to review, as well, all the nonverbal messages that his reporter mind could recall. Running through it all was a musing about the encounter with Lily at this particular time in his life, and a seeming question about his life, but available to him in only the slimmest outline.

The woman Lucius was currently seeing in Washington, D.C., was white. Though they both attended Duke as undergraduates, he did not meet Claire Bolton until she was introduced to him as Senator Fawcett's legislative aide. Claire said yes to going for coffee with Lucius and, then, to much more as they explored their relationship with each other on the Hill.

Lucius described Claire as bright and courageous—the same adjectives Claire would choose for Lucius, though using a different rationale and definition for his courage than he would use regarding hers. Claire was from the West Coast and had never been south of the Mason–Dixon line before college. Her parents met while attending Cal Berkeley and, though they openly supported their children's dating choices, Lucius was an adventure Claire had not yet had. This was, also, Lucius's first experience of serious dating outside his race. They both committed to keeping the relationship real insofar as anything could be real given the enchantingly self-important atmosphere of the nation's capital, second in working-glam only to Manhattan.

FEARFUL OF FALLING INTO THE GAP between her world and the one she just entered, Lily mustered a plan to hide out in the women's restroom inside the meeting hall for as long as she could. The sharp contrast between her current life and the urgency of events now facing her were too much to confront in such a harrowing setting. If possible, she'd wait until the service and meal following concluded, find Hugh, make apologies, and catch the next flight back to New York. It seemed right in terms of self-preservation—and even plausible. The sounds of nylon hose rubbing and a voice talking to herself roused Lily into instant recognition of the woman from the kitchen known as Aunt Evie. Her presence exposed what seemed like betrayal in Lily's stratagem. The people filling Mt. Sinai Church of Deliverance were not a monolith—they were individuals, some of whom Lily had already met over biscuits and gravy.

"The church look like to burst it seams today," said Aunt Evie. "Likely to come off itself when everyone start to teeterin' and shoutin'—Dr. McGhee start the sermon yet?"

"Uh, no," said Lily. "And I don't want to miss that."

"You better finish up your bi'ness here and get on back then," advised Aunt Evie. "Dr. McGhee don't like no comin' and goin' durin' the preachin', 'cept for the Holy Spirit!"

"I'm on my way." Lily drew in a resolute breath filled with mixed emotions and walked in the direction of the front steps. She saw Lucius come out a side door of the landing at the top of the steps and begin to look around.

Their eyes signaled each other: Lucius, for Lily to proceed in his direction and Lily, for Lucius to stay right there. In that moment, Lily had a clear idea of Lucius. One question from him set off a collision of the present with her past—broken parts now flying dangerously—things she hadn't thought about for years had become projectiles which she could identify only just before impact.

Her father's admonition figured prominently in the shower of bits and pieces from her childhood and teen years: She would not endanger another's life. Her decision scrubbed from her imagination any consideration of a suitor of another race as a romantic interest—not even as a friend or companion, at least in any true sense. Lily was coming to grips with both the cost of her color in America and the cost of maintaining the color line—only barely, but barely felt monumental to Lily. She wondered now if considering marriage to her boyfriend Ethan was not only about who he was but also about who he was not.

Lily managed a quick smile, as Lucius opened the same side door from which he had moments ago emerged, anxious to find Lily and make sure she was all right. "You okay?" Lucius whispered into Lily's ear as she brushed past his lips.

"I'll let you know," said Lily, walking through the door and into the church, which by now had warmed up with singing and praying and all the preliminary gettin' ready for Mt. Sinai's preacher to ascend the pulpit.

It occurred to Lily, as she contrasted what she was immediately witnessing with the vigil the night before—each prompted by the same violent event—that Sam Jefferson and Vernon Hammond were sons of two different communities, but of the same culture that made both objects of its practice of racial sacrifice.

St. Luke's service was about a parishioner's boy who acted out the wishes of others, but who was cast as a soloist in the drama, an individual acting beyond the pale of polite society. Mt. Sinai Church of Deliverance held the life of Sam Jefferson, as well as his surviving family, in the middle of the community with a safety net so strong and of such fine mesh that no individual could pass through.

During the dialogue between preacher and congregation, Lily leaned into Lucius and asked, "Have you talked to Sam Jefferson's wife yet?"

"No, Lily . . ." demurred Lucius. "I . . . I don't know what I could say to the wife of a lynched man." The stark statement brought Lily to ground zero. There was no need for more conversation between her and Lucius the rest of the service—only silence and the deep honoring of each other's humanity.

IT TOOK NEARLY HALF AN HOUR for the church to empty and the pastor and his flock to relocate at graveside for Sam Jefferson's burial. Lily had forgotten about this part of the service but was well past needing an excuse to duck out early. She happily accepted Lucius's invitation to ride with him to the cemetery.

"I assume cremations aren't all that frequent in the Black community?"

"You assume right," said Lucius. "Burials are just that. And, given the history, are another exercise of freedom not enjoyed during slave times. People had to sneak out at night to give the dead their props. Societies formed during slavery to ensure that the gone-on would be put away proper—it might be nickels and dimes, and they might not be able to pay their other bills, but people would stay current with insurance premiums."

"Lucius, I really appreciate you spending time giving me context and explanation for what's going on."

"As long as you don't think you're getting the whole story—Black folks like to tell just enough so you think you're inside the house when you've scarcely set foot on the property. The art of evasion."

"Hey, I've been fogged in for the last, not even twenty-four hours, but I don't think it's your evasive behavior—it's *my* lack of historical perspective . . . basic awareness—at least your talking to me lets me know I'm not totally out of contact with this other world."

"This other world—you mean like a Dark Continent on this continent?"

"Yeah—that's precisely what it's like. I feel like I just walked into the pages of a US history textbook I've never seen before."

"And—is it whetting your appetite or scaring you away?"

"Truth?" Lily looked straight at Lucius. "An hour ago, I almost called an airport shuttle."

"But you didn't."

"Plot was foiled right as it hatched. Busted in the ladies' room by Aunt Evie, one of the women I talked to in the kitchen before the service—made me think I'd be missing something if I didn't get my butt back in church in time for the sermon."

"True?"

"Close enough."

Lucius pulled his tan compact rental into a space beside a parked maroon Lincoln Continental. "Some brothers know how to ride."

"Yeah, and you probably have one of these and a driver back in D.C., chauffeur you around from scoop to scoop."

"With a flag on the hood to simulate officialdom."

"Take me for a drive?"

"Anytime."

Lucius and Lily walked over to the rows of folding chairs but stood behind when they discovered there was not enough seating for everyone. The sun shone the brightest it had all day. The Reverend Dr. Otis McGhee turned his leather-bound King James Bible, softened from use, to the Book of Revelation. He began reading: "They shall hunger no more, neither thirst no more . . . And God shall wipe away all tears from their eyes . . . And I saw a new heaven and a new earth: for the first heaven and the first earth were passed away." Lily knew the passage well after poring over the text two weeks prior for a paper in New Testament theology, but today it took on flesh.

"What remains to be done on the story, Lucius?"

"A recitation of lynching history. Profiles of individuals and communities within the community. Some unfinished business for Washington, for the statehouse to comment on in a follow-up—I don't know what remains till I do mop-up back in D.C. How about you, Lily—where do you go from here?"

"I sense some new directions I can't really make out yet—I just know they're out there," said Lily. "Or maybe same direction with a better map."

"When does your plane leave?"

"I think Hugh got us on a seven thirty flight. How about you?"

"I have a seat on a flight," said Lucius, looking at his watch, "that leaves in two hours. Seemed reasonable when I booked according to *The Sentinel* copy deadline—now it seems a little rushed. I'd like to have more time with you."

"Then it sounds like we better get back to the church and grab a chicken leg before you take off—you hungry?"

"You dissin' me?"

"No. I put you on hold."

Exaggerating each word now, Lucius repeated: "I-want-to-have-more-time-with-you, Lily."

"I heard it the first time—I was being coy," said Lily. "Look. Here's the deal. You gotta' get back to where you came from and I gotta get back to where I came from."

"In what sense?"

"Okay. Yes, I wish we had more time—but we don't, so that's how my mind works. We don't, so we won't."

"You kill me with candidness—can we go back to the 'more time'?"

"Are we talking immediate—or future?"

"Let's start with now. I have a plane to catch and so do you. Any possibility you could change your flight?"

"Lucius, I'm seeing someone in New York," said Lily. "In fact, we're engaged. Sorry."

"No sorry needed. I'm with someone too. What's his name?"

"Ethan. A dislocated Midwesterner whose family roots are in Germany and Wales. So, what's her name?"

"Claire." Lucius cleared his throat. "Claire's a California girl who switched allegiance to the East Coast in college. Have yet to meet her parents. Dad is English, mother French with some Black Creole from a grandparent, so under the one drop rule, Claire is Black."

"The one drop rule?"

"The definition of race in America—but only for Blacks."

"Not Asian? Not Latino?"

"Exclusively for Blacks."

"You're kidding."

"The trick, of course, is to identify by appearance or whatever, someone one sixty-fourth or one eighth—or even one quarter Black—but then white superpowers have claimed infallibility in race IDing since they created the law. Even if trumped by federal legislation, that one drop rule still blatantly functions as a grandfather clause in a lot of places."

"If not formally, informally," said Lily. "You're right. One drop . . . not in my history book."

"Slave owners legislated evasion of their parental responsibility toward children they fathered by only recognizing the *black* blood inherited. Exceptions made if the baby came out of the cooker white."

"I know it wasn't even acknowledged as infidelity—"

"Owner-man produced *workers* with slave women— plural, but fathered *heirs* with a spouse. Can you imagine seeing your child working in a field, being beaten for not moving fast enough, and then selling that child off because you don't need or want him anymore? Auction block was a useful salvo for keeping family matters in perspective—got rid of the evidence and turned a profit besides."

"But not all plantation owners were cruel."

"Ms. Lily-beration. You mean to tell me that forced labor for no pay—no matter how nice massah is—isn't cruel? Add to that, not enough food, little access to timely and decent medical care—hey, let's walk and talk," said Lucius as he circled an arm around Lily, steering both of them toward the car.

"Other people have been exploited in this country, and women—of any race—are still being exploited."

"You might wanna take that up with a sistah," rejoined Lucius. "You do have sistahs at your seminary, Lily?"

She winced. "Uh . . . probably? . . . Not yet?"

"Could it have something to do with the fact that among hyphenated Americans, only Africans were forced to be citizens while systematically denied the rights of citizenship?" hammered Lucius as he pulled open the passenger door for Lily. "And, when given their rights after the Civil War, were denied the exercise of those rights?"

"So, I guess Vernon Hammond is just—"

Lucius paused the conversation, telling Lily to wait a sec, as he closed her door and went around to the driver's side.

As he started the engine Lily began again, "I was gonna say that Vernon Hammond is just following in the footsteps of his forebears."

"Who found an effective way to control the Black man and at the same time uphold the honor of the South," Lucius snapped. "Yeah, Vernon Hammond got the message all right."

"How could he not, growing up in Dixieland?"

"The North had its ways of discouraging life, liberty, and the pursuit of happiness, too—hell, of limiting access to basic necessities. Even border states like Maryland and Missouri had their share of lynching.

"And not just the Vernon Hammonds were responsible either—you probably know that the Ku Klux Klan was started by a starving Midwestern Methodist parson who got other clergy and people in business and politics interested,"

Lucius continued. "The KKK has never been just common, rural whites."

"But all men of God, right?" asked Lily sarcastically.

"Boys. All good ol' *boys* of God who allow the violence to continue by not taking murderers into custody and by avoiding investigation. Or if the suspect is picked up, not getting a conviction. Or if a conviction does happen, by letting the bastard off with a small fine or a suspended sentence, which was probably minimal in the first place."

"Vernon Hammond seems like someone from another era," reflected Lily. "When was the last lynching in this state . . . or anywhere?"

"Racism creates its own time warp. According to statistics there have been 4,709 lynchings—defined as 'slaying for racial reasons'—in forty-three states since records originated. From the years 1882 to 1968, Texas, at almost five hundred, holds the number three spot behind only Mississippi and Georgia.

"As for this state's last lynching," Lucius went on, "about a year ago there was a strange disappearance of a man whose body was discovered a month later with evidence that he had been tied to a tree with barbed wire and burned. Typical story: Authorities hauled in some suspects, members of the local chapter of a hate group, but refused to prosecute the kidnapping and murder as a federal crime. Instead, they pitched it as a drug deal gone bad. History is filled with surprises. Sam Jefferson's murder, case in point, shows not just backwater Blacks in Georgia get lynched. In fact, uniformed Black Americans returning home from the World Wars were lynched and otherwise persecuted."

"So why hasn't there ever been more Black retaliation against whites—more than, say, the slave revolts or even the riots after King and Malcolm were assassinated?" Lily asked.

"Blacks are no more inherently violent against their own human species than whites, number one. And number two,

Blacks in America would rather outwit whites than kill 'em. I suppose that has something to do with their practice of religious tradition, which sure didn't come from admiring the behavior of the plantation owner or his goons. Or from the mistress of the house—compliant out of fear, perhaps—but, compliant, nonetheless. Protecting white southern womanhood—the bogus justification for lynching after slaves were freed, even though there exists no record of white women being molested when Johnny Reb went off to fight for the Confederacy and left them in the company of those same Black men."

"It's still used," said Lily. "I mean, I was raised to fear Black maleness as something malicious that required wariness on my part, which I think comes from the same myth—or is it? That all Black men desire white women."

"I can speak to that, but, right now, I gotta turn in here and find a phone."

Lily saw the announcement of Sam Jefferson's "HOME-GOING" for the first time on the church's signboard.

As he opened the door and extended his hand to help her out, Lucius said, "How 'bout we continue this inside—go grab that chicken leg while I call American."

Feet on the ground, Lily thanked Lucius and watched him walk in the direction of the pastor's study. Then she turned and walked to the meeting hall, where women familiar to her from socializing in the kitchen asked, "How you doin', hon?" For the first time since the morning, Lily took notice of Hugh's presence.

"Hi stranger," said Hugh. "Either I was slow, or you were fast—I looked for you after the service."

"Here at the church—or at the cemetery?" Lily asked.

"Both—but by the time I spotted you, you were pretty wrapped up in conversation," said Hugh. "Didn't want to interrupt."

"How are you doing?" Lily moved the locus of conversation back to Hugh.

"A little tired—this kind of thing . . . maybe it's years of tired," said Hugh. "You must be starving—go grab a plate."

"Oh, I will," said Lily, looking at the door expectantly.

"Come sit with Otis and me," said Hugh, gesturing to the table at the head of the room. "Here—I'll get a chair."

Lily walked over to the gray-haired pastor who rose to greet her. "Otis McGhee. Nice of you to join us—Miss Wallace, is it?"

"Yes, Lily Wallace, thank you," she said, extending her hand, which was met by one of the pastor's, his other patting her shoulder in a kindly welcome.

"We're well-fed here at Deliverance." Otis McGhee's eyes looked down at his middle, then lit up in a laugh.

"I had a chance to meet your kitchen crew before the service," said Lily. "They let me do some tasting—great cooks!"

"Have you been introduced to Mrs. Jefferson yet?"

Lily had to stop and think of the name just given and its connection with the widow's first name: Cyrl. Hoping to cover her pause with a confession, she replied, "No, I'm afraid I haven't had—or made—the opportunity."

"Well, why don't you go fix yourself a plate and then we'll see to the how-dos. She's a lovely woman—a lovely mother. We're not going to let her get too far from us," said Reverend Otis, his eyes looking to the other side of the room. "It seems God wasn't exactly watchin' the shop. Seems He step outside and for that little bit o' time he out, the devil do his mischief with the Hamm'n boy and his friends. Then they do they evil mess with Sam Jefferson.

"We've lived through terrible days before," he continued. We know they come—we know they do come. But we know His eyes on us in our trouble as they be on the sparrow. Go on now. Fill up that plate. If there's a hunger can be easily fed with food the good Lawd and good cooks provide—up to us to do the rest an' get it from the hand to the mouth!"

But before Lily could take the pastor's advice, Hugh walked up in the company of two other men about his age, also in clergy collars. They were talking and laughing like they shared boyhood secrets, as, indeed, turned out to be the case.

"Lily, I'd like you to meet Farley Johnson on my right and Howard Pickett on my left," said Hugh, nodding to one side and then the other. "Gentlemen, Miss Lily Wallace, my aide who hails from the great state of Texas."

As Lily stuck her hand out for shaking, Hugh said, "Farley's dad was my history teacher in high school. I did my best to make sure he earned every dollar of his pay. I'll tell you, it was as hard-earned as I was hard-headed."

"Yeah, we had us some times, some do-right times, but mostly it was do-wrong. And look at us now," Farley laughed, shoulders shaking, bent over at the waist. "Sorry, Miss Wallace, for actin' like a buncha silly old men. But that's jes' what we are." Farley cracked himself up again. "This one here," Farley indicated by pointing his thumb sideways to Hugh, "he's got tuh come back and eat some greens and get in touch with his soul now and then. Man lose his soul up Nawth. Trade one set uh circumstance for 'nother. He went off to college and next thing any us know, he become Episcopass. Traitor to the AME. But you back home now, Hugh." Farley doubled up again with Howard egging him on saying, "You tellin' the God's honest truth, Farley, you tellin' it like God planted it."

"Yeah, if it weren't for these two hit men," said Hugh, "I'd still be in the South. Just couldn't take the grilling. Had me on the spit all the time, layin' on that sauce—you can see they have no mercy."

"Not for some Black expatriate," said Howard, "who only comes back on official business once in a blue moon."

"But, seriously, Miss Wallace, we glad you're here, keepin' track o' this ol' man, make sure he don't pass for young as well as white," said Farley, winking at Lily. "This kin' of thing known to you all in Texas, Miss Wallace?"

Lily was confused. Was he talking about older men teasing, trying not to act their age? Having a meal after a funeral? To what was he referring? She didn't want to appear ignorant, but she couldn't keep up with the friendly ribbing and reminiscing. She smiled and raised her eyebrows and bobbed her head in a sometimes-yes, sometimes-no fashion.

"So, you know someone met same fate as Sam Jefferson in the part of Texas you raised in?" asked Farley.

All eyes were on Lily. She could admit mistaking Farley's earlier question, admit giving a wrong, if not ambiguous, response. Or, she could lie. But she didn't want to dishonor the group surrounding her. "I wish that I could say I am more informed about this sort of violence around where I grew up, but it wasn't a part of my world," said Lily.

"Now, I didn't mean to put you on the spot, Miss Wallace—"

"You couldn't put me on the spot any more than the last twenty-four hours have," said Lily. "I've been thinking a lot about why I didn't know more . . . it just wasn't something I knew about."

"I appreciate that," said Farley. "'Preciate the candor. You rather an exception, Miss Wallace. Don't get many young white female sistahs come travelin' all the way that you traveled to be here in this serious mess."

It's my job, thought Lily, knowing that Farley was pressing for more. *Why her? Lucius's question again: Why was she here?*

"Actually, I feel like I've awakened a decade too late," said Lily, *and shades too light to understand.*

"Again, we don' mean to put you on the spot, Miss Wallace. Just interested in what you seein' these old eyes might be missin'."

"Murder is no less unpleasant in New York, certainly. But here . . . here it's out in the open. *Race* is out in the open," said Lily.

"It tends to give that impression," said Hugh.

"In New York, race as a motive seems more subtle. But against the immediate backdrop of the South . . ." said Lily, "something I've seen as not all that amazing—Hugh's position as Executive Officer to the Presiding Bishop—suddenly stands out." Lily shrugged her shoulders and turned empty hands upward. "I bring nothing new to the table."

"It's the bringing that's most important," said Howard. "Don't care new, old, or neither! Like Farley said, we glad you're here. And I wouldn't worry too much 'bout the color line, the Good Book tells us, we go where we want to fin' pasture. Now let's see about somethin' sweet to finish off this fine meal. You have some fine cooks in your sheepfold, Otis."

"Better count 'em 'fore we leave," Farley added and, with that, stoked the laughter again.

"WHERE'S MY CHICKEN LEG?"

Lily started, almost dropping the plate she had begun to fill with items she had been looking forward to since the pretasting earlier in the day with the women in the kitchen. "Every man for himself."

"In New York, maybe. But in the South," said Lucius, "a concept as foreign as riding the subway."

"I'm so hungry I need a second dish just for myself. Look at *all* this food," said Lily as she moved a pile of candied carrots with a biscuit to make room on the plate for rice and fried chicken gravy. "Any luck changing your flight?"

"Yeah," said Lucius. "Wanna ride with me to the airport?"

"Chicken leg or no."

"I'm a forgiving kind of guy."

"Well, yeah. I mean if you're going in time for my flight."

"You said seven thirty before," said Lucius. "Can have you there and checking in at six thirty—whenever you'd like."

"Thanks."

"Where are you sitting?"

Lily indicated the table where Hugh and Otis looked to be in conference and said, "I'm gonna set this plate down and come back for dessert before they start closing down."

AS IF THEY COULD TELL something about her character by what dessert Lily chose, the women of Mt. Sinai Church of Deliverance watched to see if she would go for deep dish apple pie or a stout stand of chocolate cake. Or would it be a bowl of Ms. Emmett Woods's cobbler, made with peaches put up the previous summer to be opened up at just such a time as this, when winter lingered past the secular and religious rites of spring.

As soon as Lily made her selections, cutting precut pieces in half so as to sample more, there was a flutter of aprons to get to her with tea or coffee, and did she want one lump or two of sugar, and could she use some cream in that coffee, and why not take herself another plate to hold all the treasures the women of Mt. Sinai had to offer of things out of season as well as in? Strawberry jam thumbprint cookies, rhubarb crisp, slabs of pound cake, candied cherries and pecans, buttery golden rounds with maple icing. Lily bit into a bar of shortbread containing nuggets of black walnuts, elegant and liqueur-tasting, reminding her of her own grandmother's baking as well as the deli around the corner from where she lived in New York. She was glad for this small connection between parts of her life at seeming variance with each other.

She thought about how her life centered on people talking about appropriating, not living, life. She flashed on second grade and a field trip to the Dallas post office, where employees told with pride how fast letters could be sorted. Every envelope had a slot, because the system could only accommodate slottable mail.

Perceptions that had shadowed Lily much of her life had changed overnight in a place previously unknown and unknowable. The shift had no place to lay its head in Lily's wearying and changing world. She would need a guide and looked over at Hugh, still with his boyhood circle of friends. Lily wished that she had a similar group of bonded allies, as she faced her return to the melting ice of spring in New York City.

"Lily Wallace and Lucius Clay, I'd like you to meet Cyrl Jefferson," said Mt. Sinai's pastor. "Lily is aide to Hugh Lovelle, here, whom you've already met. Lucius is a journalist with—is it *The Constitution?*"

"*The Sentinel*, the *L.A. Sentinel*," said Lucius, extending his hand to Cyrl's, which had just let go of Lily's, the two women looking into each other's eyes. "I'm very sorry, Mrs. Jefferson."

Cyrl Jefferson parted her lips as if to speak but no words escaped. Lucius's condolence was acknowledged with only the slightest tip of her head.

SOON IT WAS TIME FOR CHILDREN and food containers to be rounded up before saying goodbyes. Lily clasped the hands of the women she had just met that afternoon, hands that had prepared the sacred meal that followed the sacred farewell to a treasured son killed by unloving hands, hands fearful that God was partial after all and needed human intervention to correct the divine way gone awry.

Hateful hands were in the hands of the law now, but it would take a stretch of courage to believe that justice would be served. Courage for Samuel Jefferson's community and family to believe that this kind of violence would not be tolerated. No matter. They were used to peeping around corners for their own survival, seeing what no eyes should have to see.

They would remain in the homes their parents knew, the ones grandparents built, continuing the attempt to settle in the midst of what could always be unsettling. They weren't going any place but back and forth between home, work, and church. Marrying, raising families, celebrating the one child who made it through high school and then college, and mourning the loss of that same child moving to seek their professional destiny in a place far from the home where they grew up. But these losses were easier to take than the loss of a child—no matter what age—by death.

"We'll be here, Lily, any time you want to make your way back to pay us a visit," said Aunt Evie.

"Yeah, we always heah cookin' and cleanin' and makin' do wid what the good Lawd give us," chimed Tildie.

Puddin' warmed her send-off: "You take care y'self, Miss Lily, in dat New Yawk City!"

". . . LITTLE WHITE SOUTHERN BOYS suckled by black breasts told at a not-much-older age that it's time to treat their Black mother like hired help and her to treat them like lord of the manor—that's gotta fuck with the psyches of both the boy and his bio-mother, who allows, but at the same time resents, black maternal surrogacy."

"Anything published on Black surrogate mothers' influence on white kids' sexual development?" asked Lily.

"There may be, but I haven't read it," said Lucius. "Ironic, isn't it? The historic white dependency on black caretaking, while imagining any influence to be nonexistent, because white minds, *some*, render Blacks in caretaking roles, invisible. But have a Black child sit next to a white child in school, drink out of the same drinking fountain, use the same facilities—might lead to handholding or worse."

"Interesting," returned Lily. "Before I actually lived there, my impression of New York City was that there was a lot of racial mixing, but now I think it's just as segregated as that little burg in Texas where I came from. There are just a lot more people is all."

"The Supreme Court only a few years ago overturned laws against interracial marriage. Virginians Richard and Mildred Loving appealed their state's statute."

"When was that?" Lily blushed at her ignorance. "I mean, *how* recently?"

"1967. Six years ago. With sixteen states still endorsing white supremacist doctrine."

"You know, I did a project in seventh grade, which involved reviewing local ordinances and state laws about marriage," said Lily. "It's when I learned the word *miscegenation* and thought how weird that interracial sex had its own word."

"Specifically, *black and white* interracial sex—allowances were made for Pocahontas and John Rolfe's descendants. With black, only takes a drop."

"Impressive that it only took one drop to create a whole idiom that manufactured categories of coupling privilege and progeny—an entire canon that superseded the Constitution. And for so long," said Lily.

"So, how effective was the canon in Greenville, Texas?" asked Lucius.

"Oh, I'd say almost one hundred percent effective. Only one bit of gossip about a friend of a friend's father. The family lived in Dallas and had Black help, and, supposedly, one maid was pregnant by the father," said Lily. "But I think you're asking if there were any consensual relationships that would have been impossible to keep secret. No, can't think of one instance of *Guess Who's Coming to Dinner?* in Greenville. How about Galveston?"

"Well, as a city on the gulf there was a lot more flux between those who lived there and those stationed there or, otherwise, in port for a while. High school sports is when I started seeing the world in black and white. I played basketball, and I can tell you, firsthand, that my buddies and I were definitely interested in mixing it up. I don't know that much permanence was attached to any of those combinations. I think it amounted to a lot of talk, some dark-alley sex—no real credibility given to any kind of future relationship.

"And, I only knew of white girls pursuing black boys," Lucius went on. "Some reason, not the other way around, which reinforced the assumption that for a white guy to hook up with a Black chick was not just a step, but a whole lotta steps down. Didn't matter how poor, puny, or ugly the white guy was. Just the reverse for a Black dude gettin' it on with a white princess. She gonna be that Black boy's ticket to somewhere. 'Course in the sexual frenzy of all that mixin', we were never sure where that somewhere was."

"Still?"

"Oh, yeah, that assumption's still out there, sure," said Lucius. "Only now it's put in more perspective. Chasin' that forbidden fruit, those girls had no concern for the danger their attention exposed us to. Now, there's more acknowledging the danger of Black males getting involved with white females—the self-loathing of 'white is right, black get back.'"

"So, before Claire, did you ever take a chance on a white girl?" asked Lily.

"Not many white girls *to* take a chance on comin' up in my neighborhood."

"Same experience in Greenville," said Lily. "All the Black kids lived in Hamilton Park; all the white kids lived everywhere but."

"And now that you're in the Big Apple?" asked Lucius.

Lily caught her breath and held it a beat before answering softly, "I've been wondering the same thing," was all Lily could muster to plug up the holes punched by Lucius's question.

"I have a vision," said Lucius. "Of all us colored folk— from pink to chocolate, pale lavender to sapphire black—all passengers on the same train going down the same track. The scenery, which is all our past history, goes by us in a blur. We don't talk, we just listen to this original, pervasive, irrevocable Rhythm in us, between us. And then, there's this monotonous background noise—*white noise?*—that competes with the Rhythm. Though unsuccessfully."

At once, Lily looked at Lucius. "My God, you're pretty."

"Where did that come from?"

"I don't know, just the way the sun is hitting your face. You're like a painting that looks like a single, solid color at a distance but up close there are particles of different colors."

"A man of many shades."

"You are."

The airport exit sign showed Lucius where to get off the highway, but not how to bring the conversation to a satisfying conclusion.

"Lily, thank you for riding with me to the airport," said Lucius. "This wasn't a routine assignment to begin with, and meeting you made it all the more unusual."

"Too little time," said Lily. "Thanks for making it go a little further."

"May I write to you?"

"You'll have time?" said Lily, not wanting to be direct about his current relationship.

"I have time, but will you answer?" asked Lucius, dodging the same concern about Lily's relationship with Ethan.

"I could do that," said Lily.

Lucius pulled into the car rental lot, stopped the motor, and dug out a card from his wallet. "Here's my card. I'll write down my home number—you can call me at home." Lucius jotted down the ten digits of his number in Georgetown.

"Here's mine," said Lily. "It already has my home number on it."

THE SHUTTLE STOPPED AT AMERICAN FIRST. "Well, I guess this is my stop," said Lucius as his eyes moved to meet Lily's.

She watched him get his bags, turn to say another goodbye before walking down the couple of steps and out the door of the shuttle to the curb, where he turned and said goodbye, again. The lights of the shuttle came on as the driver pulled away and headed for the United Air terminal and Lily's return home.

———

CONSULTING THE ARRIVAL/DEPARTURE schedule, Lily located her flight and headed for the gate. Coming toward her, pushed in a wheelchair, a man cradled socked and shoed prosthetic legs like a pair of salami. *Poor man,* Lily commiserated. Then, rushing on, worried about missing the plane, her pity turned to envy. *Lucky man. Having someone to push him where he needs to go.*

"Thank God this isn't La Guardia," said Lily in out-of-breath puffs as she approached Hugh, sitting in a chair in their boarding area. "I'd have never made it."

"Relax, Lily," said Hugh. "You're in the South. Where time slows down—and waits for you."

"Some things are definitely at a standstill here," said Lily, observing Hugh as only one of three Black passengers waiting for the flight to Atlanta. "How do you do this, Hugh?"

"Do what?" asked Hugh, as two white pilots with duffle bags and four white flight attendants carrying overnight cases breezed past the waiting passengers, exiting through double doors held open by an older Black man.

"Slog through the *whiteness* every day," said Lily.

"You make *white* sound monolithic, Lily. There *are* distinctions, you know."

"So I'm seeing, more and more. Twenty-four hours ago, I could've only named one. White *trash.*"

"Media's favorite."

"At least it saves us from being *totally* invisible to ourselves."

"Big cost to pay for those shouldering such an unasked-for burden. Uhp—that's us," said Hugh, when the counter attendant summoned passengers in the back rows to line up, right after first-class.

After finding their seats and stowing their carry-ons, Hugh said with a flourish of his arm, "After you, Lily. My legs are happier on the aisle." When she told him about the man with removable legs, her tall travel partner smiled. "With these stilts, that would be a handy option. But, now, getting back to your question about *race*. And the options I *do* have, relative to your question about how I deal with this construct of human machination . . ." Hugh ducked into himself, then reappeared, saying, "Funny how we always have to find some way of making our little bit of human matter more important than another's.

"White Americans, though, have gone about it with a *peculiar* vengeance. And with no small help from Mother Church parsing her children into light and dark and proclaiming it the ordering of God Almighty. The same God who, in 1954, was added to the Pledge of Allegiance, just before the word *indivisible*. The same year *Brown v. the Board of Education* reversed 'separate but equal,' schoolchildren began to recite: 'One nation under God.' The truth is, America is one *mulatto* nation which, for most of its history, has precariously held the self-evident truth of 'inalienable rights' in one hand and the slave master's lash in the other."

Then, reminding himself of another part of Lily's question, Hugh continued, "Every day, was it? Every day I plant both feet on the ground, say my prayers standing up, usually while shaving and looking in the mirror at this black mug, and thank God for the help I know I'm gonna need that day. Same thing my mama and daddy do, though the mirror is my own wrinkle. My parents haven't always had a mirror, nor would they use it, perhaps, in the same *siddity* way I do," said Hugh, cutting his grave words with humor. "Sounds like your eyes have been opened a slit or two, Lily."

"And that's about all. I'm wondering how I'm gonna get them open wider."

"Well, you have lots of material. Stuff always goin' on, and you're young. I guess I've just grown accustomed to the stuff I do and the stuff I don't do, last decade notwithstanding," said Hugh. "I probably learned to draw the line from the cradle. A lot of generations of suffering before mine—could have been something passed on to me even *before* the cradle."

"I learned to draw the same line," said Lily. "I just never saw it so clearly as I have on this *excursion* outside home borders."

"What was happening with you the last five years or so?" asked Hugh.

"You mean civil rights–wise?"

"You were at Brown, if memory serves me."

"Oh. There was lots of civil rights activity on campus," said Lily, "but I wasn't part of it. For me, it was like watching the news on TV. Something I could opt to do or not. I gave more thought and reflection to my senior thesis than to what was immediately happening."

"What was that about?"

"You mean my non-activism?"

"No—your senior thesis."

Lily laughed nervously. "I was looking at strands of feminist thought in nineteenth century American literature."

"And was the expedition successful?"

"Actually, yeah," said Lily. "I was ready to continue on in grad school."

"And did you find any of those feminist strands twisted with race?"

"Among abolitionist women," said Lily. "But when they became suffragists, feminism was out the window. The vote for women was argued more as a right of race than of gender. Which, of course, left Black women out of the equation completely. It appeared as though white women became *white* overnight," reflected Lily. "Kind of how I'm feeling."

"Black has always had a whitening effect," said Hugh. "Black inferiority defining white superiority has been written into American culture since the Constitution. It is *the* most successful commodity, from entertaining to selling pancakes, from 'separate but equal' to anti-miscegenation laws. Like Tide," quipped Hugh, "one drop of black can 'make your whites whiter.'"

"That's some of how I see sexism. *Female* used to define *male*; *masculinity* needing *femininity* to define itself."

"I can't presume to know what it's like being female—"

"I *tried* to avoid knowing what it's like to be female," said Lily with a laugh that was half disgust. "I thought that if I didn't gender-ID myself, nobody else would bother with it either. Until I was turned down for a fellowship. They said 'sorry' and that it was 'highly competitive—lots of good candidates.' All that. So, at the time I thought I wasn't as well qualified as another Tom, Dick, or Harry. Today, I'd say it's because I *wasn't* a Tom, Dick, or Harry. I think I wasn't selected because I'm a bigger investment risk. Males marry, if they *must*. But they're not gonna get pregnant and drop out of school."

"The assumption being," Hugh filled in, "that you can't be a mother and have a career at the same time."

"Oh, I think it's more than an assumption—an assumption that, by the way, has been disproved over and over again," said Lily. "I think, like race, it's a deeply embedded, self-serving ideology. Crazy-making."

"I hear that," Hugh sympathized. "I, myself, try to lay the race thing down about every six months so I *don't* go crazy. Try to fool myself into thinking, like popular opinion, that discrimination has been dealt with, because it's no longer 'legal.' Doesn't last but about five minutes— and all in my head. No, Lily. Though we can't escape our flesh, neither does it define us. And, especially, are we bound to resist another's notion of how gender or race might hold us captive."

"There's so much to come to terms with . . ." said Lily.

"Could be a sign of longevity!"

"Thanks for giving me the benefit of the doubt here," said Lily. "My choice of friends, college, where I eat, which theaters in which neighborhoods I frequent . . . whom I consider *experts*. Who speaks for me and for whom I'm spoken—the list is endless."

"You were *spoken for* long before you were even born— unless your parents were exceptionally open and skilled at dodging racist bullets," said Hugh. "It's a matter of reproduction rights: not only *who* is allowed to reproduce, but also *with whom*—and, very importantly, reproduction of *what* ideology."

A flight attendant in pressed navy-blue uniform crisply asked for their dinner preferences: Would they like the roast chicken and new potatoes or the Salisbury steak and mixed vegetables? They both chose the steak.

"I never liked *mixed* vegetables," said Lily, looking out the window and realizing she was about halfway home, whatever that turned out to be. "May have to reexamine that one!"

"Well, like I said, you have lots of material to work with," said Hugh. "Speaking of reproduction rights, what are your thoughts on *Roe v. Wade*, Lily?"

SLEET ASSAILED THE WINDOWS OF the plane the closer it got to LaGuardia, where passengers had to walk between plane and terminal due to a backup in United Air bays. Lily was unprepared for the onslaught of wind and cold that ripped through every layer of clothing, exposing her to the freezing reality of being back home.

Lily felt a wistful twinge, as she remembered leaving Texas and her mother the last trip home. She may have been *grown* there, but the East Coast was more in step with her own rhythm and sense of what the world was about: all-night delis on sidewalks that never emptied, long-haired flower children in Greenwich Village, love-ins at Central Park. Women on Fifth Avenue walked dogs better groomed than most of the city's population. They looked neither left nor right, as if nothing was worth their concern save the fur ball at the end of a rhinestone leash.

Lily made New York her home in every way possible: a job for now, ordination sometime, a suitor she may marry. She had her own flat with her own neighbors and corner grocery, in a colorful, but safe, block. Sundays, she worshipped at a church that was like, or so she thought, a smaller version of the United Nations. Though her life in the city was, in fact, circumscribed, she appreciated having the freedom to go anywhere, anytime.

Bright lights assaulted Lily as she stepped onto the carpeted ramp leading into the waiting area. She saw a grin move toward her, first appearing as an apparition, then becoming more recognizable as light reflected off her boyfriend Ethan's wire-framed glasses, making the flesh of his forehead shiny.

"Good to see you too—means the cab's still running," said Hugh, acknowledging the ghost from her past, one bare, cocoa hand clasping the gloved hand of Ethan's vaporous body, the other patting its woolen arm. "Well, all right then. See you back at the station day after tomorrow, Lily. Thanks for all your help on this one."

"Thank *you*, Hugh," said Lily, inwardly saying, *Don't leave me, don't leave me here with this stranger.* "I'm not really sure I did help."

"We'll talk more on Monday. PB'll be back from Jerusalem Tuesday, and he'll want to know all about it," said Hugh. "I'm counting on you to remember what I don't."

"God's witness," said Lily, raising two fingers in mock oath. Then, as she used to do with a certain tree at the park near her home when it seemed like the most permanent thing in her life, Lily wrapped her arms halfway round her mentor, saying, "Thanks, again, for everything."

Lily watched Hugh, until the river of people closed behind him and a bouquet of lavender thrust in her face startled her out of a lingering reverie that had time left on its meter.

The fruity sweetness of her favorite lilac-gray roses replaced conjured aromas of fried chicken and baked ham, cologne and pomade. As lips touched her lips, Lily smelled the spicy cheek of the man who knew her preferences. Some of them. She responded, detachedly, as a customer finally able to transact business upon reaching the front of the line.

"Geez, can you do better than that?" complained Ethan.

Realizing the teasing reproof was directed at her, Lily, regardless, offered little more feeling, mechanically punching Ethan's lips with hers in the same way she might turn off a morning alarm. She began reconciling herself to the wakefulness of being home. Though she had to deboard, Lily resolved to leave some bag packed, in order that some part of her might remain on the journey that, in her mind, had only just begun.

"I thought you'd be glad to see me," said Ethan, grinning with too much golly-gee. "I mean, last time I checked, you were still my girl."

Taking some time to study his face and its expression, Lily breathed out, "Hi-i-i . . . Ethan." Then, surprising herself, finding a warmth she would have thought misplaced, she added, "Long time no see."

Suddenly, the flow of bodies picked up Ethan and Lily and carried them downstream to the escalator leading to the baggage claim, an area more crowded than the one they left. People compacted around the baggage belt, bumping into the couple in whom a strangeness began to settle.

"That's mine. The one with the wine-colored band," said Lily. "Can you grab it?"

Ethan easily lifted Lily's suitcase off the conveyor. He took Lily's free arm and steered the two of them out to a blast of ethane and hailed a cab.

"Would you mind?" A well-dressed man, fiftyish, asked to share the taxi, *their* taxi. Lily checked her ambivalent reaction to the stranger inviting himself into their company with no apparent concern over where they were going or whether they would even be heading in the same direction. Seeing the same concern register on Ethan's face, Lily didn't know if she were being reasonable or shameful. The man saw their ambivalence and felt their guard assume its position. Nevertheless, he, too, needed a ride on this icy night.

"I'm sorry to seem so presumptuous, youngblood, but recognizing you from the building we both call *home*, I assumed a common destination."

Irked that the recognition wasn't mutual, Ethan proceeded at curbside to interrogate the supposed neighbor, thus prolonging exposure to the below-zero wind chill. The older man's answer only increased the younger one's clenched irritation. Priding himself on a faculty for observation and detail, Ethan was exasperated that he and this other could be residing at the same address for three years without his notice.

Suddenly, the bone-chill overpowered Ethan's attempts to regain his presumed edge. He peevishly opened the front passenger door to his newly identified neighbor, "After you." The gesture helped Ethan feel as though he might still have a narrow advantage. Remembering Lily only then, Ethan opened the back door. The cabdriver had already relieved

Lily of her carry-on bag, putting it in the trunk. Yet another detail had fallen annoyingly outside Ethan's notice.

Though travel-weary, Lily became reenergized by this simple request to share transportation; her return assumed a new complexity. Lily had not originally intended to go to Ethan's place; rather, she wanted to be in her own apartment and use the dark of night to retrace thoughts of the last forty-eight hours. But the recent exchange piqued Lily's curiosity. She decided to accompany the two to see how it all played out in the cab and, then, alone behind closed doors with Ethan.

Lily had everything she needed still packed in her suitcase, since the next day was Sunday and not a workday. All this was quietly discussed in the upholstered back seat, which reeked of cigarette smoke and hair tonic. The front seat passenger gave directions to the cabby, denying Ethan yet another opportunity to be the alpha man.

WHEN THE TAXI ARRIVED AT ETHAN'S apartment, a single fare was paid the driver with a "Thanks," and "Keep the change." A stammering Ethan protested, struggling to free his wallet from the pants pocket inside his coat. By the time Ethan pulled out two twenties, the Black neighbor had taken his leave with a "See you around, perhaps," to Ethan and a playful wink to Lily.

"I be glad to take all y'all wanna give me, sir, but the other gentleman done taken care all y'all." The driver laughed like this was the best joke he'd heard all day.

"Yeah, well," mumbled Ethan.

Lily told Ethan to *just* get out of the car. She passed the neighbor's wink along to the driver and told him she hoped he didn't freeze to death moving people from one part of the city to another.

"'Preciate your concern, miss. You an' your mister have a nice night now. Don' give no 'cicles chance tuh start formin'! G'on now, git yourselves inside the door," said the taximan, having the last laugh.

The wind whipped the hair around her head as Lily, hoping to see the elevator to identify which floor the mystery neighbor lived on, backed out of the cab and ran up the steps to the front door.

"Damn!" Ethan had just removed Lily's bags from the trunk and was attempting to make his way to the curb, when he stepped in a pothole of icy water.

"Are they new?" Lily yelled over the wind to Ethan, now scrambling up the steps. "Your shoes, Ethan. Are they new?"

"First time out—damn!"

"I'm sorry. Here, get your key out and I'll open up." Lily put out her hand to take the key, but first laid it against Ethan's cheek, saying, "Thanks for meeting my plane, Ethan. Thanks for being here for me after this trip . . . and, sorry if I seem out of it," her voice dipping, "the truth is, I am."

———

THE WEATHER IN NEW YORK was miserable. If it just stayed mounded on the ground, it would have been beautiful. But rain turned the rogue snowfall into spring slush.

When she got home to her apartment the following evening, Lily went right to her desk with all of its talismans: a small bear representing endurance; a decorative inkwell inspiring expression; a diminutive Tara given by a Buddhist friend for the never-ending pursuit of wisdom. And, finally, her eyes lit on her grandmother's paperweight: millefleurs encrypted in a hemisphere of clear glass.

Lily called her sister, but Dee was out. Her brother-in-law Craig said he'd have Dee call Lily back, because he knew she was anxious to talk to her younger sister. He wouldn't say what it was about, just that it was something that would take getting used to, which put Lily on edge.

Opening her suitcase, Lily took out a toiletry bag and a nightgown. As she took off her eye makeup and rinsed the rest of her face, brushed her teeth, and massaged face cream into her forehead and cheeks, Lily thought about her time away. Before unpacking the rest of her suitcase, she toured the flat to see what, if anything, had changed.

Magazine covers displayed white faces. She had tapes of Jimi Hendrix and Gladys Knight and the Pips but the rest were white performers: Beatles, Stones, Doors, Fugs, Turtles, Cream, Who, Jefferson Airplane, Janis Joplin, Carole King . . . of course, her classical collection was all white, and she realized as well, all *guys*.

Lily had no country music, didn't like "hick" tunes. She thought again about knowing who she was by what she wasn't—definitely not *white trash*—the only distinction of whiteness she knew. The rest of the spectrum of whiteness being—well, normative, Lily assured herself of being *normative white* by going down a familiar checklist: no plastic-covered furniture, no Elvis paintings on velvet, no tacky knick-knack collections. Instead, Lily had eclectic furniture, live plants, and interesting framed prints on her walls. And books. Lily thought her library reflected broadmindedness, that it was fairly extensive given her shoestring budget for buying mostly used books. Some were books that everyone of her generation seemed to have, like Kahlil Gibran's poetry. Others like *The First Six Centuries of the Christian Church* were specific to her current theological studies. The one Black authored book she owned was Eldridge Cleaver's *Soul on Ice*, assigned in the only political science class Lily took at Brown. *I am white*, Lily thought, *because I am not Black?*

As she unpacked a skirt to hang in the closet, Lily thought about her makeup and shampoo and every other product used on her body and hair. Wondering what the difference might be if she were Black, she considered the product availability at the corner store. She doubted there was much demand; all the folks in her building were some derivative of white. Lily had never seen any hair or skin products whose packaging featured Black models at Martinelli's Grocery.

Lily thought about how she lived where she did by design. Though she didn't make that much money, she had connections with people at Church Center. If she were Black, would her connections hold up in this apartment complex, this neighborhood, or would race negatively supersede any employer-provided reference? What if, over the phone, she said her name was LaToya? Would the manager have made an excuse, sight unseen, not to rent to her? Or what if, also by phone, she made the rental inquiry *for* a darker-skinned friend? Would the manager have changed his mind about renting when the friend showed up to sign the papers?

Lily knew a lot of nasty, unrespectable white people who, nevertheless, if they had the money, could be her neighbors. Examining the assumption that same race meant adherence to the same values code, Lily observed herself feeling no safer because all the tenants in her building were white. She knew there was stuff going on in other apartments—like that freak with yellow rat teeth and eyes that licked at her every time she walked past. *He's probably running some racket inside the doors of this respectable tenement, in this respectable neighborhood*, thought Lily.

Picking up *Cosmo* from the floor where she'd dropped it, Lily thumbed through the latest issue of her continuing sex education manual. All the models, all the contributors—all color encoded. *Must assume a white readership*, she thought, making a mental note to check out the newsstand for Black magazines the next morning. *I live north of the Mason–Dixon line by design*, thought Lily, the rain hurling against the window like it wanted to come in. *Yes, I'd rather live North than South. But the difference isn't all that dramatic. No matter where I live, the market is segregated.* And then the thought came to her that, by design, all Americans might be consumers, not just of a segregated American marketplace, but of *segregation*. The very thing, itself.

LILY'S SISTER CALLED BACK THE next morning, sounding like she was announcing the academy award for Best Picture: "Test results are in." Then shouting into the phone, "It's twins, Lily! We're having twins! I was stunned—must be Craig's genes."

"Sure?" asked Lily.

"My doctor detected two little heartbeats. And you know how big I am and getting bigger by the minute—eating for *two* like I thought. Now it's the three of us, plus daddy Craig, making it reservations for four!"

Lily told Dee she couldn't be more excited, and asked if they knew the sex yet—or did they want to know? Dee said not until she went through a new procedure called amniocentesis, and, yes, they'd just as soon know now, what equipment each was coming with.

Putting on her makeup, Lily mused what it would be like if the human gene pool became mixed to such an extent that it would be possible to have a child expressing features of any race, regardless of the parents' racial makeup. Painting brown eyeliner on pale eyelids, Lily thought about children and the "great divide." She had heard of Blacks wanting to pass for white . . . never the reverse. Never heard any friend say, "To get that job, I need to be Black; to ever get a foot in the door, I need to be Black."

Lily wondered if, by putting on darker makeup, she could pass for Black. Why would she want to? She couldn't think of a single advantage. She thought about testing the divide by applying increasingly darker makeup, perming her hair, then one day announcing Black Wallace ancestry. Wondering how long her landlord would allow her to remain in the building, Lily concluded maybe if she kept bringing only white men . . . but, if she *did* date Black men, how would her life change?

Harlem seemed like the place to begin—who would go with her to meet a darker shade of male? Already, Lily felt guilty: *my experiment at the expense of his safety.* She didn't really know the history or extent of Northern violence against Black men. Even though she wouldn't intend anything bad to happen, it could.

Besides, Lily thought, she might have to go to extraordinary lengths to meet eligible Black men in a natural setting.

Black men weren't in her world, or was it that she wasn't in theirs? She considered how, on paper, she had rights, but how, in actual day-to-day living, racism abrogated those same rights. Lily wondered how she, as one individual, might bridge the gap.

And what is the Church doing about this? Most white congregations aren't going to call a Black priest—would a Black congregation even want a white priest? Despite rumblings about *Black* or *Native American, Hispanic, Asian* or other so-called "designated" ministry, Lily saw the Church, also, as a consumer of segregation.

And, if recognition of cultural differences *were* a good thing, she wondered, who got to define and set in place those differences, and by applying what kind of spin? She considered family. The Church was always talking about itself as "family." Was valuing family above all, in fact, a good thing? Or was *good* a racist-relative term? Maybe *good* only applied when family behavior stayed within segregation's—since segregation was no longer legal—*norm*s. The valued family, then, was always being qualified by race. *White* family: 2.4 kids, new station wagon, picket fence, tree-shaded, flowered property on which sits a newly constructed house with built-in kitchen appliances. *Black* family: Lily saw a whole different picture. *How racist am I*, she thought, *assuming one circumstance for white and another for Black?*

RIDING THE CROWDED SUBWAY TO work, Lily noticed how each person pressed against the next. *The only way to separate us by race*, thought Lily, *would be separate cars.* Although the passengers all breathed the same stale air, Lily reflected, she had no idea what other passengers' lives were like, especially if they were Black, Puerto Rican, or Asian. She read her ignorance not by *Constitutional*, but by human design.

*Categories of inferior and superior—like a seesaw; if this one's up, the other's—*a second thought halted the first. Wait, Lily reasoned, the unamended Constitution's singling out Black Americans from Africa as "non-citizens" *was* by human design. *How long has this been going on?* As she looked around at fellow passengers, words of Marvin Gaye's song started playing in Lily's head.

LILY CALLED ETHAN FROM WORK and arranged to meet at his place that night for pizza. Ethan said again how glad he was that she had made it home safely. Lily was not sure to how much safety she had, in fact, returned. Undergoing changes she could not anticipate or prepare for, she had a hard time finding the ground under her feet.

Ethan had been assigned a big project at his investment firm. With a Midwestern family that was certain about how life was to be lived based on cycles of planting, harvesting, and putting up for the winter, Ethan was as steady as they came. Never getting too far ahead of God's own provision, and definitely never falling behind. A life of getting ready for the next season, each year repeating itself like a caged mouse pedaling a wheel but never really going anywhere.

Ethan's family and friends were the ones testing new product viability not only for the Midwest, but for the whole country. And with the exception of Chicago, maybe St. Louis, the country's breadbasket was overwhelmingly white.

Even before her trip, Lily had become increasingly annoyed with Ethan's predictability, his blinders, his seeming lack of curiosity about anyone outside his investment firm cubbyhole. As many reservations as she had about ordination, Lily had three times the number regarding Ethan's adjustment to being a priest's spouse. When asked, Ethan said he didn't know how he felt about her becoming a priest. She had no reason to doubt the truthfulness of his response, and that's what bothered her. Have some idea, some thought—not nothing, Lily grumbled inside. Ethan usually didn't *feel*, unless it was factored into his day—and then, only *outside* his workday. God forbid anything emotional and unscheduled should claim his attention during the sacred hours of financial analysis and deal-making.

On the other hand, if he didn't know how he would feel married to a priest, maybe Ethan wasn't totally predictable after all. Of course, it could be a lack of imagination. Ethan, not ready to abandon his calculating approach to say, "I think it's going to be the coolest thing I've ever done . . . or the most bizarre, scariest, dumbest." He didn't have a range of emotional descriptors.

But he *is* my intended, Lily thought. Afraid, the way things were going, that marriage might become just a destination—the last stop—Lily worried that already the relationship was the best it might ever be, with Ethan never questioning how they got to where they were: sharing pizza, shopping for rings, comparing calendars, choosing a wedding date and a common residence. That scared her.

Lily more and more saw marriage to Ethan like a privileged couple's consolidation of resources. Wedding guests wishing them health and wealth—mostly wealth? Wishing them well—*well, what*?

"WHERE HAVE YOU BEEN?" barked James from behind the receptionist counter at the gym, as Lily tried to sneak past.

Wary of James's appreciation for matters beyond the daily gossip, Lily answered simply, "Work."

"Well, you have a big group tonight," volunteered James. "Linda's back after maternity leave and Sandra, after husband leave."

"She left him?" asked Lily.

"Divorce. Two weeks old," said James. "Wants to get back into circulation."

"James, you must be the source man for *The Times* —you get it all, the full scoop on everyone," said Lily. "And now you're getting into matchmaking too?"

"Getting into—where have you been, Lily?" James snorted. "And all the time thinking I'm so obvious."

"So, tell me, Yenta, where *have* all the flowers gone?"

"The prettiest is standing right in front of me."

"Yeah, yeah. You know how to bullshit a girl up one side and down the other," said Lily. "But after this week of work, it's probably just what I need."

"Hi ho. Hi ho. To exercise you go."

"Hey, James—who was the last Black member you signed up?"

"You must have us mistaken—we have other branches if you're looking for Kodachrome."

"Is that right?" snarled Lily. "Then what does the C in YMCA stand for?"

"Not colored, that's for sure," James replied, then added, "have a good one, anyway." But Lily, already halfway down the hall, was out of earshot.

THE EXERCISE ROOM WAS FILLED with all manner of female bodies endlessly reflected in the mirrored walls surrounding the encampment of women cloistered every Monday, Wednesday, and Thursday night for the purpose of self-improvement. Isometric and aerobic exercise, set to music crossing racial lines, helped tune up physiques, some newly liberated of bras and girdles.

Lily thought about romance, as she knew it growing up from records heard on the radio or played on her sister's phonograph. "Baby, baby, sweet baby . . ." No boy had ever called her that. "Will you still love me tomorrow?" Lily, not wanting to jeopardize her career, never risked doing anything with a boy to prompt such a question. And "chances were," she doubted any boy thought her heart a "valentine," despite what Johnny Mathis crooned over the radio waves. Connie Stevens, Connie Francis, Ed "Kookie" Byrnes, and Bobby Darin aside, Lily realized it was mainly black expressions of physical love and affection that tutored her preteen and teenaged heart in romance.

And, Sal Mineo—in the days of flats and petticoats, his exotically dangerous looks were somewhere in between the two color poles. Pat Boone? Never. But James Darren—another Italian boy-man who knew something about love—he qualified. Influenced by sound more than sight, Lily knew Sam Cooke had to be her long-lost uncle; Mary Wells, a second big sister, was teaching her how to dodge love arrows while maintaining her reputation as "a good thing." Doin'-the-splits, "Johnny B. Goode" behind-the-back-up-side-down-and-sideways guitar-playin' Chuck Berry and his rock-and-roll peer Little Richard were as comic in performance as they were sensually thrilling, moving as they did all over the stage and sweating like country preachers just getting warmed up.

Seated with legs up in the air, bicycling, Lily thought about Jimi Hendrix's buttery bass "foxy lady"—no one had ever referred to her as *foxy lady*–and Janis Joplin's gravelly "Take it! Take another little piece of my heart . . ." She was glad to have seen both live in concert before they drugged themselves to death. Hendrix in Central Park, complaining about the "amps," and Janis at NYU, one of her last concerts with Big Brother before she slipped into Southern Comfort's eternal rest.

By the workout's deep breathing finale, arms lifting and legs pliéing, Lily made a decision to research other branches of the Y—maybe go uptown to Harlem—in her quest for the bigger American picture.

"I NO LONGER APPRECIATE ETHAN," Lily confided to her sister late one night on the phone. "I cannot for the life of me find passion for his struggle."

"Funny, I've never associated *struggle* with Ethan," Dee responded.

"That's just it," said Lily. "The boy doesn't have it. Partner by twenty-eight? The tumblers are rigged to come up plums, straight across, just a matter of time."

"He talks often enough about beating the odds," said Dee, not as eager as her sister to cross Ethan's name off the list.

"There are no odds to beat when they're all in your favor."

"Whoa. You're on a tear about something," said Dee, "but I'm not sure it's Ethan. I think he's an innocent bystander who just got in the way. You *are* still engaged to the boy, aren't you?"

"I don't know—"

"What do you mean you *don't know*?" snapped Dee.

"I mean, I don't know that I wanna walk down the aisle into some results-oriented future as a corporate wife."

"Some people would call that *good*," said Dee. "What if the Church doesn't start ordaining women?"

"Oh, so that's how you see this," said Lily. "I'll be taken care of like I'm some dipshit bimbo, in case one of the only two options I have falls through."

"I didn't say that."

"Yeah, well, I'm not that desperate," said Lily. "Besides. There's every indication that women's ordination is an eventuality in this decade."

"And if it isn't?"

"I'll teach American Lit or race motorcycles or design dams," said Lily. "I don't see the limitations like you do."

There was silence, then Dee spoke disapprovingly, "Baby sister. It sure sounds like you don't need anybody and their stability. You can just move around the planet at will, and hell to pay for anyone who tries to point out a few likely obstacles to your illusory, charmed path of no resistance."

"Maybe it's a generational thing," said Lily, "and Ethan is your generation."

"Oh, like I'm some old stuffed shirt," huffed Dee.

"Look," said Lily. "I'm just not ready for settling down to a life of straightening my husband's tie and brushing dandruff off his shoulders, being left bored with an ironing board as he heads for a board*room*."

"And how ready is Ethan for living on the clergy male spouse frontier?" Dee asked, as much for herself as for Lily's fiancé.

"Then God help us all," Lily fired back. Another silence took its pause.

Feeling the strain, Lily moved first to end the conversation with her sister on a conciliatory note. "Thanks for putting up with my rantings and ravings, Dee. Sorry—you must be tired."

"I take naps—have to. I don't know what I'll do when there are two permanent guests in the house," said Dee.

"Am I hearing a confession of uncertainty from my older and wiser sister?" cajoled Lily.

"Yeah, and you're not even ordained yet," Dee said, moving to an accord with her sister. "Can't wait for you to baptize the twins."

"That's the nicest thing—you're making me cry." Then, before her sister could get back on her high horse, Lily quickly asked, "Call me next week?"

"Unless there's a power outage."

"I haven't heard about any energy shortage."

"You're talking to it—g'night. Love you, Lily."

"Love you too. Sweet dreams of those babies and their extra fine daddy."

LILY WAS THE YOUNGEST AIDE in both the Executive Officer's and PB's offices, until the arrival of Ayana Davis whose father had defended the purple-and-gold of Miles College and his quarterback friend some forty years ago. There wasn't anything Hugh wouldn't do for Armet Davis, the person who had his back on and off the football field through four decades of friendship.

Though distressing to parents already contending with a preteen and two teenaged children, Enola Davis's unplanned pregnancy was a welcome distraction for their close friends, the Lovelle family.

That autumn in Birmingham, Hugh's wife, Cherise, took a nasty fall outside their home, which was close to being an empty nest with the last of the Lovelle daughters making plans for college. While Tracy finished up a junior year at Villanova and middle daughter Faith completed her sophomore year at Georgetown, the youngest girl, a senior in high school, received attractive offers from Spelman and Talladega. Cia couldn't wait to get away from home and parents. But the diagnosis subsequent to her mother's fall changed all of that.

At the same time Cia giddily anticipated the magic of prom night, the raft of hope on which Cherise and the rest of the family floated from Christmastide into spring was shored. The fourth and holdout medical opinion gave up its optimistic prognosis, joining the others, who, from the start, had predicted their vivacious patient would succumb to an inoperable brain tumor. In and out of consciousness, Cherise postponed death until a week after Cia graduated, when the whole family gathered to say their goodbyes.

Though Cherise's leaving coincided with Ayana's arrival, new father Armet was at his grieving friend's side. "Only twenty-eight summers with my beautiful coffee-no-cream woman," wept Hugh. Holding God accountable for his wife's death, Hugh took personal offense at God's failure to intervene. The offense remained an irreconcilable difference between creature and Creator who, in the course of his wife's illness and dying, became somewhat less almighty. *If God had the guts to show his face*, Hugh thought, *it would look like my friend Armet Davis.*

"AYANA WILL BE WITH US for the summer," Hugh announced at the close of Monday morning's staff meeting. "Please make her feel welcome. Anything you can do to get her acquainted with the city and our little corner of it is much appreciated."

People started filing out, greeting Hugh's new recruit as they moved toward the door. The weekend now seeming a distant memory, each made a mental list of all that needed to get done during the hectic week laid out in the meeting just ended.

"Boy, can we use you around here this summer! With Convention coming up, all of us are swamped. The crunch of pulling together arrangements for ten thousand Episcopalians and friends for home-of-Kentucky-Derby Louisville *feels* like a damn horse race. Hi, I'm Lily."

As she reached out to shake the towering new kid on the block's hand, Lily instead got swept up in a long-lost-pals embrace. "I'm glad to finally meet you—Uncle Hugh has been talking about you behind your back," said Ayana. "I think he sees you as my mentor."

"You're sure you have the right person?"

"If you're the Lily enrolled in seminary, then you're the 'courageous young female' I'm supposed to hook up with," said Ayana. "I get the feeling Uncle Hugh hopes you'll rub off on me."

"I wonder which *part* of me he was thinking of." Ayana's confident laugh made Lily feel as if the mentor–mentored roles should be reversed. "Don't know if I can live up to the commendation," said Lily, "but I'm definitely flattered that your . . . Uncle Hugh speaks in such glowing terms."

"What will you do with a seminary degree?"

"*If* I make it to a seminary degree," said Lily. "General, the Episcopal seminary, isn't terribly supportive of my taking up space in their classrooms, so I fill out studies at Union. Much more pleasant there—none of the rude remarks I get from some of the would-be princes of the Church at General who'd have an easier time dating than having me sit next to them in homiletics."

"Oh, please," said Ayana. "This sounds like the place I just came from. Only in Birmingham, it was about nappy hair and everything else nice white kids might catch from *cuhl'ed chi'rn.*"

"Believe me, New York has that, too. Families stacked up in segregated high-rise projects," said Lily. "We don't have any busing problems, because we don't have any busing." All of a sudden, the reality of Lily's tenement intruded, and she added sheepishly, "I confess having no Black neighbors myself," which brought the female bonding to a dead halt.

Then, in a lame attempt to recover a sense of shared gender experience, Lily said, "Even some of the most liberal white men would have the same problem with you as they have with me—we don't have the right gender stuff." She knew the other foot was in her mouth before she even finished speaking.

"See, that doesn't even faze me," Ayana replied, much to Lily's relief. "Because race, which is no longer supposed to be an issue—and especially among folks calling themselves *Christian*—is so big and ever-present, it takes all the steam out of the gender thing for me. *Let* the men wear dresses and set the Lord's Table. Before I'm drafted by God or anyone else, I'm getting a degree in journalism."

Lily grabbed the lifeline. "Journalism, yeah? Hugh said you'd be starting at Cornell in the fall but didn't say in what."

"'Cause he probably didn't know. He's watched me like a hawk—I guess, from birth. But there are still some things Uncle Hugh doesn't know about me," said Ayana mischievously. "And his move to New York made keeping close tabs on me impossible—though he probably has informants back home!"

"Doesn't Hugh have three girls?"

"Yes. Though I call Hugh *uncle*, his daughters are more like aunts than cousins to me," said Ayana. "They all have a good thing going—two have stayed active in the Church. One doesn't want a thing to do with the 'brood of vipers,' as she calls it."

"What's kept you in the Church—or are you?" asked Lily.

"Yes, I do attend Sunday services," said Ayana, "not just weddings and funerals. I kind of took a long vacation through high school, except for going to a Baptist church with my girlfriends once in a while. I don't know—Anglican tradition just doesn't do it for me like when I was younger, running around, playing hide-and-go-seek in the basement on bathroom breaks during Sunday school. I just started going again this spring, but I want to give myself some freedom in New York to explore other traditions."

Lily envied Ayana's uncommitted future, her openness to a path, which, relative to Lily's, was as yet undetermined. Though she saw New York with different eyes since her trip to the South, still, Lily wished for more of the sense of adventure Ayana expressed about her new home. "So, tell me. Why work at the Episcopal Church Center for godssakes?"

"Well, because it *is* a center," said Ayana. "I figure it might serve the same purpose as the UN—my first choice—and it seemed a helluva lot easier to get a job here with my connections to Uncle Hugh."

"You are on your way, girl," said Lily. "I'll be coming to you for mentoring."

"I figure, here I am in New York—I want to find out what's it all, you know, about, *Alfie*."

"You must have been a baby when that movie came out," Lily hooted, to which Ayana returned a dirty look.

"Anyway, I'm lookin' to find my groove in the North," sing-songed Ayana.

"Oh, you will. You definitely will," said Lily. "Where are you living for the summer?"

"With Uncle Hugh, for now. Cornell said I could move in just after the summer session—they shut down for cleaning between semesters. But it's cool for now."

"Yeah, I understand he has a nice place," said Lily. "Ever visited before now?"

"Once with my dad. You know, he and Hugh were gridiron buddies in college."

"Where was that?"

"Miles—in Birmingham. Small, all Black student body," said Ayana. "I did *not* want to go there, though my oldest brother graduated from law school there and is doing well—you gotta meet Rodney."

"He sounds interesting."

"He'll be visiting in June, so you can judge for yourself. To me, he's just an older brother and a generation gap, but he has a cool ride that he lets me drive once in a while."

"Thanks," said Lily. "I'd really like to meet him when he comes."

"You'd like him—he actually had a white girlfriend his senior year in high school. Well—mostly white. Tuwanda. Sounds like she should be Black, right? But Tuie definitely acted white," said Ayana. "We always teased him that she was gonna leave a milk moustache on him when they kissed."

Still curious, but afraid to probe what Ayana meant by *acting white* for fear of causing yet another awkward moment, Lily followed up with a different question. "Whatever happened to Tuie?"

"I don't really know. I just know that after graduation, she stopped calling our house, which wrecked all our fun," said Ayana. "My sister and I used to make up all kinds of shit—oops, sorry."

"Please," Lily said, gesturing for Ayana to continue.

"My sister Sharon and I used to crack up telling that girl Rodney couldn't come to the phone, because he was out slaughtering a hog. Or that he was upstairs trying to get a comb through his nappy hair. Meanest thing was telling Tuie that our brother just took off, all dressed up, to pick up his date and didn't she know anything about it? We'd be all innocent, saying, 'We thought he's goin' to pick you up, Tuwanda—he sure looked good!'"

"So what did your brother do—I assume he found out?"

"Oh, he found out all right. He always found out. We tried to stay invisible until our mother came home. Then we just hid behind her. She didn't believe in siblings hitting or kicking each other . . . Sharon and I knew we were safe." Her easy laugh once again drew Lily in, but she proceeded more cautiously this time, not wanting to make the same blunder twice and leave a bad first impression with Hugh Lovelle's *niece*. Lily checked her watch.

"Well, come on, Ayana. I'll show you how to get started around here and what to work on."

"I'm on it."

"Have you gotten any instruction so far?"

"No, just that Uncle Hugh was depending on you to show me around and get me going, I guess, on whatever you're working on."

"You're a lifesaver, Ayana—do I have projects for you!" said Lily. "My office—the box I work in—is right down the hall." *Cubicle buddies*, Lily thought. *This should be interesting.*

"Oh, I don't mean to crowd your space, Lily. Maybe there's another—"

"Don't be silly. I got over it the first day. Nobody has an inch to give in New York, but everyone acts like the other guy is holding out on them," said Lily. "You know about attitude in Alabama?"

"Whaddya mean—'Bama folks put the *A* in *attitude*," said Ayana. Knocking elbows coming into Lily's cubicle, the two laughed as they pulled up chairs facing each other, and with pencils and a legal pad between them, began mapping out their plan of attack on work needing to get done that week in their compartment of the Church Center.

DONALD GENUINELY ADMIRED THE LADIES working out at the 135th Street Y, and they, in turn, appreciated his sincere attention, which sweetened the more disagreeable aspects of his administrative duties at the five-hundred-member-strong Harlem branch of the now coed Young Men's Christian Association.

"Hi my name's Donald. How are you ladies doin' tonight?"

"Actually, this is only our second time using the equipment. Will helped us out last week, but I don't see him around anywhere," Ayana flirted. "Do you think we could get a refresher on gym equipment orientation?"

"Sure—that's what I'm here for," said Donald. "Were you circuit training?"

Ayana looked at Lily before replying. "I'm not sure what that means, but I know Will had us, first thing, hang full body weight on the bar there, then we warmed up on these bikes."

"Okay, so you're probably ready for—"

Just then, a pair of buff males working out next to them began to have words about music playing from a tape player on the floor. Their voices quickly reached yell-decibel before Donald intervened. "Can I help you two gentlemen?"

"Yeah, asshole here—"

"Hey, hey. Watch the mouth," said Donald.

"Okay, *dog* here's stuck in Motown."

"I just asked him to switch to somethin' grabbin' more beat, know what I'm sayin'?"

"Put a lid on it or both y'all's asses are outta here, and I mean in a New York minute," said Donald. "Know what *I'm* sayin'?"

The arguing tempered and continued, as Donald signaled for the women to join him at the rowing apparatus.

"Who's first?" asked Donald. Lily pointed to Ayana.

"Okay, you're gonna have a seat here, but first I'll show y'all how it works," said Donald, proceeding to sit down and demonstrate the correct movement of the chest-opening exercise while Lily counted the striations of his exposed back and shoulder muscles. Motioning to Ayana, Donald said, "Okay now, your turn—three sets of twelve. Hold on . . . we need to adjust the seat. See the knob on the right?" Donald showed Ayana how to change the height of the seat before she started her pull-down reps with the horizontal bar. "That's it. Now squeeeeze those shoulders together. That's right. You got it, sister," encouraged Donald. "Rest in between sets—get a drink, stretch your arms, whatever."

Lily liked Donald's patient instruction, the care taken to ensure Ayana's having a good workout. "Okay darlin', let's get you—"

"Lily."

"Huh?"

"My name's Lily."

Donald whistled. "Excuse me, *Lily* darlin'—"

"I don't do well with *darlin'*," bristled Lily.

"Yeah, sorry. Then Lily—*what*?"

"Lily Wallace."

"That right? I was in Philly with a cat named Wallace. Afro up to here," said Donald, grinning and holding his hand a foot over his head. "We all had 'em back in the day. Full name was John Henry Wallace—any relation?"

"You never know," said Lily, returning Thomas's grin. "Where were his people from?"

"Can't tell you that. Philly was the end of the line for JH and myself. I had to get out of the Black Power business when dudes started asking what kind of piece I carried," said Donald. "As a kid, I was terrified of my daddy's shotgun—never owned a gun, never will. Leaving Philadelphia, I wanted to go someplace where guns are kept in a locked case, not stuck in a belt."

"So, you came to New York?" Lily chided.

"Yeah, well, a guy in Philly got me into Y work there and when this opened up, I jumped on it, and, fortunately, the folks doin' the hiring here jumped on me."

"I can see why, Donald, you seem good at what you do," said Lily. "You're a trainer, right?"

"No, though I keep up my certification. I'm actually where the buck stops around here."

"Director?"

"Yes."

"I feel honored getting assistance from the *di*-rector himself."

"You sassin' me, *Lily*?" Donald smiled. "I don't do well with sass."

"Excuse me and touché," Lily smiled back.

"So, Lily—what do you do when you're not pumping iron?"

The unevenness of Donald's teeth balanced the orderliness of the rest of him: neat mounds of muscle, straight part faded into short-cropped hair, Tide-white socks against plumb-black skin. Lily tried to think of an ambiguous, yet truthful response. "Well, kind of like yourself. Working for the social good of . . . of all. Through an agency, philosophically Christian, like the Y." Then, seeking more impersonal ground, Lily said, "Can you get me going on this machine, Donald?"

———

LILY ALLOWED ETHAN'S BUSYNESS AT work to take the rap for *her* immediate lack of interest, telling him it was fine with her if he needed to work late or overtime on weekends. But, even as she appeared generous in accepting Ethan's repeated apologies, she knew that sooner rather than later, questions about their future together would need to be addressed.

Things were busy at Church Center, as well, coordinating the divergent needs of thousands of General Convention attendees: bishops, clergy and lay deputies, support staff, vendors, security, the press. It was a daunting task for so few hands on deck.

Despite female deputies allowed to be elected and seated in the proceedings with voice and vote since the prior Convention held in Houston, Episcopal Church Women (ECW) proceeded, doggedly, as before the change, with plans for their separate, all-women Triennial.

Lily was annoyed with ECW's seeming unwillingness to get on board and confused about why a majority of its all-female membership would continue to insist on holding their females-only meeting concurrent with the Church's official deliberations. Church business was now conducted by women, as well as men, in the House of Deputies, with pending hopes, Lily's included, of a similar gender mix in a future House of Bishops.

Anticipating increased female numbers at the upcoming Convention, Lily and other staff recommended making additional restroom facilities available by changing some of the men's room signs. The recommendation died, however, for lack of support. While some in the denomination feared *feminization* to be a terminal disease afflicting the Church, others saw female assumption of traditionally male roles in the reverse: a step toward wholeness and the restoration of, ironically, "God's *king*dom."

The clash between opposing camps on the issue of women's ordination was expected to be noisier than three years prior. The clergy vote, then, consented to a female diaconate, but withheld its approval of female priests and bishops, leaving the question still in hot debate. Some thought granting diaconal ordination only was like a placating bone thrown at lukewarm voters to gnaw on during incendiary times.

Less than two years before, pro-women's ordination members formed the Episcopal Women's Caucus (EWC), which, despite its name, included men. The EWC worked with Church Center to provide speakers and publications countering anti-women's ordination arguments. To: "If God wanted women priests, then Jesus would have chosen female disciples," the EWC rejoined: "If God wanted the Church to replicate Jesus's selection, then all candidates for holy orders should be thirty-one years of age or younger and Jewish." The Caucus planned to come to the Convention in Louisville armed with bannered T-shirts: GOD IS NOT A BOY'S NAME; FAITH, HOPE, AND PARITY; A WOMAN'S PLACE IS IN THE HOUSE OF BISHOPS.

Lily found herself at a historical loss, as she got up to speed on current arguments pro and con for linking gender and race. Those seeing the two as mutually exclusive competitors for justice opposed others who saw racism and sexism as two forms of a single canker destroying the Church.

She reviewed how, in the sweltering summer heat and humidity of the Church's *Special* Convention held four years earlier, bishops and lay and clergy deputies came face to face with demands for African American reparations. A prominent group of Black Philadelphia clergymen excoriated the gathered body for refusing the opportunity "to rise up as men of God," saying white Church membership was "afraid to love, afraid of freedom, afraid to be beautiful."

The white PB's response had been left hanging in midair when a young Black pastor, also from the City of Brotherly Love but outside the denomination, yanked the microphone out of the PB's hand—the same Presiding Bishop, who, only two years earlier, took heat for radically setting aside planned agenda to deal with more immediate issues of injustice fomenting violence across the land.

Lily, along with other staff, had been keeping tabs on the growing apprehension that this now outgoing leader might, again, allow disruption of Anglican process, because, as everyone around Church Center knew, race and reparations was still a hotbed, regardless of civil rights progress.

Church leadership and staff prepared for the prevailing point–counterpoint to animate the Louisville meeting: those wanting the Church to take responsibility for its participation in perpetuating racism and sexism versus those pointing to the presence of more color and females among current conventioneers, while continuing to maintain, "These things take time."

LILY WATCHED VERA COUNT AND recount wafers for the midweek communion service. The older woman made stacks of twenty-five and rolled them in precut rectangles of waxed paper. Next, she took an oversized priest's host from a plastic bag and, setting it to one side of the chalice and paten, opened the drawer labeled "Pentecost."

"Vera, these come in whole wheat or rye or anything browner?"

"Oh, Lily," sighed Vera. "Why would you ask such a thing?"

"I bet the real body of Christ was browner than these wafers."

"Maybe, but I haven't seen one darker than those," said Vera, as she inspected an olive-colored sateen square. "Too drab," she muttered, replacing the swatch in the far end of the drawer and fishing out another. "We'll use this one in your honor—looks to me like *lily* pad green."

In a rhythm all her own, Vera began the quiet ritual of layering and centering each piece that went into the sacramental sculpture. Though she had constructed the same miniature tower, hiding it under its drape of liturgical color time and time again, Vera took such care, as if she were preparing the veiled column for the first time.

The sacristy stayed cool as a small cavern hewn out of the mass of stone that was the Cathedral of St. John the Divine. The room adjoining the Lady Chapel held sacred vessels and was outfitted with a drain allowing unused consecrated wine to return to the ground.

Seventy communicants gathered round the chapel's altar every Wednesday noon, praying the ancient canon and sharing essentials of what the group affectionately called The Lord's Lunch, and former Catholics, Lunch Lite.

"So tell me, Lily dear, do you think they'll share their fancy wardrobe and their place at the Lord's Table with you before I die?"

"Depends upon when you're planning to go, Vera."

"Maybe it should be announced before the vote is taken, so's they get the urgency of the matter."

"Kind of like the end-of-the-world freaks in the fifties."

"Yeah, that oughta shake 'em up," said Vera. "Just want all you fellas—"

"There are women in the House of Deputies now, Vera."

"Well, they can listen in too. Vera Cartwright is planning to meet her Maker at quarter till two this afternoon—oh, no, they won't go for that. Anyone knows me, knows I'll be watchin' my programs from eleven to three thirty, four o'clock."

"So, what happens on Wednesdays when you're here?"

"Nothin'," said Vera. "Not a darn thing that won't get repeated the next day. Those soap op'ry people are in a time warp. I s'pose so's they can sell more hair products or floor wax."

"So, Vera, let's say the vote *does* allow women's ordination to go forward—will you set up my altar debut as priest celebrant?"

"I don't know, honey. What kind of life is that? Whatever happened to that nice boyfriend of yours?"

"Ethan?"

"Yeah, Ethan. He's crazy 'bout you. Why don't you marry him and have a nice family? That's what kind of *Mother* makes sense."

"Vera, whether I'm ordained or not has nothing to do with Ethan."

"Well, I would'n wanna be a priest. Would'n even wanna be married to one. People watchin' yer ev'ry move. I can't see how it's any kind of life for a man," stated Vera, "and I sure as shootin' can't see it as any life for a woman either. We gotta answer to enough menfolk, Lily—why do you wanna have to answer to one in purple?"

"Unless *he* could be a *she*—"

"Oh, go on! Women bishops? I gotta stick around just to see that!"

"Promise?"

"If we don't get that altar set up," said Vera, "we won't even have *this* job."

"But if not us women, who *would* prepare The Lord's *Supper*?" Lily cajoled. "Vera, you need a Women's Caucus T-shirt."

"An' why's that?"

"'Cause it's time you came out from under wraps and showed your colors as the original feminist."

"Yeah, I'm a women's libber all right, and Pat Nixon is still gonna be First Lady when all this mess is over," Vera harrumphed. "Come on now, make yourself useful and bring these two cruets if you would, please. We got to get this show on the road."

"Yes, ma'am," said Lily. "You know Vera, *you'd* make a good bishop."

"No, but you bring that boy Ethan by and I'll show you some supper fixin'," said Vera. "I wanna talk to you and him together."

"Give us some of the gospel according to Vera?"

"That's right. That and a piece of my feeble mind."

"We'll see," said Lily, unwilling to commit. "So, Vera. You never answered my question."

"What's that?"

"Will you help me when I preside at my first Eucharist?"

"I don't know just yet, Lily. Like you tell me . . . *we'll see*," said Vera. "We'll just have to see about that."

"Way to keep me on hold."

"It's 'cause I'm on *old*."

"You're a hard woman, Vera. A hard woman," teased Lily. "I don't know why I put up with you."

"Same reasons I put up with yer nonsense—'cause we love each other, honey."

As they finished setting the Lord's Table, Lily asked Vera, "What's your favorite in a T-shirt color—black, burgundy, or navy blue?"

———

THE TREE BOUGHS ON LILY'S street looked like the wind-blown hair of giant pedestrians whose legs were forever fixed in cement. Lily's first-hand experience of racial violence seemed likewise crystallized. Each day she examined a different facet of her sojourn in the South; she used new eyes to bore into lives around her to dig to the taproot that drank from the common human well, invigorating the soul's capacity for joy and sustaining its reserve during periods of great sorrow.

This morning, Lily and Arthur Benson observed the same sunrise, as the young woman jogged past her older neighbor walking his fox terrier Mister. Mister was more the master of both the retired bus driver and his wife Rose. Because she had no children of her own, some of Rose's family believed marriage to a non-Italian to be the cause of her several miscarriages. Mister was, for all intents and purposes, the couple's only child.

Like a preview of the summer day's advance from morning chill to warm afternoon, the sky went from purple to fuchsia, pink then gold, before turning into a solid blue canvas with no more distinct colors. Lily took advantage of the cooler temperature at dawn's light to be in the open air before, once again, becoming captive to her workday and the conditioned air at Church Center.

Her hours were so long now that when she did make it to the Y, each workout felt like her first.

"You ignoring us, Lily?"

"Would be hard to ignore you, Donald."

"Then why we not seein' you 'round here a whole lot lately?"

"Because a whole lot lately I've been working a whole lot late."

"Sorry to hear that. Just don't want anything we say or do discouraging the pleasure of your sweetness showin' up every now and then."

"You're layin' it on thick tonight, Donald."

"God's truth."

"God's truth is, I've been getting more exercise on the *office* treadmill than this one."

"Not twenty-four, seven."

"No—I take a sabbath."

"How far your sabbath stretch, Lily?"

"Well, we actually take the last call at four on Fridays, but then we have to make some order out of the week's mess, so we don't have to eat too many in-basket leftovers Monday."

"What's it you do again, Lily?"

"I told you already, Donald," said Lily in mock annoyance.

"Maybe—but tell me again."

Hesitating, Lily said, "I make phone calls, write memos, go to meetings, hold meetings, make copies, collate and staple, send out for lunch—"

"So, what's all the mystery?" asked Donald, his voice lowering. "Sorry, Lily, maybe you don't want me all up in your business."

"It's not like that—"

"Hey, if you work undercover," grinned Donald, "I can respect that."

"This is silly of me," relented Lily, "I'm an aide in the Presiding Bishop's office at the Episcopal Church Center on Second Avenue."

"Not familiar with the place. Anything to do with the big stone church on Amsterdam?"

"The cathedral. It's like the county seat. I work in the office of the *national* head of the Episcopal Church—kind of like the West Wing, but, of course, on a much smaller scale."

"I'm impressed."

"No more questions—stop while I'm ahead!"

Ignoring any serious intent in her statement, Donald asked, "This head figure is called *what*, again?"

"Presiding Bishop," said Lily. "Elected for a twelve-year tenure."

"Who elects?"

"Both clergy and lay."

"So, which are you?"

"No girls allowed to play with clergy boys—yet."

"So, you're a wannabe?"

"Hopefully, a gonnabe."

"When you *gonna get* the magic?"

"Soon's the church votes 'Yea.'"

"How does that happen?"

"Are you really interested in all this ecclesiastical rigamarole?"

"I'm interested in you and where this hangs for you, so hit me again."

"Do you want Theology for fifty or Politics—also for fifty?"

"How 'bout both. Fifty-fifty, Church politics *and* God."

"You got it," Lily laughed. "The Church playing God, reading the mind of God . . . then the Church, *er* I mean, *God* changing his—or is it, *her?*—mind."

"Know the talk well: 'God doesn't mean a blessing over *all* creation. Some only deserve a partial blessing.'"

"You sound like a feminist, Donald."

"No, if anything, just a man trying to survive—in living color."

"Is that really how you feel—I mean, you *look* better than survival."

"Oh, so now *you* doin' a little mind readin'?"

"No, seriously—I apologize if I offended you. I don't want to come off like I know what your life—I mean, as if I could even know what your life is like . . . *living in color*. Besides, I hardly know you."

"On the other hand, Black men and white women been tangled up for years. Ten years ago, it was Laura and Titus. Hundred years, Lucinda and Theodor."

"Interesting thought," said Lily. "I doubt if Lucy and Theo's conversation was anything like ours."

"Maybe, maybe not. Different institutions maybe, but same shit," said Donald. "Speaking of institutions, come to think of it—remember I mentioned being from Philadelphia?"

"Dimly."

"Glad I made such an impression—"

"*Anyway*—"

"Anyway, priest there, Black dude let us use his church for meetings, organizing demonstrations, anti-shit shit," said Donald. "I can't really claim to know how the Episcopal capital C-*Church* does business, but this man was straight up with us and pretty much joined our cause. Getting all-white Girard College to open up Black admissions; the don't-shop-where-you-can't-work campaign; monitoring police violence. Then Jim Forman started making church rounds, demanding reparations. I know the Episcopal Church—your boss, maybe?—was approached for its share of a modern day, much-less-than forty acres and a mule equivalent. Any of this familiar? By the way—how old are you, Lily?"

"Ten years ago, I was the same age as the fourteen-year-old girls killed in the Birmingham church bombing."

"Where were you at the time?"

"With my family in Texas—I grew up in Texas," said Lily. "But I was at Brown when the *Black Manifesto* came out, asking five hundred million from white churches and synagogues."

"Fifteen dollars per Black—fifteen dollars!" said Donald. "I know our worth is low in the eyes of some, but that's a *pitiful* sum."

"Yeah, I was astounded by the numbers: thirty-three and a half *million?*"

"Kidnapped, bred, bought-and-sold Africans cleared and cultivated *how much* land? Built *how many* homes, levees, canals, schools, government buildings—entire cities? How *many* white families were cleaned, clothed, and fed with slave labor?" said Donald. "Like Martin, I'd say payment of the bill is past due, *way* past due."

"But I don't see there ever being enough support," said Lily.

"And among those who stand to benefit, as well. Some of my brothers and sisters want nothing to do with *too-little, too-late.* Deh body's bin layin' in deh col', col' groun' too damn long tuh git dug up now."

"Even though it could redress some of the wrong," said Lily, "I can see where it would bring up a painful history for Blacks."

"There's only *one* history, Lily."

"And I just demonstrated how easy it is to dissociate from it. Sorry."

"Easy as 'I don't own slaves and neither do my parents' releasing white folk from further considering, much less acknowledging, the extent to which they and their parents benefit from their land-holding, voting ancestors' citizen status."

"Male ancestors."

Donald's facial expression asked for explanation. "Okay. White *male* ancestors' legacy. White *females* by extension," Lily replied. "Black men had the vote before women."

"Point taken. However—"

"However. I know—it's a difficult objection to sustain."

Concurring, Donald smiled then asked, "Your boss holding office in '69?"

"Same PB—but he's not my immediate boss," said Lily. "His executive officer is. First Black man appointed to the position."

"He ordained?" When Lily nodded, Donald said, "Maybe you'll be the first woman."

"Prospect looms more and more likely. Church meets in convention every three years. This year, we're on for fall and voting for the full ordination of women—priests and bishops, in addition to the female deacons Convention authorized three years ago," explained Lily. "Our office is in the throes of coordinating thousands of attendees and support personnel. I can tell you every Louisville hotel's room capacity."

"I *remain* impressed," said Donald. "Been there before?"

"Last year, locating accommodations, meeting sites, lay-of-the-land type thing."

"You travel much for your job?"

Donald's question came too close for Lily's comfort. "Some," she answered.

"Where else have you been?" Donald continued his inquiry. "For the job, I mean?"

"A few trips to D.C., some local diocesan—sorry for the churchspeak. *Diocese* is like county. I've been to some diocesan conventions along the East Coast. I haven't been with the PB's office that long . . . a trip to South Carolina in the spring." Then, feeling as though she'd already disclosed too much of herself, Lily looked at the wall clock behind her interviewer and said, "Hey, this has been great talking to you, Donald. I almost forgot why I'm here."

"Pleasure's all mine," said Donald. "Nice to discover where you and I might connect."

"And I thought I was coming here tonight for exercise. This was a lot more interesting."

"Do it again?"

"Absolutely."

Lily did a couple more miles on the treadmill before calling it quits. Exchanging a friendly goodbye with Donald, she went into the night air of Harlem, dashing to the corner just as the bus pulled up to its stop.

LILY NO SOONER GOT IN THE door before her phone started ringing. Throwing keys on the pine crate serving as a table in front of her best Salvation Army bargain, a pair of raspberry moquette upholstered chairs, Lily caught the phone before the answer machine picked up.

"You sound out of breath," said Ethan. "Are you okay?"

"Yeah, I'm fine. Just got back from the gym."

"So did I, but I didn't see *you* there," said Ethan, sounding like an irate parent. "Where have you been? I called your office and they said you left for the Y, so I went there. Where the hell were you?"

"I was at the Y—just not the branch you went to."

"Since when did you change?"

"Since I started going to the one on West Hundred and Thirty-Fifth with Ayana. And what's all this interrogation about, anyway, *Ethan*?"

"Hundred and Thirty-Fifth. Is that Harlem, Lily? Don't tell me—your white guilt's driven you over the edge. Are you nuts? I don't know what happened to you on that trip, Lily, but I'm about over the edge not knowing who you are sometimes."

"Do you want to talk about it or just hear yourself yell?"

"Yeah, I wanna talk, that's why I called your office and then went tracking you down."

"Nice metaphor."

"Say what?"

"Tracking me down, like I'm your prey? Is that how you think of me, Ethan?"

"Now you really don't make sense," Ethan fumed. "I go looking for you—sorry if my words don't mesh with your *fem* sensibilities—because I love you and want to see you and you're not where I'm expecting to find you. So, yeah! I'm mad and I'm worried, and, so far, I don't hear anything from you that might change that."

"Since when do I need to check in with you, Ethan? And for that matter, who says I need to anticipate—in order to soothe—your *worry*. Maybe you *should* worry."

"What is *that* supposed to mean?"

"It means, some emotion now and then might indicate a human inside the suit . . . a little talk to go along with the *worried* would be an improvement too."

"Oh, so now I'm an emotional mute."

"However you name it."

"Okay, okay. I know I've been super busy at work. But so have you. That's *why* I was trying to grab a couple of hours with you. I feel like we've been going in opposite directions the last month and a half. I miss you, Lily."

"How would I have known that?"

"You wouldn't," said Ethan, "I'm just saying it now."

"You're just saying it *now* to cover your butt. I mean, yelling at me is just not cool."

"I'm sorry, Lily. But you shouldn't be—"

"Apologies don't have *buts*, Ethan—this is one of your flimsy attempts at passing off blame-Lily rationale as an apology. I'm not up to it tonight, Ethan, so if you want to talk as in *talk*, it will have to be some other time after you've calmed down."

"But Lily—"

"There you go with the *buts* again. No more buts. I'm tired. I'm going to bed. Goodnight."

Lily hung up the phone. Filled with anger and nowhere to discharge it once she dismissed Ethan, Lily called Dee to grouse about her fiancé. Line busy. She got her book and tried reading. Couldn't. Picked up pen and journal. Writing helped. Who was she these days, anyway? On that point she agreed with Ethan. She had changed, but how? Fighting with Ethan didn't feel good. Lily dialed his number and got a busy signal. Was Ethan talking to Dee? I'll give him five minutes to get off, thought Lily. Then I'll go talk to him in person.

LILY'S MOTHER HAD OPPOSED her post-college decision to remain East instead of returning to Texas. By settling in New York, Lily widened the family breach made first by Dee moving to North Carolina, then further away to New York. Their father's death during Lily's college sophomore year made the break especially painful for their widowed mother whose loyalty to the Lone Star State surpassed that to her daughters. More painful still, though, was Lily's growing realization of the divide between her and persons leaving a divide in her soul.

Wanting no part of Texas's rigid separation of people into racially superior and inferior categories, Lily felt glad, more than guilty, that her own resourcefulness and the hospitality of others had kept the life of her mother's choosing at a safe distance. By culling other furnishings from what neighbors threw out or left behind when they moved, Lily satisfied both artist and nester in making her flat a home.

The one significant Texas article Lily held onto was the log cabin quilt that lay on her bed as far back as she could remember. With its red patch of chimney being the only color and pattern repeated, her mother called it a crazy quilt. But a sociology class surveying symbolic value of household items rendered new meaning for Lily. The log cabin design signified a safe house for escaping slaves headed North on the Underground Railway. Who made the quilt, bought at a garage sale by her mother, remained a mystery. Perhaps, mused Lily, that's where her propensity for used, rather than new, came from. That and maybe her ability to put colors together in oddly pleasing combinations was all Lily allowed as maternal inheritance. Though she challenged parental rearing in the way she lived her life, Lily was not sure she could, in fact, change her entire social encoding. What was certain, however, was the feeling that returning to Texas was not and would *never* be an option for her, especially as, more and more, Lily recognized estrangement from others as estrangement from her own self.

WHEN LILY CALLED HIM BACK after six minutes, Ethan picked up on the second ring.

"Yes."

"You sound like you knew it was me."

"Yes."

"*Yes*, as in 'I'm glad you called?'—or, '*Yes*, I'm an idiot and I'm really sorry, with no *but*?"

"Both," said Ethan. "Lily, I need to see you."

"I would say yes, but it's a work night—"

"For both of us," Ethan cut in. "I know we're both still employed. I'm wondering if we're still engaged."

"Serious question demands a serious answer," said Lily. "Ethan, this is no quickie at my place. We really do need to talk—but not tonight. Look, how about dinner here Friday night. Can you manage that?"

"Theoretically."

"Good," said Lily. "And, Ethan, sorry about the fangs."

"Sorry I'm such a madman."

"Ooh, bring some of that madmanness Friday night."

"And wine? Riesling or Chardonnay?"

"Chardonnay, dry, at seven," said Lily. "That way I can guarantee being here. Work has been crazy."

"Same here," said Ethan. "Let's just order out and eat in."

"Okay with me," said Lily, adding, "Love you, Ethan."

"I love you, Lily. Thanks for calling back to say goodnight."

"Goodnight."

Resolution of their immediate relationship assuaged his fears enough that by Friday night, Ethan forgot his questions about the status of their engagement.

"THIS MAN OF YOURS HAS some serious potential, Lily."

"You're talking about Ethan, 'this-man-of-mine'? I thought you two had met before."

"Not in person," said Ayana. "I've just taken messages. You two serious?"

"Off and on."

"Now?"

"Now, I've sort of put our future as a married couple on hold and renewed my resolve to proceed toward ordination. Ethan is equally determined to make partner before thirty, so I don't know if we're before or after the fork in the road right now. And if *after*, if we've taken the same fork," said Lily. "I don't know if we share the same commitments."

"He acts glad to be here with you now," said Ayana. "What more are you looking for, girl?"

Just then a man rushed into the kitchen, hugging a brown grocery bag with his left arm and supporting the bottom of the bag with a hand nearly as broad as the sack's bottom. "Perspiring drinks for perspiring people comin' through. Sorry ladies. Gotta lay my burden down."

"Always grabbin' the attention," said Ayana. "Lily, meet Rodney."

"The brother."

"Yes, indeed. I am a brother." Rodney wiped his hand on his pants and reached out to Lily. "Nice to finally meet you, Lily. I've been hearing a little something about you. You the person my baby sister wants me to meet."

"And so we have. I'm flattered," said Lily, eying Ayana.

"He's not just a brother, he's *the* brother. Number one brotha-man in our family. Why he's so spoiled." Ayana hugged her big brother and asked, "Did you meet everyone else in the living room?"

"Not yet. Was looking for a place to park the cold goods," said Rodney.

"Would you ladies care for a margarita? Piña colada?"

"Was that what you ran out to get?" asked Ayana.

"Gotta have a holiday drink for a holiday celebration," said Rodney. "How's Hugh doin' on the ribs?"

"Under control. The barbecue king's got it all under control," said Ayana. "I'll go see if he wants an umbrella in his drink," said Ayana, wanting to give Lily and her brother some space.

Pulling a bag of miniature Old Glories out of the grocery bag, Rodney said, "I have something better." Then, opening the bag and handing a flag to his sister and one to Lily, Rodney took up his own small token and acclaimed: "In honor of emancipation making us citizens and potentially freeing white America from continuing to dehumanize their Black brothers and sisters."

This was Lily's first Juneteenth celebration and first time entertained in a Black home. Hugh and Ayana made sure Lily was coming and that the invitation got extended to Ethan. Lily was fairly certain the party was a first for Ethan as well. His firm had yet to hire a Black trainee, even as clerical support, much less a female of *any* color. As was explained to Lily, management wasn't opposed to the idea, they just had a *preference* for hiring the *best* person. And if that person turned out to be white and male, well. . . .

Ethan's peers reacted with tense silliness to Lily's presence at the firm's social functions, especially when she disclosed her field of graduate study and *vocational*, rather than career, aim. The junior moneymen all-dressed-for-success couldn't help themselves from disparaging comments, Lily sensed, to relieve their discomfort. Just how offensive depended upon the speaker, most remarks being a variation of *women* uttered in the same breath as *dick*, *dyke*, or some other sexual term.

Figuring her only means of survival was treating Ethan's peers as subjects under study, Lily mingled liberally at her first company business party. Another female declaring a career rather than a strictly domestic agenda sleuthed through the evening with Lily, cracking the code of male business. The two wagered how long a particular male could keep up nervous laughter before feeling outfoxed, finally having to move out of their perimeter.

One of the firm's hopefuls, however, defied the women's typecasting. Albeit liking money as well as the next kingpin-in-the making, Stuart Benjamin's appeal lay in what he wanted to *do* with a six-figure income. As Stuart described his vision of establishing a foundation to provide learning and nutritional support for poor children, Lily recalled the wisdom of an African tale read to her as a child: Animals with full bellies don't look at others as their next meal. As an adult, she translated the tale to mean: Persons satisfied with their own lives don't prey on others.

At the next firm function, when Lily asked why her new friend Danielle wasn't there, Ethan said that her boyfriend dumped her. Failing to find a replacement sidekick, Lily cheerlessly endured each subsequent gathering with its manufactured jollity of backslapping over gimlets and highballs.

"THANKS FOR INVITING US, HUGH, Ayana," said Lily, raising her glass. "And Rodney—great to meet you after all the good things Ayana has said about you."

"I pay her plenty to shine my star," said Rodney.

"And happy Juneteenth, everyone—I like the West Indian touch. You make a smooth piña colada, Rodney."

"Back in the day of slave and mistress, you'd have to be wary of me slipping a quarter jigger poison in your rum—"

"But he'd have to think twice about doin' in a mistress as pretty as Lily," said Ethan, just joining them at the door.

Embarrassed by Ethan's talking over her, Lily reinserted herself into the conversation, "This was fun. I really appreciate being included."

"My thanks, also," said Ethan. "Turns out your neighbors have family in my hometown. And Terrell's *laugh*. The jokes and stories were good, but the *laugh*—guy had me goin' all day long."

"Glad you could make it, Ethan. We don't see enough of you and what we get is always day-old and warmed over," said Hugh, casting a glance at Lily. "We want to see the real thing, live and in person, more often."

"You can and you will—in fact, let the Fourth of July be our treat," said Ethan, checking Lily's face to see if she agreed. "Can't guarantee the eats will be anything like today, but we're pretty good at popping open those deli cartons. Right, Lily?" Ethan winked. "We'd like to think it's in the presentation, so we keep lots of parsley and radish roses on hand."

"Let us know what we can bring," said Hugh.

"Leftovers from today—if there are any—would do fine," joked Ethan.

"Better get the freezer wrap out now," laughed Hugh, feigning movement toward the kitchen.

"Will we be seeing more of *you*, Rodney?" asked Lily.

Rodney looked at Hugh and Ayana as he replied, "Yeah, I'm scheduled to come to y'all's office—Monday, is it?" Hugh and Ayana nodded confirmation. "My plane leaves in the afternoon."

"Well, maybe we can all grab a bite for lunch, big brother. After the grand tour, of course."

"Of course," Rodney repeated. "Looking forward to seeing the celestial heights of church business and those cubicles you described, Ayana—I don't need an oxygen tank or anything, do I?"

"We'll let you puff on our air supply, long as you don't go over the metered limit for visitors," said Lily.

"Yeah. Give us your tired, your hungry and all that, long as they don't suck up too much of our air," quipped Rodney. "I don't know how you people live here!"

"It's the hotdog vendors on the street," declared Ethan. "That's what keeps me here. Once a day. I'm a two-dog man, unless it's baseball season and game day. You like baseball, Rodney? I can usually pick up a pair of tickets at the office."

"About as much as I like waiting for ketchup to run," teased Rodney. "No, it's good, it's good. It's not basketball, but it's good. Thanks, man. I'll take you up."

"I don't know if I could survive without it—truly, I don't think I could get through an entire year without a substantial amount of time spent in the stands. Hell, I'm like an old man—transistor plugged into my ear. Whatever it takes. Long as I get my game."

"Now that you've revealed your deepest self, Ethan, I think we should take our stuffed selves and waddle down curbside to flag a cab," said Lily, waving the tiny Stars and Stripes from her drink. "Souvenir. Really, thanks."

Before leaving, Lily and Ethan exchanged hugs and handshakes with their hosts, reiterating their turn at hospitality for the Fourth of July.

MONDAY, THE SAME CONVIVIAL SCENE repeated, sans Ethan, after Reuben sandwiches at a favorite deli and before Rodney left for the airport, promising to be back to check up on his baby sister once Cornell's fall semester got underway.

"Maybe we can figure out something more fun than an office tour for your return visit," suggested Lily.

"I've got some ideas already, Lily," said Rodney.

"Well, okay, then. Just make sure it doesn't fall between September twenty-two and twenty-two October," said Lily. "I'll be on expedition to the *Kentucky Republic*."

Rodney looked puzzled.

Hugh spoke up. "Church convention. For all of us who couldn't figure out anything better to do with our lives than tinker with prayer books and sing hymns loudly, though in order."

"Put that way—why *would* I wanna be ordained?" Lily gibed.

"If you change your mind about the priest thing, Lily, I can write a fine recommendation for law school," said Rodney. "When you get out and pass the bar, you can come be the first female—the first *white* attorney even, in the office of Hampton, Waters and Noble."

"Sounds forbidding," said Lily. "Or foreboding."

"Either way, Lily, you're making history," said Ayana.

"We'll see."

"What my daddy always said when he wasn't sure if he wanted to grant permission," said Rodney. "Don't wanna keep yourself on a string like that, Lily."

"Anyway. Again, great to meet you, Rodney, and I hope to see you when you're up this way again," said Lily.

"As delighted to make your acquaintance, Lily—see you on the rebound North." Rodney's use of the word "rebound" gave Lily an ominous pause.

"Yes, well. I better get back upstairs. Have a good flight, Rodney." Lily turned to Hugh and Ayana. "In a bit, you two. Fun lunch. Thanks."

Questions, all beginning with *What if . . .* crowded the elevator ride and walk to her office. *What if I had been raised in a mixed neighborhood, gone to a racially mixed school— what would the dances have been like? What if I had had a Black dance partner? Lab partner? Worked on projects, done presentations with Black students? What if I had made the same effort getting to know people of other races in college as now?*

———

HEARING THE PHONE RING, LILY called out to Ethan, "Can you buzz them in? My hands are covered with chicken fat."

Lily and Ethan had split party preparations; she got kitchen duty, he got vacuuming and making the rest of his apartment presentable—or at least clearing enough accessible space for invited guests plus any last-minute surprises. Finishing his chores, Ethan began organizing music for the party. He had just settled the needle arm on the Stones' *Goats Head Soup* LP when the phone rang. Ethan called back to Lily, "You mean, we actually have friends showing up on time to something?—must be yours."

After buzzing them in street-side, Ethan opened the door and waited. Shortly, Ayana appeared with a friend Raquel from Birmingham and two twentyish males toting full grocery bags and introduced as Clarence and Darby. The girls took the grocery bags into the kitchen while Darby, explaining his name to Ethan, quipped, "My pops was part Irish—we're still trying to figure out *which* part." Continuing to hold his audience's attention, he said, "Used to think that if we took a slice outta him, it'd be like a cake with green and black layers. He told me, only way I was gonna get a cross-section of those bones was payin' the coroner for an autopsy. Muh pops died of asthma last year and I still haven't found out if *biracial* means *bicolored*—all the way through."

Wiping her hands on a dishtowel, Lily walked in as the laughter slowed and abruptly cut off. "I won't ask you to repeat. Sorry about the hands," said Lily, introducing herself to each stranger and getting their names in return.

"That's cold, man. Sorry about your dad," said Ethan. "He must've been young—was he young?"

"Hell, yeah. Him and my mom had me when they were my age," said Darby. "Bitch of a thing. No one saw it comin'."

"You have family?" asked Ethan, as Ayana and Raquel reemerged from the kitchen.

"Moved out here from Indiana to live with my pop's ma. She works at NYU," said Darby. "Me and Clarence'll be startin' there in the fall."

"So, how'd you two meet?" asked Ethan.

"Our parents have known each other all our lives," said Clarence.

"Cool. Parents were best friends?" said Ethan.

"Somethin' like that," said Darby.

"Cool."

Then, "Aw, we're jes' messin' widdya, Ethan," said Clarence. "We're twins."

"No. No shit? You got me, man," said Ethan. "Didn't see that comin'."

Laughter relieved the prior heaviness of Darby talking about his father's death.

"'S'okay man," said Clarence. "We're fraternal."

"Damn. Saved my ass on that," said Ethan. "I thought you were gonna tell me you're identical."

"We don't know you well enough to unload on your ass like that, man," said Darby, still laughing.

Lily asked Raquel how long she'd be visiting, as Ethan took the brothers in the kitchen to see about drinks. "Give you a hand with the cooler, man?" volunteered Clarence.

"Uh, yeah . . . sure," said Ethan. "All kinds of cans and bottles in the bags on the floor by the fridge. Thanks, if you could pack 'em in and pour the ice already in the cooler on top."

"Where do you want it?" asked Darby.

"Yeah, good idea to set it in place first. Up against that wall. Thanks," said Ethan.

"No problem. We got it," spoke Darby for his twin, also.

"NEVER HEARD OF THEM," SAID Ayana, picking up a Cream album cover. "These either—The Who?"

"Who *dat*?" joked Raquel.

"How could you not know The Who?" asked Ethan.

"'Cause it's white music," said Ayana, "and my integrated school had segregated dances."

"Like sock hops and after-school shit?"

"Like *all* dances," said Ayana.

"Is that even legal? How is that still legal after the '60s?" asserted Ethan. "Not prom—"

"Most *especially*, prom," said Raquel.

"Why?" Ethan was incredulous.

"Tradition," said Ayana. "Black and White Ball in Birmingham means a black ball and a white ball, all separate."

"Well, it's about time you hear some of this *white* music for yourselves," said Ethan, placing a disk on the turntable.

After listening to "My Generation," Ayana snickered to Raquel, "Must not only be white, must be a generation *thing*!"

"You're saying I'm old?" whined Ethan.

"No, I'm saying just give me some sweet-sounding Marvin Gaye. The Temps. You know, a little Sly. You heard of my man Marvin, Ethan—I know you got to've heard of brotha-man Marvin."

Ethan grinned. "In fact, I've got him sitting on this shelf
. . ." said Ethan, thumbing through his albums. "Oh, yeah.
Here we go. Mercy, mercy me. Marvin, show your face."

"And I see you still have a turntable," flirted Raquel.
"No tapes?"

"Old school," said Ethan. "Got tapes, too, but we old
fogies got to hold on to our collectibles. They'll be worth
something someday. This turntable, ladies—and these speakers—bought the system college freshman year. Paid cash.
Glad to have it. Glad to have anything back then."

"So, you made this purchase once upon a time . . . when
you were *our* age," said Ayana, also enjoying flirting.

"Hey, it wasn't that long ago. We haven't put that many
more men on the moon—"

"Or women," said Raquel. "You're right, Ethan. Things
haven't changed *that* much."

"Nice. I like that, Ethan," said Lily, entering the living
room without their notice. "How come you never put it on?"

"You never ask," said Ethan. "Ayana and friend Raquel,
who've been giving me guff here, requested it. Just glad I
have some playable inventory for these larval-stage women."

"Yeah, that's it, *old man*. By the way, where do you keep
your respirator—don't want you turning blue on us, tryin' to
catch your breath every time you get excited," teased Ayana.

"And don't let us keep you from your afternoon nap,
graybeard," chimed in Raquel.

"You're in trouble now, friend," Lily teased, enjoying the
bite in her tone maybe a little too much. "Watch out these
girl-larvae don't have a feeding frenzy on your *boy-ego*."

"Hot town, summer in the city," sang Ethan. "Women's
lib on the rise."

A KNOCK ON THE DOOR JUST then produced a roomful of people. "You planned this, right?" asked Ethan. "A meeting of New York minds is as rare as Halley's Comet."

"Then we're actually *early* by a dozen years—last was 1910. Check it out, Bro—every 75 years," said one of Ethan's colleagues. Seeing Ayana, he said, "Hi, I'm Garrett." Ayana introduced herself and Raquel; everyone else followed suit.

"Now that everybody knows everybody," said Ethan, "glasses, ice are in the kitchen, straight ahead twelve paces and to your left. For everyone besides two-left-feet Phil, that is."

"See if I share any Mr. Daniels with you, chump."

"Bottle's probably half-emptied on the way over, cheapskate," said Ethan.

"Chef recommended it with omelets this morning—and whatever else she was serving," said Phil, tilting his head toward the giggly redhead reaching to cover his mouth with her hand as she tugged on his arm with the other.

Before the swarm got moving, another face appeared at the back of the crowd. "Hugh Lovelle, everyone," said Ethan. "Help him make your acquaintance." Heads turned to identify the stately new arrival and smile their acknowledgment. The nearest couple introduced themselves and offered to get Hugh something to drink.

"Actually, I brought some tonic water. I think I ate something last night that's getting back at me today."

"Sorry to hear that," said the younger man whose hair curled at his paisley shirt collar's edge. Dressed in a red, white, and blue grannie dress, the girlfriend reached out her hand, saying, "Here, I'll fix it for you—want ice with that?"

"That would be lovely—thanks."

Making his way to the back of the group now beginning to unclot, Ethan extended his hand to the newest arrival, "Hugh, glad you could make it. What can I get for you?"

"Nice young lady beat you to the punch. Believe her name is Sherry?" said Hugh, looking toward her date for confirmation. "And you're Shawn. With a *w*."

"Two for two."

"Remembering names and doing crossword puzzles," said Hugh. "My strategy for delaying senility's onset."

"I'd say you have a long way to go before having to worry about that."

Sherry returned with Hugh's tonic water. "So kind of you. Thanks, Sherry."

"I hope it's okay, Mr. Lovelle."

"Please. Call me Hugh—makes it a little easier to pretend I'm not the oldest person here." Then looking at the host he asked, "Unless Ethan has some more of us hiding in the kitchen?"

"You're it, buddy. I don't know if Lily's hiding out, exactly, but she *is* in the kitchen."

Hugh excused himself and headed for the kitchen, greeting and being greeted by guests enroute. "Smells good—can I help with anything?"

"Oh, Hugh. Thank God you're here. Any trouble finding the place?"

"No problem—your directions were very clear. Can I give you a hand?"

"No, I think between the oven and the grill outside we managed to fit all eighteen TV dinners," laughed Lily.

"This is a nice place," said Hugh. "Any view?"

"Yeah, got lots of view—red brick on this side and gray cement on the other. Just no blue sky or green leaves with this lease. The lighting is good though."

"It seems very comfortable," said Hugh. "Well, let me know if I can give you a hand with those aluminum covers on the TV dinners."

"Maybe in a little bit. Let me introduce you around now."

"Unless someone new has arrived, I think I met everyone. We came as a package deal, all at your door at the same time."

"Maybe it's me, then, that needs to go out and see if there's someone *I* don't know."

"Do you have a drink, Lily?"

"I had a glass here somewhere," said Lily, her hands moving items on the tiny bit of counter space. "Well, it was here a minute ago. I'll have a beer, though. There's a cooler on the side. Opener should be on top or somewhere around there. Thanks."

"My pleasure, ma'am." The eyes behind Hugh's glasses twinkled.

Ethan was at the cooler, too, so Hugh asked, "Take you long to find this place?"

"Fortunately, no. A guy in the firm was moving and told me about it when I first came on. The rent was just affordable, and the space accommodated my easy chair," Ethan said, pointing to a well-worn wingback. "And my custom-made bookshelf—like the bricks and two-by-fours?"

"Seen a few of that type construction in my day," said Hugh. "In my own house."

"Storage would be a problem, if I had any real goods to store. I have an allotted cubic yard in the basement, but I wouldn't put anything valuable down there. People consider it free pickins."

"It's very pleasant. Nice neighbors?"

"Hell if I know. I don't see them very much," said Ethan.

"No socializing?"

"Not at all."

"Well, I guess you keep pretty busy."

"Chasing my first million," said Ethan playfully.

"Remember me, son, when you come into your kingdom!"

Lily emerged from the kitchen pointing to a table set up at the room's edge and saying, "If I could have some assistance carting the food from here to there, we can eat."

A cheer went up as everyone rushed her. "Let's change that last directive—how about we do this fireperson-style. Form a line and I'll start handing out food."

"There goes my tip," said Hugh. "I took her order and never returned."

"Oh, Lily's forgiving—at least she should be," declared Ethan, "if priesthood's really gonna be her thing."

"I'd be interested to hear more about your perspective, Ethan. Perhaps another time when you're not in the middle of hosting a party."

"Oh, I'm her strongest supporter," said Ethan. "I mean, if that's what she wants to do."

THOUGH FIREWORKS WERE ILLEGAL IN the city, there had been firecrackers popping all day. As dusk neared, several guests departed for other Independence Day venues such as Central Park's fireworks display choreographed to music or Yankee Stadium's dazzling program, including traditional cannons fired to accompany "The Star-Spangled Banner."

Hugh, Ayana, and her friends were among those who stayed to watch the city sky light up from the roof of Ethan's building. Whistles and applause hailed intermittent booms sounding every time a projectile shot onto night canvas, spattering its color to exaggerated *oohs* and *aahs* from the growing and diverse group of sky watchers.

Focusing on Hugh and Ayana, specifically, Lily thought, *What if I had Black neighbors at home as well as work?*

NEEDING TO PUT IN EXTRA HOURS at work, Ethan, at the last minute, begged off meeting Lily, Ayana, and her friends for dinner at Sharky's Grill. Told to go ahead and get a table and Lily would follow, the four young diners watched as the hostess seated party after party coming in after they did. Inquiring, they were told no tables were available, though none of the tables just seated displayed "Reserved" placards. Asked when the next table would come open, the middle-aged hostess first had Darby repeat his question, then answered while walking away with menus in hand to lead another group to a table for six, "Could be half an hour or more."

"Hey, I don't need this shit," said Clarence, turning toward the door.

"Hold on, hold on," said Ayana. "Lily won't know where to find us, if we leave and go someplace else."

"Well she better come quick 'fore I make a scene with Betty here and her system of black diversion," said Darby.

"Yeah, we came here to eat, not hold up the joint," said Raquel. "We're the ones being held up—at *shun*point. When Lily comes, I'm takin' my money someplace decent."

"Hell, Indiana's got its problems but I ain't been told my money ain't worth shit like this lady done," said Darby. "Maybe we should just park our black asses right here and scare ol' Betty's customers off the rest o' the night. Serves 'em right. Missin' out on their Friday night special. Like to show them a Friday night special—"

"Sorry, you guys," said Lily, entering the restaurant and waving to the hostess. "You just get here, too?"

"Not exactly," said Ayana.

"I told you it was okay to go ahead and get a table," said Lily. "No need to wait—"

"It seems you can't get a table here, unless you have the right skin color," said Darby.

Stunned, Lily sought to redress the wrong immediately. Signaling to Betty, she turned with an aside to her new, younger friends, "I'm really sorry if she gave you that impression. We've never had a problem."

"It's the *we*, Lily," said Ayana. "We *here* is not the usual *we* Betty sees you with."

"There's a table opening up—" said Betty, directing her announcement to no one in particular, before shouting to a miniskirted waitress with hair dyed jet black, "Number six, hon', you take 'em on number six." Turning to Lily, while ignoring the others, she said, as if doing a favor, "Jessica'll take you on number six. Oh, and here are some menus."

Lily led, while Ayana coaxed her friends to follow "just this once" to a noisy table near the kitchen's swinging doors. If not for Jessica's humor and getting their order in, cooked and served without further hassle, the group would have gone elsewhere, they said. With or without Lily.

Embarrassed by the hostess's treatment of Ayana and her friends, Lily volunteered picking up half the group's tab. Telling her it wasn't her ass needing cover, the four divided the entire bill, leaving Lily responsible for the tip only. "Okay," said Lily, "but you all can just step outside, please, while I have a few words with the hostess."

"Naw," said Clarence, "you might need us to watch your back."

"If I need you to watch my back," said Lily, "then it'll be the police having a few words with Betty, not me. Just let me do this my way, thanks."

The hostess missed the departing quartet's cold stare but not the tone and substance of Lily's complaint, which, nonetheless, got dismissed as soon as Lily was out the door. Figuring her job secured by staying mum about the grill owner's occasional trespass whenever his wife was off visiting relatives, Betty didn't feel the need to take the grievance seriously, much less apologize. And, anyway, Sharky wouldn't want her causing trouble for the Grill, making nice to race mixing.

THE DAYS OF SUMMER STRETCHED into early fall. At the Episcopal Church's sounding call, planes, trains, and cars delivered advance staff and, finally, conventioneers to Louisville, Kentucky. The weather was unseasonably warm at the start of the triennial meeting and the agenda longer than usual, in order to accommodate the election of a new Presiding Bishop amid all the customary legislative business.

The vote for women's ordination was even more disappointing than three years previous, some of the failure owing to the shopworn argument purporting competition between movements for gender equality and racial justice. Like pitting contenders of a land grab, only instead of the fastest, it was whoever was the weakest, most threatened by the potential for peer relationship—white males and their female sympathizers—who came out winners, securing their holdings for the time being with a tight fist. Those women already ordained deacon waited most patiently of all for church polity to catch up with what was blowing in the wind.

MEETING FOR BREAKFAST THE FIRST week, Lily showed Hugh a glossy "plantation tour" brochure picked up from the hotel rack. Photos depicted white guides dressed in period costume, while text caricatured owners as American nobility, with no mention of slavery as the economic basis for white wealth yet on display for paying visitors. Appealing to seekers of Old South romance, the brochures wisely avoided history's bloodier details inscribed on slaves' backs, mutilated and castrated body parts, and children born of rape.

"It's a national amnesia, Lily. Not just a few individuals, but as a whole culture we know, but easily *forget*, what drove American agricultural and later industrial dominance in world markets. Then the forgetting is media-generated, reproduced in everything from travel brochures to the daily newspaper, along with the conditions and attitudes that supported slavery, near slavery, and prevailing, persistent though illegal, discriminatory practice. Yet today, you can glimpse white family luxury, but the absence, as the brochure suggests, of the enslaved families who made white privilege possible. The concept, practice, and reproduction of white *superiority* always has and still does depend upon the concept, practice, and reproduction of black *inferiority*."

"How can you stand being in this city, at this hotel, where Blacks are still the maids and bellhops—not front desk staff or management?" asked Lily.

"Louisville and this hotel are neither more nor less discriminatory than other cities and lodging in America," said Hugh. "Why does the Episcopal Church patronize discriminatory practices to the Convention's tune of thousands of thousands of dollars?"

"What's the alternative?"

"We have yet to know, because other than bus boycotts and sit-ins, we as a country have not availed ourselves of methods as persistent and popular as racism to achieve its opposite: racial equality. Methods have limited utility. What we need is a change in the basic contract of America that clearly and punishably removes race superiority and inferiority from the center of American life. Of course, denial that it *is* central to American social as well as economic commerce helps keep it at the center; and whether subtly or obviously, race remains the commodity of choice."

"Well, I for one will be happy to leave Louisville and get back to familiar territory," said Lily. "Of course, having said that, I have to add that the familiar territory of which I speak, whether that's the Church Center or my neighborhood or New York—they're all stakeholders in maintaining race at the core. If not, things would be different."

"A simple truth simply stated," said Hugh, "is eloquence."

———

BOOK 2

Not the hucklebuck as in do-the-hucklebuck, do-the-hucklebuck in some five watt blue bulb stomp down street alley dance hall place and she with too much make-up on getting maneuvered into a dark corner thigh on thigh and nothing romantic and nice about it. But Charlie Parker doing "Now is the Time," coaxing from her something muscular and daring, something borrowed first . . . till she earned it for her . . . learned to listen to linears and verticals at the same time, new time, rhythm bam.

—TONI CADE BAMBARA, *The Salt Eaters*

A CHANGING OF THE GUARD came with the arrival of a new PB in January of the following year. Hugh Lovelle left Church Center and was called as rector of Harlem's St. Philip's parish. He invited Lily to do field training with the congregation of six hundred members. Including grants from the national EWC and the local activist group in her own New York Diocese, Lily secured enough funding to be a full-time student spring semester, receiving her Master of Divinity at term's end. She and the bishop talked about the possibility of an early June diaconal ordination. Remaining in place at St. Philip's after she was made a deacon, the plan was for Hugh to continue mentoring Lily as she prepared for priestly ordination.

All was going quickly and smoothly for Lily until Easter. A call from her uncle in Texas delivered the sad news of her mother's sudden death. The coroner recorded the cause as an "allergic reaction to new medication," and Uncle Bob added, "with no one at hand to rescue or call for help."

Lily called Dee and began crying when she heard her sister's voice. "I didn't go home at Christmas and now Mom's dead. I should have gone. I should have found the money for a ticket. . . ."

"Lily, Lily. Remember Mom was invited to spend the holidays here—Craig and I weren't going anywhere with new twins, and, especially, in the winter," said Dee, trying to assuage her sister's guilt. "Mom said she'd come visit in the spring. We were *all* okay with that. Including Mom."

"But I haven't been home since the summer after I graduated from Brown," continued Lily. "She always asked, and I just kept putting it off."

"Because Texas no longer runs through your veins—that is, if it ever did," Dee calmed. "And while you're at it, feel bad you're not a self-made millionaire with your own private jet which you, your favorite sister, and the rest of her family could have used to go back and forth to Texas or wherever else, at will."

"I could use that jet now," said Lily. "Are you going home for Mom's funeral? I guess there'll be a funeral."

"I can't. We don't have the money for all of us to go, and I can't travel by myself and leave the twins at home with Daddy. Daddy's gotta work to put food on the table and pay the rent that keeps going up, since we don't have any friggin' rent control in the 'burbs."

"Isn't Uncle Bob doing pretty well?"

"Yeah, but I can't ask him to underwrite a quick trip home for all of us. Besides, I think he plows all his profit back into the insurance agency."

"God, I haven't talked to him in ages, either," groaned Lily. "Dee, I can't find myself—I feel like parts of me are floating detached around the room. I'm not handling this well at all," said Lily, starting to sob.

"Look, baby sister," said Dee decidedly, "we can give you some of the airfare and Uncle Bob can probably put in the rest to bring you home to say goodbye to Mom. You're almost a deacon—heck, you could do the service."

"Yeah, right—I'm not ready for that. For any of this," said Lily, an anger starting to brace her body as if defending against an invisible enemy.

"We're never ready, as ready as we want to be, for anything

it seems," Dee philosophized. "Knowing what I know now, I could have used five more years before I became a mother to twins. I need a double doctorate in twinology and sanity, but you know what? They're here and I'm as ready as I'm gonna get. And, Lily, *I* need you to go. Be there for me too."

"I know I need to go. So, what do I do first?"

"Call Uncle Bob and ask him to put a ticket on his credit card. He's out there in business for himself. He'll know how to get a good deal, especially if he's paying for it. Let him know we're good for fifty dollars."

"Let me see what he says first." Then, remembering her mother's death as the reason for the call, Lily said, "Dee?"

"Yeah, sweetie."

"Thanks for being such a good sister. It's you and me now."

"It always has been," Dee said, putting her final seal on the sisters' relationship. "I love you, now go call Uncle Bob."

"WELCOME BACK," HUGH GREETED LILY. "How was it?"

"It was," Lily hesitated, "the saddest trip I've ever made home."

"I'm sorry, Lily."

"I don't think I'll be going back," said Lily, tearing up.

"Don't you have other family in Texas?"

"My mother's younger brother Bob, Billy Bob as his friends still call him. He's there with his wife and my cousins—who are lots younger—but Mom was my real family. I'd have about as much reason to go back as Billy Bob and his buddies would to leave."

"What drew you out of Texas in the first place?"

"I think ever since I saw my first *National Geographic* at the public library, the world got a whole lot bigger. So, whether it was Africans' dyed bodies or a pile of silvery-orange salmon fresh out of a Norwegian fjord, it didn't matter. I was ready to take my Brownie camera and hop the next train. We did actually have a train going through Greenville," considered Lily, "just that none of my family ever took it. I wonder how far I would have gotten!"

"So, attending college out of state was an easy decision for you, I suppose."

"Not only out of state," declared Lily, "out of the South."

"I still get a kick out of people referring to Texas as the South. It's west of Birmingham and that means cowboys and cattle and home on the miles and miles of range."

"Y'all may think that," Lily drawled, "but we all know where we're from. South and east of the *real* West which is actually north of Texas. Dodge City, Durango—you been to any of those places, Hugh?"

"No, these wingtips haven't taken me too far out West as yet. I'll have to see more of the country one of these days—for pleasure, not business. Do you think they're friendly to East Coast types like me?" mused Hugh.

"All depends on who sees you first!"

"There can't be too many Texans gendered like you who got the call for ordination," said Hugh. "You must be the exception, Lily."

"Or the tip of the Texas iceberg," asserted Lily. "The Church might need to think about preparing for a Second Coming . . . of the flood. 'Cause when she thaws, there's gonna be a deluge."

"You mean I should start investing in women's clergy shirts—or would it be *blouses*?"

"Now you're thinking like a smart man. But, then again, you always do," said Lily with obvious admiration. "You know I'm depending on you to get me through this."

"Thanks for your confidence, Lily," Hugh responded. "It's tough losing your mother."

"Well, that, too. But I was talking about my ordination.

My poor mother has been dead, all but buried in the ground, for quite a few years now. As if she'd been running on fumes. It wasn't just my father's death. I think the tank got emptied somewhere before my dad passed," Lily explained. "The coroner's report said she died instantly. Probably didn't know what hit her, which was pretty typical of my mother. She didn't want to look too far ahead or too much beyond the immediate periphery. I think something must have scared her good when she was younger. Maybe in childhood even, as a girl growing up in Texas."

"Funny how like, but also unlike, our parents we are," said Hugh, using what Lily said to relate to his own life. "My father couldn't read or write, but he had a good memory and a sharp mind for details. Unfortunately, I got the details-observer part without too much of the memory. So many times, I've wished my father were still around. I would just like to be able to talk to him. And especially when Cherise died. He was already gone then. He had a way of putting things in perspective that I, in my sophistication, have somehow lost."

"I'm only beginning to realize how little account I took of my mother's mortality," said Lily. "A mother is supposed to be there. Like the mother of the bride. My God! I'm not even married. My mother won't be at my wedding," Lily cried. Hugh reached out his hand. Taking hold with both of her hands, Lily held on tight before reaching for a Kleenex to blow her nose. "She won't be there, scared as she was, to put the deacon's stole on me either."

"Not in the way you wish her to be, Lily," comforted Hugh, "but in ways that remain a mystery. The love never goes. The love triumphs."

"Thanks, Hugh. Maybe it *is* more about my mother's death than ordination," reflected Lily. "It will be an ordination without my mother. I don't know what it's like without a mother. Thank God I have a sister who mothers me. She can help vest me after the bishop gives the word."

"There will be many of us to help you, Lily."

"SO, ETHAN, ARE YOU SAYING YOU *don't* want to be at my ordination?"

"No, that isn't what I'm saying, Lily. If you'll just calm down, maybe you can get it right. I *can't* be at the ordination *that week*—I'll be out of town."

"If this is about getting it right, you haven't been getting it, *period*, Ethan," her voice lowering to Ethan's voice rising.

"What do you want me to do, huh? Just tell Fred, 'No, I can't go do the presentation to the biggest account I've handled to date'—and just kiss making partner goodbye?"

"You seem more committed to being the *firm's* partner than *mine*. And if that's how it is—if that's *really* how it is—I need a simple declarative statement from you, saying, 'Yes, that is so,' because if it *isn't* so, I need to see a little more interest on your part—or at least a better act."

"Lily, you know I love you—"

"You say that like I'm forgetful."

"I love you, Lily," repeated Ethan, "but where is all this ordination business going anyway? I mean, what's down the road for me? *Clergy spouse?* Am I gonna be putting on bake sales, keeping your halo polished . . . making sure your wings are back from the dry cleaner?" asked Ethan, sounding desperate. "Because I have no training in *clergy spouse support.*"

"Why not try basic support—as in the *other party* in this what-we've-been-calling *relationship*," said Lily in exasperation. "My God, I'm not even ordained yet. . . . But since you brought it up, what does the future hold for *me* as *corporate spouse*? Look good, say nothing. Is that gonna be my formula to your success? 'Hi, I'm Barbie's friend and I keep Ken's friend, Ethan, super happy!' Gee. What a reason for being."

"A runaway train."

"A what?"

"You. You're like a runaway train."

"Then you're the engineer and it's time to hit the brakes after climbing aboard with me."

"Yeah, yeah, I know. The 'Mr. Cautious' business," said Ethan, annoyed. "Can we maybe try a new approach, since neither of us knows what the end of the line looks like?"

"If *this* is the end for us, we do."

"Let's just say it isn't. Can't we work it out like the creative, intelligent people we are?" Ethan asked, following quickly with a solution. "What's involved in changing your ordination date to either the week before or the week after—the invitations haven't already gone out, have they?"

"Verbally to a few people," Lily snapped, "including the bishop who came up with the date in the first place. His calendar is scheduled a year, two years out. I can't just bump it up or back a week because my boyfriend—"

"I thought I was your fiancé."

"As soon as you act like it," said Lily sarcastically. "Until then, I'll call it as I see it. I mean, you say *clergy spouse* like you wanna puke."

"Thank you," Ethan continued acidly. "I'll consult that instruction manual before I make another bad move. Commitment . . . commitment? Wasn't somebody around here just lecturing about commitment? Oh, but I guess the rules are different if you're ordained or about to be ordained. You can confirm with the bishop but not with the fiancé. I can call it as I see it too."

"Much as I hate admitting," Lily slowed, "you have a point, Ethan. But being the person of integrity that I am—"

"And on the verge of taking *holy* orders—"

"See—how can you miss the chance of seeing me take orders, holy or otherwise, from anyone?"

"Because I have—"

"I know. Big important business to take care of."

"One of us has to be the materialist."

"I suppose."

"And I'm best suited. So, as a purely pragmatic matter, can we get back to the calendar and when the damn ordination could, might, maybe take place?"

"I'll have to check with the Holy See."

"How soon?"

"At a decent hour in the morning. If he is in town."

"I can come any time, night or day—"

"So, where's your hot stuff been hiding?"

"Just waiting for sex kitten to retract her claws," said Ethan, planting his hands on Lily's shoulders and drawing her in, "or should I say, *lioness?*"

Putting him off a while longer, Lily said, "The bishop and I had, also, discussed the Visitation of the Blessed Virgin Mary as a possible alternative. . . ."

"*Now* what are you talking about?"

Lily continued pedantically, "May thirty-first. It's the fixed lesser feast of Mary's visit to her cousin Elizabeth who, though elderly, was with child and knew that Mary, though she didn't look it, was pregnant too."

"Sounds auspicious. You wouldn't be trying to slip something into the conversation, would you?"

"Many things I am, but cruel, hopefully, is not one," said Lily. "No coincidence of spiritual and biological motherhood in this ordinand."

"Well I'm just saying—I mean, I would be happy, of course," backpedaled Ethan, "as well as surprised. You *have* been taking—"

"Precautions?" Lily scoffed and continued edgily. "Yes, I believe we're calling them birth control pills these days. No, Ethan, we won't be celebrating your first Father's Day in June." Returning to the previous topic, Lily said, "Now if I had the *ordination* in June, I'd have my pick of martyrs: on the first, there's Justin who bought the farm at Rome, then martyrs, plural, of Lyon are on the second, followed by Ugandan martyrs on the third."

"How do you remember all these dates?"

"Had to, for a class in seminary and for my examination by the bishop's academic cleric appointees. But wait, there's more. . . ."

"Save me."

"That's what the martyrs said—maybe that's what your sacred calling is. Saint Ethan martyred by his beloved's ordination relegating him to lowly clergy-spouse status. You could join the ranks of Bernard Mizeki, martyred in Rhodesia—when it was Rhodesia—honored on June eighteenth or Alban, a Roman soldier who impersonated a priest and became Britain's first martyr—maybe in *York*. So, hey, Ethan! You could be the first martyr of *New* York."

"Stick with May thirty-first," said Ethan. "Pregnant cousins comparing due dates over tea and lavosh sounds more congenial than male martyrdom. By the way, are *all* the noted martyrs male?"

"Historical footnote, in case you missed my last fem go-round rant. Whereas, a*men* is usually the last word punctuating an assertion . . ." Lily said, hands diagramming as she spoke, "ah-*woman* generally begins a wearied lodging of complaint and *femaligning*. So, whether martyred females are overlooked for canonization or, worse and more likely, their case for sainthood never made it into the historical record in the first place, them's with the right gender-tender are them's doin' the choosin'. So, a long-winded answer to your question—yes, most martyr berths are taken, thank you ma'am, by men."

"I know you don't mean to, but sometimes your comments about the son-of-a-bitch males responsible for patriarchal oppression are directed at me. Do you think I'm oppressing you, Lily?" asked Ethan.

"You don't get it, do you," Lily said flatly. "My comments are not directed at you *personally*, but it would be hard to tweeze your particular male privilege from the whole corpus of perks and benefits of male privilege. And that's just present day with how much of it derived from historic male prerogative—"

"Okay. I got it," said Ethan, cutting her off. "I know it must be frustrating for you—"

"I doubt it—"

"Doubt what?"

"You knowing my frustration."

"Can we just get beyond the boxing ring?"

"A male metaphor."

"Okay. You want I should scrub all masculine references from my speech before *attempting* conversation with you?"

"No," said Lily. "I just ask that you be aware when you're using them, as I am made to do as a female American."

"Fine. I'm aware. More than aware, thanks to you."

"You're welcome."

"What I wanted to say three reels back was, thanks for accommodating my work schedule, Lily," Ethan spoke softly. "And I *do* want to be at your ordination, because I love you and want to see our partnership work."

"It must be my turn to say something."

"I was wondering when you'd abandon your shy demeanor and speak up," teased Ethan. "How 'bout using body language?"

THE OFFICE OF THE BISHOP was, indeed, able to move the ordination to the thirty-first of May. Because it fell on a Saturday, even more people were able to attend, and from as far away as Alaska, Oregon, and California. The attendees included women about to be ordained, as well as those who had been ordained deacon on the heels of Church approval almost four years before. Lily was pleased that the most veteran among females ordained deacon, a woman who sensed her priestly calling as a child, came from Minnesota, adding her witness to the laying on of hands making another, but considerably younger, sister deacon.

More wonderful still, a classmate four years her senior accepted Lily's invitation to serve as deacon. Nan read the Gospel lesson for the service bestowing on Lily the title "Reverend" with the characteristic boldness Lily had come to appreciate in liturgy and homiletics courses taken together at Union Seminary when the same courses were off limits to females at General Episcopal Seminary. It was this classmate who, during the opening chapel service on the first day of classes, openly declared her feelings in whispers loud enough that even hard-of-hearing professors couldn't miss her message: "We've *got* to do something about the 'he this, men that' language!" Nan, though labeled "radical" by the establishment Church, was on her way to gaining respectability as a theologian now that her first book chapters proposing God be let out of the patriarchal box, and asking of Jesus, "Can a male savior save women?" were featured in academic journals.

Ordained the previous summer, Lily's outspoken friend and mentor joined the thirty to forty other women deacons eligible for priesthood to agitate for canonical change allowing women to preside at the Lord's Table in God's Episcopal house. Though happy her own ordination would add to their game-changing numbers, Lily wondered how many more "non-Caucasian" women's vocations simply went unacknowledged. She knew of only one exception: sixty-three-year-old Black attorney, author, educator, Pauli Murray, a founder of the National Organization of Women. Out of the country at the time, this extraordinary woman had enrolled at Virginia Theological Seminary only the prior fall. She sent an encouraging note that arrived the day before more of the Church's history-in-the-making conferred deacon holy orders on Lily.

The ceremony was both joyful in the combined St. John the Divine Cathedral and St. Philip crowd's acclamation, and painful in her mother's absent voice when the people resounded, "We will!" to the bishop's question: ". . . uphold her in her ministry?"

Dee and Craig were there, however, each dangling a twin. When the time arrived for Dee to proceed to the lectern to read the Old Testament lesson, Harry cried and would not release his hold on his mother. At the reception following, Harry was the chuckled-over metaphor of those in the Church who, with an equally tenacious grip, sought to keep women in the pew and out of the pulpit.

THE MEMBERS OF ST. PHILIP'S in the Harlem neighborhood of Manhattan and St. John the Divine Cathedral, two congregations not used to mixing, notwithstanding, were mixed together like a well-shuffled deck of cards as they passed through the greeting line. A well-built woman, who wore an elaborate affair of a hat that included bright red cherries and variegated green leaves spilling onto a wide black straw brim, led the parade of alternately boisterous and reserved well-wishers greeting Lily at the church door after the service.

"We'll see you in the mawnin', honey, with a new spahkle in yaw eyes!" said the woman. In a hat at risk of being as potentially attractive to hungry birds in the immediate vicinity as ten years ago it was to its purchaser, Vernyce Washington was one of the church mothers at St. Philip's.

Though a smaller package than his wife, Neville Washington shared her large affection in marking the occasion. "I guess we goin' to need to change how we refuh to you from here on out, Rev'n Lily! No more plain jane. No sir. You got some-a that sacred sass now!"

"Yeah, yeah," said Lily, inspired by Mister Washington's humor. "You got to be on your best behavior now. Unfortunately—me too!"

"We like you any way you come, Lily," said Neville, smiling God's own sunbeam. "And we *all* are glad you came to Saint Philip's. Good for us be shaken up a little—got some of us, at least, shiftin' in our seats. No, Rev'n Lily, you just awright with us."

"That means the world to me," said Lily. "I still have a lot to learn. I thank God I have you and Mother Washington as teachers. Thank you so much for being here today. When I looked out to give the dismissal, I thought, you two are where the hymn 'Blessed Assurance' got its name. And, definitely, I'm going to be seeing you tomorrow morning for another dose."

"We love you, honey," said Vernyce Washington, as she enclosed Lily in her soft motherly arms, leaving a kiss of peace on her cheek.

Next to last in line, Robbie and Tony, one of the Cathedral congregation's least reserved couples, each had an affectionate go at endorsing the new deacon. "Finally!" said Tony with voice and hands in exaggerated exasperation. "Lily, sweetheart, this is worse than standing in day after Christmas Macy lines."

"I appreciate your devotion," said Lily.

"My feet are screaming for some of their own 'Ave Maria.' Can't wait to get out of these heels," joked Robbie. "Are you ever going to return to us at St. John's, Lily? You know we're the only *divine* in the city. We miss you."

"Miss you, too, you divine twosome. Maybe I'll let you do my liturgical colors."

"We've got some great ideas."

"Oh, I bet you do," Lily returned.

THREE QUARTERS THROUGH GREETING LINE duty, Auntie Lily had been happy to have nephews Harry and Spencer burst on the scene, restoring levity to the unearthly moment, their chocolaty hands profaning her new silk skirt and begging, "Up! Up!"

Fortunately, Ethan came to her rescue. "*I'll* pick you two ragamuffins up!" The two toddlers squealed in delight, their adoration unconcerned with whether the man was officially attached to Lily as their uncle. Ethan easily scooped up the two knots of wiggly muscle and proceeded to the small patch of grass, where he recognized Ayana but not her afro, which was bigger than the last time he saw her. She and her brother Rodney stood in the midst of several unfamiliar faces. Glad to see someone else he knew, even if only somewhat, Ethan said, "Hey," lowering his two charges to the ground and putting out his hand in greeting.

"I didn't know you and Lily were already in the family way. Radical!" whistled Rodney. "Now I know my chances of gettin' wid da new deacon are slim to none."

"Been damn hard keeping it hushed, but their nanny had the day off and, since I had to be here—what're *you* doin' here, Rodney?" Ethan asked. "You still in Birmingham?"

"Here to witness the deed. Same as you. Male as we are, figure my sister here could get me through the gilded doors," said Rodney, looking anything but second class. "Gotta stick together, bro Ethan. These women got some crazy ideas. Here for mutual support, my man. Thanks to a client. Glad somebody wants our business—know what I mean?"

"You talk so much trash, you sound like *baby* instead of big brother," said Ayana, breaking into the boy banter. "Hi Ethan."

"Hey—I'm still the one opening doors, pulling out chairs, getting the lady a drink. I know what my manhood is made of," said Ethan, enjoying Rodney's male camaraderie, unready to make room for his sister just yet.

"Well, thank God, we still got room when they ask us to move our male tushes over a few more inches," breezed Rodney, "we're not on the edge of the cliff yet."

"Yeah, well, I may have to join you in Birmingham, this thing gets any hotter for me here."

"Done gone. Invited to be on the yellow brick road to partner with some law school buddies now in Atlanta," Rodney said, relieved to be on the safer turf of shop talk. "But you're welcome in Atlanta. Any time. Ever been to the Peach State?"

"Through there, not to stay any length of time. Only saw the newsstand at the airport," said Ethan. "Like it?"

"Yeah, yeah, I really do. Got a lot of promise."

"Business-wise?"

"Business-wise and people-wise, both. A lot of people our age have relocated to Atlanta, especially Black professionals or wannabe, gonnabe professional types. Nights, weekends— the city's hoppin'. You oughta come down."

"I'll definitely have to check it out. Maybe when I get some time to waste, Lily and I could head down for a weekend."

"Do. I even have decent accommodations for visitors. Can I get a witness?" Rodney said, looking at Ayana.

"More like, can I get a word in?" Ayana said hotly.

"Sorry, baby sister," Rodney said, falsely contrite. "Light's green. Your turn. Go on and tell Ethan how smooth my pad is."

"It had possibilities," Ayana said, her brother's humor unable to budge her peeved expression, "when I was there in the spring. Most of his stuff was still in boxes, but that was good, because that's all we had to sit on."

"Well, see now. That's why you have to come back and see the place in its slammin' glory."

"I wish I had a sister," Ethan mused.

"You don't have a sister in your family, Ethan?" asked Ayana, surprised by Ethan's admission of want.

"Just brothers," said Ethan. "And none of them are like a sister. Not in any way, shape, or form. Corn-fed and contented."

"Rodney! I thought that was your handsome self, sitting with your sister second pew on the right." Lily's face lit up as if she were reuniting with an old and dear friend. "What are you doing here?"

"Missed you when I was back in the fall—besides, you being my only *white* sistah, I wouldn'a missed it."

"Oh, stop! Your sister had to come. She knows I'd kill her if she didn't," said Lily, giving Ayana a look. "But you—I can't believe it!"

The twins, failing to keep the attention of the next adult group they'd tottered off to, came wobbling back over to their aunt like two little old drunks, imploring, again, with upraised hands, "Up! Up!" This time Lily obliged but gestured for Ethan to pick up Harry while she reached for Spencer.

"When did you get in?" Lily asked Rodney, who looked at his watch as if calculating the answer to his question. "About eighteen hours ago. Caught the last flight out of Atlanta. Or what people *acted* like was the last flight out of Atlanta . . . *ever*."

"A real mob scene, huh?"

"Yeah, but worth all the scars to be here firsthand. This is your day, Lily. Congratulations," said Rodney with gracious sincerity.

"I didn't know if I could pull it off. I feel like one of the first explorers to the South Pole. Aren't too many of us in this cold-shouldered wilderness. I wonder how long it will take Father Church to make up his mind about our status as humans, so he can ordain us as priests."

"And bishops," Ayana added. "I think you'd look good in purple, Lily."

"It's been in the oven awhile," said the new deacon, "you'd think it'd be ready to serve."

"Critical mass," said Rodney.

"Nice pun," Ayana complimented.

"No, serious. Slave emancipation would never have happened without numbers of people in opposition, including the slaves themselves. They took off, leaving massah to his plantation prison at their own peril."

"And, I'm sure had a lot more unknown and dangerous territory *out there* as an untraveled slave than I will as a lady cleric."

"Nonetheless. Takes a lot of courage to do what you're doing, Lily," offered Rodney. "And I will be the first one at the altar rail," looking at Ethan, "after your man, here, when you do your thing—or get the thing done to you that makes you a priest."

"Thank you. I know y'all have my back," kidded Lily. "But seriously, it means a lot to have you here. All of you. After Dee, you're the ones'll have my unlisted number when the threatening phone calls start coming . . . and, Rodney, you're the lawyer I'm calling to my defense when the time arrives."

"Women been getting those?" asked Rodney.

"Some. You know Church people can get pretty vicious defending their little dogpatch of belief."

"No need 'splainin' that to a Black man; got it the *first* time—up close and *personal*: 'No offense meant, Rodney, but my mama says we're fruit from different trees and God created us that way.' No offense, my ass. Using God to justify some cracker's bigotry passed on to a child."

"Sorry. How easily I *blanc* out." The three looked puzzled. "*Blanc*—French, for 'white.'"

"So. I have a baby sister who's Black and one who's white," Rodney declared, "I'm ready for Atlanta's next Black and White ball."

"Atlanta?—I thought you were in Birmingham," said Lily.

"Already been covered. Before you arrived," Rodney declared. "You and Ethan are coming to visit me and my new place in Atlanta."

"Gee-oh-gia," finished Ethan.

"You got the accent down, Ethan," Ayana encouraged. "You're halfway there."

Then, spotting Tony and Robbie, Lily called, "Hey you two, get over here. I want to introduce you to a couple of friends of mine—Ayana is Hugh Lovelle's surrogate niece . . . and Rodney, from *Atlanta*, is her brother," pulling the siblings in closer for Robbie and Tony's greeting, each in turn. "And you know Ethan?"

"As much as you let us," ribbed Tony before the two trilled in unison, "Hi Mister Deacon!"

"Thanks, guys," said Ethan, "way to cast me in a supportive role."

"Sweetheart, we nominate you for best in a supporting role," said Tony.

"And we think you're just as good as a leading man," said Robbie, openly flirting with a less game Ethan.

Ethan wondered how it worked with two guys in a relationship: Did they take turns leading and following, or were their roles static? He thought Tony the more take-charge of the two, but maybe they cooperatively wore the pants in the family. Ethan caught himself comparing his relationship with Lily to theirs and was silently mortified by that thought. What did that make him? He didn't know yet what to make of all the hoopla around Lily's "set apartness," how it would work with Lily and him when she was in clergy collar.

"If you're in the neighborhood, stop by later on. We don't leave for the opera till sixish," said Tony.

"You need to stop by for old time's sake, Lily—before you become a complete stranger," said Robbie. "I'll bake cake and Tony'll pop champagne."

"Don't look at me," said Ethan, "I have a plane to catch and a meeting back at the office before departure, but you all go ahead."

"These days have to make sure it clears Ethan's travel calendar—this month he's away more than at home," said Lily. "I better not commit. I think going back to my place and taking off these heels sounds like a great idea for starters; and Ethan may have more ideas . . . before his before-departure meeting."

"Ooh, you are too hot, and did we mention what a statement you made in that red dalmatic?" said Robbie.

"One *foxy* deacon," said Tony. "Bye, love. Bring your travel-widow loneliness over this week and we'll pop corn *and* champagne."

"GUESS I'M THE PARTY CLOSER!" announced Hugh, hugs and handshakes having already made it around the circle before he walked into their midst. "Lily, it was a wonderful service today. Now, I'm looking ahead to being part of the ordaining group making you priest."

"We'll see if I have a full set of teeth and can still walk without assistance to the altar and kneel for my vows by the time the Church decrees women eligible for altar duty," said Lily.

"I'm an old man already," said Hugh, "and not dying till it happens. So they better hurry up and decide, or prolong having to look at this ugly mug getting older and uglier!"

HAPPENING SOONER THAN ANYONE THOUGHT it would, at the end of July, three maverick bishops ordained eleven female deacons, priest. The Diocesan trio, two retired and one nearing retirement, said they had little to lose compared to what the Church would gain. One of the rogue bishops whose own daughter was among the eleven, said that whether people thought the action precipitous or protracted, the wait, both for his own and for the larger Church family, "had been long enough."

He and his brother bishops had recently endured yet another special meeting of the fraternity continuing their hot pursuit of a theological rationale that could keep the lid on their Pandora's box of women's ordination. Tired of hearing their fellows apply the same justice-just-not-yet rhetoric to women's ordination as they did to African American reparations, *these* Church fathers eagerly jumped at the opportunity to hold the regular-just-not-yet ordinations in the predominantly Black Philadelphia Church of the Advocate.

The Church at large broke out in a national sweat, calling for more meetings in the House of Bishops, while groups like the Women's Caucus cheered and strategized their next move, spurred on by the boldness of what had just occurred in the City of Brotherly Love.

The next year in September, yet another retired bishop ordained four more women at the Church of St. Stephen and the Incarnation in the nation's capital. The ordinations of the Washington Four, as they came to be called, were the final shove needed to "regularize" women's ordination by once again changing canon law in the following year's General Convention legislative process.

Lily was glad to be an observer rather than support staff this time around at the Triennial held in Minneapolis. Going between debates in the House of Deputies and the House of Bishops, she experienced firsthand institutional history in the making. In the midst of celebrating the successful final vote that would validate women's ordination, Lily did a quick visual inventory of race represented in the two groups responsible for ecclesiastical oversight and polity. Vowing never to forget the picture of inequality caught in her eyes right then, Lily found her initial excitement at a future, more equally gendered leadership, in fact, damped by the Church's lack of diversity.

LILY'S WAS ONE OF A STRING of ordinations coming on the heels of the bicameral Church mandate. Having full support from her mentor Hugh Lovelle and the people of Saint Philip's, and with all due pomp and circumstance as befit such an occasion in uptown Harlem, the sacramental laying on of hands made Lily a sister priest. When the bishop appointed her vicar of a smaller, needier congregation after Easter, Lily had to leave the people she had grown to love and respect. Lily was sad, having to let go of their ministry together, with the members of the "kingdom done come," as Mother Washington and her Mister liked to say, of bringing God near. Like the psalmist, Lily sat down and wept: How could she sing the Lord's song in a "foreign land," the land of poverty-stricken South Bronx?

Making it even more difficult for Lily was transitioning without Ethan. Lily got the message on a Tuesday morning after her day off. The church secretary had taken down Ethan's message "just as he had given it, in a voice not sounding like himself."

"When I asked if there was a number where he could be reached, he just told me, 'Not yet,'" Deidra reported to Lily. "What did he mean by that, honey?"

"I don't know what he means by *any* of this message: 'Something came up. Must go away for a while. I'm sorry. Ethan.' Deidra, where was he calling from?"

"I don't know, and he wouldn't say. He in some trouble, Lily?"

"The only trouble Ethan's ever been in is the day he wore an unmatched pair of socks to the office. I can't imagine . . . I just saw him here at Saint Philip's Sunday for the ten o'clock service, but he said he had some work to do in the afternoon, so I had the rest of Sunday afternoon to myself. This is very odd."

"Well, I hope that boy calls back to clear up this mystery," huffed Deidra.

"In the meantime, I'm calling his firm."

Lily felt as if she were being rushed by bodies hurtling themselves at her, trying to knock her down. Going into her office and closing the door behind her, she sat at her desk to recompose herself before dialing the firm's number.

"Hello, Linda. This is Lily Wallace. . . ."

"Oh, Lily—you're Ethan's—"

"Yes. Ethan's whatever. Is he there?" Lily asked, trying to keep the panic out of her voice.

"No, he isn't in today. I think I better have you speak with the boss, Mr. Minion," said Linda. "Oh, he's in a meeting. Can I have him get back to you?"

"Yes. Please. My number is . . ."

THE NEXT FORTY-FIVE MINUTES before Fred Minion returned Lily's call were tense. What he had to say added more confusion to the tumult already knocking around Lily's head. "Ethan took some liberties and . . . rather than prosecute, we thought it best to let him go."

"Go where?" Lily almost screamed in Minion's ear.

"I wish I could tell you. Hopefully, to get some help. You can imagine our disappointment—Ethan had such promise. Maybe you will be able to—"

"Mr. Minion. My first order of concern is for Ethan's

mental health and what desperate thing he might do. Do you have any idea where he could be?"

"I'm afraid I can't help you, Lily. You would know more about Ethan's personal life, surely, than I or anybody here would. What he did—and uh, I'm sorry I'm not at liberty to discuss details, but what Ethan did seems to confirm a very private side. Frankly, we're all in a state of shock."

"I understand," said Lily, not sure she did. "I am . . . more than shocked. Please. If you hear anything else or anyone at the office finds out something more, please call me either at this number or at my home. . . ."

Disbelieving what she had just heard about the man she thought she knew well enough to marry and raise a family with, Lily hung up the phone. Certainly, like any relationship, theirs had its bleak moments of doubt overshadowing love. But from the little that Fred Minion was able to say about Ethan's present circumstance with the firm—ironically the compass Ethan credited for giving his life direction—*this* was more than the usual flux of doubt emerging and retreating over seasons in their relationship. This was off the charts.

Lily left her office and went looking for Hugh.

"Is he in?" Lily asked Deidra.

"Father Lovelle? No, he had to go to Ithaca to see about—well, I'm not quite sure. Somethin'-somethin' 'bout Ayana."

Lily panicked. "When will he be back?"

"I think tomorrow. Hold on, lemme check his calendar." Deidra went into Hugh's office and in a loud voice called out to Lily, "Yeah. Least that's what his calendar says. Wednesday morning, he has a meeting here with Jenkins to go over the housing proposal."

"What time?" Lily asked.

"What time what?"

"His meeting with Jenkins—what time is his meeting with Jenkins?"

"Oh, sorry. He has here nine a.m. And he usually gets here a little earlier, so I'd say around eight thirty he'll be in."

"Thanks, Deidra. Sorry I'm so short," Lily apologized, then explained, "I feel like a madwoman in a house of mirrors. I feel like I can't find where to put my next step."

Deidra came back out to the foyer and in a calm, normal tone asked, "Ethan have any close friends?"

"Outside of me?" asked Lily. "No, I'm pretty much it. Not a whole lot to go on in that department. Good idea, though."

"Well, honey, let me fix you a cup of tea or something. You want some hot cocoa?" asked a sisterly Deidra.

"I don't know if I can sit still long enough to drink it," said Lily, "but, yes, thanks Deidra. That would be nice."

"Okay. I'll just be bringin' it into your office in a New York minute." Deidra winked in Lily's direction like they were a pair of detectives about to sort through clues.

"Thanks," said Lily. "I'm calling my sister. I hope *she'll* be home."

As she dialed Dee's number, Lily reflected on how many talks she had had with her sister revolving around Ethan and the bigger picture she thought was slowly coming into focus. Now, still at the center of conversation, Ethan was mysteriously not in the picture at all.

"Dee, I don't know where Ethan is."

"What's going on, Lily?" asked Dee.

"I don't know. When I came to work this morning, there was a cryptic message from Ethan: 'Something came up. Must go away for a while.'"

"Go away?" shrieked Dee. "What came up that you wouldn't know about?"

"Oh, he closed the message: 'Sorry. Ethan,'" added Lily. "Church secretary, Deidra, took the message. Said he wouldn't say anything else. I'm really afraid for him, Dee."

"Sounds bizarre. Did you call his apartment?"

"No, but I called the firm and was quickly told that I should talk to his boss, who was in a meeting but called me back to say that Ethan committed some impropriety. A prosecutable impropriety. That, rather than take him to court, Fred said they let him go."

"Where?"

"My question exactly. They don't know. I don't know. Where do *you* think he'd go?"

"I don't know, but I hope it's not in his car with windows rolled up and a running motor pumping carbon dioxide in."

"Oh, God," exclaimed Lily. "Where is that jerk-off?"

"Okay, calm down. Let's think," Dee said, returning to reason. "Have you called any of the emergency rooms?"

"No. I mean, I just got in and got hit with this ton of bricks, Dee. Hugh's in Ithaca till tomorrow morning. . . ." said Lily, diagramming the situation for her sister's benefit, as well as her own.

Deidra tapped on the open door and came into the office where she set a steaming cup on Lily's desk, gesturing that she would be at her desk and mouthing for Lily to take her time.

"Look, Lily, you need some company. Why don't you take the train out here?" Dee encouraged. "I can't believe he did this. I'm so sorry, baby sister. Promise me you'll throw some stuff in a bag and come on out on the train."

"But what if he tries to reach me," wailed Lily. "I don't know if he has your number or would think to call me there. If he's even going to call."

"Waiting there or waiting here—what's the difference?" Answering her own question, Dee said, "The difference is, I'm here. I want you to come, Lily. This must be horrible for you."

"It's totally out of the blue, Dee. I've been turning over and over in my mind how he was acting on Saturday," said

Lily. "And when I saw him briefly after the service here Sunday, he said he had some stuff to work on. So, what the hell. I enjoyed my time off from The Boyfriend. Come in this morning and BOOM! Where is that fucker?"

"Lily. Go home. Get your little bag packed and get over here. Please."

"Okay. I just want to make a couple of phone calls. Some guys at the firm. I can't stand not knowing."

"Call me when you get home. I want to know that you're okay and that I'll be seeing you within the next couple of hours—at the latest!"

"I will."

"And if I don't hear from you—soon, I'm gonna call you. Okay?"

"Yeah. Thanks, Dee. Thanks for being home. I guess you're right. I guess I need to be with family right now."

"HEARD FROM ETHAN?"

It took Lily a minute to put the voice with the person and another minute to believe it was that person on the other end of the line. "Is that you, Rodney?" asked a surprised Lily.

"One and the same, your Atlanta brotha," said Rodney.

"How'd you know he was missing?" Lily felt in some way an accomplice to Ethan's misstep, whatever it was. Like she needed to explain. Fill in the details of what happened. But she had no details and no clue as to what needed explanation.

It did not occur to Lily that Ethan would not act judiciously, which meant returning to confess and make amends for whatever wrong he did. Like a woman assuming a seafaring husband's safe return, unaware that she has, in an instant, become a widow, Lily went about her daily routine believing Ethan would call any moment and begin to fill in the holes of his sudden disappearance. It was too out of Ethan's character for her to believe otherwise.

"He's not coming back, Lily." Rodney tried to put all the gentleness he could into telling the abrupt truth.

"You sound sure. Do you know something?" Lily punched out the next words, as if each deliberate syllable was jabbing at Ethan: "Tell me, Rodney. Do you know something about Ethan?"

"Only what he told me when he called on Monday looking for some legal advice. Which," said Rodney, "he ended up rejecting. So convinced that what he did was no big thing. He was saying things like: 'People do it all the time and get away with it.' And that he didn't deserve being let go. On and on, till I had to excuse myself for a client meeting."

"Back up, Rodney. You're saying Ethan called you *Monday*?"

"Yeah, and I asked if he had talked to you. He got real huffy and said he'd 'handle it.' Said he has a friend out in California who owns a string of car dealerships. He sounded real fucked up, Lily, so I waited a couple of days before calling to see if Ethan had, in fact, talked to you himself."

"Yeah, well, if he's *handling it*—just what *is* it he's *handling*? I talked to his boss Fred Flintstone and all he could say was, he couldn't say. Just that they could have prosecuted. What did Ethan do?"

"From what he told me, sounds like he was playing around with clients' money behind their backs. Thought he could increase his percentage of return by investing in some venture capital scheme without their knowledge. Guess the risk was higher than Ethan calculated. Higher than the moral ground he *thought* he was standing on."

"Moral ground on a slippery slope."

"He was cocksure of both precedent and prerogative—claimed having 'client benefit foremost in mind.'"

"Ethan in high finance," mused Lily. "How did the firm discover his *questionable* business practice?"

"He said it all came down Friday. He was asked to pack up his things and leave before the morning break. When he threatened with 'his attorney,' evidently, the boss laid a fatherly hand on Ethan's nonsense, telling him how disappointed he was and advising him to get some help."

"I can imagine he went off on that, or would have, if you didn't have an appointment."

"Yeah, he was pretty damn sure he was right, and they were wrong. 'Their problem,' kind of thing, 'not his.'"

"So he said he was going to California?"

"With a banjo—or was it a Band-Aid—on his knee."

"What a jerk! Go off and sell used cars—or maybe he'll pan for gold. What the hell. I wish I felt like I lost a love instead of something more personal like my self-respect. How could I not know? Asshole!"

"He didn't want you to know, Lily."

"Oh, that's consoling. The man I've batted around marriage with didn't want me to know he's a thief and a liar."

"At least he had that much integrity."

"So when did he say he was westward ho? I've been over to his apartment different hours of the day and night these last three days, except the night I spent with my sister Dee after Ethan left an obtuse message with the church secretary."

"What'd he say?"

"Surf's up. Gotta go. Sorry. As ever, Shmuckhead."

"I'm sorry, Lily."

"Yeah, and we never made good on accepting your invitation to Atlanta."

"Invitation's still open."

Lily drew in her breath and held it, not knowing what message to send with her next exhalation.

"Lily—you still there?"

"Trying."

"Sorry. All this about Ethan has got to be chasin' you down. I didn't mean to come at you so fast. Perhaps . . ."

"It's okay," said Lily. "Even appreciated, since honesty seems to be on back order with my fiancé, past tense. Guess I'm the only one not seeing what's so damn obvious to everyone else."

"Doubt it. He fooled the firm for who knows how long," said Rodney. "I was going to say, perhaps you're free for dinner—I'm going to be in the city this weekend. Weather report says the snow has thawed."

"Like someone took a blow torch to it."

"You available?"

"My guess is yes. What do you have in mind?"

"Dinner. You pick the place."

"I'm a real dud these days."

"A slow, easy table dance is fine with me."

"Oh, you're gonna have nothin' *but* slow—I've been in slow motion since Tuesday," said Lily.

"I'm not too mercenary?"

"I'll show you mercenary. Bring some packing tape and tips on moving."

"Where?"

"South Bronx. I'm gonna be the new priest in charge of a little mission church."

"Can't wait to see it," said Rodney. "With you."

"I almost forgot! Asshole Ethan. He always did have great timing," seethed Lily. "This is my last Sunday at Saint Philip's."

"I know. I was going to surprise you," said Rodney, "but I figured you'd had enough surprises for one week."

"Surprise me?"

"Something like that," said Rodney. "Hugh phoned a couple of weeks ago, and then I got Ethan's call Monday, so I guess the surprise is on me. I'm glad we're having this chance to talk and that on the weekend you can make time for me—"

"Perhaps *with* you."

"Oooh, you're gonna have me fannin' muhself, Rev'n Lily. You are one saucy woman."

"Well, before *you* disappear on me, where and when?"

"My ETA is two forty-seven, so I could probably make it to your place by four, four thirty?"

"If your cab driver's Raphael Parnelli Jones," said Lily. "I'll be ready by five."

"Lily, I want to assure you that I do come equipped with brakes."

"Good, 'cause we're gonna take this thing out for a spin and see what it can do."

"In that case, lemme get with my travel agent, see if there's an empty seat on the next flight—"

"For all you know, I might be all talk."

"Anyone's crossed the gender line and lived to tell about it—I'll take my chances."

"Keep pourin' it on, Rodney, and bring some more of the same with you this weekend," said Lily.

"Sorry to be the bearer of bad news. I hope, in some way, it was helpful."

"Helpful? Rodney, you're the first person with real information," said Lily. "I really appreciate you calling. And, I am really looking forward to seeing you this weekend. There's gonna be a lot more salt in my tears come Sunday saying goodbye to Saint Philip's and all the people who helped raise me."

"I'll be there, Lily," Rodney assured, "with my big hankie."

NEW YORK'S LATE SPRING REMINDED Lily of that time four years ago, when she made her way back to the North out of a fresh wounding of America's soul in the South. Lily marked being at Saint Philip's as a time of reckoning. Between her arrival and departure, she felt as if she had moved from a naive place to a more knowing place among old souls and still older spirits, descended from the fertile depths of a plenteous continent many cultural miles away.

Try as she might, Lily could not remember her first Sunday with Saint Philip's congregation, save for the sensual memory of, by now, familiar things: lemony furniture oil used on old altar wood, decades of incense caught in the maroon folds of the *reredos* drape, and, of course, the coffee hour that was much more than a coffee hour. Whatever empty space needed filling, all left Saint Philip's weekly party with their hunger satisfied.

News of Ethan's disappearance having passed from parishioner to parishioner on the eve of her departure, it was Lily's turn to be the object of Saint Philip's particular caring. And, since most of the church membership had been expecting to stand in as parents, aunts, uncles, and cousins at their unconventional bride's wedding, Ethan's vanishing meant a double loss. Her adoptive family blamed Ethan for making more bitter the already bittersweet parting, a testimonial to the love hunkered down deep in the hearts of those who loved Lily and whom she loved in return.

On her goodbye weekend, however, Lily's emotion flattened, spiking only to remonstrate about her missing fiancé. Undeterred, Rodney remained patient like the knobby trees dispensing wisdom outside Lily's window: Leaves would reappear; the dead season would not last forever.

The mechanical activity of packing up Lily's apartment temporarily relieved the heaviness that had rolled in and settled in the place left by Ethan's absence, now going on a week. Taking her request seriously, Rodney appeared at Lily's door late Friday afternoon with packing tape in one hand and a quartet of her favorite lavender roses in the other. Together, they worked their way around Lily's studio, boxing pieces of her life. Each closed and secured box sealed the finiteness of being sheltered at this address of circumstance and identity.

"I may not have to call in favors from friends, after all," said Lily, appreciating Rodney's focused effort. "You've obviously had drayman experience in some former life."

Rodney chuckled. "Moving office, as well as body and soul from Birmingham to Atlanta padded my résumé a bit," he said. "I'm just glad you were willing to accept my offer of help."

"Are you kidding? I owe you."

"You owe me nothing, Lily. But we do owe it to each other to find a stopping point, so we can go grab a bite to eat. You hungry?"

"Oh, yeah. Food. I forgot what that was this week."

"I snooped in your refrigerator. Looks like you're reducing inventory for the move."

"Well. That, too."

"How about we blitz that bank of kitchen drawers and then get cleaned up. I want to take you out for a nice, relaxing supper. Notice I said 'supper.' Not 'dinner.' No pressure. Low key."

"Here I thought it was me and my low-key stupor. Now you're telling me you get the credit?"

"Hey—I'm a smooth ride."

"Rodney," said Lily in a whisper, "I'm not sure what I'm doing."

Rodney's eyes played over Lily's face. "You don't have to be sure, Lily—you don't have to be anything."

"Except first in the shower," said Lily, moving toward the bathroom. "Get yourself a beer, glass of wine, tall drink of water . . . I won't be a minute."

"Take your time. We got lotsa time."

THE NEXT MORNING, SAINT PHILIP'S parishioners turned out in their Sunday finest. Lily vested in white, the color for Christmas and Easter festal seasons, as well as baptisms and funerals. Preaching the homily, Lily focused on their short life together at Saint Philip's: first, when she was a seminarian doing field education; then, as one of the early women ordained deacon, and, now, as a priest on the way to her own cure, Grace Church in South Bronx.

Lily identified with the spiritual thirst of the sermon story's woman at the well. She said that her own request for "living water" had been satisfied by Saint Philip's water, scooped up in a drinking gourd of history, and offered time and again to slake the thirst brought on by painful circumstance and unexpected grief. Indeed, she proclaimed, it was happening, yet again, that morning, as Lily stood among her church family, giving as well as receiving.

The party afterwards sent Lily off with a full stomach and enough leftovers for the first month in her new home, half of a two-family brownstone two doors down from the church in a struggling neighborhood. Because Lily did not have the money to take a vacation between cures, her first Sunday at Grace Church followed her last at Saint Philip's. The vicarage, which did double duty as an office, had been burglarized even before Lily could move in. A typewriter and tape player were taken, along with the phone.

Despite the break-in, signs of welcome greeted Lily when she brought her first load of goods. Someone had planted geraniums in the freshly painted window box hung to one side of the door. Never mind that the bars on the windows reminded Lily of a jail, the inside of the house had a fresh coat of paint which, like the neighborhood, was a mixed palette. The kitchen's mustard yellow contrasted with the turquoise of the dining room; both were a vivid contrast to the quiet ivory some godsent person had thought to use in her bedroom before dipping the brush into a pail of bubblegum pink for the bathroom, which was finished off in lavender trim. *Girl colors*, thought Lily. *At least they know what gender they're getting. . . . They seem more ready for me than I am for them.*

Though the call to be their vicar was set up from downtown, Grace Church and its priest began their dance with hopeful curiosity, each a little hesitant about taking the lead or where to place their hands. The shyness resolved a month later when the service of Holy Communion ended with a bang. *More of a pop*, Lily thought on reflection. A small cartoon sound that did big damage to a fourteen-year-old kid who lay gripping his bloodied leg and grunting angry threats of revenge for "the muthah-fuckah who capped him."

"Don't call the cops, man! Jus' don't call no cops!" Despite the boy's protests, Lily had a church volunteer do just that, but had conflicted feelings herself when the squad car pulled up like it was a donut stop. The officers treated the violence as if it were all in a day's work. "Somebody don't like you, kid," was the extent of the uniformed concern.

The predicted "big shock" she was to be "in for" hit Lily in that moment of irritation that quickly turned to rage. *If this is routine*, thought Lily, *what* does *get the attention of those responsible for civilian protection?*

"Paramedics down't the fire station, next block. Somebody wanna run down there?" said the younger officer as if it might be optional to get help for a child bleeding from a gunshot wound. "Lucky he ain't killed"—the consensus was the same, whether bystanders gathered by the sound, then sight of the police car or those gathered by communion bread and wine earlier inside Grace Church.

Lucky he ain't killed? Lily thought, then questioned anyone listening, "What do you mean 'Lucky he ain't killed'? This happens every day or what?" Lily said with fear that emerged as anger.

Someone from the crowd yelled: "Yeah lady, we pop people around here, so you better stay in that little stone hut ah yours." At that, the older officer drew out his billy club and started into the bunched onlookers in the direction of the menacing voice, but the jeering crowd blocked his way.

They like cops less than they like crime, thought Lily. "Good thing the bishop issues bulletproof vests. And double-padded for females," said Lily, trying to make light of the situation. "The Church can't afford losing us, you know, 'cause we're so few in number."

"You tell 'em, Lily," said Leon with a whistling sound caused by his missing teeth. "Ain't nothin' we gon' let happen to you, Father Lily," Leon's title for the new head of God's household at Grace Church. "Son, you bettah let no more tha' dirt fly outta yoh filthy mou' or we gon wash it out wi' moh than soap." Leon yelled his counter threat toward the younger-voiced heckler who most likely had already left the scene when the officer drew his club from the loop at his side.

THE QUESTION OF LEADERSHIP WAS further resolved and established as a pattern of alternating initiative and cooperation when Lily made an agreement with Leon's son Ray-Ray. It was midweek, and Lily was reading the Evening Office shortly after suppertime. The church doors were open, even though it was rare to have anyone else join her in prayer at the close of the day. "My dad said you were—" his voice startling Lily, "Sorry ma'am, I uh," said Ray-Ray, quickly apologizing when he saw Lily's reaction.

"Hi. I'm the priest here," Lily said officiously in defiance of her heart's pounding, her body starting to quiver. "Can I help you?"

"I come to help *you*," said the boy . . . man? quietly. Dressed in jeans and T-shirt with cutoff sleeves, the visitor continued, "My dad said you were pretty shook up by the drive-by and some chicken-ass fool callin' out his threat from behind the skirts of the neighborhood elders."

"Well, yeah. Guess I was sent here to get an education," said Lily, relieved to find him friend, not foe. "You might be one of my teachers."

"I don't know nothin' 'bout teachin'. I just come here to tell you, me and my buddies got your back—"

"You said your dad put you up to this?" asked Lily. "I'm embarrassed that I don't remember. . . . Who's your dad?"

"Leon Dell. I'm his son Ray-Ray. But it ain't like you say. He di'n put me up to nothin'. He just say you was shook up. It was my idea to come talk to you."

"I'm glad you did, Ray-Ray Dell," said Lily, breathing more easily. "What do you and your buddies get out of 'watching my back?'—and what does that involve anyway?"

"We take care ah bui'ness. Whatey' i' takes."

"Guns?"

"I said, whatey' i' takes. You in our hood, ma'am. We protec' you now."

"Ray-Ray. I am so . . . well, thank you, first of all, for your concern for my safety. I guess your father could pretty well read me. I'm trying to understand what it's like to live with a certain level of violence—or potential violence."

"You're livin' it now," said Ray-Ray, "but you may not ev' understan' it, smart as you are ma'am, if you don' min' my sayin'."

"I appreciate your politeness in calling me 'ma'am,' Ray-Ray, but I would feel your respect just as much if you called me Lily."

"Don' matter to me. You the rev'n."

"I don't mind 'reverend' either, but here's the thing we need to talk about. It's the 'using whatever it takes,' including guns, for my protection. Now . . ." said Lily, unsure of how to proceed, "I know I'm the new person on the block—so new I squeak. Maybe just a little too loudly. But . . . I can't have you and your friends pledging to 'have my back' when that could mean guns. You're too young to be risking your life with this kind of violence."

"We risk our lives every day jes' livin' here, Rev-er-end. Nobody axed us if we wan' live somewhere else. This is our place an' we gonna defen' it like we can."

Lily studied the turbulent face of the proud young man. "I have no response, other than thank you for being honest, Ray-Ray, and I'm sorry if I try your patience. I believe I have a lot to learn."

"'s not all tha', Rev'n Lily."

"Would it be possible, just to help me understand more, for you and your friends to meet with me here at the church? Just to talk?"

"Mos' them ne'r darken da dohr. I ain't sayin' it you or this church. They got no problem with white folk, what I'm sayin'."

"Could you ask them? For me?"

"Wha' you wan' bunch ah hoodlums comin' roun'? I think I scare you 'nough tonight."

"You did that. And, *and*, I really enjoyed talking to you. I hope I'm not scaring *you* away."

"Naw. I'm jes' messin' wid you. I'll ax 'em—get back to you later."

"Ray-Ray, thanks again for stopping by to offer yourself and your friends as my protection. Nobody has ever done that before for me."

"'Cause you prah'ly ain't never needed it," returned Ray-Ray with a grin displaying a silver tooth.

BETWEEN GETTING SETTLED AT GRACE Church and doing a long distance "thang," as Ayana referred to Lily's relationship with her brother, Lily rarely left the neighborhood, where life was lived loudly and on public display: Old people sitting on front stoops or porch chairs, fanning themselves and hollering at kids playing on the asphalt street, which was hot and bubbly like some emergent life form.

In addition to families in the neighborhood, including the Greek grocer and his seven kids, Lily got to know children and grandchildren from out of the area when they came to visit their long-time resident relations. She became acquainted with vendors selling legal, as well as boosted, goods and the beat officers, a couple of whom winked at petty crime, but were the first to call a social worker if they thought a child was in danger.

When the school year started, Lily introduced herself at the first PTA meeting, first to the elementary school principal and then to the teachers. She had already met the parents active in PTA, because they were also the force behind the community association of owners and renters from the sixteen-square block known as "Myrtle."

Almost ten years prior, encouraged by the civil rights movement, mothers and fathers and grandparents pulled together to advocate for a park on a vacant lot that had been heaped with trash for as long as anyone could remember. Myrtle Park got its name from the crepe myrtle trees planted by hands already working fourteen- and sixteen-hour workdays.

Establishing Myrtle Park was no small thing; keeping it weeded and safe was an even larger testimony to the neighborhood's commitment and self-reliance. Like other districts, Myrtle Park kept a tight rein on city water and public works departments, at the very least to ensure the uninterrupted delivery of rightful services.

"LILY, I WANT YOU TO COME to Birmingham for New Year's with my family."

"Can I think about it?"

"Yeah," said Rodney, pausing, "I'll set my stopwatch for a minute. Ready? Go!"

"No, I'm serious," said Lily. "I haven't had any time by myself away from this place. I might be weird company. Wouldn't wanna make a bad impression on your family."

"That wouldn't be possible," said Rodney. "And even if it were, I'll be there to run interference."

"Actually," said Lily, digging for information on any already-formed impressions of her, "they must already think I'm weird."

"No, just white."

"Oh yeah. That too. What does your mama think of our liaison?"

"As a collusion of color to add nuance to the family, she's all for it; as a conspiracy to blanch our family's heritage of *negroism*, she's not sure if you're down for cookin' collar' greens. . . ."

"So, she doesn't care about the collar-wearin', it's the collar'-cookin' she's concerned about."

"Now you're talkin'," laughed Rodney, "like Black folks. See, you could do some more of your anthropological inquiry with my family—see how us Black folk ring in the new year, 'Bama syle."

"Long as it's not *Bombingham* style," said Lily.

"Missy's read her history, I see," said Rodney. "Workin' on your sistah thang."

"Okay, okay. 'Nough nonsense," said Lily. "Where would we stay?"

"In my father's mansion," quipped Rodney, "there are many rooms—"

"Yeah, so will I be bunking with your kid sister?"

"For two nights, max," said Rodney, continuing before Lily had time to protest, "See, my plan was to first get you down South and then take you away due east, to the coast—where you can bunk with me. How does that sound?"

"More better."

"So . . . what do you need to make your decision?"

"Well, as I said before—time. I need to think about this some, Rodney."

"Okay, but I know you. You can take anything and after it's put through that wringer of a mind, it comes out the other end completely unrecognizable from its original form. It's a simple invitation," said Rodney, feigning desperation. "A simple lecherous invitation!"

"I understand the novelty of my saying 'Yes,' right away," said Lily. "I'm even aware that it could be mood altering . . . for the better."

"What's up with your mood, Lily?" asked Rodney with genuine concern. "Are you depressed?"

"I think I am," said Lily. "I think Ethan's been *haintin'* me lately. You don't suppose he's in town, do you? I really get the creeps sometimes."

"Baby, you need some chocolate therapy."

"Deep, *dark* chocolate therapy," said Lily. "Sometimes I wish you were just down the street—"

"Down the street. Hell. In your bed, more like it," teased Rodney. "How about this weekend?"

"Just like that," said Lily. "You can take off just like that."

"My jets are already firing up," said Rodney.

"See, that's what's weird about what I do," said Lily. "I love it, but I have all of these people depending on me, and whatever I do has to be scheduled in advance or else they think I'm gonna leave for good."

"Well, you will one day."

"I don't even think about *that*," said Lily. "My nose is so firmly wedged in between the here and the now. That's the real reason I can't give you an answer right away."

"I already got my answer about *this* weekend—hearing no protests," said Rodney, "I'm comin' up."

"But I'm still gonna think about New Year's."

"Think as you will, think as you must," said Rodney. "Just don't think it to death."

"By the way, we haven't talked about Christmas or Thanksgiving. Where are you gonna be?" asked Lily, as she looked at the clock.

"Anywhere you want, baby."

"Well, maybe we can talk about that this weekend."

"Grab that fig leaf," said Rodney. "Don't show me anything I haven't already seen and fallen in love with."

"I'm glad there's one romantic in this relationship."

"What's your role, then?"

"Resister," said Lily. "You must get tired of the Ethan excuse."

"True. He's one sorry-assed excuse for a—" Rodney said, cutting short his comment about Ethan out of respect for Lily. "But he's former. What's to resist about us in the present?"

"Admitting," said Lily. "I resist admitting I've fallen in love with you."

"Always intellectually sidling up to the thing, aren't you, Lily? You think you're always buttoned up to your neck and down to your ankles, but, baby, you got a whole wardrobe of *see-through*," said Rodney. "So, you've fallen in love with me—what does that mean to you?"

"It means, I would consider a state of love, more permanent and less precarious than 'falling.' I hate to sound dumb, but I'm not sure if I *loved* Ethan."

"Or maybe you did and still do," said Rodney. "Doesn't concern us, Lily. Anyway, I analyze for a living, I don't wanna do it with you. It doesn't make any difference."

"Except for driving you crazy."

"You, worse."

"Okay, so you're coming to the 'hood to do a little time with this crazy priest-confessor." Then continuing more slowly, Lily said, "I'm already writing this down as we speak so I don't forget: I . . . promise . . . to be . . . spontaneous . . . when *Rodney* . . . lands on my doorstep."

"As long as your hands are free by Friday afternoon."

"What's that?" Lily laughed.

"You have four days to memorize what you wrote. I don't wanna see no scrap of cheat-sheet in your hands when I come knockin' on your vicarage door."

THE NEW YEAR BEGAN WITH two major changes for Lily. After the bishop's approval of a congregational vote, Lily was formally installed as vicar of Grace Church. And, informally, during her post-Christmas introduction to Rodney's family, Lily became engaged. A series of incidents, concluding with a Thanksgiving weekend mugging, prompted Rodney to move his marriage proposal ahead of a more prudent timetable, out of concern for Lily's safety. The assault stoked Rodney's desire to more personally care for Lily as his wife.

Midday after an evening snowfall blanketed streets and sidewalks, Lily was walking from the church back to her place. She leaned against the wind, struggling to maintain her footing as she made her way down the street. Her purse slung over her left shoulder, and her arm hugging a stack of manila folders, Lily sensed a shadow before being knocked down, folders flying and purse yanked from her arm.

To Eddy Connor's dismay, Officer Duggan was just starting up the street to walk his beat. Pulling out the radio clipped to his belt to call for backup, the officer, meanwhile, dragged the mugger, appearing to be in as much shock now as his victim, to where Lily was attempting to catch the files curlicuing in the wind. The file contents danced from one side of the street to the other, clear up to Lily's doorstep.

"This the guy that hit you?"

"Couldn't identify him, unless he hit me again," said Lily. "But *that's* my purse." Then looking directly at the nabbed man, "Next time, why don't you ask?"

AS SOON AS HE HEARD, Rodney flew from Birmingham, where he had spent Thanksgiving day and night with his parents and two sisters. The third sister Mariyah was in France on a fellowship and was not expected back in the States until the following fall. Rodney used the time alone with his family to prepare them, and himself as well, for Lily's visit the week between Christmas and New Year's.

Rodney's mother, Enola Tuttle Davis, had been blessed to know both sets of her sharecropper grandparents. Their greatest gift to the world, Enola thought, were the babies that grew up to marry and run a general store before parenting their own. Willie Pinker Tuttle, surviving her husband Clifford, reluctantly gave up housekeeping and came to live with her daughter after the last grandchild, Ayana, went off to college.

"We're not old people," Willie said, "we're people aged to perfection." Nicknamed "Mother Wily," because she didn't miss a beat, Grandmother Willie regularly complained to 'Nola about the lack of "greats," and the abundance of degrees among her, as she referred to them, overeducated and undersexed grandchildren. When Rodney and his siblings deferred to their first cousins' procreativity, Grandmother Willie wouldn't let them off the hook. "I'm not passing from this life to the next," she said, "until you produce some'f y'own."

So although Rodney knew he had an ally if he started talking "wedding" to his grandmama, he also knew that his ally would turn into a she-bear guarding her young if she got wind of his intended's color. Shuddering every time he thought about his grandmother's fierce attack when he even broached the idea of dating a white girl in high school,

Rodney and the rest of his family were evasive when Grandmother *Wily* started digging around the edges. "You met this girl? Where huh folks from? You have a pitcher a'Rodney's fee-an-cée—he say he don' ha' no pitcher. I don' un'erstan' you young folks. No pitcher! No word on this gal! I don' b'leeve you gettin' married."

"Oh, you'll believe it when you see her at New Year's, Gramma."

"Well, I hope I lak whut ah see."

"I *love* what you're gonna see, and *I'm* the one marryin'. But I am countin' on your blessing," said Rodney, as he kissed his grandmother on both cheeks, then loudly planting a drawn-out kiss on her twitching lips, added, "'cause you're my oldest flame. You know that, Gramma."

His grandmother's hand flew up to cuff his shoulder, but it had all the strength of a hand brushing off lint. A sign, Rodney hoped, that her reaction to Lily, also, would be checked by old age.

AS IT TURNED OUT, GRANDMOTHER Willie felt poorly and, so, was in bed for the duration of Lily's visit. Insisting that Lily remain at the door so she wouldn't catch whatever was "playin' roun' wid her system," and not wanting to be bothered with glasses, examination of Rodney's future bride was from a blurry distance. The older woman heard Lily's "white-sounding" voice as confirmation not of race, but of the girl's education and culture from living "up North." Another "country," known only secondhand, but known enough that the family matriarch didn't see any need to go see for herself "the mess of smoke and dirt" that couldn't be much different from what Birmingham's steel mills gave off.

Rodney's family breathed a collective sigh of relief that Grandmother Willie was out of the picture. With no one forewarning her about the wolf in grandmother guise, and because the wolf herself never had the opportunity to bare her teeth, all Lily experienced was a respected elder, temporarily under the weather, being cared for by her loving family. Lily felt at ease around her future in-laws, who seemed put-together in a way she had never experienced with her own parents and sister. Like the difference between centripetal and centrifugal force.

Lily asked and was shown photos of both sides of Rodney's family. Thoughtfully, she had brought along some of her own, including a recent snapshot of Dee and Craig with the twins at Thanksgiving. "So you have twin genes in the family, Lily?" Enola's eyes lit up, and she chuckled as she said, "Rodney may make up for lost time with his grandmother yet. She's been giving him the business for years."

"How about the Tuttles and the Davises?" asked Lily. "Any twins hiding outside the family photos?"

"If there are, they're either so far back or else there wasn't a picture made."

"Or . . . one twin might have died before being recorded on film."

"True," mused Enola. "But not to my knowledge. No, I think it would be a first in Rodney's line. I've always wondered if the condensed version, two babies for the price of one pregnancy, might not have been easier. Maybe you'll be lucky!"

"My sister had a hard time with all that baby growing," volunteered Lily. "Made me think of the story of Cain and Abel already fighting in the womb. I don't know how I'll do with one. . . . Twins, I think, would have me really scared."

"You'll do fine, honey," said Enola, laying a gentle hand on Lily's. "And we'll be there for you every step of the way, whether it's one, two, or ten!"

"Oh, no. Not ten—I'd be a basket case," said Lily. "Don't be prayin' behind our back, Mother Davis!"

"You know it's all in God's hands, Lily. We can only agree or disagree with how He shapes the clay," said Enola before excusing herself to go check on the turkey casserole.

"Need any help?" offered Lily.

"No, I'll be fine," said Enola. "Rodney and his father ought to be home any minute, and you all can have a chance to visit before dinner."

LEFT ALONE, LILY THOUGHT ABOUT what Dee had said when she told her about her developing relationship with Rodney. "Are you sure you want to put yourself through all the stares and snubs and . . . well, I hate to say it, Lily. But you know as well as I do, it's still open season on *mixed* couples in America. You and Rodney will be targets for all the crazies whose mission it is to maintain bloodline purity, as well as the even larger number who do the same, only *undercover*, as upright citizens."

"Dee—"

"And what about your kids? You and Rodney, at least—"

"Dee, we already are."

"Pregnant?"

"No. We already are a 'mixed' couple, whether we're legally declared as married by the state of New York or not. As long as we're together, *whenever* we're together, we're Black and white."

"So, this is serious."

"So far."

"I guess I should have asked that first."

"You already had me marching down the aisle into the maternity ward."

"Remember what we used to say jumping rope? 'First comes love . . .'"

"Okay, okay. And it's not as simplistic as a rhyme," said Lily. "I'm still on the 'First comes love,' and just getting used to it after Ethan. Wondering if he and I ever made it to square one of love."

"Where is he now?"

"Never heard from him. Never even heard—from him—that he was going to California. Rodney told me."

"Rodney told you?"

"Yeah. Idiot was probably really calling up Rodney to find out which direction was west. Probably never made it to California. Probably hiding out in Mexico right now."

"Made a wrong turn!"

"*Another* wrong turn."

"Enough about the fool that gave up being my brother-in-law," said Dee.

"Scary thought."

"At least I'm not scared for you with Rodney in the same way as if you had stayed with Ethan."

"You mean, if *he* had stayed with *me*."

"You think you'd still be together if Ethan hadn't left?" Dee asked.

"Well, we *thought* we had the 'First comes love' under our belts. . . ."

"I don't doubt something was going on under your belts. But I wasn't convinced it was love."

"Hey, I can remember when you were his strongest lobby."

"My memory isn't as long term as yours."

———

IT WAS A QUICK "YES" and a long engagement. Neither Rodney nor Lily could see giving up residence and position in their respective cities. The prenuptial period extended over time and distance, until Rodney's call almost two years after promising each other a mutual future.

"Baby, how does Oakland, California, sound to you?"

"It sounds like Black Panthers and Raiders."

"How does 'Shooks, Tribault, Moore and Davis' sound to you?"

"Well, for a department store, it's a little long."

"How 'bout for a law firm in which your beautiful Black man is junior-most partner?"

Lily yelled into the phone: "Get out of here!"

"My buddy Preston called out of the blue to say he was faxing his firm's annual report, wanting to know if I'd be interested in moving out West."

"And?"

"And, so I'm calling you . . . you still wearing those ten carats on your right fourth finger?"

"I've been meaning to speak with you about that. The band is turning green."

"The color of money. Means the ring is worth more!"

"Couldn't be worth more than you," cooed Lily. "So, Rodney, are you saying you're excited about moving to California?"

"No, baby, I'm saying I'm excited about marrying you and then moving to California to spend the rest of my life under one roof wif' ma woman—can you handle that?"

"Gee, I don't know. Just when I've finally gotten used to the F-word."

"Plenty more of that to get used to."

"You know what I mean."

"You'll have plenty of time to get over 'fiancée' and get used to 'wife' with me, Lily—we'll be together! And, in the land of opportunity—"

"And tolerance?—How do races mix in Oakland?"

"Plus two when we arrive."

"This is really true then. . . ."

"Not only true—with your word, can already be in process. This is happening. All I need is a word of encouragement from you," said Rodney. "Baby, let's do it. I know you don't need any big wedding, Lily. I'm cool with that too. The gold's out West. This is a break for us, baby. This is our golden opportunity to finally be together. . . . You still—"

"Yes, I still. So when are you talking about moving?"

"We. I'm looking for the 'we,' Lily."

"Okay, when would *we* be moving?"

"Whenever we want. Preston mentioned the start of the new year."

"And a new decade."

"All that. But we can move as fast or as slow as you need. Preston's not gonna right away pull up his bucket and let it down in someone else's well. He knows how seriously I'm considering his offer . . . and he knows about you."

"That's good news," said Lily. "What's Preston's last name? What's he like?"

"Preston Shooks is my age but with skin as thick and smart as an old Black man. *De facto* top of our class."

"*De facto*?"

"Law schools in America teach law by the book and bigotry by example."

"Sounds familiar," said Lily.

"Maybe forty acres and a mule are waiting for me in California."

"For *us* . . ." said Lily. "Naw, on second thought, I think the mule done died. And the forty acres are tract homes. Rodney . . . I believe I neglected to tell you something earlier in the conversation—"

"Can't think what you left out. . . ."

"Congratulations, pardnuh!"

"I haven't said 'Yes' yet."

"But you will."

"Yeah, if the 'us' just uttered is for real."

"Absolutely—this is going to be a great adventure, moving cross country."

"How soon can you be ready?"

Lily laughed. "I'll call in my order to Father Uncle Hugh right now."

"Baby, I love you."

"Can't wait to show you the same in person," said Lily. "And, really, congratulations writ large. . . . I better start working on what I'm gonna do in California besides get a tan and a season pass to Disneyland."

"Other end of the state."

"Whatever—"

"You're not worried, are you?"

"Moving across country with no job as a clergygirl—what's to be worried about?"

"Glad for your optimism," said Rodney, then more seriously, "It's gotta be good for you, too, baby."

"It will be. It just may take some time."

"My salary should cover—"

"It's not the money, Rodney. Believe me. If it were about the money, I wouldn't be playing dress-up in Father's clothes in the South Bronx every week trying to fill church-daddy's shoes."

"And this *Black*-daddy? Am I a stumbling block on your path to success? I hope you're not—"

"Rodney, stop. You are . . . the love of my life," Lily choked on her tears. "And love conquers all."

"Some trite white bullshit. How are you really feeling?" asked Rodney. "I'm a big Black man made in America, remember Lily? I can take it."

"Paranoia understandably comes with the territory—but take this, big Black man. You are strong and beautiful and if anybody is a liability, it's me, with you. It's my female whiteness that poses a threat to your life."

"Lily, Lily. The liability is not you, and it's not me," said Rodney. "The liability is the thinking in this country that persists in its pursuit of a race and gender meritocracy. Love may not conquer all, but it may transgress a little piece of the race-rules monstrosity that wants to keep us apart. Lily, you are the love of my life. I like who I am with you. I love seeing my strong, beautiful Black reflection in your eyes. Plead guilty to the high crime of love if you need to, but I am not going to listen to self-accusations of becoming my wife making you an accomplice to my foreshortened life."

"You asked how I really feel. I really feel scared. For you, for me. Mostly for us. People say and do cruel things. And my white, female skin is *not* thick."

"Lily, I have known you over the course of the last seven years. You are not 'The Reverend' in title only. I add myself to the number of people, all different kinds and ages of people, who respect your courage and the grace you offer up to a horribly hurting world every day. I'm glad your skin is white. Definitely glad it's female. And thick? Would be gross to the touch. Your skin breathes, Lily. It breathes life. We are all going to die someday. However long we have, I want to spend my life with you."

"You should have been the preacher," said Lily.

"Already am, so to speak. I'm a lawyer, remember?"

"Let's get his thing movin' then. I'll call Hugh and my sister. Could you talk to your family and see when would be a good time for them to come to the city?" asked Lily. "I'm shaking."

"With excitement, I hope," said Rodney. "My strong and beautiful black arms can hardly wait to hold you, Lily. I have a meeting tomorrow, but I could be in the air afterwards and get to your place late afternoon. How does that work with your schedule?"

"What schedule? Do I have a schedule?" said Lily with new lightness in her voice. "Don't forget to talk to your family. And call me right away when you know something. Or, even if you don't. Call me."

"It's gonna take me a little while."

"Hey, I know how fast news travels in your family. Anyway, I'll call *you* after I talk to my sister and Hugh. I love you, Rodney."

"I love you, Lily. I'll be up late tonight if you think of anything else."

———

BOOK 3

Either you will
go through this door
or you will not go through.

If you go through
there is always the risk
of remembering your name.

—ADRIENNE RICH

FOR THE MARRIED AND RELOCATED couple, the eighties went by as a blur of babies born, Rodney's success in the law firm that made him partner, and Lily's satisfaction as part-time priest at jewel-windowed Saint Mary the Magdalene in San Francisco's formerly Italian-Catholic Castro district, now considered a gay mecca.

Identifying and naming the HIV virus informed a mid-eighties public about how the virus was contracted; everyone was less sure about how to deal with the excruciating pain of serially losing friends, colleagues, and partners. Mother Lily, as members of her congregation and the larger AIDS caregiving community called her, was asked with increasing frequency to be at bedsides of the dying and, subsequently, conduct memorial services for their survivors. Despite all the death and dying in and around the small Church of the Magdalene, parishioners retained their humor, referring to themselves as the "dying live" and, using television's comedy show, joked: "Saturday Night Live, Sunday morning dead."

WHEN THEIR YOUNGER SON Wylie got accepted at the same school his twin siblings, Desmond and Zora, attended, Lily accepted the call to full-time parish ministry at Holy Innocents' in Oakland. Twelve years after their move from the

East Coast, Lily would finally be working in the same community as Rodney with a fifteen-minute commute from their Oakland home. No more having to massage tight schedules to be on the right side of the bridge at the right time of the right day.

In her new position, Lily, now going by her middle name, Vida, inherited the congregation's dispute with its former priest, along with its undisputed claim to fame. John Hartwig was raised up in the parish's Gospel progressivism and elected to the US Senate in November after securing his party's nomination two months after the start of Lily's tenure in Eastertide of 1992.

Hartwig appealed to the sensibilities of a changed 1990s electorate. An American near-majority challenged the military's "Don't ask, don't tell" policy for gays in uniform. Church-going Americans, somewhat more ambiguous in number, debated formal acknowledgment of gays in the pulpit.

While rates of HIV infection slowed among gay white males in the mid-1990's, every other demographic saw an alarming increase. Internationally, death rates continued to rise and were predicted to reach 25 percent of Africa's sub-Saharan people by the new millennium. Gathering in symposia, the world health community found neither tactical agreement on stemming the epidemic's advance, nor broad-based support giving even one of the several proposals on the table financial and political viability.

During the same time, America's other and embedded epidemic spiked. The stir caused by a white presidential-contender's daughter marrying a Black son of the urban ghetto was felt, in ways good and bad, by citizens of all fifty states, who were united as much in their common history of racism as by their claim to ideals put forth in the Constitution and its Bill of Rights. The Klan, on the visible move again, issued public statements denying domestic terrorism despite current incidents of Black church burnings bearing the Klan's hate moniker all over them. Emboldened by no federal designation as a hate crime, arsonists, as with lynchers, continued having to answer only to local authorities, who were reluctant to find the motivation to investigate, much less charge and convict.

———

A MAN MADE A CALL from a phone booth in Contra Costa County, California, to a younger man in Hale County, Alabama. Their business was as brief as the first chill of sundown.

"Whatcha got for me?"

"Don't have shit, Hank. Whadd'ya expect I got? I'm down here with spooks and cops and nothin' else."

"Hold up, dickbrain," said the steely-cold voice. "Lee's gonna be gettin' in touch with you just as soon as everything is a go."

"Meaning what?"

"Meaning you better have your ass ready to ride—you with me, son?" snarled his mentor, uninterested in the boy's answer. "Now, look, I can't stay on long. Just listen to what I'm tellin' ya."

"Fine, jes' as long as it's b'fore they're up my ass with a warrant," said the boy, puffing on a cigarette.

"Who? What're you snifflin' about now?" The man studied the younger man with his words, knowing exactly what to say to worry his charge into complicity.

"I don't know, I don't know," bobbled the young operative, before taking a drag on his cigarette. "I jes' wanna do it and get th'hell outta here."

"Well, can ya wait for his call?" The voice stabbed and proceeded to turn in the younger man's gut, saying, "Do ya think you can just hold up on your weak-ass, crybaby tears? You a Ranger or not, Jesse?

"We ride proud of our heritage, son," the voice exhorted. "Person by person, hour by hour—that's how this war is waged. We got to do it to turn this country around—you with me, son?"

"I know we got to do it. I hate 'em," said the boy as if reciting an oath, "and I hate bein' here in Spadeland. Don't worry 'bout me," said the boy, deepening the pitch of his voice, hoping to convince his mentor of his manhood, the same as he had convinced himself. "I'm stayin' honorable—I'm here, man, ain't I?"

"You're alright, li'l Jesse," said the voice, bandaging the wound made by previous words. "Your daddy be proud of you—you know that? You bringin' a new nation to birth— we no longer gonna be somebody's whippin' boy."

"Yeah. I loved my daddy. I love you, Hank," spurted the boy-man. "Thanks for trustin' me with this mission. I'll get it goin'," he said, dropping his cigarette on the stained asphalt and mashing it with the steel toe of his boot. "Jes' as soon as Lee calls, I'll get it goin'."

"Ride with God, son. You make me and your copatriots proud—you doin' real good."

———

HE KNEW WHERE HIS BLACK male body was in relation to surrounding bodies. His posture was instinctual. Lily stared at the back of his neck and the vigilant seated length of his ramrod-straight spine and knew exactly who he was.

Lucius Clay had all eyes on him as he spoke for the first time. "Senator, will you and Mrs. Hartwig be entertaining the family of Thomas More at the White House?"

Action, reaction. His whole life was paying attention to harm's way. Though his reaction had matured, it remained reaction. Intellect civilizing fierceness, journalist Lucius tended to his childhood rage to preserve his family and, now, to get his copy published.

Lucius's grandmother worked for an old white lady who lent her out like an appliance. *The colored woman.* The day he heard that old, cane-leaning woman refer to his gramma as *her* colored woman—"Oh, yes, dear, you can have my colored woman on Tuesdays"—Lucius wanted to whip her ass with that cane, just like his dad would whop him if his son showed disrespect. What held Lucius back was his mother, the second-born and first daughter of seven Cooper children. Sassing the dowager would have shamed his mother and, besides, his gramma could still lay a forceful hand on an impudent child.

Mathilde Cooper started working for Miss Spencer as a child, running errands. She kept on working, barely stopping to celebrate her marriage to Lucius's grandpa Eli, right on through to the birth of her last child, Lucius's Aunt Cecile. By that time, her kids were having kids. When Lucius's mom worked at a local diner, he hung out with his Gramma Mattie.

"Most certainly," said John Hartwig, straining to understand the question behind the question. "But please be assured, *Mr. Clay* and other esteemed members of the press, that you don't have to marry the senator's daughter to have a seat at the White House dinner table. Mrs. Hartwig and I are proud to have reared our children to be colorblind." Knowing he was in trouble with this word choice, Hartwig attempted more certitude in what he hoped would be the final coat of polish needed to address Clay's question. "What I mean is, Mrs. Hartwig and I have done our best to instill our values of human dignity—that human talent and companionship are not a function of skin color."

Clay bristled. "And what about recognition of human talent and companionship *as* a function of skin color?"

The senator was transported back to the mat of high school wrestling days. He was chosen all-state over the more excellent talent of his peer, Emmett Williams, most probably because of skin color. A white boy getting ahead fulfilled expectation; a Black boy showing talent provoked revenge. Hartwig sidestepped Clay's thrust: "On my staff, recognition and utilization of human talent, Mr. Clay, is not a function of skin color. I am proud to have more African American staff, including top-drawer advisors, than any of my predecessors." Hartwig hoped he was as convincing to Clay and the other journalists as he was to himself. "I am proud to have supported the campaigns of Senators Longview and Walston—both now claiming D.C. residency while representing their Ohio and New Jersey constituencies in the chambers of the US Senate. And if elected to sit in the Oval Office, my support for Black representation can only increase."

The expression on Clay's blue-black face only slightly revealed his thinking, now interrupted by a White House staffer's five-minute warning of the conclusion of the senator's press conference. *Will I ever hear anything more original than "just as good as"?* Lucius steamed inside. *Anything more relenting than "what I did for the just-as-good-as Black person"?*

As the senator's wife and mother of the bride Carol Hartwig began to speak, Lucius's thoughts turned to his own marriage. Claire was William and Josephina Bolton's third child. After their second meeting, William told Lucius to call him "Bill." Jody nicknamed herself at first introductions, and the informality of her name was characteristic of the woman herself. Despite a mutual show of friendliness, the awkwardness of meetings between Claire's "colored, or-do-you-prefer-*Black*?" fiancé and the family continued into marriage. Claire seemed urgently bent on proving her choice of mate as the exception to Black male stereotyping. She never really got it, that it was her ceaseless defense of his racial difference—not *her*, that grew tiresome.

The issue of defending, rather than loving, the difference between Lucius and Claire came to a head after they became parents. With Miles's arrival, Claire had new reasons to bolster her argument for not only her husband but, now, their son being the model of Black racial exception. Any sense of pleasurable accomplishment in their coming together to create a *new human being* was quickly overshadowed by Claire's panic that she and Lucius had been outed as interracial lovers.

Blues began playing in Claire's postpartum head and continued sounding their racialized key as background to her unilateral decision that the marriage would produce no more children. But it wasn't until their "exceptional boy" faced insensitive taunts from his kindergarten peers, Black as well as white, that Claire found the courage to declare herself to

Lucius. She told him she was unable to defend and, therefore, felt she was unfit to have any more earthy-brown children. The quick initiation and processing of their divorce belied the profound pain lying beneath Lucius and Claire's agreement to undo their marriage.

———

"WELCOME TO OAKLAND, MISTER CLAY."

Lucius turned in the direction of the voice. "Lily?" Her face was immediately pressed into Lucius's chest by his squeezing embrace. "Used to be," Lily muffled into his jacket lapel. "Now I use my middle name, Vida."

Lucius released his hold yet remained connected by sliding his hands down her arms to take her palms in his. Regaining balance, Lily continued her explanation. "Comes from a grandmother I only knew by family legend."

Lucius held Lily out at arm's length. His eyes examined the whole person in front of him before settling on just her face and, then, her eyes in particular. "So, this is your church."

"More or less."

Lucius dropped Lily's hands, but she remained captive as he dropped his voice to a whisper, "I never knew what happened to you, preacher-woman. You never called."

"You never wrote, writer-man."

"And we're all here for a wedding . . ."

"The ultimate *personal-as-political*."

"Still delicious in your delivery."

"So, you?" queried Lily. "You're in working clothes, I see. And badged. 'L.A. Times–Washington Corres.,'" Lily whistled. "You're a coast away from home, Mr. Clay."

"Bride's church home isn't in D.C., Rev'nd *Lily*," said Lucius. "I go where the potential First Family goes—when it's making history. And now it seems," said Lucius, grinning and wagging his head side to side, "you're the icing on the cake."

"So why *didn't* you write, Lucius?" asked Lily, reassigning her immediate pique at feeling too openly admired to a past mostly forgotten.

"Well, Lily . . . *Vida?*" began Lucius, responding to Lily's question seriously, with emotion more honest than she used in asking.

"*Lily* works," she said with less swagger. "Let's keep it simple."

"I wish I could. Anyway, it was a long time ago," said Lucius, reversing Lily's false offensive. "What's the point?"

"That's why I didn't call," said Lily, joking. "I couldn't figure out the point of calling someone who didn't write." Lucius was glad Lily took the initiative to further the conversation, no matter where it went. "Still, we were an interesting couple."

"*Couple?*" Lucius bucked. "*Were* we a couple? That committed? This ol' newsman definitely missed something in this story," Lucius chided himself, wanting to extend debate on the subject.

"Well, maybe by poetic license," humored Lily, searching Lucius's face for a shared interpretation of the past.

"We didn't allow ourselves any more," Lucius conjectured, with Lily surprised at his pronouns boldly presuming to speak for her as well. "But now, I feel we're allowed another opportunity—like I just found a winning raffle ticket, buried away in a drawer."

"And I'm the prize?"

"You're the sur-prize," quipped Lucius. "Don't know that the *prize* is still claimable." Then looking at the ring on her left hand, Lucius asked, "You're married?"

"Happily."

"Kids?"

"Twins, boy and girl, and a single. Son." Lily checked for his reaction before putting the obligatory same questions to Lucius. Hazy amusement played over his face, as he blew a resigned yet admiring sigh into the space between them. Lily asked, "And you?"

"Was," Lucius reminisced, "past tense."

"I'm sorry."

"No need," Lucius backed off in unconvincing lightness. "Some good years and a great son is what I got away with." Regret tinged his hair gray and crinkled the corners of his smile. Lucius cast half-closed eyes down at polished black shoe leather.

"Was it Claire?" Lucius stiffened. His eyes gazed into Lily's and exited out the back of her head, but his mouth stayed mute. "Claire," Lily repeated softly. "Is she your son's mother?"

"I'm amazed you remember." Lucius deemed her remembering proof of trustworthiness. "We had no models for an *interracial thing* then."

Lucius's words opened the hatch for Lily's thoughts to escape into the "interracial thing" that happened when she met Lucius so many years ago. "And no muse," she absolved. "Or at least one that would abide, as we made up who we all were as we went along."

Before it occurred to Lucius to be confused as to which relationship they were talking about, he was already halfway down the path with Lily. "Maybe the muse was there," he reflected, "just couldn't get a word in edgewise between all the fear."

"Spoken or not," Lily said, laying her words alongside Lucius's.

"I know I was scared . . . I remember that. I definitely remember that." Lucius checked his watch. "Not to appear more evasive than I am, I gotta go. Round two of *Meet the Press*. This round, first up, First Lady-in-waiting."

"Oh, you mean Carol?"

"First name basis!" It was Lucius's turn to cluck. "Maybe I should have gone into the ministry—how does the Reverend Lucius Clay sound?"

"Serious," said Lily. "But serious*ly*. Would you like to join me for lunch with Carol *and* John?"

Lucius bowed his head and rolled his eyes upward to Lily, aping obeisance. "You would do that for me, Miss Lily—a lowly *House*boy?" Lily shot him a disgusted look, mildly annoyed that her grandiosity had backfired. Helping her recover but not fully, Lucius popped, "Yeah, I could dig it . . . you're okay disclosing association with this ol' Texas boy?"

"Not just okay," asserted Lily. "It's one of the highlights of my life. Just never thought I'd get so personal a reminder of the fact."

"Aw, you never gave me another thought once you got on that plane back to New York," capped Lucius. "We do need to talk, but no need to scrap lunch plans with Him and Her after the dog and pony show. Besides, I know you want to hear what your friends have to say, officially, about their daughter's headline-maker?" teased Lucius. "And one good turn deserving another, I'd even offer to get you into the press conference—but I see you already have connections."

"Well, sure," Lily said, feeling foolish for suggesting the alternative arrangement for lunch and grateful for Lucius's finessed cover, facilitating her changing back into a crisper demeanor.

Lily's retreat into professional guise ruffled Lucius's confidence in his ability to navigate the channels of any relationship. "*Reverend Lily*—I always wondered how I'd react, seeing you in collar."

"Well?"

"Suits you," said Lucius. "I don't know what this *Vida* is like, but Lily, thank God, clearly remains on the premises."

"And still keen for the last word," Lily finished. "Go do your thing, writer-man. I'll find you afterwards."

"Lily," began Lucius, "this is a sweet, sweet moment."

"I'VE ASKED AN OLD FRIEND, Lucius Clay, to join us for lunch," Lily informed John and Carol Hartwig as they stepped into her office following the press conference.

"Oh, we've known Clay for years. Splendid," voiced the senator. "Mind is hard-cast. Good journalist, even better investigator—tough on people in high places." A side glance to his wife, "We pay attention to what comes out of his pen—" A rap on the door interrupted the senator.

Lily opened the heavy antique door, one hand on the knob, the other waving her visitor in. "Welcome to my sanctuary, Lucius. No need for introductions, I hear." Lily shot Lucius a look as if to ask what other personal history he had up his cagey sleeve. "We all seem to know each other."

Senator Hartwig stood and grabbed Lucius's right elbow at the same time he began pumping the journalist's hand. The senator's wife rose and turned her head slightly, indicating where exactly on her cheek she wished Lucius to place the courteous touch of his greeting. It all happened quickly, before moving on to arrangements for getting to the restaurant.

"You and Lily come in our car, Lucius. Agents all know where we're going."

"Probably, months ahead of time," said Lily. "I thought the *Grille* downtown would be appropriate after getting questions fired at you here at Holy Innocents'."

"Good choice," said the father of the bride. "And speaking of good choices—may I say how glad Carol and I are that you will be God's agent at our daughter's nuptial altar—"

"Yes," Carol interjected, "Heather *and Thomas* are in good hands."

"Thank you for the confidence. It's been just a little daunting doing premarital counseling with an about-to-be US president's daughter and her fiancé."

LUCIUS BEGAN, "SENATOR—" BUT WAS interrupted. "Always have loved Lake Merritt," said the senator, gazing out the window of the limousine. "Look at those blossoms. What is that tree?"

"Flowering plum, I believe." Carol Hartwig followed her husband's lead in keeping the conversation light and, when necessary, redirecting the flow away from politics.

Undiscouraged by the closure of one entrance, Lucius tried another. This time, he took a running start, propelling his question more forcefully into the center of the couple, seated opposite one another. "Being that all eyes are trained on what has got to be one of the most important days of your and Mrs. Hartwig's lives—seeing your daughter exchange vows with Mr. More at Holy Innocents' Church—what will you be saying to those whose churches are no more?"

The mother of the bride looked nervous, as if she'd not done her job. Lily, on the other hand, had been waiting for the subject of Black church burnings to surface—twenty-something in the last eighteen months, was it? She knew from her own public life that no matter how hard they tried to protect it, the Hartwigs' family time was never their own.

Attempting to blunt the pointed question aimed at his public official's conscience, Hartwig used first-name informality in his hale and hearty reply: "I believe you to be a plant from the Congressional Black Caucus, aren't you, Lucius? Lily—how much they pay you to introduce Clay, here, as 'an old friend'?"

"She hasn't yet found the time to count all the pennies and nickels of their offering," countered Lucius, happy that race was at least introduced with the senator's remark.

"Look," said Hartwig, "I'm immediately nervous about Holy Innocents', and whether or not some idiot extremist is going to light a match to express his political views on my daughter's interracial marriage—" *It's Thomas's* interracial marriage *too,* Lily thought. *And just maybe he and his family are in the most danger.*

"Forgive me, Senator, sir—you think it's a matter of *politics,* nothing larger?"

"Well, of course, it's something larger," wheedled presidential nominee John Hartwig. "Why the hell else do you think I lose sleep at night worrying about how my daughter and son-in-law will fare *after* the 'I do's.'"

"Even more reason to have the eyes of the world looking to you in the dual capacity of bride's father giving his blessing on racial mixing, and world leader, guarantor of a Constitutional freedom from threat to life, liberty, and the pursuit of happiness," said Lucius. "What do you say to all those who are less than satisfied that federal law enforcement is doing all it can to bring the perpetrators of this conspiracy to justice?"

The senator felt trapped and wanted to hedge his answers. "First of all, Mr. Clay, we don't know these burnings to be conspiratorial by design or execution."

"Hell, racism *itself* is the conspiracy which for too long has had *both* the sanction and protection of the law!" Lucius jeered.

Hartwig checked street signs for evidence of proximity to their downtown Oakland destination, while mentally constructing an answer that might open the jaws of his bulldog captor and secure his release. He was about to speak when Lucius cut him off, continuing his barbed interrogation and reprimand, "What *is* clear from the evidence is that every arson arrest has been white males only, with an age range of—what is it?—sixteen to sixty? Some less-than-optimistic figure that things have changed . . ."

"I believe the House Judiciary heard a range of sixteen to forty-five—"

"Forty-five or sixty, doesn't change matters," Lucius thrust.

Clay had caught Hartwig hiding behind quibbling. The senator sat up straighter to face his contender again. "The real truth is that *ninety-year-olds* are complicit—"

"Then, respectfully, *Senator*," jabbed Lucius, throwing a punch to the gut, "when *are* you and the Administration going to come out and say, '*Race* is behind the burnings'?"

"Soon," Hartwig shot back. "Damn soon, Mr. Clay."

The journalist, used to lobbing questions from a seated sea of inquisitors below the podium, was suddenly stunned by the immediate volley, eye to eye and toe to toe, in the back of a limousine.

In the abrupt silence punctuating the end of the quick exchange, the tension visible in Hartwig's constricted neck muscles began, as visibly, to subside. As an inflatable object relieved of having to keep its walls rigid, the senator volunteered a concluding statement: "The president meets with NAACP, National Council of Churches leadership, and some of the affected pastors next week. I'm prepared to say more at that time." The silence spoke a loud amen.

Lucius met the senator's avowal with grace, saying as a benediction before the car pulled up to the curb, "I admire your courage, sir."

"Well, is everyone hungry?" asked Carol Hartwig, reclaiming her place as mother of the bride and hostess of the luncheon at Frank's Downtown Grille.

"I hear they burn a mean steak here," rejoined Lucius, signaling the all-clear.

"And do we know if your sources are reliable, Mr. Clay?" quipped Lily, still sorting through the peppery exchange to which she felt a party, if only because she first extended the invitation that resulted in their all being in the same car.

"Very, *Reverend* Wallace." Lily thought she heard respect between Lucius's teasing words.

"Well, then," said Hartwig, "by presidential-hopeful fiat, I say we get to it."

RESTAURANT PATRONS STARED AT THEIR table during lunch. The looks and buzz were for the senator contending to be the nation's leader and his wife, certainly. But for those in the small urban community who knew or knew of Lily, a portion of the interest was about the man whom they did not know. For them, Lucius, more than the couple *célèbre*, was the hub of animated conversation.

After declining coffee and the Grille's famous caramel mousse, the trim set of senator and wife excused themselves. They took the pleasant burden of their daughter's wedding in stride, simply adding the event to the multiple demands of their everyday schedules. They knew how to go about their business with one eye on themselves and the other on the rest of the world.

"I NEED TO APOLOGIZE, LILY," Lucius began.

"What for?" returned Lily, pouring cream in her decaf. "I saw or heard nothing outrageous in your behavior or remarks with John."

Lucius laughed. "As a matter of record, neither did I." Lily paused to blow on the steamy liquid and to question Lucius's mirthful eyes across the table. "No, the failure of investigative duty I was about to confess, Reverend Lily—"

"That's the second time in the last hour and a half you've called me that," interrupted Lily, stirring a little conversation dust. "Do you like the title?"

"As I said before, it suits you. Besides . . ." Lucius

hesitated, ambivalent about whether investing in the present with Lily would improve or disturb his comfortably resting memories of the woman who aroused his interest so well in the past. "I don't have another. I mean, after you interviewed *me* over two decades ago, I failed to ask for the name that took you from back then to happily married with kids. So you? You marry that boy you were engaged to—Evan or Ethan or something like that?"

"Yeah. 'Something like that' was probably the best name for him," said Lily, sipping and looking into the decaf as if looking into the past. "No. Didn't work out."

"I'm sorry," said Lucius quietly. "My recollection of you has a 'committed' sticker on the tab," Lucius poked, then switched to geniality. "You must have found a better man."

"'Deed I did, and you'll meet him Saturday—I assume you're staying for the wedding?"

"Wasn't planning to," Lucius said, turning his perspiring glass of ice water round in circles as he hung his head in mock oppression and continued, "I don't have a pew."

"I can fix that," chirped Lily. "It's my priestly duty to welcome the stranger in our midst," she said, sitting up straight as if called to official business. "And you, Lucius Clay, are the long-lost stranger. Of course, you won't be able to see a thing sitting in the section behind the two-foot diameter marble column."

"Boy, git to the back o' the bus."

Lucius noticed Lily's face redden. "I'm just messing with you, Lily. I know you didn't mean it like that—"

"I'm sorry—I forget to examine my teasing for thorns every now and then," said Lily. "But also, practically speaking, the one place left unoccupied is—"

"Lily, hang it up. No offense taken. Really," said Lucius, keeping both hands on his side of the table, unsure if what felt natural for him at that moment—reaching out for her hand—would be misconstrued. "Just wanted to see if you still light up like a Christmas bulb when you think you've stepped on black toes."

"You're not a nice man." Lily relaxed into easy talk again, her hands encircling the warm mug. "I might have to rescind the sincerity of my offer and let the clumsy humor stand."

"No, if I start neck-craning exercises now, I might survive. And if not," said Lucius, tapping the back of her hand with his index finger, "I can go sit in the john till the reception."

"You *can't* remember that far back," Lily said, eyes blinking and opening wide as if trying to bring the man sitting in the booth with her into sharper focus.

"Hard to forget a female fleeing outta church."

"You made me nervous back then."

"It was my pleasure."

———

FROM WHERE LILY STOOD AS officiating priest, the color line stood out all too clearly, as tradition was maintained in the seating of a bride's side and a groom's side. Though grains of contrasting color were sprinkled here and there, the distinction between guests invited by the Mores and those by the Hartwigs was obvious. The entire congregation was on the move, however, when it came time for the nuptial kiss and passing of the peace. Attendees from both sides crossed the aisle to extend a hand, bestow a smile. For Lily, the peace-passing gesture in a yet color-banded America symbolized more than a friendly greeting between wedding guests.

The goodwill continued into the reception held in the ballroom of a renovated hotel in Oakland's newly beautified Old Town harbor district. The project had taken years, the city's Black administration taking time to ensure that none of its citizens would be displaced from even the humblest of their homes. At the same time renewal plans were being developed for environs fit for Oakland's new convention center, social services kept pace advocating for Oakland's port population.

Lily grabbed Rodney's hand and took off across the room, explaining along the way, "Rodney, there's somebody I want you to meet."

"Hey, hey," Rodney mildly resisted. "You pullin' me up by the roots like this—must be a Mr. *Big* Somebody."

"So you assume a 'mister'?" asked Lily, lightening her grip.

"I *educe* a mister," said her husband, the judge. "From behavioral evidence—"

"That obvious?"

"You obvious, baby," teased Rodney, cutting himself off as he spotted a tall man with mahogany complexion darker than his own turn away from conversation with a squat older man and toward the approaching couple.

"Lucius Clay," said Lily, pivoting between the men, "my husband, Rodney Davis." Then, turning to the raw honey–colored senior of the pair and gesturing with outstretched hand, she said, "And this is Eston More, Thomas's most notorious relation."

Rodney didn't have to guess which of the two gener-ated Lily's current of excitement. "Pleased to meet you," Rodney said, shaking Clay's hand more stiffly and forcefully than Eston More's. Then, with no subtlety, Rodney turned a half-shoulder to Clay and picked up the morsel Lily dropped in her introduction.

"So, what makes you the notorious one, Mr. More?"

"You a young man, Rodney, like this captivatin' Mr. Clay I been wastin' time with, here." Uncle Eston smiled broadly, continuing in poetic cadence, "You think I'ma old man, but I tell you the truth. I found the fountain of youth. So while I mebbe long ah tooth, I got no lack ah juice!" Uncle Eston, his own best audience, bent over, sputtering and choking over his own humor. With that, the man whose expansive girth suggested that he missed neither a good meal nor a good laugh temporarily diffused most of the younger men's charge.

"I'm going to leave you three to figure out why you should get to know each other, while I work the room." Lily turned and immediately joined a cluster of Hartwig relatives nearby, easily inserting herself into their conversation.

"I don't quite know what she meant by that," began Lucius, "but I can demystify her parting remark by saying that Lily and I met some twenty years ago on a somewhat grimmer occasion."

"And I'm the one Lily met around the same time," asserted Rodney. "The hound at her heels, until she agreed to quit running and marry me."

Lucius sized up the man in front of him. "Persistence dogged as that—gotta be a lawyer or judge."

"Gotta be right," returned Rodney, uncomfortable that Clay pegged him so easily. "I'm sentenced on both counts. What keeps *you* pluggin' away?"

"Probably my hard head," fronted Lucius, immediately regretting his glibness with Lily's husband.

"A person of the cloth, also?" ventured Rodney.

"No. Mr. Clay writes," the rotund Mr. More answered, pleased to have personal knowledge about one of the two men circling each other, while continuing to assert his presence. As a referee anticipating having to separate locked egos, Uncle Eston added, "For the *L.A. Times.*"

"So it's Lucius Clay the journalist," said Rodney, backing off his mark.

"Ever since they offered me money and a desk," finished Lucius. Then, feeling like he wanted to be more transparent with Rodney, he said, "Hoping—but usually with all evidence to the contrary—that what I write may have an impact on somebody, somewhere."

"You seem to have had quite an impact on my wife," said Rodney, acting like a score having to do with Lily's past and this other man needed to be settled.

Lucius laughed uncomfortably. "Debatable."

"How long for it to *take*?" asked Rodney.

Registering confusion about Rodney's question, Lucius's eyes narrowed as he shrugged his shoulders and shook his head.

Rodney asked more pointedly, "How long were you and Lily together?"

"Look, Rodney. Lily and I were never 'together,' in the way I think you imply," dismissed Lucius. "I happened to be investigating a hate crime—you might have heard about the Jefferson lynching—outside Greenville, South Carolina— early 70s? Lily was there on church business."

Lucius perceived trust in the husband's eyes, as Rodney became more interested in Lucius's story and less concerned about any former relationship with Lily. "In fact, I don't know that you were even in the picture then," recalled Lucius. "Older man. Hugh something. He and Lily flew in from New York for the funeral and the mayor's event preceding."

"Okay. This is sounding familiar," said Rodney. "All but you. Lily never mentioned—"

"I'm sure I was an insignificant part of that whole fucked-up scene," said Lucius. "It was something like less than twenty-four hours—we were in, we were out, and, for a small part of that time, I remember enjoying some solid conversation with your wife . . . well, not your wife then. Lily."

"Sounds like a powerful time for forgin' new bonds's what I'm hearin'," observed Uncle Eston. "You two never stay in touch?"

"No," said Lucius, unfolding his arms, his hands finding immediate cover in his pants pockets. "That's the thing. This meeting up with each other again is as much out of the blue for me as for Lily. In fact, it's doubtful I made *any* impact at all. When we talked on Thursday for the first time, there was no indication from Lily that she had ever read one of my bylines, much less sought communication with me."

Lucius, sensing the rivalry, if that's what it was, de-escalate, felt at liberty to speak of Lily as their mutual friend. "I have to say, I was a little hurt by Lily's confession of disinterest . . . but meeting you, Rodney, explains all. You must have swept her off her feet, man."

"I tried my damnedest," said Rodney. "She resisted mightily, though. Every step of the way. A tough woman."

"I'll take your word for it," said Lucius, graciously stepping back for Rodney to wax proud over the long term of his and Lily's marriage.

"She is an amazing woman," beamed Rodney, "and mother. She tell you about our three rugrats?"

"Not in detail."

"Well, before you leave, you'll have to be introduced," said the proud father. "They're around here somewhere."

Inviting Rodney's comment and version of the story, Lucius prompted, "Lily failed to mention what brought you to California." Conveniently responding to a wave and hello from the next party over, Uncle Eston excused himself, saying it was nice to have met both of the two "young men," and asking Lucius if he'd be joining him when the bride tossed her garter.

"Not my thing, Uncle. I'll leave it to those less ornery and stuck in their ways. Those with more spring, like yourself Eston," said Lucius. "Been a pleasure meeting you, though. Look for me in your corner, when you go hand-to-hand for that garter!"

"Likewise," said Rodney. "I'm throwin' all my support in your direction."

"Cain't jump like I used to, but my timing's still pretty good," Eston winked.

"You gon' outfox all that youngblood with your moves. Throw a few elbows at 'em, Eston. We know you gon' take home the prize!" said Rodney, including Lucius in his encouragement. The older man took his leave, satisfied that his self-appointed mission with the two former strangers had been accomplished.

As Uncle Eston walked away, Lucius spoke. "I hope I have half his optimism when I'm that old. I tend to wring the world dry with cynicism."

"Tell me about it . . . you with a pen, me with a gavel—the world discharges a lot of shit," said Rodney. "But back to the question you laid on the table, concerning making California my home—*our* home. A good opportunity brought us here." Rodney twisted his torso and popped his spine, clearing his body of tension before launching into the story. "My family's all in Alabama—Birmingham. I moved a little east of them when I went with a firm in Atlanta. But then a buddy of mine from law school wanted to hook me up out West, and I came riding. Eager to have more autonomy. Though I don't know if I've achieved the desired end."

"Wielding a gavel—now that's gotta give some sense of satisfaction."

"True. But you know my professional black ass is *every* black ass," said Rodney, waiting for Lucius to nod in agreement as permission to continue. "You know, the celebrity that comes with public service—takes its bite out of you, representing the race. Not forgetting where this Your-Honor black ass came from, and on whose shoulders it sits." Rodney felt comfortable sharing himself with Lucius. "How about you? Where're your people from?"

"Same African coast as yours, brother! After emancipation from their South Carolina captivity, a branch of Clays made their way to Texas."

"SO DO YOU KNOW EACH other's hat size by now?" Lily interrupted the two men's flow of talk and easy laughter.

"Yeah, but we lie about that too," said Rodney.

"I take what he gives me and add four, 'cause I know he's addin' two," said Lucius.

"Must be the drink talking," said Lily, realizing she was not part of this fraternity.

"No, I believe it's the barbershop," said Rodney. "You can take a Black man out of the barbershop, but you can't take the barbershop out th' Black man."

"Thassright, brother." More laughter rolled out of the two mouths, witnessing to Lily how vitalizing relationship only took recognizing kinship, whose roots were established long before any present circumstance.

"Well, I can see all the *chairs* in the shop are full!" Lily tested the pair to see if she even had a toehold between them.

"No, there's always room for you, babe." Lily was relieved that her husband was first to offer hospitality.

"Room, especially, for the one who made room for me . . ." added Lucius. Rodney, half-joking, threw Lucius a menacing look. "Today," qualified Lucius. And to ensure his remark would be taken in jest, he added further clarification for Rodney's benefit. "Thanks for saving me a seat in your church, Reverend Lily."

"My pleasure, helping a reporter get his scoop."

"And if you were the Reverend's mister," said Rodney, punching the air with his words, "you'd not only have a seat, but your own parking place too."

"Some days, two," said Lily. "I get my money's worth out of Rodney as informal legal counsel, as well as mate."

"I can see you're a dynamic duo," said Lucius. "Feed my jealousy. Tell me more."

Lily hesitated. Enjoying the flirty conversation, she was reluctant to switch subjects to the parish trouble already taking up too much of her time and emotion. Rodney, though, glad for Lucius's attention, whether the journalist was just being polite or not, happily occupied the space Lily held back.

"Parishioner diverted funds intended for PWAs— People with AIDS—until the bulge in his pants got too big.

Investigators wanted to know if it was dirty money or was he just glad to see them."

"Big standing in the church?" asked Lucius.

"And in the community," Lily chimed in. "But I think I feel most sorry for his wife. Here's a woman, just a minute ago proud of her husband's recognition for charitable work over the past decade, now seeing him pose for mug shots with the Oakland PD. The cognitive dissonance is too much for everyone, really."

"That's some white shit, right?" Lucius said, fingerprinting the crime.

"One hundred percent guaranteed white shit," said Rodney.

"Wait a minute . . ." said Lily, "how can you color-code a *particular* crime?" The two men looked at each other, then Rodney said, "Now I *know* you're the one stenciled E-R-A-C-E on the wall of that freeway underpass over by the kids' school. Name me one Black man doin' time for white collar crime."

"Marion Barry—"

"Crack and women more his rap," said Rodney, "but I'll give you half for Barry if you come up with a second name."

"Father Divine."

"Never proven. Didn't do time," said Lucius.

"Okay, so what's your point?"

Both men spoke at once, then both stopped. Rodney signaled for Lucius to continue, saying, "I yield my time to the gentleman from DeeCee by way of Lozangeleez."

"All I was going to say, Lily, was that it may not be so much the case here in Oakland, but in most of the country, crime reporting *is* color-coded," said the journalist. "In fact, Black or Latino suspects are still identified by color and not by name more often than you'd like to believe in our *e-r-a-c-e* enlightened times."

Lucius said thanks as he grabbed three glasses of champagne off the tray wielded by a server half their age. Passing out the champagne and lifting his own glass, Lucius proposed a toast. "And here's to you two for pulling it off . . . may today's bride and groom do it with such style!"

"Here, here," said Rodney, clinking his glass against the others. After taking a sip and remarking about the champagne's and the father of the bride's good taste, Lily commented, "I don't know how they'll do it. Hard enough being a senator-maybe-president's daughter and son-in-law."

"They'll do it by being spun by every pundit around the country. Around the world. And that's just what's in print and visible." Champagne not being his drink of choice, Lucius set his glass down after the toasting sip and looked around for a waiter to take his order for scotch.

"You suppose white sheets are on back order as good Christian brethren sound the 'Heritage Violation' alert?" asked Rodney. "Course, the mills probably already started upping production first of last year with all the burnings . . . what are we up to now, Lucius? You must have your finger on that pulse."

"Depending on the source," said Lucius, "high 20s, low 30s. Of course, that figure needs adjusting for all the underreporting by authorities maintaining local investigative control."

"The Episcopal Church and other National Council of Church members are working on resolutions—" Lily began.

"The situation demands a watch brigade equipped with fire extinguishers and NoDoz," interjected Rodney, "not a committee drafting resolutions—"

"If you'd let me finish," said Lily, "the resolutions are the mechanism for marshaling resources for prevention as well as rebuilding—money, volunteers, public outcry. . . ."

Just then, the call sounded for eligible men to proceed to the courtyard for the tossing of Mrs. Heather Hartwig More's garter.

"You don't want to miss this, Lucius," said Rodney, suddenly desirous of Lily's long-lost friend to return to his singles category. "Man of your maturity must play some pretty good catch."

"The trick is to hold on to what you catch," said Lucius, pulling up his coat sleeve slightly to consult his watch.

Wondering what Lucius's comment was about, but reluctant to pursue it then, Lily opted for silly banter: "Bring your glasses, boys. Testosterone refills comin' up."

"I can hear ESPN's color commentator now," mused Rodney. "Blacks have it. No, Team Pale's hands are goin' up. But a brotha comes in to grab it."

Lucius laughed. "My money's on Brotha Eston, long as he catch good as he lie!"

———

"HEY, BABE. TIRED?" **RODNEY PATTED** the sofa cushion and clicked off the TV. "C'mere and let these beautiful black hands do some magic on that neck. What're you stressin' about?"

Lily put her hand up. "I'll be right back. Let me change out of these church clothes." Lily began to remove the metal studs holding her plastic Clericool collar in place as she walked toward their bedroom down the hall of their split-level home built in the early 50s.

"Yeah, enough church for one week!" Rodney threw after her departing form, admiring what he still thought was her "best side."

Lily reappeared in jeans and gray T-shirt with the kids' school logo in navy blue block letters. "Do *you*, sweetie pie, for an entire year—"

"You already get my 'Do Me' renewal for another year?" Rodney's smile slid off his face.

"I'll do you, all right," said Lily, swiveling toward the sofa in a burlesque queen feint. "Be an honor, Your Honor."

"I sit on a pew bench all week, baby." Then acknowledging Lily's glare, added, "Metaphorically speaking." Seeing her look dissolve, Rodney piled some tuna salad he found in the refrigerator on a cracker and handed it to Lily, saying, "Does it really bother you that I don't make it to church every Sunday?"

"Well, yeah. You're part of the package, you know. And how do I get the preacher's kids to come if their daddy's home watchin' the NFL triple-header?"

"C'mon—it's not *every* Sunday," Rodney objected.

"True," returned Lily. "Some Sundays, Daddy's playin' golf."

"Long as I give you support at home, baby . . ." Rodney suddenly turned the page from playful to serious, "don't tell me it's not plenty enough."

"I've never done a comparison—"

"That you'd tell me about," Rodney said, looking directly into Lily's eyes.

LILY BROWSED THE ROOM'S VINTAGE farmhouse furnishings. What she called worn, Rodney described as just getting comfortable. Her eyes traipsing over the schoolbooks piled on the amber-colored corner work unit, Lily mused how her family had come of age along with the computer. Zora and Desmond, having recently gotten their learners' permits, wanted to drive everywhere. They agreed on little these days, except being the first in line at the DMV to take and pass the driver's licensing test the minute they turned sixteen. Lily knew that automobile use would be the least of Rodney's and her negotiating worries.

Though they were twins, Zora was lighter than Dezzy, her hair thicker and more loosely coiled. Lily recalled the awe and absolute peace when the nurses placed each swaddled infant at her side, simultaneously drawing her arms around the warmth fresh from her body. Her sister Dee, unsure of what to expect, remained in quiet attendance, while Rodney's mother and sisters, Mariyah and Ayana, speculated on how the twins' color might finish up "once they done baking!" Any of the prenatal "what-about-the-kids?" alarm still hanging around quickly dissipated and was replaced by family love and wonder. Race was mixable, their firstborns beautiful; Lily was confident that they *and* their parents would be able to deal with any opinion to the contrary. She did not, however, anticipate her children being at variance with themselves.

Lily remembered the day Zora and Dezzy came home from school to report their respective embarrassment and frustration at having to choose between *African American, Caucasian* or *Other* when asked to designate their race on a school demographics form. They wanted to know why their parents didn't have better foresight about problems their kids would have to endure and wondered out loud if their mother and father cared more about themselves than their kids.

Rodney still at work, Lily took the blow to her maternal heart alone, reacting first with guilt, then with a defense meant to bolster her children's egos. "In all honesty, no. I'm sorry your father and I didn't put a lot of thought ahead of time into what our kids might be up against," Lily had said, thinking to herself, because it was daunting enough considering what, as husband and wife, the two of *them* might be up against. "I think, quite frankly, we didn't try to script out every battle our kids might encounter, because we presumed their resourcefulness to be more vigorous than their parents' *self-absorption*." Lily made sure the discussion continued with their attorney father, taking notes on how he listened and asked questions first, leaving it to Dezzy and Zora to puzzle out their own solution.

Depending on the circumstance, Lily experienced her mate's reserve as either enhancing or obstructing honest communication. Perhaps it was only a matter of timing, because no matter the situation, Rodney's judiciousness always seemed to have the win over Lily's impatience.

Lily came back to the lazy afternoon and the man who had kept his promise to "make diversity fun," asking Rodney in return, "Am I *plenty enough* for you?"

Rodney reached out to take Lily's hand. "Hmmm, let me see now," he said, as he scooted down to her end.

ONE OF THE RED LIGHTS started blinking on her phone simultaneous with Jules's buzzing Lily in her office Tuesday after the wedding. With Rodney's persuading, she had taken the previous day off. "*Luscious* Clay, line 2 for you—says he's an old flame. Or did he say 'friend'? Know him?"

"Lucius. Yes, Jules," said Lily, tapping the worn pencil eraser on the yellow legal pad. "Thanks for checking."

"Just looking out for you, sweetheart. Churches attract too many crazies like me." When he lost his partner while Lily was still at St. Mary Magdalene, Jules increased his participation in the HIV-AIDS support group that met at the church, and eventually became a member of the congregation. Knowing that the voice on the phone was usually the first Holy Innocents' voice people would hear, Lily chose Jules's spontaneity and intelligent compassion over a roster of otherwise qualified applicants.

"You're a jewel."

"You know, that was my parents' original spelling, but I changed it so the bullies would beat me up only every *other* day in kindergarten."

"Another sad story. So many, I don't know which to believe."

"Dahling, they're awl truuuuue," Jules twanged in his Carol Channing best. "There must be a Bible around here somewhere to swear on."

"Well, while you hunt, I better not keep my old friend waiting."

"I still think he should change his name. If he's as delish as he sounds—"

"Yes, Jules," Lily laughed appreciatively, as she always did at her admin assistant who preferred his own titling: "Hester's Court Jester" (after Hester Prynne, when Jules found out the earlier history of Rodney's home state, Alabama, not recognizing interracial marriage) or "Jules-of-all-trades" (and always adding, "And I do mean *all*, honey").

Though he dated after Charles died, Jules hadn't yet found, as he quipped, "the real fling" again. He stayed a resident of San Francisco, making the commute across the bay six days a week in the period Volvo that had served as coach for his "Cinderfella" romance with Charles.

"I HOPE I'M NOT DISTURBING ANYTHING."

"No, oh no," chirped Lily.

"I called yesterday, but your Boy Friday said you were off on a cruise."

"Ten demerits for Jules. He didn't mention your call. You made it back to D.C. okay, I take it?" asked Lily, cordially.

"Yes, thanks. Uneventful flight." Lucius felt his moustache curl up in a smile.

"So how're things in our nation's capital?" Lily was eager to get his take on the preceding week's events but was uncertain about the level of familiarity to assume with Lucius. "You and Senator Hartwig have a chance to continue your discussion?"

Lucius laughed deeply, saying, "No, I think he had more important folk to knock heads with . . ." Lucius looked at the time on the clock radio as he switched his cell phone to the left ear and picked up to scan the front section of *The Greensboro Watchman* bought earlier at the airport. "Or wishing *he* were the one on a cruise right about now. You heard about the latest burning?"

"Another 'Green' place." Lily worked to retrieve that morning's CNN coverage. "Greensville? Greensboro! Yeah, Greensboro, Alabama."

"Bingo."

"News said there was a 'race-charged' election today, but investigators are loath to implicate race in the fire."

"Indeed. Any chance you're for hire?" Lucius's tone belied how disturbed he was by only five arrests out of the thirty or so Black church arsons reported by the media in the last seventeen months. And maybe more disturbed that the count was unofficially higher, given no federal law requiring local officials to report Black church incidents, however suspicious.

Lucius and others' investigations had examples, too indecently numerous, of how Black churches had been targets of white supremacist vandalism and destruction for years, without notice from anyone outside local jurisdiction and with the majority of cases still unsolved or dismissed as alcohol-related pranks.

"I'd be too rich for your blood, the big bucks I make as a cleric," Lily said, sardonically.

"You must do it for the clout, then . . . I assume that's what secured me a seat at the wedding of the century, and for which I *again* wish to express my appreciation." More importantly, Lucius said, he wanted Lily to know how delighted he was that threads of their personal history had, after all those years, been reconnected.

Lily reciprocated, adding that she had wondered off and on what became of his agitating pen, and if the importance she had attached to their meeting was justified.

"And the verdict?"

"My marriage to Rodney warrants a yes," began Lily. "I don't think I would have considered a suitor shift under my own steam. So, yes, I think our meeting was all-important, not only in long-range, personal terms of marriage partner—"

"Kind of your *de facto* best man, then?" teased Lucius. "Seems to be a beautiful thing you have with Rodney—really happy for you. You wanna give me credit for any of it, there's always more room in my ego!"

"Well, yeah. I feel like you played a part," said Lily. "But—or, maybe, in addition—I was about to say something about the more immediate result of our meeting back then . . . and its circumstance." Lily felt her fingers tingle, her heartbeat increase, as her words called Lucius to more rapt attention.

Laying down the newspaper as if Lily had actually caught him distractedly scanning for articles related to the last night's church fire instead of listening to her, Lucius apologized. "Sorry. You were about to say something about our circumstance. . . ."

"Well, Sam Jefferson's circumstance, our timing—or the timing of our meeting." Lily paused to gauge Lucius's interest before proceeding. Satisfied that he was with her, she continued. "That experience was a watershed for me. Like going to sleep one night seeing the world as usual, and the next morning waking up hypersensitive . . . seeing slavery's legacy everywhere."

"Not so beautiful. . . ." said Lucius.

Lily wasn't prepared for his response. She was expecting a journalist's question to help drive her next train of thought. "No," said Lily, "not at all. Frightening actually. I was more frightened than anything. But my appreciation of gender and race as civil rights crossovers increased dramatically."

"There's a lot of history between then and now we could catch up on," said Lucius. "I was impressed that when your church put a miter on a woman for the first time, she was Black."

"And divorced," said Lily.

"Personal friend of yours?"

"Let's just say Barbara Harris and I are friendly acquaintances—members of the same small club," said Lily. "Female *and* Black, Bishop Harris is, actually, in a club of her own."

"How many Episcopal female clergy are there now?" asked Lucius.

"In the hundreds—deacons, priests, *and* bishops," said Lily.

"A few more than when we met," Lucius observed, "and you could only theorize about change. But—always hopefully so. I remember you being very positive, very determined about women's ordination happening sooner rather than later."

"We still have a long way to go as far as gender parity. Race is even worse," Lily rued. "Though the Church tries to eke out more diversity in the numbers."

"Unlike current qualified church arson reporting: it's either a Black church or a white church. Have to dig a little to find out that a white church may actually be multiracial and, hence, the reason for the crime," reported Lucius. "Yes, we like our diversity where we likes it. . . . Olympic torch just made its way to Indianapolis as another church is torched."

"Yeah," Lily continued, reflecting on the contradictions Lucius brought up, "such deep-seated hate of diversity makes the reverse—which should actually be the human *norm*—stand out as anomaly. Take for example in the early movement for women's ordination, these two prophets, both Black males—"

"So we're not the sons-of-bitches women make us out to be after all," interrupted Lucius.

"Sometimes—"

"But," Lucius interrupted a second time, as if finishing his own previous comment, "sometimes we are?"

"Actually, *my* 'sometimes' had a 'we' referent. As in, sometimes *we women* overstate the case. But," said Lily, "there's probably more truth in your interpretation."

"She slices . . . she dices!" rapped Lucius, before apologizing. "Sorry. I should have let you finish."

"Must be hard, when there's so much that needs defending," Lily teased.

Then, sensing a mood change and fearing she'd missed a cue from Lucius, Lily stopped the banter and checked out her intuition. "Does your silence mean I shouldn't continue?"

"Talking about *special* Black men?" Lucius finished her question sarcastically.

"It sounds like a 'yes,'" said Lily. "Do you mind if I ask what that's about?"

"Forget it," said Lucius. "I'm being an ass."

"We've picked up where we left off back in South Carolina," said Lily. "With me *still* not understanding."

"Forget it. Really," Lucius snapped. Then, contradicting himself, let fly more red words. "My awakening was a little less glorious is all. *I* went to sleep on my wedding night and woke up six months later, *un*able to recognize. When I finally figured out that the woman I thought I wanted to spend the rest of my life with was pimping me to her family and friends as her *special* Black man, we already had a son," Lucius saddened. "I saw her game more clearly, when she played it with *him* . . . should have taken action before that. To this day, I feel guilty, letting my son down like that," sighed Lucius, spent by his outburst.

"Not an easy call to make," Lily consoled. "Where did you find the courage to stop being 'special'?"

"When she started eliminating friends from our social register," said Lucius, his voice dropping sadly. "She'd already alienated most of my family."

"Not beautiful," Lily repeated Lucius' words back to him. "Takes guts reclaiming the right to define who you are," sympathized Lily. "Especially when you're breaking down barriers and the line becomes real blurry between one person's genuine commendation and another's self-serving drivel."

"Sounds like you speak from experience," said Lucius calmly.

"I know that I'm tolerated as a priest by some," explained Lily, "because in their minds they can justify making an exception to their gender-bound rule by making me an *exceptional* female."

"They may be right," toyed Lucius.

"Yeah, all of us female firsts quickly found out how *special* we were—" Lily scoffed, "as targets of special *harassment!*"

"Initiation rites of the 'small club' you joined," said Lucius, "with the assistance of that dynamic duo of—what did you call them?—'Black male *prophets*'? "

"You mocking me, Lucius?" laughed Lily. "You're mocking me."

"No, just jealous of the attribution," said Lucius. "But I may get a piece of your prophet thing yet," said Lucius, drawing up the canter to a walk. "I'm in that *Green* place now."

"Where the fire just destroyed that Baptist church?"

"Yes." Lily heard the gravity in Lucius's voice, as if he were telling her his own home had just been destroyed. "I was invited to be part of AP's—Associated Press's—*special* investigative team, whatever the hell that means."

"Speaking of *special* . . ."

Lucius huffed. "Yeah, with all its hidden land mines."

"So they're taking you off the campaign trail and sending you to cover bigots in Alabama."

"Not entirely. Hartwig's campaign stump includes a visit with the president to Greeleyville, South Carolina, next week when they dedicate the rebuilt church torched there a year ago. He and our sitting Chief Executive might finally be feeling the pressure to say something more definitive about racial motivation for these arsons."

His words suddenly triggering a concern for Lucius's safety, she asked if he couldn't just pass.

"Lily, you know this ol' ebony-faced boy has never been able to *pass*."

"You know what I mean," protested Lily.

"Maybe, but do I know the meaning behind your meaning?" said Lucius, half-serious in his play on words. "Sorry. It's an inside thing—this special team was created to 'get the news behind the news,'" explained Lucius. "Anyway, I *want* to do this. In the same way you wouldn't *pass* on your commitments as a religious leader, I won't pass on mine as a journalist."

"Well, your commitments are really none of my business, anyway . . . it's just that yours, in this instance, seem a hell of a lot more dangerous." Lily asked soberly, "What is the official count now?"

"Still depends on who's counting—somewhere between twenty-three and fifty-three."

"And there's no conspiracy," Lily jeered. "Yeah, right."

"House Judiciary Chair would say you're rushing to judgment. 'How do we know one Black church isn't burning its crosstown rival? C'mon now—you know those connivin' Black boys up to their ol' gamin' pin-the-tail-on-Whitey's ass. Prob'ly torched 'em themselves to cash in on the two-bit insurance policy.'"

"Insurance—another color-coded racket," segued Lily. "Rodney is hearing a case now—evidently, one of several developing around the country—history started out in the South—intentionally overcharging Black clients and, *then*, not delivering on contracted services. But you've heard this before, right?"

"Yeah, but what's the status of state legislation requiring insurance companies wanting to do business in California to prove they have no history of underwriting slaveholding property?"

"I'd have to check," said Lily. "But I'm sure your sources have a quicker turnaround than mine!"

"I don't know about that—I'm not the one married to a judge."

"I'll ask," said Lily. "Hey—I see the president continues taking a beating from the CBC."

"Earned every lick," said Lucius, detecting silence on Lily's end. "The man doesn't have my vote, not even my sympathy vote. So worried about race becoming a *campaign* issue. Try tellin' that to folks kneelin' in ash."

"Then, what about his visiting the rebuilt church?"

"I didn't say the man was dumb," said Lucius. "Of course, he's gonna go where he has some place to set his uncommanding Commander-in-Chief ass."

"It took them a year to rebuild—I can't imagine the disruption," said Lily. "It in no way compares, but it took Holy Innocents' a year just to remodel its little closet of a sacristy."

"In the meantime, all these poor rural churches been renamin' themselves: 'Holy Incense,' 'Holy Incineration.'" Lucius joked.

"Where are all the flag-waving Americans?" Lily railed. "Where were they when this year's Martin Luther King Day bonfires—well, you know this already—made it thirteen arsons around the holiday, alone, since 1990."

The last General Convention deputation meeting flashed through Lily's head, especially the Church's decision to hold its next national meeting in Arizona, a state still refusing to honor Martin Luther King Day. "It's not just the rebuilding, even if there were enough to cover the cost. Irreplaceable pieces of American history are being destroyed. I know some of the churches were built by freed slaves, free Black farmers—why has it taken so long to get to the bottom of this?"

"White supremacy's a powerful lobby in this country," declaimed Lucius, pulling back the curtain in his budget hotel room and feeling the heat off the window's glass. "Look at the World Trade Center bombing. Federal investigation was immediate and funded. A piece of scrap metal was enough to indict ten men.

"What if these were all white churches?" Lucius continued. "Agents be all over the place—look at the numbers: something like over a hundred federal agents and one million dollars committed to the standoff for a relatively few number of wacko Montana Freemen at *day* sixty-six compared to maybe fifty-three or more Black and interracial church arsons in the past seventeen *months*," Lucius fumed, "representing hundreds of terrorized Americans—still waiting for the Feds to investigate the threat to and the Constitutional protection of *their* religious liberty."

"So, Lucius, what is your part in all this?"

"To make a dent in the silence," said Lucius, straight-voiced. "To quote Lowery, 'The fifty-first state in this nation is the state of denial.' Local media is mute, and national is slim to nothing. And how many investigators—who, by the way, have only declared one case of conspiracy—might be part of the Good Ole Boys Roundup—"

"Wait, you said only *one* case?"

"Alabama. And the Black judge's home was shotgunned on the day of sentencing."

"Didn't even get a sound bite here," said Lily.

"'Cause it's repeating, not *making* history."

"Back up a minute, Lucius—what were you saying about a 'Good Ole Boys Roundup'?"

"You mean California police and fire boys don't sell licenses to hunt Black folk or wear King masks with a bullet hole in the forehead at an annual beer slosh, like they do in Tennessee?"

"You are kidding!"

"I know better than to kid a woman of the cloth," said Lucius, soberly. "The Good Ole Boys was special agent Gene Rightmyer's creation in 1980. Been drawing up to five hundred attendees in some parts every year since. In '92 ATF agents designed and promoted a T-shirt featuring a Black tot peering out of a pocket. The hunting licenses, along with T-shirts showing Dr. King's face targeted in a rifle's crosshairs, were among '95's souvenirs."

"This is outrageous!"

"First Amendment rights," said Lucius. "Two of Tennessee's Good Ole Boys are reportedly part of the local investigating team," said Lucius. "Doubt if we'll hear any report of an organized reign of terror out of that state any time soon, 'cause they don't see themselves as organized—and media goes along with the charade."

"Seems like they're as organized as they need to be—I hear changes are proposed to make civil rights arrests easier?"

"It's definitely in the works with good support in both the House and Senate."

"So, if it passes, the president's *gotta* sign off."

"He'd be halfway to getting my support in print."

"And what does he need to do to get the other half?"

"Money. The man needs to put some money into his late-ass effort. Anyway, enough of this—what's stirring at your house of worship?"

"No flames, thank God. We do have some Aryan activity on the other side of the tunnel from Bezerkeley, but I haven't heard of any plans to replace the Golden State's bear with Johnny Reb on California's flag."

"And no Klan memorabilia stores?"

"Now, you've *got* to be kidding!"

"No, Reverend Lily. But I could probably get you a catalogue. From the shop that opened up around the corner from the rebuilt church Hartwig and the president will be visiting next week."

"That creeps me out."

"That's the basic idea. Black folks been menaced for decades," said Lucius. "Even though every law enforcement officer right up to the president himself swears to uphold the Constitution, placing their hand, so-help-them-God, on the same Good Book Black hands got cut off for touching, and tongues cut out for reading."

"How do you stand it, Lucius?"

"By *taking* a stand and inciting others to do the same, hopefully—with my pen."

"Well, thanks, writer-man, for taking the time to call me," Lily gushed, then yelped, "Oh! I just looked at the clock! I gotta go. Sorry I'm so abrupt—I'm late for an appointment!"

"Don't let me hold you up—"

"I'll be praying for your safety, Lucius. And your mission."

"Thanks for your prayers and concern, preacher-woman," Lucius said, then added, "*and* the good conversation."

"As my kids would say—'It's all good.' You're a good man, Lucius."

"And as Flannery O'Connor would say, 'A good man . . .'"

"'Is hard to find.' I know. It's Rodney's favorite line. Or something close to it."

"May I call again, Lily?"

"You *better* call again. Just to let me know you haven't been killed in the line of duty. Actually—how *would* I know if somebody made you disappear?"

"After a few days my decomposing body would begin to smell and someone with a nose for missing Black men would come looking."

Lily needed to bring the call to a quick goodbye, but not without speaking her piece. "Okay. Enough morbidity. So far, except wood and upholstery, no fatalities are associated with the burnings. Well, that's not true, either—the number of cultural fatalities is huge. Anyway. What am I trying to say? Just please be safe, Lucius."

"Absolutely."

"Catch me again, and . . . God keep you safe, Lucius."

"You, too, Lily. Give my regards to Rodney."

"I will. Goodbye, Lucius."

"And Lily," Lucius tacked on, "if you don't hear from me in a week, please do *not* call the Texas Rangers."

"I know," whimpered Lily. "More childhood heroes struck down by their ambivalent history, which goes along with their ambivalent name. Got it, Mr. Kent. Got your cape?" Lily tossed into the phone, as she opened the desk drawer where her purse was kept. "Okay, gotta go."

"GRAMMA CALLED," SAID ZORA, barely looking up from the TV.

"And?" Zora had already forgotten that her mother was in the room. Lily walked over and stood in front of the screen. "Zora—child! What did your grandmother say?"

"I don't know. Just about us comin' down this summer." Lily was reminded of her promise to check on flights for all three kids to spend the first two weeks of July in Birmingham with their Davis relatives. "I really, really don't wanna go. I think I'm gonna be busy."

"We'll talk about it when your dad gets home," said Lily, glad not to have to make any decisions or act as patient listener for maybe the next half hour. "Gramma 'Nola say anything else?" Lily tried holding Zora's attention until she got her second question answered.

Clicking the remote control, the daughter gave up only the time it took to make a one-word response to her mother. "Nope." Lily decided it was a minor battle and moved out of her mute daughter's viewing line. Finding the juice pitcher left in the refrigerator empty except for a swallow, Lily swore under her breath and filled her glass with ice water instead.

Lily had suspected Zora's lack of enthusiasm for the annual summer visit with Rodney's family. Dezzy seemed lukewarm also. Perhaps this would be Wylie's time to have the stage all to himself. His cousin Troy, Sharon's boy, was a year older, but shorter, making the age difference moot in terms of compatibility. It would be interesting to see the two together now, with another tick on the growth chart and Wylie's official entrance into puberty.

Lily thought about how boys seemed to handle it better. Girls still, upon reaching their teens, her own daughter no exception she was sorry to say, began setting a hierarchy of beauty in place and foregoing female friendship, if a male date were floating around as even a vague possibility. No wonder the high suicide rate among gay teens, she thought. Acceptance was hard enough for so-called straight kids.

As she sat on the end of the bed pulling socks on, Lily heard the garage door open. She yelled down, before appearing on the stairs that led down to the kitchen, "Rodney, is that you?" *If we can just get through the next five years with our sanity intact*, Lily concluded her maternal ruminations.

"Hey, sweetie pie," Lily said, kissing Rodney and knocking him off balance.

"Whoa, kisses still pack a punch," said Rodney, stooping to pick up his briefcase. "How was your day?"

"Before I go through my litany, do you have Wylie with you?"

Rodney set his case back down, kicking it flush with the kitchen counter, saying, "My turn? Sorry, babe. I forgot." And picking his keys off the counter, he said as he opened the door, "I'll go get him right away. Sorry."

"Pick up a pizza? I'll call in the order."

"Round Table or—what's the other? Chicago style?"

Lily had left the room and reappeared with coupons retrieved from her purse. "Take these. I think they're still good. What's today?"

"Fourth."

"Yeah. These are good till Friday. Thanks, sweetie." Noticing her mate's sagging shoulders, she added, "I'll ice the beer mugs while you're gone."

"That'll help."

Lily came closer and, putting her arms around Rodney's neck, moved into her husband's manfragrance.

"Woman, you want pizza or more of me?" Rodney smeared his generous smile all over Lily's lips.

Coming up for air, Lily replied, "Both."

Rodney drew back and sighed, "I know. Wylie's waiting."

"Sorry, sweetheart."

"THAT WAS EASY. THANKS FOR dinner," said Lily, running her eyes slowly over Rodney. "All that and providing pizza too."

"I'll give you a pizza, woman, wid awwwl the toppings!" said Rodney, his hunky chest leaning halfway across the table. "No extra charge."

Just then, Zora entered the room, interrupting her parents' tabletop foreplay. "Can you sign this?"

"I think I can manage," said Lily, moving items around in the drawer by the stove, looking for the pen always kept there. "Well, I guess I spoke too soon."

"Here," said Zora, sullenly. "Use this one."

"What is this for, again?"

"Field trip. Lawrence Hall of Science. Next Tuesday."

"You'd be great in a hostage situation, Zor'," said Rodney. "Wouldn't give up any secrets to the enemy."

"Very funny," Zora said snidely. Recently, she had gotten her hair cut short and permed, achieving the desired look of cute corkscrews popping out of her head, kept somewhat in check by one of a new wardrobe of colorful scarves and twisted wraps. Lily worried that her very hip daughter looked too mature for fifteen. For the moment, however, she submerged her deeper motherly concern by taking inventory of her daughter's body piercings, knowing, even so, how superficially assuaging it was. So far, Zora had no rings or studs in her eyebrows and no other new decoration "bolted to her person," as Rodney would say. When Lily refused to give Zora money for navel-accessorizing on her last birthday, the girl used the check sent from Rodney's parents. Lily prayed for Zora's discretion in writing that thank-you note to the grandparents.

"I think what your mother is trying to say, and I agree, is that we'd like to be able to have a decent conversation every now and then with you."

"Over signing a form? Why you always doggin' me?"

"Sorry," Lily said, returning her daughter's irritation. "Are we boring you?"

"Whatever."

"Well, if we don't see you before the moon, have a good sleep, Zor'," Lily twittered, followed by instant self-reproach for following suit with her adolescent daughter's annoyance. Knowing it was the wrong thing even as she was saying it, Lily hastily added, "We love you." It sounded like the afterthought that it was.

"Can I go?" Zora replied.

Lily and Rodney looked at their daughter leaving the room as if she couldn't get away from her parents fast enough, and then looked at each other. They held their laughter until Zora's peevish form was out of sight and earshot.

"It's not us," issued Rodney.

"No, it's not us," Lily agreed. "Most definitely not us. Let's hope the research is true and our daughter develops beyond the one-word response."

"Hey—I caught some twos and threes in that last interchange," said Rodney, still laughing.

"I'm glad you can laugh about it."

"Hell. The crap in human disguise that comes across my desk every day makes our daughter look like teacher's pet." Cocking his head to one side, Rodney set his eyes on Lily and vocalized his thoughts. "The daughter follows the mother. And the mother is a *beautiful* woman." Rodney liked seeing Lily's face flush. "What were *you* like at Zora's age?"

Opening the refrigerator door, Lily asked, "You want another beer?"

"Split one," said Rodney. "You stalling?"

"No. I'm actually just trying to remember," said Lily, wondering if memories lagged because of the usual suspects— physiology, the "generation gap"—or was it something else? Could there be a *race* gap with her daughter?

"Okay. Here's one little something my brain just squeezed out. Me, a year younger than Zora, at the one drive-in in Greenville, Texas, sitting between my sister Dee and her boy-friend in the front seat of his '58 convertible Chevy, eating a paper-wrapped cheeseburger and embarrassed at slopping ketchup on my new shorts from the squatty bottle Deke would *borrow* from the outdoor counter."

"Pretty vivid."

"How about you?"

"Nothing I can recall as a fourteen-year-old female." Rodney grinned at Lily. "But I do have distinct memories as a contentious roustabout just starting to get a whiff of himself—"

"That expression!" pounced Lily. "That is such Black idiom."

"Suth'n-Black idiom, please," Rodney corrected. "So, yeah. Any more on that page?"

"Yeah," said Lily. "I've never heard you use that before. Actually, I hardly hear you use *any* 'Suth'n Black idiom.' Are you intentionally decoloring your speech for the benefit of our inter-color family?"

"Wait a minute," Rodney bristled. "Where is *that* coming from? I say one thing, and I'm indicted for not saying more."

"Well, sometimes I wonder if in normalizing our life together, we haven't sacrificed distinction. And, I've never heard that 'at the age of smelling one's self' applied to females."

"That's 'cause you didn't grow up *Afro* American."

"This household isn't *Afro* American enough? Don't forget, this white mother-girl's *still* growin' up," said Lily, reclaiming the right to her opinion. "Seriously, though, did your mother talk that way about your sisters when they reached puberty?"

"Along with my grandmother, aunties, and all the church mothers. We might have been uptown in style, but we was down-home in our, what did you call it? 'Black idiom.'"

"Speaking of Black expression, before I forget, Lucius Clay called today. He sends his regards to you." Lily waited to read her husband's face for reaction, before going on. Rodney finished off the last drop of beer and swiped his moustache with a napkin, right side first then left, more crisply than usual, Lily thought. Continuing, as if answering a question from Rodney, she said, "Yeah. He's part of an AP special investigative team looking into Black church arsons in the South."

"Where did he call from?"

"Ashes of the latest fire. Greensboro, Alabama. Rising Son Baptist—burned to the ground."

"Any suspects?"

"None so far. And, they say they won't be able to determine the cause without 'more examination of the evidence,' which was gathered while there were still hot embers just before dawn."

"Insurance?"

"Undetermined how much it will cover, or at least he didn't say. Pretty good-sized congregation, though. Two hundred fifty members. There was a service scheduled for tonight. Supposedly being held at a community center."

MEMORIES OF THE *TWO* SERVICES that sad spring in South Carolina flooded Lily's head. Saint Luke's furtive afterword in the parish hall that evening. White pockets hiding conversation that hushed at Lily's approach . . . next day, grim faces of pallbearers conveying Sam Jefferson's casket out of Mount Sinai Church of Deliverance to the cadence of voices backed up by a cheerfully mournful organ. "Black idiom"— too much Black idiom back then for Lily's breaking heart and ignorance about slavery's broad legacy.

"Jesus. I wouldn't want that smoldering mess in Oakland's backyard. Arson's hardest to prove, because most of the evidence is destroyed," said Rodney. "Proving it's motivated by hate's even harder."

"The media and investigators both seem to exploit that fact. By the way, why *does* a *white* seventeen-year-old choose to set fire to a *Black* church?"

"You and a whole host of other folks askin' the same question, since things heated up more, pardon the pun, in February."

"Yeah, like history can just be set aside."

"We claim to be a people innocent until proven guilty."

"Unless you happen to be gay or Black or some other permutation of white heteromale people," finished Lily.

———

THERE WAS NO MOVEMENT OF air that night. The smell of burnt wood hung over the neighborhood for a ten-block radius. It was old wood they burned. Old growth cut and hauled by horse-drawn dray from the hills to the east.

Rising Son Baptist was built by hands that knew hard work. Building the church was a labor of love. Renovations had been made over the course of a half century: classrooms added, and a meeting hall. Groups from within, as well as outside, the congregation used the hall to conduct business, to stay sober, to commemorate passages, to plan the next church social.

Reverend Ellis Greene began the service with a prayer: "Bless your people, Lord God Almighty, as we gather here with the smell of betrayal still in our nostrils; betrayal of your almighty purpose, Lord, to make us one with each other, O Lord, and one with you. The smell of the enemy still in our nostrils, as we mourn the violence that set match to our building and took it, ash by ash, floating heavenward. Redeem this act of violence, Savior Jesus, 'cause we know you have the might to heal. . . ."

The congregation answered, "Yes, preacher. . . ."

"We know that you do not willingly inflict your wrath on us or whoever did this. . . ."

"Yes, Lord. . . ." hummed the congregation.

"We know that you are a God of compassion whose almighty hand can come down and lift us up!"

"Ohhhh, yes!" was shouted from the back of the hall.

". . . right now, can come down and lift up your people!"

"Yes, Lord!"

"You took the Israelites through the muddy waters. . . ."

"Yes, He did . . . yes, Lord, uh-huh. . . ."

"You opened up the way. . . ."

"Uh-huh!"

"Whatever stood in their way . . ."

"Thassright. . . ."

"What*ever* the obstacle—you moved it aside. . . ."

"Yes, He did, yes, He did!"

"You parted the waters, your mighty arm quick to save. If you wanted to, you could resurrect that building before our very eyes. The temple of Jerusalem—I say the temple of *Jerusalem* . . ."

"He know. . . ."

"The temple of Jerusalem destroyed by the enemy and Jesus say, 'I raise it up—in three days I raise it up again.'"

"Yes, Lord!"

"Whatever our sorrow, whatever our loss—whatever vengeance come knockin' on our door, sayin', 'Let me in,'— we see the tares of the enemy for the scrawny weeds they are, and we re*buke* the one tryin' to sow his seed among us now!"

"Thassright!"

"We know you can turn our mourning into dancing . . . wipe away every tear. This injustice will not stand!"

"Don't He know it!"

". . . does not have a *hambone* to stand on. God will not permit the wolf back in our midst—lickin' his big ol' dirty chops, thinkin' he catch one of us sleepin' an' not watchin'. . . ."

"Yes, Lord!"

"You gon' have to show your teeth. 'You be snarlin' an' growlin'—but you cain't have none of my sheep!' saith the Lord. 'You be circlin' 'round, *hongry* hangin' awwllll *over* your pitiful face. But you can't have none of my sheep!'"

"No, sir!"

"You try awwllll your cunnin' tricks—but you cain't get to the sheep. . . ."

"No, he can't, uh-huh. . . ."

"Because the Good Shepherd has your number! Maybe the police don't have it. But the One who sees awl and knows awl has it!"

"He know . . . He know. . . ."

"And is attendin' to our sufferin' right now . . . is answerin' our cry right now."

"Yes, He is. . . ."

"Thank you, Lord, for bein' with us right now, exorcisin' the hate that burned our church—keepin' the wolf outside the door. We will not let him in! We will not let him in!"

Clapping, the congregation began shouting out the chant, some improvising their own descants. Those able got up out of their seats and marched. Suddenly, all gettin' happy stopped. "Call 911!" screamed one of the sixteen-year-olds posting watch outside, as he ran in and down the center aisle. "Fools took a shot at Stevie!"

Ellis dialed 911 on his walkie-talkie phone, while the deacons circulated in the community center hall telling everyone to stay down and keep calm. "Be here'n a minute. Ms. Johnson's boy on duty, gon' come see 'bout this mess any minute now." One mother, both hands full of youngsters, was making for the door, but was told, "You jus' stay put where you are . . . bes' be prayin', not leavin'."

A police siren could be heard screaming up Fourth Street. Lieutenant Johnson got out of the squad car and ran into the meeting hall. He saw his grandmother, arms raised, beseeching "Lawd-God-Almighty" to end the violence disruptin' her and her brothers and sisters at Rising Son Baptist Church.

"WE NEVER ATE COLLARDS IN the summer." Lily overheard the small woman counsel her walking companion whose right leg was bowed, causing a dip in her step. "But when the first frost comes, that's when you eat 'em. Otherwise, you get indigestion."

Just then, before Lily could go around the pair walking in front of her, a streak of black spandex with hot pink elbow pads and matching inline skate wheels passed Lily and the ambling women of another generation on the left, cutting Ss as she danced to some internal music.

At 15th and Lakeshore, downwind of Merritt Bakery, Lily remembered the order for her son's birthday cake: a baseball diamond with Wylie's number seven painted on the miniature first baseman. Thank God he had agreed to celebrating his thirteenth birthday after Saturday's game, requiring minimal parental effort. On Monday, Lily had found on the kitchen table the piece of notebook paper inscribed with signature variations of "Scott Davis" in Wylie's handwriting, as if by using his middle name, he was trying to reinvent himself upon reaching the age of reason.

Now that Confirmation was, if at all, typically an older teen or adult rite of passage, there was no *bar mitzvah* comparable, signifying Wylie's—or "Scott's"—rite of passage in the Episcopal Church community. Pony League would have to do for now, Lily mused, watching Korean elders perform *their* ritual early morning exercise, gently sculpting the air while a modern-day Pan played his flute, sitting cross-legged on a bench just outside the white wood-framed gazebo.

ON THE CURVE OF THE HEART-shaped lake's left half, the old Alameda County Court House smiled through its Loma Prieta cracks. Lily smiled back, wondering what was happening with the news-grabbing case being heard in her husband's courtroom a couple of blocks away.

The president had appointed Rodney eighteen months into office with little opposition, both sides of the aisle feeling a solid win in the attorney respected as a Constitutional law expert. Rodney hadn't been able to leave his desk until late every night that week; this evening would be no different. His meticulous research, and better, his ability to focus upon a case's defining issue amidst all the legal clutter often meant the difference between life and death for poor Americans represented by overworked, inexperienced government-appointed counsel who did not or could not do right by their clients.

" . . . **THE POWER OF FEMALE** sexuality poses a threat to the existing order and authority. One way of controlling the threat is to label women prophets as somehow immoral . . . out of *social* order." Lily heard her own voice addressing the mostly female audience, larger than expected for the Center's first brown bag lunch in the middle of summer session opening week for the Graduate Theological Union.

The Center for Women and Religion was established as a necessary corrective, an outpost to Berkeley's consortium of theological schools at a time when women from all denominations were sensing and wanting to act on a call to public ministry. A call, however, not all seminaries were eager to validate.

"Even though women are entering ordained ministry in greater numbers—when they enter the pulpit to preach, there is not the same sort of institutional support to do so . . . often clear that women are *heard* in a different way than men. This has both positive and negative aspects. . . ." Lily looked out at her audience, thought of her daughter Zora, as well as her good friend Fran, and longed to see more women of color. Though fifteen years her senior and a prominent daughter of Oakland's Chinatown, it was almost a decade more than Lily that Fran Toy was the first Asian American woman ordained priest. Optimists could say more were enrolling than when she was in seminary, but Lily, detesting the whole business of statistical objectification of persons, anyway, knew that "more than one" was hardly a laudable number.

"Being aware of subtle and not so subtle social, political, and cultural forces of dualism increases consciousness about how women's words are received without feeling *personally* undermined. Women colleagues can assist the development of this critical consciousness."

As she finished, Lily wondered about the extent to which even she, married to a Black man and mother of biracial children, assumed a mostly white audience. Like the demographics inventories that used to frustrate her children in school, because of no accurate place to record their Black-and-whiteness, what of her own thinking and expression did she need to reexamine and update?

THE SOBBING CALL CAME THAT evening in the middle of Lily's macaroni and cheese supper with the kids. Rodney was working late as usual. LaVerne Tubman's call had been expected any time in the last several weeks as her only son lay dying. Lawrence was survived by his partner, Keith, and his mother's furious sadness.

LaVerne's so-called son-in-law was rendered invisible by family whose experience narrowed the definition of love to what worked for their heterosexual lives. As they saw it, sex between a man and a woman was God-issued regulation. Anything else was sin, punishable by God's ways. Ways as mysterious as the AIDS epidemic and the HIV virus that spawned it.

Laverne's family spoke out their opinion but stifled their questions. They feared putting a crack in their orthodoxy and being sucked out through that crack. They did not want to risk becoming outsiders to the world as they believed it to be.

Though her family observed John's gospel, "In my house are many rooms," for comforting mourners of God's "deserving," Lawrence's mother wanted no part of their quibbling with the One who created her baby boy. LaVerne presumed her boy's occupancy in God's "house," and his partner Keith's too. How else could their love have survived the nastiness still shaking its threatening fist?

"I never thought I would lose him before he lost me," faltered LaVerne. "I feel so bad. Like there was something I didn't do or didn't do right." LaVerne drew in a breath and continued, "But I think I did everything I knew to do. And still, it wasn't enough." Her voice breaking again, "Oh, Vida, I just hurt so much. He was my baby. The only one God gave me."

"And he always will be," said Lily, "and Keith?" She had been in almost daily contact with Lawrence's partner in recent weeks, both giving and receiving help. At the same time he lived with his partner's imminent death, Keith was parish legal counsel. He advised Lily and the vestry as they dealt with another parishioner's illegal use of charitable funds that had been collected in Holy Innocents' name.

LAWRENCE TUBMAN'S SERVICE WAS scheduled for Friday afternoon. That morning, as she did sit-ups, Lily watched the CNN report on a fire intentionally set in Charlotte, North Carolina. ". . . destroyed a ninety-three-year-old church sanctuary about to be renovated and turned into a wedding chapel, making this the twenty-ninth arson since 1995."

Lily sat up straight at the interview with the young white mayor expressing his confidence in local police and fire officials to solve the crime and hoping, on camera, that the fire at the Black church surrounded by mostly white subdivisions might remain "a strictly local concern."

Another spokesperson for the segregationist-hyphen-American platform, thought Lily, as she watched investigators on-screen sift through the church's ashes for clues, while a voice overlay reported on other agents "continuing to look into fires in Tennessee, Louisiana, South Carolina, Mississippi, North Carolina, Virginia, and Georgia, which African American leaders have charged were racially motivated."

She felt the hairs on her neck rise as journalist Michael Fomento launched into a refutation of the Black leaders' statement. He focused anecdotal remarks on the *exceptional* arsonist and failed to note how few arrests had been made. *Lucius is dead on*, she thought. *If white churches were burning . . .*

LONELY HOURS DRAGGED THEIR FEET preceding her son's church funeral and cemetery burial. Happier hours followed at the reception held in the parish hall, gathering friends, fellow parishioners, and whatever family relations able to declare themselves available to God's tender show of mercy. Still, Lawrence's mother wondered how she would make it through the night, the next morning, and the next evening.

"I fixed you a plate, Mom. If you do a good job on your dessert," Keith cajoled, "we'll see about some meat and vegetables." He set down a paper plate divided into quadrants by a square of brownie, two different kinds of cookie, and a lemon bar in front of LaVerne. He placed another one featuring the same items on the table in front of the chair next to her. Bringing her one-spoon-of-sugar coffee order, Keith then moved his mother-in-law's cane to another chairback and returned to sit beside her.

———

"**GRIDDLE ME THIS, DAD. WHO** you got goin' against MJ on the boards, game three?"

"Well, if I were a betting man—" began Rodney, intently installing blueberries steaming their own sockets in pancake batter.

"Which you are!" hooted the boy named after his paternal great-grandmother.

"What number are you as *Scott*?" asked Rodney, angling for a catch of his son's laughter on the boy's thirteenth birthday, while plopping another quartet of pancakes in the cast iron pan that was a wedding gift from Wylie's namesake.

Rodney chuckled every time he thought about the family-designed flow chart supposedly leading up to his grandmother finally accepting Lily as Rodney's future wife and newest branch, by marriage, of the Davis tree. The family had deftly sidestepped an encounter between Gramma Willy in bed with the flu and Rodney's fiancée, during the New Year's visit when they officially became engaged. But the wily matriarch discovered Lily's problematic "culluh" on her own.

After snooping into thank-you notes with photo enclosures sent by her daughter 'Nola's future daughter-in-law following the visit, the old woman demanded a private audience with Lily. Arranged at the grandmother's convenience, Lily, then priest in charge of South Bronx Grace Church, had managed to find coverage during the busy Lenten season.

"The girl's sensibilities" were what tipped the scales for Willie Pinker Tuttle almost a decade after civil rights legislation was enacted more quickly than it was implemented or enforced. "The girl has a head on her shoulders equal to Rodney's," issued from Gramma Willie following her closed-door meeting with Lily. "Enola. You still have my bridal veil? Let's see if't fits Rodney's girl."

She was too infirm to travel to New York for the wedding, not that she would have if she were able. The family had learned their lesson not to leave correspondence lying around. Gramma Tuttle passed on before Lily's priestly vocation was ever disclosed.

"If you don't know and you're the coach, then I got nooooo respect for my elder!" boomed Wylie, laying out the pink, blue, and gold Monopoly bills in stacks. "You *know* the Cats have never had nothin' on first 'til Lucky Number Seven!"

The banter always about sports, like their complicated system of betting on teams and individual players—and for particular games—was all part of the father and son's Saturday morning ritual. Lily protected its sacredness by claiming the need to sleep in "just another half hour" and synchronizing her kitchen entry with Rodney's laying out the still-sizzling bacon on folded sheets of paper towel.

"Happy Birthday to you, happy birthday to you, happy birthday—" Lily sang to her new teen, until he stopped her, saying, "Okay. You've proven for the thirteenth year that you can't sing."

"Wait a minute," laughed Lily. "How would you remember what I sounded like when you were a one-year-old . . . or two or three for that matter!"

"Present performance reflects the past," said well-named Wylie. "That's what the judge say."

"The judge *say*, sit down and eat your pancakes and quit sassin' the woman responsible for your birth," said his father.

"Beautiful Momma, how many of these custom-made cakes you want—you got your number 7, age 13, a W—and my personal favorite, a blueberry baseball diamond—"

"And an S."

"Thassright. Cain't f'get the S," smiled Rodney. "Lily, you know our boy's changed his name?"

"Haven't changed it," declared Wylie. "Scott's my middle name."

"Okay, so how many and what kind can I get you, little lady?" asked Rodney, spatula poised to flip the four pancakes already in the broad cast iron pan. "And don't forget the Brown 'N Serve. Got yours browned just the way you like 'em!" Rodney leered.

Lily indulgently shook her head at the man and looked lovingly at the child who, of their three creations, inherited more of their dad's mahogany and all of his large personality. She remembered how closely she had inspected the nine-pound, two-ounce naked newborn for evidence of her maternity. She had to look no further than the splotch of red on the back of his neck under the fuzzy fringe of Wylie's perfectly shaped head to know this one was hers, also. Rodney thanked Lily, still groggy from the exertion of delivering such a big baby, saying every family needed at least one "redneck," and, now, theirs had two.

It was different when she was a new mother of twins. Though even small identifying traits like mole placement were of utmost interest to Lily, immediately after their delivery she was too exhausted and relieved to take inventory of which characteristics came from whom. She laughed now to think it didn't take long to notice how, well before big teeth replaced baby teeth, the twins' smiles seemed cut and pasted from their grandfather Wallace's photo.

"So, Dad, you never answered my question," Wylie took up the matter of betting again.

"About my pick?" said Rodney, back at the serious matter of his Monopoly-money bet. Since his son had the Bulls, he was forced to choose from his second-best Seattle Supersonics. "Jump-and-grab Kemp. Unless I go with Never-Late-Nate, steady-as-a-Stockton McMillan. Of course, we also have the Oakland's fine native brother. My man, first-in-steals, tenth-in-assists Payton. The Gluuhhhve. Might need till the *end* of your birthday 'fore I can let you know, son."

"Sure," said Wylie, anxious to leave with his coach dad for pregame warm-up at the field near Mills College.

"You guys get going. I got the dishes," said Lily, as eager to have them leave so as to have a slice of the morning to herself. "I'll be there by the first pitch—promise! With BBQ stuff: hotdogs, buns, chips . . . anything I've left out?"

Wylie looked up, startled out of readying his backpack. "I thought you said you ordered a cake?"

"Oh, thanks for reminding me! I'll swing by and pick that up first. It's from your favorite bakery over by your dad's and my offices."

"You're kind of ditzy sometimes, Mom."

"But you love me, right?"

Wylie pulled his lips tight and gave them a twist to ensure that nothing sappy would escape from his thirteen-year-old mouth.

"Better get going, guys," Lily shooed. "And don't forget the bat!"

"Touché, Mom. Very funny," said the child for whom trips to the orthodontist would soon be added to Lily's already-bulging chauffeur schedule.

LILY LISTENED TO THE NEWS on her way back home from getting the matches forgotten on her first trip to the baseball diamond. Cokie Roberts announced the names of the two

Black pastors from burned-out churches flanking the president in his regular radio address on the heels of the latest arson. "It is clear that racial hostility is the driving force behind a number of these incidents," the president stated forcefully. "This must stop."

———

THE NEXT MONDAY, LILY HEARD from Lucius again. "Two more arsons."

"In my hometown."

"Greenville, Texas? I knew that. Did I know that?" Lucius spun. "We must have talked about that back in the other Green*vile*—no, that's too harsh. Appears to be a nice place other than two charred churches. One's got about a thousand bucks worth of damage; the other, the one with insurance, is burned to the bones."

"Thank God it wasn't the reverse."

"I'd have *more* reason to thank God if the burnings would stop altogether."

"Like the president."

"Yeah. I'm glad to see some action, finally," fumed Lucius. "Something productive may actually come out of the weekend meetings with our president and his attorney general."

"CNN reported her promise, at least, that the administration would devote whatever resources necessary to solve the crimes—"

"We'll see what happens today when Black leadership meets with the whatever-resources-necessary people at the Treasury."

"I expect more strong words'll be exchanged."

"And so there should be," said Lucius, flaring. "I was still in South Carolina last Wednesday when the governor toured some of the burned churches and pledged his support to fight racism. Maybe he could start by lowering that rag that's flown in the face of decency and the Black community since school integration days. Like the wolf needs a reminder that its teeth are still sharp," hissed Lucius. "South Carolina's historic Confederate *legacy*—damn fool knows very well— who the hell doesn't know?—just whose historic *legacy* from which side of the color line he's referring to."

"Yeah, certain pastors complained about investigations making members of their flock feel like suspects. I'm sitting there listening to this in disbelief and trying to imagine being in their collar. . . ." Lily's voice drifted off.

"It's not the collar; it's the color," Lucius rejoined. "Double jeopardy. Burned out congregations defending themselves against local law enforcement that failed to do its job in the first place. Same beast—only now, the wolf's in charge of protecting the sheep *inside* the fence."

Continuing his monologue, Lucius didn't hear the cellar door close as Lily pulled herself in to quietly wait out the storm and dab at the fresh scrape of his upbraiding. "To date, only *Black* church burnings have included racial vandalism . . . and only *whites* have been arrested in those cases. You can't convict *juveniles* of hate crimes, you know, like the thirteen-year-old missy responsible for Thursday night's blaze. And they're playing up the satanic beliefs angle with her, 'cause in this new civil rights era we don't wanna *re*call the recent past. . . ."

His words pressed into her ears like wads of cotton, losing their individual distinction. "Add *those* uncounted numbers to all the *unsolved* crimes against the Black church. No suspect, no arrest. No arrest, no charge and no conviction for the record. *Plus*, nobody monitoring the record. Crime pays big dividends to white supremacists seen as individuals committing random acts."

Lily wanted Lucius to know that she understood the female-nonetheless-a-white-female facts of American life.

That she was up to the race-trumping-gender battle. None-theless. She felt suffocated by Lucius's cutting response to her attempt to sympathize with the pastors of violated churches. Finding an air bubble, Lily said, "I can't know the depth of your frustration, certainly. . . ."

Her stilted voice jolted him to retrieve his audience. "By the way, where did you live in Greenville?"

Albeit embarrassed at Lucius's apparent notice that she couldn't take the heat, Lily was glad the billows stoking the fire of his complaint were temporarily idled. "Our house was on Sayle Street, but I reckon it's long gone now. Probably torn down to make way for the Texas equivalent of a Jack-in-the-Box."

"Or a church," said Lucius, realizing the potential utility of Lily's Texas roots. "Was there only one Catholic church when you lived here?"

"Yes. Which made it one more than the number of synagogues," said Lily drily. "See any Stars of David on Greenville's skyline?"

"Neither skyline nor Yellow Pages."

"Must still be the same as my last visit."

"How many times have you been back?"

His question sobered Lily; she had not thought about Greenville *wholesale*. Only bits and pieces. "What I meant was my last visit—*ever*. I buried my mother about twenty years ago."

"I'm sorry," said Lucius. "What did she die of?"

"She had an adverse reaction to . . . life."

"A sad heart?"

"Depleted," said Lily. "Actually, it was a reaction to medication. If she hadn't lived alone . . . well, anyway, that's in the past. So, Lucius. *Greenville*. Do you think it budged from the fifties?"

"Not if most of Greenville was divided up into something like seventy Protestant congregations back then. . . ."

". . . each tagged with its own doctrinal and racial assertions, purportedly biblical, that gauge whether you're going to heaven or hell," she finished. Then, thinking about her church youth group and camp experiences, added, "And a set of rules for calibrating your head and heart."

"No wonder y'all took the train bound for New York." Lily took his comment as a compliment. "So, Lily. *Oaktown.* How're things in your port o' call?"

"Parishioner's funeral clobbered everyone's emotions Friday. He died of AIDS. One of the unlucky ones who couldn't tolerate drug therapy. We anticipated his death . . . still, I always pray for a miracle."

"It sounds rough. You close to the family?"

"Very. It's tough when a kid, even an adult kid, precedes a parent, especially an only child like Lawrence." Lily recalled LaVerne's smile at Keith's attentions. "But Lawrence bequeathed his partner. Lawrence's mother loves Keith like another son."

"And, how's *your* family?"

"Usual teen–parent dynamics. Plus one. Our youngest, Wylie, turned thirteen Saturday, immediately after the Wildcats—for which he plays shortstop—whipped their rival, the Yankees."

"Congratulations on his maturity . . . and your and Rodney's youth."

"Hey, hey," returned Lily. "We're gonna discount the *best* seat in the house next time you're out our way. Oh, and by the way, I asked Rodney about that legislation, you know, about insurance companies seeking to do business in California needing to prove they'd not previously done business with slave-holding entities."

"And?"

"He knows about it. There's talk the ACLU could bring a test case to Rodney's courtroom." Lily shuddered at her husband's high-risk work; since the violent sixties, California judges were allowed to carry a gun. "Did you hear they're going ahead with that lawsuit in Georgia? Multimillion restitution for overcharged *non-white* policyholders."

"Hell. Their *survivors* be lucky to see any of that settlement before *they* die!"

As quickly as she had brought it up, Lily changed the subject. "Where are you staying?"

"There's a Double Tree Inn on the outskirts of town. Nice enough." Lucius was glad to be on the hotel's third floor, where he was less accessible to anyone who might have a problem with his being in Greenville. Of course, similar precautions didn't save King from a sniper's bullet. "Three white boys were arrested last night, then released, after the second church burned while they sat in a holding cell. No other suspects beyond those three."

"Meaning, the arsonist or arsonists are still at large . . . creepy times."

"When aren't they?" Lucius returned. "I'll hollah at y'all though, if there're any new developments."

"Well, watch your back," she said, vocalizing her body's tremor. "Y'all travel in pairs?"

"Yeah, we special AP dicks are on the buddy system, *y'all*."

"*Y'all* take care then, Lucius. And thanks, fer the cawl," Lily drawled. "Got me lookin' forward to that next press conference . . . all the way from *Green-vull, Texas*." Then, as an afterthought prompted by hearing the name of her hometown in her own Texas accent, "Hey—do you think in your *special* investigating, you could do me a *special* favor?"

"Been waiting to return the one done unto me in Oakland," smiled Lucius.

"Really, Lucius. That was no big deal—not even big enough to mention again," Lily laughed. "So, pleeease, make this the last time you bring that triflin' mess *up*."

"As you desire, Miss Kitty—now what can my smokin' gun do for you while I'm *in town?*"

"If it isn't too much of a bother, could you check out whether the old Ritz Theater is still standing? And Jack's Drive-In—also, Robbie's Drugs?"

"I could do that. Anything else, Rev'nd Lily?"

"For now, thanks," said Lily. "Call me if you find them."

"I may be calling *on* you, said Lucius. "To fill in some of the gaps as another point and person in Greenville time."

"Any way I can help you, ask," she quickly obliged, "though it's been awhile since I've poked around in that attic."

"Thanks, Lily. Hasta luego."

"Yeah, hasta lumbago to you. Be safe, Lucius."

LILY SAT IN HER MINIVAN at the curb, waiting for Desmond to emerge from the small shop down the street from the gated south entrance to Mills College. She recalled a visit to Birmingham a few years before, when she had watched a red-throated linnet fly in and out of the hanging baskets of the lavender silk morning glories dotting her mother-in-law's patio. Requiring no watering, the artificial flowers had freed up the widow's time for water aerobics and tap and line dancing. Rodney's mother reported to Lily that she had taken those three baby birds making their flying debut from the colorful baskets outside her kitchen window the week before as a sign of blessing on her pragmatic aesthetics. The way *she* saw it, if God's own natural creatures couldn't tell the difference between a turnkey nest and a more labor intensive, built-from-scratch one, who else could?

But as they continued their conversation, a hummingbird making a pit stop hovered, frantically inserting its beak into one and then another of the attractive pale purple centers before flying off again. "That's right, baby, don't keep goin' after what you want from what you know can't give you what you want," Enola admonished. "That li'l, itty bitty thing just proved that some birds are smarter than humans." The lesson had stuck with Lily and for some reason, came to mind as she waited for her son outside the hair parlor that had done 'dos from forties conks and marcels to nineties fades, twists, and weaves.

"LIKE 'EM?" A BEAMING DESMOND pivoted for his mom to admire the full three-sixty of his newly planted cornrows, before climbing into the passenger side.

"Looks good," said Lily, detecting new inches added to her son's height, as her sides pulled when she reached over to finger the tight braids on his head. "How's it feel?"

"Like a *new man.* . . ." Lily automatically filled in the *Black* modifier, realizing yet another experience she'd never share with her children, something she seemed to have been doing with increasing frequency ever since Dezzy and Zora hit their teens. "Who did it—Angie?"

Pulling down the vanity mirror to bask in his changed appearance, Desmond replied, "Nah, this other girl Rhonda worked on me." Lily watched as her son's fingers followed the length of each braided row. "Go for it, Moms."

"Pffff," scoffed Lily, all of a sudden business-like, shifting her attention to starting up the car. "A lame Bo Derek–wannabe? That's *just* what you need."

"Just 'cause you're *white*—"

"Exactly," snorted Lily. "Exactly why cornrows look good on you, and not on me."

"Dang, Moms! Somethin' got your goat!" hooted Desmond. "Wanna talk about it?"

Desmond had her priestly persona down. Enunciating each word, Lily flicked her son's ear with her reply. "Very . . . funny."

"Hey! I *like* your red-beige look. It's unique!"

So my son thinks I'm unique. "Well . . . thanks. I feel encouraged," she said, leaving her thought unfinished as to what she felt encouraged in or as, out of parental embarrassment that she might appear too much in need, reliant, even, on her child's approval. "You hungry?"

Desmond threw a look at his mother, making her check herself in the mirror. "Now what?" she asked.

"You *know* I live to eat," Desmond teasingly rebuked his mother's silly question. "Let's get a roll on it, over to Wendy's."

"You sure Rhonda didn't tighten your hair too tight?" Lily knew it was a dig. But she wasn't ready for anything or anyone making her fifteen-and-a-half-year-old son feel like "a *man*," much less, "a *new* man."

"Thass cold—it's not like braces, Mom!"

Lily noticed that Desmond dropped the "s" on "Mom," and with it, she sensed, the man-boy affection so easily displayed earlier in their parrying back and forth. She messed up with her son. "Dezzy, you have your permit on you?" Lily asked, intentionally leaving off the diminutive "learner's." When he nodded glumly, she stopped the car and switched places. "I think you know the way," she encouraged, dropping the key in his palm. Desmond accepted his mother's apology, saying, "Thanks" and flashing her a smile still full of orthodontic silver.

WHILE LILY WAS OUT WITH Desmond, Rodney's mother had phoned again, this time leaving her message on the answer machine: ". . . wondering when I could expect to pick up the twins and their younger brother, and on what airline?" Since the previous month, when a 4.8 quake shook the earth from San Francisco to Sacramento, at the same time the Midwest experienced perilous flooding, and the East Coast a deathly heat wave, naturally-occurring disasters and disasters of depraved human nature conspired to make Lily uneasy about their kids traveling as usual to Alabama the first two weeks in July.

Lily waited till she and Rodney were alone to voice her concerns, which ran the gamut from plane crashes and weather reports to Polly Klaas's local kidnap-murder and church burnings in the South. "I don't want our kids subjected to the kind of hate that could just as well burn down a full church as one that's empty. Like that sign your mother saw at the gas station: 'Negro read and run—If you can't read, run anyway.'"

"Lily, that was way back in the fifties."

Lily locked eyes with her husband and hurled back, "Yeah, and so were church burnings and attitudes about *race mixing*. Sorry, but I just don't feel comfortable letting the kids go to Alabama this summer."

Rodney's set jaw provoked Lily's equally resolute stance. Planting hands on maternal hips, she continued her reproach as if chastising a recalcitrant toddler. "Rodney, you know those attitudes still prevail—I mean, Alabama *still* hasn't gotten rid of the interracial clause that the Supreme Court said couldn't even be enforced for the past thirty years, for chrissake."

When Rodney turned from her gaze and started unbuttoning his shirt, Lily followed up with a final emotional appeal. "Besides. As I mentioned last week, I don't think Zor' and Dezzy are too hot on the idea, anyway—and I *don't* want Wylie going by himself."

"You mean, you don't think it would be good for him to get out of his older siblings' shadow?"

"I do. Just not in that venue. Not this summer," insisted Lily.

"Your journalist friend call again, gettin' you all riled up about the big bad South?" Rodney badgered.

"I resent the implication that I can't think for myself."

"Well, if the kids don't go, my mother'll be heartbroken."

"I've thought of that . . . still, it's not a good time," said Lily, firmly tamping more words around her argument, hoping to hold it in place. "How about an alternative—like, maybe we could all go for Thanksgiving."

"You're changing the whole thing now," Rodney huffed, then chided, "You sure it isn't Lucius that's got you spooked?" Not waiting for her answer, Rodney continued on the offensive. "Maybe this overriding desire to protect our children is really a desire to protect Lucius—where's he now?"

Lily's eyes filled. "Texas," her voice breaking. "Greenville."

Rodney's broad arms enfolded her into his chest, as he whispered, "Sorry, baby. I knew that—I mean, I heard on the morning news that's where the latest fires were."

Lily's head lay tucked in the crook of Rodney's neck. After a few minutes of her temple's drumming matching beats with his heart's pulsing, Lily poked her head out and asked, "Do you think he's in danger?"

"Who—Lucius? Of course he's in danger. But maybe only a little more than me."

"What are you in danger of?" she asked in a knee-jerk defense against the threat of potential harm to her husband. Lily knew very well how controversial Rodney's bench decisions were. Even more so now that cheaper, faster DNA evidence, gathered from as small a sample as a single sneeze, hair, or drop of semen, threatened to overturn an inestimable number of cases remanded back to Rodney's courtroom. Every time someone was exonerated meant that the guilty someone was still out there—not all of Rodney's detractors were white; families hungry for retributive justice, no matter whose innocence was expensed, came in all colors.

LILY WAKENED TO A FREE morning after going into the office for part of her day off the day before to counsel a couple whose marriage was threatened by the young wife's infidelity. She started a pot of decaf before Rodney got up to the six o'clock alarm and appeared in the kitchen doorway, running his hands over his trim Afro. "Hey, babe. What woke you up?"

"I don't know. I've just been mulling over last night's *discussion*," she responded, her lower back propped against the counter edge. "I think I'd like to propose a compromise," she continued, handing Rodney his favorite mug, "you know, about the kids going to visit their grandmother."

"And cousins," he added, as he reached out to take the mug and hoist a thanks in her direction. "Remember, Mariyah said she'd be bringing her three to my mother's around the same time." Rodney took a sip of the steaming decaf, then set it on the kitchen table to cool. "And, of course, Sharon's bunch are local."

"Oh, right," Lily confirmed, having only a vague memory of his sister making summer family plans earlier that year. "Anyway, I thought I'd talk to Zor' and Dezzy again, to see if they'd be interested in going, if it were only for a week—"

"That's hardly enough to get their feet wet again, Lily."

"Better than not at all. Like I told you, the twins are really *not* gung-ho about spending half the month of July in Alabama."

"So what're you proposing again?"

"That the three of them go for one week, instead of two."

"That your final offer?"

"Hey! It's not just me. Ask them yourself—they're your kids too."

"I believe you," Rodney conceded, "I guess I'm just disappointed."

"Can't ask your kids to live your life—visiting your mother for you."

"Woman's so stubborn. If she'd just get on a plane, we could see each other more often."

"I know, sweetheart. I know." Lily appreciated Rodney's tender feelings for his mother. She agreed with a recently read *Ebony* claim that "mama's boys" made the best lovers.

"Well, why don't you go ahead and offer the twins a *reduced sentence*," Rodney surrendered. "Once they sign off, I'll call my mom with the details."

Lily was bothered that Rodney seemed more resigned than content with her proposal, but she wasn't willing to reopen the can of worms. "It's coming up soon."

"When did we give time permission to speed up?" Taking her mug and setting it on the counter, Rodney then proceeded to take both of Lily's hands and wrap them around his back as far as they would go. Settled in her embrace, he kissed her forehead, alternately stroking and pulling out wisps of her hair, as if to inspect each beloved strand.

BACK IN THEIR BEDROOM, THEY listened to CNN as Rodney shaved and Lily went through her abdominal exercise routine. "Did you hear that, sweetie pie? The House Judiciary Committee just approved the Conyers-Hyde arson prevention bill."

"That's a long-overdue no-brainer," jeered Rodney, as he emerged from the bathroom, toweling off his face.

"They're saying it will be forwarded to the full House later today," said Lily. "Bets on how long it will take to get to the president's desk?"

"In this life, I only bet on basketball," Rodney deadpanned. "And only with Monopoly money."

"Oh, that's right. The big game four's tomorrow night. Could be a sweep, what I hear."

"Now, now," Rodney pleaded. "My boys are gonna do their comeback thang. Got some big goldbacks, some important real estate ridin' on my Super*sonic*men."

"Oh, you bet property too," clucked Lily. "High stakes."

"Yeh, you know, take a ride on the Reading . . . stay a night or two in the penthouse suite at my Caribbean Four

Seasons," he said, smacking his lips. "Y'all didn't know your man be as wealthy as good-lookin'."

HAVING THE LUXURY OF THE REST of the morning after the kids left for school with their respective carpools, Lily dressed in a light sweatsuit and headed for Lake Merritt. Early June in Oakland provided sympathetic cloud cover for summer's advance, making it easier for students finishing up the school term to study for finals.

Lily had always been curious, but never took the time to stop and inquire about lawn bowling until that morning. "You meet some of the nicest people," declared the man in whites. "There's the coach," he said, pointing to another senior in similar attire, crouched over an equipment bag on the adjacent groomed green alley. "George'll teach you—best way to learn about the game is to play . . . we have women who play. You know, women live longer; they do less damage to themselves as kids. I think their bodies last longer." Herb nattered on, dispensing philosophy as freely as instruction. "The shape's what makes the 'bowl' when it's rolled, curve in or *draw to* the smaller, white 'jack' ball," Herb explained, as he ran his hand over the bowl's surface. "It's a lot like horseshoes, Lily—ever play horseshoes?"

"We had a pit in our backyard, growing up in Texas."

"Well, then, you know what I'm talkin' about when I say that the object's to come closest to the jack."

More members wearing pith helmets and panama hats arrived for some pregame practice before the afternoon competition. George, the coach, had just walked over to give Lily pointers on how to start, when Joe, a novice of one month, asked if he could join the match.

Lily learned "lagging the jack" down the green to stop two feet over the "hog line," using the "straight-armed release," just demonstrated by George who sported a hat resembling a tournament trophy pin display. "Guess you had your Wheaties this morning!" complimented Joe.

George concurred, offering further direction about following the track in the grass made by the gutter bowl, ". . . only with less Wheaties this time." Lily picked up another bowl and was about to step up to the mat when Ricardo, recently arrived, offered his coaching two cents which, being at variance with George's, nearly caused a rumble. She smoothed it over by saying she'd stick with the guy who had more medals showing.

After two "endings" of instructed play with Joe, Lily begged off, saying, "Sorry, gentlemen. I have to go to work." Her new Oakland Lawn Bowling Club chums thought she was making up an excuse so she wouldn't get roped into staying for their monthly birthday celebration. Especially when she disclosed the nature of her work. "You?" they exclaimed. "You're too young, honey." *Too female is what you meant to say*, Lily thought. Nevertheless, she kept things polite, with a generous thanks for introducing her to, as they claimed, "the trickiest sport devised by *man*."

LILY STILL HAD TIME TO STOP in for her cup of McDonald's coffee at the Fairyland entrance end of Lake Merritt Park. She passed a column of mothers pushing strollers on their way to Oakland's mini Disney Fantasyland. *Rodney is right*—where *did the time go?* Lily thought as she looked into faces fresher than hers.

Not so for the young woman who took her decaf order and seemed already spent—her hair smothered under too many coats of paint and skin like it didn't have enough pigment. Lily sat at a rectangular table-for-two in the back corner opposite the window with a view of both the drive-thru lane outdoors and the Bingo game in progress inside its senior-friendly doors.

"How 'bout a G, here, G-forty-eight, four, eight . . . and a B-nine. How a-bout I-twenty-two . . . *two*-two, *two*-two," the caller cuckooed. The seventyish Korean caller held the Bingo seniors' rapt attention for another few minutes, until a woman with beautiful braids squealed "Winner!" and cards were emptied to begin a new round.

A nickel a game per person netted winners a medium-sized coffee. Some players kept the same card; others changed boards after every "Bingo!" hoping their luck too would change.

A heavily made-up, forty-something woman got up to demonstrate a salsa dance step for her friend. "Yeah, every Monday night, can you believe I stuck with it?" The only dancing Lily and Rodney did was at the occasional fund-raiser—for charity, not for themselves.

"Okay, now—triple layer. Top row, middle and bottom lines. Playboard? How many you want there, Ruby?"

Somebody's cell phone rang. "Hello? McDonald's . . . No problem. Bye." Another male voice answered his phone with a loud, "Dear Jesus" for everyone else's benefit. Lily hated that kind of public display but couldn't stop listening and watching, as he groaned into the phone while tearing open sugar packets with his teeth, shaking three into his cup before unwrapping his McFish sandwich.

"O-*kay*. Here we go! A diamond. Middle, top, and bottom—center, sides . . ." *How many games has that been since I got here?* Lily wondered. *Where does the time go?* "First number, we have an N-forty-two . . . How 'bout a G-forty-nine. Four, *nine*?"

Lily put her wadded napkin into the empty coffee cup and got up to leave just as the Bingo maestro and his entourage were collecting their winnings. Assessing the dozen or so seniors to take their fun seriously, she mused what kind of an old lady she'd grow to be.

"BLACK PANTHERS RODE INTO TOWN yesterday. From Dallas."

"Was there a showdown?"

"Of sorts. Dudes came packin' some sizable heat," Lucius whistled. "Guys with automatic weapons set up a patrol at the church service last night. Their leader, this dude called Khallid Abdul Muhammad, drew a line in the sand, 'Catch a cracker lighting a torch to any Black church, or any property of Black people—we are here to send 'em to the cemetery.'"

"What was the reaction?"

"Mixed," said Lucius, "as you can imagine. Violence these new-styled Panthers represent versus King's legacy of *non*violence. But I saw even some of those church mothers sit up straighter, sayin' 'Amen' when the man spoke. What was it like in Oakland when Brother Huey fell in '89?"

"Kinda tame. Some protests. The funeral was a spectacle," Lily reminisced, remembering to herself how she and Rodney had, at the time, supported Panthers' radically pragmatic justice: organizing meals, education, and healthcare for Black neighbors but were as unable to support Panther, as they were Oakland Police Department, violence. Then, returning to Greenville's immediate concerns, she asked if any more suspects had been questioned.

"Not a one, and in the meantime, another firebomb planted on a Black church pew in Florida," he groaned and asked if she'd seen the lead article in *USA Today*.

"Sorry, don't subscribe. So, anyway, what's it say?"

"Came right out and called the burnings 'acts of terrorism . . . apart from old-time lynchings,'" Lucius read from the national daily, "'there is no more calculated act of racial hatred than burning a church.'"

"Strong language," Lily approved, "I like it."

"*USA*'s rumored report's due out end of the month."

"And when does yours hit, again?"

"Day after Independence Day, but it's largely *not* mine. I think I remain one of the few skeptics on the team at this point. Everyone's looking for the here-and-now, superficial explanation," Lucius reproved. "I like what my South Carolina colleague Brinson says about working on complex stories—gotta *know* the community, needta keep working *back*wards till you get to the deep beginnings."

Lily agreed, "I'm so sick of hearing 'no clear indication, no clear indication'—what *is* the magic threshold that makes race crime *clearly* a conspiracy of hate, anyway?"

"There'll never be a hundredth monkey with racism," Lucius spit into the phone. "This country resists relating one hate crime to another—it's an outrage. And *state*-perpetrated hate crime—the president's sure been takin' it in the neck, *this* week," Lucius chuckled. "Who does he think he is, promoting the idea that same-sex couples in America have the same Constitutional guarantees as the next Joe Blow job?"

"That's okay," Lily played along, "the quarter of our federal Union that still bans consensual sodomy will keep us from goin' to the dogs."

"Yeh, states like Texas that don't believe in any fundamental right to private sex between consenting adults, *especially* if you're gay, got extra *special* punishment for those pariah," mused Lucius. "Oh, and being from Texas, you'll love this— two Confederate plaques hanging outside the State Supreme Court and Court of Criminal Appeals. And get this—the same two fuckin' plaques dedicated to the fuckin' Texans who served the Con-motherfuckin-federacy were re*hung* after the building was remodeled four years ago. State's NAACP keeps raising the issue but are told the memorials have to remain in place because a Confederate widows fund funded the building's original construction in the fuckin' forties."

"You know, until you said that, I was entertaining a move back to my old home state . . . I'm glad you reminded me, before I mentioned anything to Rodney—"

"Like to get his response on that one," jabbed Lucius, his deep, bass laugh chasing. "Say, did I mention Greenville's female mayor?"

"You're kidding."

"I never kid about gender."

"Any good?"

"Seems to have the people's respect as the only woman councilor in this booming metropolis. Greenville's population increased by about a thousand since the last decade."

"I wonder how much of the swell was due to babies born?"

"I can find out," offered Lucius. "Oh, by the way. On the other matter you had me look into, Ritz was torn down and replaced, and let's see—I'm checking my notes, here—"

"You took the assignment seriously."

Lucius ignored her comment as he continued to rifle through his spiral pad. "Oh, yeah, here we go. Robbie's is still upright. Though I didn't go in, looked like some vestige of a soda fountain—"

"How do you know if you didn't go in?"

"Windows. Peered through the windows. Whew," Lucius blew, "sun's hot here."

"What else did I have you look up—Jack's Drive-In?"

"Is a Drive-Thru now, no car hops."

"None back in my day either. We just ordered at the window and ate in the car. Are there picnic tables and hitchin' posts?"

"Picnic tables and bike racks. Didn't see any posts. You used to ride in?"

"Yeah. What are you laughin' at? My girlfriends and I. Mopped a lot of floor for those French fries. 'Course, I think I probably spent more on Fire Stix and BB Bats. Banana-flavored was the best. What kind of candy'd you buy?"

"So we've decelerated from church burnings to candy preference . . . it's okay, I'm just buyin' time while I think. Hmmm, lemme see now. Milk Duds and root beer–flavored saltwater taffy."

"Oh yeah, you were on the Gulf."

"Made honest money turning in pop bottles. That and delivering newspapers."

"A newspaperman even then."

"Yup, the *Galveston Gazette*. A flimsy li'l ol' thing, no more'n ten, say, twelve pages. And that was Sunday's edition!"

"Well, an interesting juxtaposition of today's news," remarked Lily, changing topics. "The president visiting the rebuilt church in South Carolina on the second anniversary of Nicole and Ron's murders with O.J. slugging his way through civil court."

"Thassright," Lucius beguiled. "You and I haven't touched upon the Juice yet."

"Gotta leave something for next time," she replied. "Now, I gotta get suited up for midday Eucharist, 'fore my posse comes looking for me."

"Your posse?"

"Yeah, there's this great young altar guild woman who keeps me looking sharp every Wednesday at high noon."

"I guess it's true. Can't take the Texas outta the girl—"

"Just you be careful down there," Lily cautioned, then responding to his repudiating grunt, added, "You know what I'm saying—you're an ol' Texas boy. Just, uh, just keep your guard up."

"I don't make for good eatin'—too tough, hard to chew. Too bitter too," Lucius cajoled. "But you're sweet to be concerned, Lily. Hey—want me to do any more snooping into Greenville's past for you?"

"Yeah. Thanks for asking. See what my old neighborhood's like—you need the address again?"

"Hey baby," said Lucius. "I still have your number."

LILY PICKED UP FLINT'S RIBS and potato salad for the family meal to be shared around TV-courtside, watching Chicago fight Seattle to win a fourth NBA championship title in six years. Newscasts before and after the game highlighted Hartwig and VP Moore's speaking at the dedication of Greeleyville, South Carolina's rebuilt Mount Zion AME Church, while around the corner, as it did over the statehouse, a Confederate flag flew in front of the KKK memorabilia store that a year prior had nearly risen out of the destroyed church's ashes.

"Fuckers," Lily heard Desmond say under his breath with only mother and son listening. Rodney had not made it home from work yet; Wylie and Zora were still in their rooms, each listening to their own particular music selections, rap and Erykah Badu.

The report went on to say that one of the older ex-Klansman, charged with conspiring to burn that church and another, along with a labor camp and a Black man's car, threatened to set fire again to the other Black church, Macedonia Baptist, once it was rebuilt. "What do you think about all this, Dezzy?"

"Wait, I'll tell you in a minute—I wanna listen to this," Desmond shushed, as the news story continued with an interview of Southern Poverty Law Center's Morris Dees talking about the previous week's lawsuit filed against the Christian Knights of the Ku Klux Klan on behalf of the Manning, South Carolina, church.

Next, Randolph Scott-McLaughlin, VP of the Center for Constitutional Rights, spoke with another interviewer in New York, saying he hoped their filing similar lawsuits in three additional states would show that at least some of the fires were the result not of individual actions, but of organized terrorism. "In the Oklahoma City bombing, they had suspects within weeks, if not days," he charged. "Why haven't we seen those types of investigations with the church bombings? I guess they're waiting until some Black people are killed in the fires, before they begin to investigate vigorously."

The TV article concluded with remarks by Carol Moseley-Braun, the first Black female senator, made earlier that day: "In submitting a resolution 'condemning the fires and declaring the investigation and prosecution of those responsible a high national priority,'" the Illinois senator called the perpetrators "'cowardly domestic terrorists.'"

"Now I'll tell ya, Moms." Desmond was the first to speak. "I think like the *Braun* woman think. You?"

"Oh, well, where would you like me to begin," answered Lily, as incensed as her son. "The Klan's calling themselves *Christian*—the friggin' Confederate *flag* flying in the backdrop of burned churches—the *dis*-United States of white supremacy. I think it's difficult to remain rational about nonrational hatred."

"I'm lookin' at the TV, thinkin' this ain't the same country as Oakland, California."

"Exactly, the Klan's recruiting point with kids your age and younger," stated Lily. "Convincing them that places like Oakland are bad, desegregation is bad, and unless they 'stop the Black man,' they will be punished for thwarting God."

"They make me wanna kill."

"Strongly tempted myself, son," Lily sympathized, "but I'm not sure how I'd answer to God—or your father."

"But you would kill in self-defense, wouldn'ya?"

"As brutally as I could," Lily vowed solemnly. "No question when it comes to defending my family or myself." Then, going over to the sofa, Lily said, "Give your mother a hug while you're still within safe stooping distance." As her son obliged, lanky arms whipping around her shoulders for a quick in-and-out hug, she observed, "I hope you're gettin' 'nough food to keep up with all these inches of bone and muscle laid down the past few months, Dezzy."

"What throwdowns y'got f'dinnah, Moms?"

"Flint's Barbecue, sweetheart."

"Extra sauce?"

"You bet," Lily reassured. Her son's sparring having run its course, Lily returned to her maternal driver's seat and asked Desmond to go tell his brother and sister that dinner was ready and, though it didn't interest Zora, that game four of the NBA finals was about to begin.

She headed for the kitchen to assemble the ribs kept warm in the oven, and looking at the clock, wondered when Rodney would get home.

THE WHOOPING AND HOLLERING DIDN'T stop until the Sonics pulled out their first win, staving off a Bulls finals sweep, and Wylie reluctantly counted out the play money owed on the losing bet with his dad. "MJ, you let me down, man," Wylie whimpered.

"It wasn't Number Twenty-Three let you down, young-blood, it was Pippen and Rodman's no-show defense. Sorry, big guy, fork it over . . ." his dad gently teased. "There's still a game five, son."

Zora had, in the meantime, returned to the kitchen, looking for more ribs.

"You little piggies leave any leftovers?" she asked, sullenly looking in the direction of the living room where, still seated, Desmond was refereeing the payout between his dad and brother.

"If you're talking to us, we can't hear you," Wylie guffawed.

"And since when you change your skinny-ass, anorexic habit?" added Desmond.

"Hey! Hey, you two!" Rodney, the first parent to speak, jumped on Desmond. "You call that meanness back right now, son, before you make me do something I might regret!"

Desmond knew his dad's threat of physical punishment was empty. Respecting the meaning behind it, he went out to the kitchen to make up with his sister. "Friends?" he asked, his embrace starting its approach.

"*No*, first of all, and second, *hell* no!" Zora replied, stepping back from her brother's reach. "I didn't hear any apology from your raggedy ass," Zora continued, head bobbling. Lily was proud of her daughter, the way she stood up to Desmond, firmly reprimanding his insult. *She'll be okay*, Lily thought, *more okay than Dezzy*.

"Whaddya want me to say?" deflected Desmond.

"Oh, no," said Rodney, rising out of his chair, heading for the kitchen. "I know you didn't just lame-dog your sister." Now, eyeball to eyeball with Desmond, Rodney said, "And I *know* we didn't raise any dumb children—now let's hear that again. Only this time, son, get it right."

Lily dreaded the day she'd heard might come, when son would not back down to father. She hoped that when Desmond hit late teens, his relationship with Rodney would be cemented such that there would be no need for the machismo display her friends had described as having taken place between their husbands and sons, or fathers and brothers.

This time, at least, Desmond recanted and genuinely apologized to Zora, then surprisingly turned and extended his apology to the rest of the family. *Big man*, thought Lily. *Maybe we* have *given him the means of survival, after all.*

That being enough drama for one night, Lily and Rodney kissed each child goodnight and went off to make final peace with the day just ended in the privacy of their own bedroom.

THE NEXT MORNING DAWNED ON the Olympic torch making its way to Albany, New York, as a more lethal flame ignited a Black church in Oklahoma. The President reacted to the latest fire by inviting Southern governors to meet with him at the White House the following week. Some state leaders, like Alabama's Rob Lames who pooh-poohed the meeting as "mostly politicians getting together to make statements to the media," declined to attend.

When Friday rolled around, Mississippi's Trent Lott was named new Senate majority leader, and the Southern Baptist Convention called for a boycott of Walt Disney theme parks, films, and other products, as it, simultaneously, pledged seventeen thousand workers to help rebuild Black churches.

As the eighty-one-day standoff between FBI agents and anti-government Freemen ended in Montana, the search for Second Missionary Baptist's arsonist ended in Oklahoma. Investigators hastily closed the case, despite the fact that the suspect was declared incompetent to stand trial, with his mother testifying that her disabled son was "too inept to single-handedly set the incendiary device that allegedly started the fire." One of the ways white-on-Black arson was undercounted.

Later that night, the NBA season concluded after only five final games. The Chicago Bulls won over Seattle's Supersonics, and Rodney handed over the play money owed to his gleeful son Wylie.

Sunday morning, Lily preached about the church burnings, appealing to her congregation's sense of duty as outrage seemed too strong an emotion for West Coast Christians to muster about something happening in the South. Many had left Dixie, wanting to forget about it and its murderous Jim Crow. Facial reactions among her racially mixed congregation ranged from concern to disinterest. Lily moved her exhortation to its conclusion. She hoped her call to action would remain ringing in their ears; the members variously coughed and fussed with antsy hands over the *Book of Common Prayer* or the service order leaflet to see what was to come next.

"The National Council of Churches, which our own Episcopal Church supports, is looking to the generosity of Christians across America to put in their two cents or two dollars toward its million-dollar goal to help rebuild the churches burned by hate. In addition to treasure," Lily urged, "you can also donate your time and talent. See me about travel expenses, those of you who feel so called."

Lily felt encouraged to see yet a few eager expressions still with her. "I hope all of us sitting here in the safety of our beautiful Holy Innocents' Church will, as God's people, dig deeply into our pockets and with goodwill, stuff some of God's provision into one of the envelopes at the Offertory. Let's help new houses of worship rise out of the ashes of despair," Lily trumpeted, finishing like a nineteenth century camp meeting reformer.

BACK HOME, RODNEY NOTIFIED LILY that their friend Corrine had called to invite them over for an early supper. "Or would you rather pack your bags and leave on the midnight train to *Geo-juh*?"

"What's that supposed to mean?" was her reply.

"Nothing, just that I believe it's what you'd really like to do. Helluva sermon, babe," said Rodney, attempting to defuse Lily's zeal with flattery.

"Yeah, a real firebrand," Lily returned, reserving a total show of relief. Hoping to keep stoking Lily's playfulness, Rodney asked if anyone had gotten fired up. "Besides me?" Lily's voice sounded tired. "The collection was actually pretty hefty."

"That must feel gratifying."

"From this crowd, yes. Almost nine hundred," Lily brightened. "Usually, a few more dollars trickle in during the week. Short-lived, though. Tuesday will probably be the end of their attention span," said Lily, her voice sounding weary again.

"What were you hoping for?"

"A cadre of steel-toed, ready-to-go boots lined up at my office door, pinching my discretionary fund for every last dime," Lily said as she kept a straight face, "no less."

"No less than with you in the lead—"

"I just wonder if we could walk more of the walk."

"Than what?" Rodney challenged.

"Well, we have it pretty good here in Oakland—"

Rodney cut her off, "So you want to go where we could *walk more of the walk*—by whose definition?" Rodney's blood was rising into his neck muscles and face. "What, like dodging slurs and bullets? Like walking the walk of limited professional advancement, limited choice of neighbors, schools, friends for our kids? We're walkin' the Black-and-white walk every day, Lily. Here and now," Rodney reasoned. "And without a cross burned in our front yard or a rock thrown through our bedroom window . . . or worse."

"Maybe I should be talking about me, not we."

"No, Lily—we *is* what you should be talkin' about, what I'm talkin' about," he said, taking her in his arms. "What'd I just say, babe—*we* is who's walkin' the walk, *together*. Mister and Missus Ebony and Ivory is why we live in Oakland."

"But don't you care about what's happening, I mean, your family's in the South."

"You ask that like, by definition of skin color, I *should* care about what happens to every other *Black* man, woman, and child." Rodney braced her with his eyes. "Baby, we're past Noble Black Men 101. *Waaay* past."

"I can still be interested in how you feel," said Lily. "How you, Rodney Davis—not asking you to speak pan-Africanly—how you, *yourself,* feel about Black churches burning in 1996."

"That's a different question. I feel . . . deceived. We turn toward a *new* South and the future with one foot, with the other firmly still in the past. And that makes me mad."

Lily took Rodney's hand, but he broke out of her palm to hammer a fist in the air. "Fuckers vandalizing and smoking churches is the lowest blow to the heart of the Black community. Yeah, I'm angry! What really enrages me, though, is the *lack* of outrage, and lazy prosecution of the fuckers! And, so, do I wanna leave Oakland—where, *yeees*, earthquake and wildfire have shaken us up in recent years—to go walk some *notion* of walk, putting our kids and us in harm's way? No! I don't want to leave where we've made our home, where Black men reside in city hall, newsrooms, and judges' chambers. And, anyway. There's enough harm's way in the adjacent county."

"Actually, there's probably enough right here in Alameda County," Lily retreated.

"Bigotry's sung everywhere, baby. It's the American blues."

ON MONDAY, LILY'S DAY OFF, AUTHORITIES investigated a suspicious fire in Georgia at the same time local forensics began collecting evidence from the firebombing of Berkeley's Center for Whiteness Studies earlier that morning. Neo-Nazi groups from adjacent Contra Costa were likely suspects. They'd claimed responsibility for pettier acts of vandalism committed within the first year of the UC adjunct research facility's founding.

Lucius called Lily mid-morning after wresting her home number from parish admin assistant Jules.

"I guess I don't have to worry about security at Holy Innocents'," Lily crowed. "Though I'm sorry he gave you such a hard time."

"Actually, I was somewhat relieved," Lucius exhaled. "Just heard about the incident at Cal. Any idea who's to blame?"

"Skinheads on the other side of the Berkeley tunnel," Lily answered. "Make a regular practice of boasting their way into the news—*ignorant* white kids."

"How close are they to you?" asked Lucius.

"You mean geographically . . . or existentially?"

"Yeah, both."

"A short joy ride away for either," her answer causing a shiver, "through the tunnel and they're on our radar screen, harassing my kids, their friends . . . usually, or so I hear, pretty emphatically sent back to where they came from, when they're stupid enough to pick a fight with Oakland locals."

"Your kids ever involved in that mess?"

"Not that they tell me," said Lily. "Wylie's the one we worry about—our youngest's got the shortest fuse."

"Say, you asked me about your former residence in Greenville. . . ."

"You still in Texas?"

"No, between arsons, immediately juggling a cup of coffee and my phone at Dallas's beautiful Love field," reported Lucius. "My flight to Atlanta's in about half an hour."

"So, anyway, you were saying . . ."

"So, yeah, your old house on Sayle Street's been transformed into a Work and Western boot store, you know, for dudes workin' on oil rigs, Harleys, cattle roundups," said Lucius. "Course, it could be the *Live Naked Girls Girls Girls Shop*, the two are practically on top of each other."

"Oh, I bet they are," returned Lily, suddenly feeling sad. "What else is around my former address?"

"A bakery outlet, looked like, and some random office buildings—insurance, chiropractor, stuff like that."

"What are the neighborhood demographics like?"

"Well, on a weekday afternoon, lower to middle class and mostly white, Ms. Mayor's remarks notwithstanding," said Lucius, sarcastically. "She maintains her incredulity over church burnings—still wondering how it could happen in Greenville, where there's been a sizable *infiltration*."

"Her words?"

"Yeh, 'a sizable infiltration of *Blacks* in government jobs in recent years,'" mimicked Lucius. "Just not in city hall—still got *those* ramparts manned."

"Or *womanned*," she pinged. "I'm still amazed Greenville elected a female mayor . . ."

". . . but less amazed that she's *white*," Lucius thumped her back.

"True," she said, yielding, but feeling the race-over-gender prick, nevertheless. "But in terms of credulousness, I think a lot of people are incredulous that churches are burning again, and from both sides of the color line. We were at our friends for dinner last night, and Corrine, who grew up in Detroit, has, I think, willed herself into believing that racism is a non-issue because, as she says, 'Blacks are making it in America.' Her white half, Brian, is the opposite; he fears a new wave of violence."

"Friend Corrine's right on one count, but it's a matter of degree—*more* Blacks makin' it, but a whole *lot* more ain't," said Lucius, winding up for the pitch. "When you start pokin' 'round the edge of *improved* race relations, which, true, has been responsible, or at least is the *stated* reason for companies like Fuji and Michelin locating plants in the South—anyway, relations may look more mauve than rosy. And some relations, still the same ol' shit-brown," he said, throwing at her a story about a man found hanging by an electric cord, and another about a decomposed body found burned and tied to a tree with barbed wire. "Moral tales: what happens in some parts of Texas when Black men date white women."

A chill ran down Lily's spine. "This just happen?"

"Springtime." Lucius only heard silence, as images of daffodils and dead men turned in Lily's head.

"So where are the police?"

"Good question," said Lucius, as if penning comment on a student's paper. "Especially now. Churches continue being victimized by arson, local authority continues touting confidence in local investigation to solve *crime*, most local authority loath to call it what it is—*hate* crime. Then we have about two hundred federal agents spread over nine states' worth of arsons saying they find no connection with other fires and, therefore, no evidence of a conspiracy."

"Official word out of Washington," inserted Lily.

"If you hang onto a lie long enough, it becomes incorporated as a way of life—at least there are *fewer* Black men being strung up by mobs these days," Lucius mocked. "As recently as a year ago, Mississippi's state senate voted to abolish slavery."

"No," said Lily, estrangement from the South yet again creeping up on her. "A hundred and thirty years after the rest of the country. You've got to be kidding!"

"And you're an educated woman. . . ."

". . . who prides herself on staying current with current events," she said, admonishing herself. "My Methodist colleagues are soliciting Black voter registrars for the South—do *you* think the burnings are designed primarily to interfere with voting?"

"They do, whether primarily designed to or not," said Lucius, pinching off discussion to go back to her question's introduction. "So, are you coming to register voters?"

"Don't think Rodney'd be too keen on the idea."

"Smart man."

"I feel like I could, or should, be doing more."

"You're a part of America's religious leadership—making sure church membership doesn't keep a silent tongue," Lucius charged. "I don't know if it's the witnessing word or the intimidated word that offers forgiveness to the person who burned them out—I don't get church people asking for leniency."

"Speaking from a limited cultural perspective . . . for me, at least, it attests to their faith stance—*not* being intimidated, *not* being overcome by violence."

"*Not* being a religious man, I haven't a clue about *faith stance*. It's just curious that a visiting fourteen-year-old boy is taken from his host family's home in the middle of the night, beaten, shot in the head, and dumped in the Tallahatchie, and an all-white jury acquits his killers. Then forty years later when Black folk finally have a hand in bringing racists to justice, white church folks do the same."

"But it's not the same," she argued. "World of difference between declaring someone not guilty and taking a stand against continuing the violence and calling for mercy—"

"I disagree," he pushed. "By not putting Little Billy Joe and his pa away for a while, they are choosing to continue the violence, in fact, are helping racists feel confirmed and vindicated in their claims—hell! Fuckers go on doin' what they're doin' for *God*." Lily tried to figure out where she had misstepped as Lucius proceeded to make his case. "Ever heard of the Church of the Avenger? How about Christian *Patriots*? Any branch of the World Church of the Creator in Oakland?"

"Look, Lucius, I'm not benighted enough to think people being cruel to other people can be neatly contained, but likewise, people's response to cruelty is nuanced."

"The National Trust for Historic Preservation just announced its annual list of most endangered historic places," he said, as if reading copy on a news broadcast, "and churches are its newest addition."

"Seriously?"

"The Trust is pledging loan money and other aid to communities with Black churches that have been damaged, calling them some of the most *significant* community institutions, at the same time some members of those *institutions* are taking the arsonist's part—my turn to be incredulous—asking the judge for the lightest sentence, and in some cases, *no* sentence. What, so they can go out and found more racist cells? Or here's an idea, Klan Kid Korp. Founded three years ago to help steer children, ages birth to twelve years, in the right direction. So they can be the Klan's next generation welcome-wagon, burning crosses in Black front yards, writing messages to wrap around bricks thrown through windows? Something like: 'We are the KKK of Mississippi. We are about 8,000 strong. You can't stay in a white neighborhood in the south. You will die. You stay, you die.' No evidence of a conspiracy? Hell! When has it *not* been a conspiracy?" Lucius's voice resounded in her ear. "Damn! They just called my flight. Sorry, Lily. No time to redeem my raving lunacy—"

"No need to, writer-man," Lily said matter-of-factly. "Keep doin' what you do best, Lucius . . . and God keep you safe."

"Check you and your God later, sweet Lily—you can teach me the Prodigal's prayer."

THE AIR OVER THE CHURCH CEMETERY was so heavy, it sweated just holding itself up. Hearing wet tennis shoes squeak, the Mount of Olives pastor spun around from his mother's, father's, and sister's graves and stared hard at the boys. So hard it scared them.

The older boy gave the minister a minute to recognize him and his friend before speaking. "We seen who done it."

"First of awl, I don' want you repohtin' this to enaone *else*." Hearing his own gruff, finger-pointing voice open up on the two young congregants standing stiffly at attention before him, Jim Beeson winced and looked down at his casual cotton pants and untucked, short-sleeved shirt.

Fear had taken hold of him for the second time that morning; he was unable to check himself once the adrenalin started readying his muscular body to fight no matter who it was sneaking up behind him. "You tell enaone else yet?" he asked, softening his tone, as he regained control over the fright that much earlier that morning had leapt onto him as he watched church flames shoot into a still-dark sky.

"No, suh," the older boy answered, taking the lead again. "We saw who done it an' we know where he live—we want yoh blessin' tuh go kick his ass."

"Yeh—I wanna take a big o' can o' gas'line and poh it awl o' that crackuh' house," added the younger boy, energized with raw emotion. "Throw a mutha—oh, sorry,

Pastuh—throw a match on th' dude's crib. With him *in* it. Toast that crackuh like he did our *church*!"

Beeson thought the youngster's talk scary; maybe there was something to be feared in the encounter, after all . . . *and what were these two doing out in the middle of the night, anyway?* The pastor, who had recently celebrated his forty-second birthday, made a mental note to have a word with their parents.

"Why they not all over th' dude's ass," the older boy continued. "*We* could be. Me an' Marcel. Shee-it. Tired bein' dogged by some crank-ass ol' lady ev' time we go 'roun' Latky's lookin' fuh somenin' tuh eat aftuh schoo'. Ol' lady awl th' time stalkin' our ass like we criminals. Like we gonna steal some a her ol' Bab' Roos candy bar," he said, looking at his younger cousin and laughing as he added, "Some bean dip off her nasty-ass shelves. *Sheee*-it."

The boys' minister used a stern voice again. "Don' say 'nuthuh word—"

"We jus' bein'—"

"You jus' bein' *i*gnorant," Beeson reprimanded. "Shut yoh mouth and don' say 'nuthah word." The boys had him scared about what powder kegs their hot anger could blow. "All your ignorant talk 'bout goin' after *him*. An' then what? We be standin' here cryin' for *you*. An' you know yoh families shed 'nough tears already."

"But we saw him. Me and Marcel saw him."

"He see you?"

"Naw, we were out by Carson's side garage, nearest the back doh to the kitchen. We saw him come 'round the corner before big ol' fireball started."

"Yeh, thass when we started Carson's hose. I' was a dribble. No watuh pressure. The fire jus' jump up th' sid' th'church an' on t'the roof. Meantime, we could see the inside awl lit up."

"Hella blaze inside, man. An' we jus' bin slavin' those pews. Look like kindlin'."

Mount of Olives's fire and the one that destroyed Brevard Congers's church four miles away made it two in one night, four in five days. Beeson did not yet know about the fire that got set the same night in a third church in North Carolina— nine arsons in June, and the month not yet over. Fire truck got to DeWitt's church over in Oklahoma the previous week. But not until flames had eaten their way through the floorboards.

Mount Olives's now charred baptismal register went back a hundred years to when the congregation was first organized. It contained all the names of those who received the water of the Spirit, including these two cousins, Marcel and Tyrone. Their daddies, Leroy and Claudelle, owned the only garage for miles, setting their business right on Claudelle's property because he had more acreage than Leroy's a mile away. Hard-working businessmen, the brothers were known for fairness.

They lost their two older brothers in Vietnam. Their mamas were so proud to see their sons taking their place fighting for their country. Those same hearts broke open, spilling their fullness, when their boys returned in flag-draped boxes.

Jim Beeson was at Morehouse when Curtis and Hench left. His sister wrote about the prayers said for the two just old enough to enlist after that Sunday worship meeting fall of '66. A big potluck sent them and everyone else off "full of they folks' food. . . . People ate a lot," Janie wrote. "But it was just to try and fill up that big hole we already felt. And they hadn't even boarded the bus yet."

Now, their nephews were coming to enlist in the fight for freedom on their own little bit of American turf thirty years later.

"You sure you haven' tol' enaone else, young Tyrone?"

The boys looked at each other, deciding who would go first. They ended up taking turns, telling how nobody but old Murdoch saw them, "comin' outta th' pigsty cottage he rent from the Carsons . . . disgustin' tobacco spit in th' corners his no-tooth mouth, smellin' nastier than ever and lookin' mean."

The boys said that they told the crazy old man who they saw "comin' real fast 'roun' the church corner," and then were afraid he'd get out his WWII gun and do some huntin' down at Felix's gas station. Instead, the boys reported, Murdoch went in his house and never came back out.

"Murdoch's crazy all right, 'cause of all the crazy he's seen in his lifetime, and this fire's just one more." Fearing retaliation should the youngsters become witnesses, Beeson made the boys promise that the only time they'd repeat the name of the one they suspected of burning down the recently renovated century-old church was when they were praying to God for his soul, "'Cause he gonna need a lot o' God right now." Reverend Beeson told the boys what to say if anyone came around asking for a name or even a description. "We don' need any more crazy operatin' 'round heah, heah what I'm sayin'?"

"But he'll git 'way and we jus—'"

The minister lit into the boys, hoping to scare off any notion of heroics in rural Mississippi, saying he didn't want anybody killed—not even the sorry figure of a man that put a torch to their church. "Let that man's name be a prayer foh mercy on yoh lips, nothin' moh."

After striking a binding silence with Tyrone and Marcel, the pastor said "Deal" as he shook each boy's hand in turn.

IN THE MEANTIME, DELORES, AN ELDERLY church member, lay dying. Her family was gathering from all parts of the North and Southeast. She had been like a mother to Jim his third year at Morehouse when his own mother passed.

Delores had spent her life lugging pots of soup, shoe-boxes filled with cookies, and foil-lined boxes of fried chicken in and out of her sister's car for delivery to suffering souls. Alice learned to drive; Delores never did.

Before meeting Delores, Beeson hadn't applied the term *calling* to matters of transportation and other needs so commonplace in everyday life. Their importance was, more often than not, overlooked. Matters of *gettin' along*, matters unworthy of others' consideration became the church mother's domain.

Full-bodied Delores had said it wasn't her callin' to be a bird—God gave her the capacity of *appetite*, for food as well as caring for shut-ins. Jim's first memory of the generous woman was at the kitchen table breaking bread with his mama. Delores, still catching her breath from trips back and forth from Alice's car, began to open up packets of savory items to share with him and his mama. "Yeah, this is good,'" she said, after biting into a turkey wing dipped in gravy. "Always makes a fool outta me," her voice jiggling, "you know food's good when the one cooked it is its most satisfied customer!"

Tensions relaxed around Delores. She knew how to get food and love into people, tending to the inside space full of sucked-back tears. It was not only the food but her companionship that was healing. "Keepin' faith" was how Delores named her calling, and she always had time for the people with whom she kept faith.

Beeson had tried emulating her example, clearing out the wasted energy between intention and action, but for him, it never seemed as easy as Delores made it look. She would take his chin in her ample palm and tell him, "Honey, you know you're gonna die sooner or later. Now I need you to make it later. So why get yourself all twisted around, analyzin' this, analyzin' that. God show you the righteous way. You jus' gotta put one step in front th' other."

He would leave the sage's session, each time thinking this to be the time he had finally grasped her wisdom for his own life. Full strength, undiluted. But then, the number of small decisions he was called on to make seemed to whittle away the totem's image, causing it to lose its edged distinction. He would forget and have to ask the big woman again.

Two handfuls chopped onion . . . his mama's meatloaf recipe. Slicing the onion one direction and then the other, he watched the pungent diced pieces fall out and thought about the questions he had posed to Delores over the years of their relationship. They were all really about one question: "How can I, a man in rural Mississippi, live as if God's Creation is one?"

"DEREK SAID IT'S LIKE THE N-word for whites."

"Can be," replied Rodney. "My friends and I growing up in Birmingham thought it was Pig Latin for foe . . ."

". . . but actually, it probably comes from a West African—a Yoruba word, which a person says to ward off danger," said Lily, inserting herself into the family's race conversation. "And since Blacks have seen whites as *dangerous*, from slavery forward, well . . ."

"So, are you an *ofay*, Mom?" Lily was startled by her son's question, but it was Rodney who spoke next.

"Son, that's *not* generally a term of respect, so, no, your mother's *not* an ofay, and I really don't want to hear the word spoken any more in this house."

Lily didn't know if she should challenge their children's father or keep still after his pronouncement. *Did he mean to protect her, because she was white?* Lily wondered. *What if I weren't here? What if they had a Black mother instead?*

As if he could read her thoughts, Desmond reenlisted his mother's comment, coaxing her to say something about growing up in Texas. "Did you have any Black friends in Greenville, Mom?"

Lily talked about Delicia and was glad that her anecdotes about her childhood friend gave Zora entrée and Scott, as her son insisted on being called, re-entrée into the table talk.

Dinner concluded pleasantly with the female Davises presenting the hazelnut torte bought that afternoon at Lake Merritt Bakery, a favorite dessert to share with the male rest of the family.

———

LUCIUS PULLED ON A T-SHIRT and went for the Mississippi daily which lay, delivered, outside his door. Nothing about arson on the front page. Instead, white hands giving and receiving an award. Self-congratulatory expressions from men who knew their place secured by the displacement of others. Lucius flipped through till he found the heading atop a two-inch mention on page seven, which simply repeated facts already known.

Lucius shoved the paper in the wastebasket as he picked up his ringing cell phone. "Happy Juneteenth, Mr. Clay."

"Lily?" said Lucius, surprised to hear her voice. "What did I do to merit a call from her royal reverend-ness?"

"It's what you *didn't* do. Three more fires and no beat from your drum," Lily fretted. "Where are you right now?"

"Right now, I think I'm still in a dream."

"You sound kinda hazy."

"Yeah. Must've been early this morning, who knows when dreams come exactly. These sisters being auctioned off. They were clothed, but then naked. Out of time . . . it could have been the thirties. I don't know. Their eyes were intense, but not immediate. Haunting. They were looking at something. Something that wasn't anywhere in the dream— least that I could see. But it was there for those women. I felt it, felt it lingering even after I woke up."

"Did they say anything, the sisters?"

"No, it was as if they didn't need to. Just their image. What they looked like all standing there on that auction block together. And their skin, their skin was this kind of rubbed-out black. As if their arms and faces had a layer of dust."

"What were they saying, Lucius . . . I mean, to you?"

"I don't know—'Where's my good-for-nothin' man? He told me he was jus' goin to the store to grab somethin'.'" Lucius tried laughing off the dream's eerie deposit. "Yeh, maybe it was just a whole chorus of angry women. Suckin' their teeth on a collective front porch, not an auction block. Maybe it was just one big bitch session about their wayward, ass-grabbin' men. What do you think?"

"I think they were on an auction block watching their men being taken away by other men, wondering if they were ever going to see their husbands and brothers and uncles again after the bidding dust settled on a new arrangement of household and kin."

With her memory's eye, Lily saw childhood friends at Halloween in Blackface and Aunt Jemima costume. Later, she and her teen peers were auctioned off as "slaves" for a day, washing cars, cleaning houses, or serving at the parties held by winning adult bidders. The implications of their "fun" held at others' historical expense never occurred to her or anyone else involved in the popular fundraising event. PTAs and church youth groups held similar "slave" auctions when she was growing up in Texas. "I think those sisters have seen something I will never see."

"You might be right, Lily." Lucius waded into the dream's swamp one last time before lighting the fuse to his outrage. "Not a peep out of the fuckers."

His anger, appearing out of nowhere, broadsided her. "Excuse me?"

Lucius continued to blow. "Not one more word in that sorry rag about night before last's fires. Not reported. Not newsworthy enough to make it into the local historical record, which seems consistent," said Lucius, disdainfully. "Some things never change."

"So, are you in North Carolina or Mississippi now?"

"Got into Kossuth, Mississippi yesterday afternoon. So many churches, now. Hard to do justice," said Lucius. "Was in suburban Atlanta Monday. Multiracial church, pretty bad. Let's see, where was I yesterday? Oh, yeah, church in North Carolina, totally destroyed."

"I heard my seminary colleague offered her church to the burned-out congregations and started a fund to help them rebuild," said Lily, seeking connection with Lucius. "Supposed to be a unity service on Sunday?"

"Yeh, between that and the Oval Office koffee-klatching strategy session, lots of togetherness happ'nin'," he sneered, "'cept with my man Lowery declining an invitation to tea and talk with an organization that fuels hate."

"You talking about the so-called *Christian* Coalition?" she asked, more for a conversational toehold than clarification. "Have you seen the churches in Kossuth?"

"You mean, what's left?" asked Lucius. "Ugly, ugly sight. I talked to one member, Orannie May Smith, who told me investigators were tryin' to pin the blame on the church's failure to put out a barbecue, said the wind blew some embers," he scoffed, thinking again about the women in his dream. "But she and her three sisters, Della, Matty, and Billie—all members of Cornerstone Missionary Baptist Church—said it had been put out 'real good.' They lost everything." Lily thought she heard his voice crack. "They'd just bought a lot of new furnishings for their church, a new piano, even. It's all gone, all burned," he said, sadly. "And the other, a much older church, had just been completely redone. Now, all they have is ash, too. . . . Happy Juneteenth."

Lily stared out the bay window of her office, remembering

her first Juneteenth party at Hugh's New York flat. Suddenly, her eyes transfixed the metal grill just outside the glass. Though they attempted a decorative appearance, the iron bars were there for security purposes. *To keep people from getting in?* Lily pondered, *or to keep her from breaking out?* In that conscious instant, Lily *felt* the race-imprisonment metaphor. Then, glad to live in a city like Oakland, whose cycles of violent eruption and recovery solidified its human core, she said, "Too bad you're not in *my* town. Juneteenth is a whole weekend long."

"It sounds wonderful," said Lucius. "I don't like being here, Lily."

"Where next?"

"Maybe a return to Greenville. Rumblings about a Klan rally in your home town."

"Mine? Don't know I still claim it," said Lily. "But I suppose it remains lodged somewhere in me . . . like inoperable shrapnel?"

"Interesting analogy," observed Lucius. "So, what's next with you?"

"Meeting at the AME church a short walk away to discuss Oakland's religious response to the burnings."

"Can I get a copy of the minutes?"

"Absolutely, and what address may I use?"

"Save for pick-up in person."

"I wish," said Lily, gazing out the barred window again. "Anyway, call me if and when you pull into Greenville again. A Klan rally, huh . . . you scared?"

Wishing to keep the remembered dangers lurking around corners to himself, Lucius was more comfortable expressing anger than fear over the phone with Lily. Abusive school "discipline"; his father's assault and premature release from the hospital; leaving home to go to college and returning that first Thanksgiving to find his mother gravely ill before her death. He would never outlive the pain of his mother's death. "Only of death by torture or cancer," he replied. "And you, what are you afraid of, Lily?"

"Harm to my family."

"That it?"

"Like there should be something more?"

"I envy the solid ground you've found, Lily," said Lucius, sounding like their conversation was a wrap. "Well, thanks for the call."

"Call me when you move tents again . . . please?"

Leaving her request dangling, Lucius moved toward goodbye. "Good Juneteenth to you, Lily—and send me a rain check on that Oakland weekend."

AS WAS CUSTOMARY, THE REVEREND Derwin Brooks opened the lunchtime gathering of Catholic, Protestant, Orthodox, and Jewish clergy in First AME's Friendship Hall with prayer: "Brothers and sisters," he said, tipping his head to Lily and in the direction of the one other female present, "I ask you to bow your heads, as we invoke God's holy spirit to come among us with tongues of fire, enflaming our hearts with compassion and hastening our step to action. . . ." Lily thought the figurative language curious, considering the purpose of their convening—to respond to Black church burnings in the South. She noticed that she was still in a gender minority among Oakland's ordained folk, those assembled being the most activist in the East Bay community, notwithstanding.

Lily had walked the five blocks from Holy Innocents', turning down offers from driving colleagues who pulled up to the curb to ask if she needed or wanted a lift. A block away from the church, though, she accepted an invitation that gave her the chance to catch up with her priest friend still ministering to the Catholic cathedral congregation seven years after

Loma Prieta earthquake damage forced relocation of the large, diverse flock to temporary worship space, while strategizing a more permanent solution and the funding to make it possible.

"Five years ago," First AME's pastor Brooks began after the opening prayer, solemnly drawing out each word, "Oakland endured its own pain and suffering when the hills were ablaze and threatened neighborhoods, businesses, schools, and parks. And two years before—we know how it feels to have the earth move, to find structures we depend on . . ." Everyone's eyes followed Pastor Brooks's to acknowledge the Cathedral priests around the table as he went on, ". . . . to no longer be dependable. Natural acts that trouble God's people where they live on this planet, that isss," again, the senior clergyman drew out the last word for emphasis, "but an island in the Creator's grand realm.

"We come together today to share what might be on each of our hearts regarding our brothers and sisters who may feel like they exist on an island, a burned-out island in the middle of the Southern savannah. Wondering if anyone out there has heard, has really *heard*, their terror. . . ."

The phrase *epidemic of terror* was used liberally, as one after another contributed some fact, some anecdote, some history to inform the proposal of how their collective voices, as a microcosm of national religious bodies advocacy, might speak out, not only within the city and county, but also on the state level.

Lily heard the difficulty of *intra*national communication, regarding the ability of one state's citizens to accurately and timely assess what was happening among other states' citizens. Her Presbyterian colleague brought up the situation of South Carolina and its governor, who reportedly denied any connection between continuing to fly the Confederate flag and the current racial climate. First Methodist's minister asserted a whole range of issues responsible for stoking the fires of racial unrest, including welfare reform, school vouchers, and carrying concealed weapons. "Don't forget the bumper stickers," the Church of Religious Science minister, the only other female, reminded. "The one with a Confederate emblem and the words 'Keep It Flying' or 'Honk—I'm Just Reloading,' oh yeah, I've seen that around Oakland—conveys a whole *arsenal* of defiant hate."

Somebody asked if anyone knew California's history as regards marriage documents and how they were recorded. "A county in Alabama up until five years ago was keeping separate books marked 'white' and 'colored'—they changed because of an AP article outing their 159-year-old practice," a minister replied. Everyone in the room vocalized their disgust, but nobody had a clue about similar historic practices in California counties.

"What would it take to put out the fires of hate that continue to be lit in America around the Martin Luther King holiday?" the pastor of the small but growing Door of Faith Church wondered out loud. "Every year there are Klan 'Homecoming' rallies around Dr. King's *federal* holiday—"

"Right to assemble, Virgil," someone answered.

"Yeah, but where do you draw the line? That kind of harassment isn't allowed in the workplace, it ought not be allowed in public spaces—"

"Hell, it ought not be allowed *any*where," said her boisterous colleague from Montclair.

"It's communication and making the hate taboo," First Methodist's senior pastor spoke again. "Even California recorded forty-three lynchings—"

"Out of how many?" someone asked.

"About forty-seven hundred between 1882, when records first started being kept, and the late sixties—that right, Mac?" he asked, acknowledging his Zion AME colleague. "He knows all this stuff like the back of his hand."

"Well, and those were just the ones put down on *paper*," Mac Jordan said, picking up where his deferring colleague left off. "So what *is* God calling us people of goodwill to do now, today, to stop the next match from being struck? 'Cause I'm tired, tired, tired of singin' the blues."

Without the lunch hour rule the group would have continued into the afternoon. Before losing any of their numbers to the clock, they scrambled to get a statement down on paper, declaring their support for strengthening hate crime statutes in California and for the adoption of federal hate crime legislation currently proposed by members of Congress.

Mount Sinai's rabbi closed the meeting with prayer, directly following the group affectionately booing their UCC colleague when he tunefully quipped from an old pop Christian song: "It only takes a spark, to get a fi-re go-ing . . ." in a (Lily thought, crass) attempt to lighten the proceedings prior to adjournment and splintering once again into particularities of tradition.

———

RODNEY, STARTING AT LILY'S HOARSE "Noooo," turned over and grabbed her. Their hearts drummed into each other, skin echoing off skin breaking out in sweat. He nuzzled her damp forehead with his lips and Lily sobbed, "I just got killed."

"No, no, baby, you're right here, safe with me."

"I caught a bullet meant for Lucius," she said, thinking she was still laying on cement outside a Seven-Eleven. "Oh Jesus . . ."

"Shhhh, baby, shhhh, I'm here, baby, i'ss okay, baby, i'ss okay," Rodney soothed, conforming his muscular frame to her nightmared body, as if he knew where it had been and what it had been through seconds—minutes?—ago. She stayed in the dream's death-dark a while longer, then abruptly left his hold to shakily reach for the lamp switch on her side of the bed. "I need the light on."

"Okay, babe, but don't go so far," he said, surprised by Lily's bolt. Then patting the warm, hollowed-out impression left in the sheet, Rodney said, "Now get back here, get right back here in the crook of this big ol' black arm."

Lily hesitated. "Oh Jesus, it was awful—it was because of me," she said, huddling around pulled-up knees.

"In your dream," Rodney said, seeking his bearings again. "This in your dream?"

"Yes, Rodney! In my dream!" she erupted. "Some *fucker* wants to off Lucius, because he's with a *white* girl—or *bitch* as he yelled it—'Move, *bitch*!'"

"How can I help?" Rodney asked quietly.

"By staying the hell away from me in this sick fuck society, because sooner or later . . . I'm gonna get you killed."

"Wait—we talkin' 'bout your boy Lucius, or your man Rodney here?"

"What's the difference?"

"I know all us Black men look the same—"

"No," returned Lily, "*I'm* the same, the same female-comma-*white*."

"That *really* your nightmare?"

Lily began sobbing again, "Yes."

"That someone's gonna come after me, 'cause I'm with you," he summarized, asking for his wife's clarification.

"Evidently."

"Well, I won't let anyone kill me, and I mos' definitely won't let my cowardly ass use you as a *shield*."

"It's not what Lucius did—"

"In your dream . . ."

"Yesss," Lily hissed. "In my dream."

"Whoa. Hold it. Hooold it!" said Rodney, pulling her toward him. "Hold *me*! I'm not goin' *any*where—just yet. Not to the South, not to heaven—and neither are you. Your *night*mare is not our scene, baby," he said, defiantly. "And I hope you're not tellin' me this is yours and Lucius's scene, Lily, 'cause that *would* rip a hole in your man's heart."

"That *scene* is public record, Rodney."

"But that's not us, baby," he cooed.

"I pray that's not us," said Lily, trembling again. "I pray to *God* that'll never be us or anyone close to us."

"How can I help you get back to sleep, Lily?"

"Just keep on doin' what you're doin'," she answered.

"I can do that," he said, hunching his shoulders more firmly around her.

"I love you so much. What if some crazy fuck decides you and I shouldn't be together?"

"Lots of crazy *fucks* already do," calmed Rodney. "But I can't live my life like that, afraid of who's in my shadow."

"I'm not asking you to," said Lily, sadly. "It was just so damn real."

"Well, here's what's real to me now," Rodney whispered, as his fleshy lips drifted and fell, drifted and fell, slowly working their way down from her face and neck, and feeling her body finally let go of the stalking fear that wakened them in the bedroom of their Oakland neighborhood that weekday night.

THE NEXT DAY, AN INTERRACIAL church fire in Oregon got added at the last minute to AP's published list tallying thirty-eight Black church burnings since January '95, a figure other sources like the hate-vigilant Center for Democratic Renewal disputed as low. The entire AP report, which Lucius and the rest of the special investigative team continued working on, wouldn't be out for another two weeks, not until the day after the Fourth of July. Regardless which count was correct, most agreed that burnings had reached a peak, while arsonist arrests remained small, begging the question: *Why weren't the best agents investigating the burnings?*

THE NEXT MORNING LUCIUS'S ROOM phone rang. "Mr. Clay," said a muffled male voice in thick Texas accent, "We don't need yer kine here. If y'all know what's good fer y'all, ya take yer Black ass back tuh whar it come from. . . . We jes' like tuh give y'all a frien'ly warnin'." Click.

Lucius kept the buzzing to his ear a while longer, as if to be able to determine the identity of the threatening caller. His heart raced, as he dialed ATF agent Rough's cell phone.

"I just heard from the local goon squad."

"Inviting you to a party?"

"Yeh," Lucius said, laughing nervously, "a lynching party."

"Doesn't sound like much fun," said Rough, "what'd they say?"

"I've overstayed my welcome," replied Lucius, adding, "It's been a long time since I've heard 'your kind'—wait, let me get it right: 'yer *kine*.'"

"You are one powerful might of a man, Lucius. Less than twenty-four hours back in Greenville and someone besides me knows you're here!"

"Some*ones*. Doesn't take a brilliant mind to figure out who the new Black man in town is."

"And here for the same reason they are, filthy sacks of Klanshit," said Rough. "I have to say, it worries me some, them having your number here at the Double Tree."

"Hell, they're probably next door, ordering up room service."

"As long as you're not it," Rough growled. "You keep a gun?"

"On me?" he asked. "Not since squirrel huntin' with my dad—why? You carry one?"

"Of course. Maybe the mayor puts stock in her lawmen, but the only thing I put stock in, especially when I'm on assignment, is gun stock."

"But you're licensed."

"And you're prey," said the Dallas-based federal investigator. "Sorry to break it to ya, old man, but the nineties are just upside-down sixties." Rough went on, "ATF has fifty-five open investigations as of this morning, forty-six of 'em in Black churches."

"Could as easily be a hundred and forty-six," railed Lucius, "who the hell knows what the real numbers are—ATF needs to get its ass in gear."

"Hey, that's my baboon ass you're insulting, don't forget," Rough joked. "But tell me about it—not enough evidently to put some teeth into an all-out sweep of high crime in little places."

"Fuckin' cowards."

"Who're ya criticizing now?" asked Rough, "The Feds or the pyros?"

"Whoever the shoe fits."

"Whomever," Rough teased, then hearing no laughter on Lucius's end, added, "You know, basic grammar—the shoe fits *whom*, *whom*ever."

"A white hood then—one size fits all," Lucius said, soberly refocusing the agent's humor. "See ya down there in thirty."

LUCIUS RUBBED HIS NECK AND WATCHED the day come through his hotel window, splashing light in his face after the disturbing wakeup call. *What the hell am I doing here?* Lucius mulled over the danger in his life up to this point, beginning with the flashback to a knife's glint and the White Monster's smile menacing him and his friends every other week on their way back from the crackertown bakery where they bought bags of cookie bits for a nickel. No matter the cookies were broken and unsaleable to white clientele, Lucius and his buddies could buy a *whole* bag with the little chunk of change earned by doing odd jobs for elderly neighbors. Moreover, the bag represented a reward for their weekly picking up the gauntlet crackertown threw down when they passed bravely by the rows of brick houses.

Lucius and his pals knew that every other week, the pimply-faced Monster would be on the lookout to pirate their goody bag, and though they entrusted its protection to the biggest amongst them, even his grip was usually no match for the older teen. Stationed two blocks before the border between their neighborhood and crackertown, the snarling Monster would bark the same demand through bad teeth, "Gimme whatcha got." Lucius recalled their discussion, how it would have been better had the White Monster taken their money on the way *to* Mr. Richie's. Instead, they would get all the way to the bakery, make their purchase, and be heading safely back to home base in the bliss of eating cinnamon-sprinkled lumps of shortbread, when the stringy-haired head with ears like cut apple halves on top of a dingy T-shirt would suddenly appear and start to growl as he clicked his knife blade into place, blocking their escape over buckled sidewalk.

Once, one of the boys claimed to have seen flames jump out of their tormentor's craggy mouth. When challenged by the others, Lowell explained that he had special powers enabling his vision—something about it running in the

Merkerson family. When Lowell reported that the bullying teen had been jailed for life, this time, Lucius and the others were eager to believe.

ROUGH WAS ALREADY ON HIS second cup of decaf tea by the time Lucius joined him in a booth off to the side and beyond where guests queued up for the breakfast buffet.

"How long you been doin' the Lipton's now, Rough?"

"Doc's visit in the hospital, two years, five months, and four days ago. Impressed the hell outta me. Gloria thought she was gonna have a corpse to dispose of. Still same ol' sack-a-shit husband though. Gave up flesh-eating, booze, and caffeine. Oh, yeah, and smokes. The hardest were steak and tobacco. For some reason, if I backslide it's with red meat. Must be some primitive genetic instinct. Smoking is non-negotiable; I know it's a loaded gun and I still have three kids to put through college so they can turn out smarter than their old man."

"Never. Maybe smarter, Rough, but not wiser."

After the war, Rough Bailey had played around the West Coast a couple of years before returning to Texas where most of his family still resided. He was a farm kid who had seen the larger world from the Marine Corps underbelly in Vietnam and had no interest in expanding his geographical horizons further.

Grinning like a car dealer ready to pounce, the waitress made her approach to their table. "You gents ready fer a li'l breakfast, now that y'all found each other?" she asked, eager to insinuate herself into the men's business. "Whut'll it be—buffet, or off the menu?"

"Buffet here," said Rough, as he got up to get in line.

"Give me a minute with the menu, *Pat*," said Lucius, grinning and reading from her badge decorated with American and Texas flag stickers.

Pat grinned back, thinking his grin was for her. As she handed him a laminated printout with "Good Morning" at the top, Pat winked and confirmed that she had heard Lucius's request, repeating, "I'll give y'all a minute."

Glancing quickly at the sheet, Lucius said, "No, I see it right here. A short stack with bacon, two eggs over easy, please. And a cup of coffee when you can."

"Want any juice with that, sir?" Pat asked, hoping to elicit something more out of her moment alone with Lucius before his less attractive, wedding-banded friend returned.

"No, thank you, Pat. This'll be fine." Lucius looked up at the same time a Black man wearing a chef's hat was transferring sausages from one large metal bin to another set in hot water on the buffet island. He looked to be about sixty-five, the same age his father was when he died. Lucius's father, however, looked older than his natural age at death. *When did his father ever take a break?* Heart trouble like Rough. But, unlike Rough, his father was only partially treated, then released. Just like with the head injury, insurance only paid so much. *Sorry, Mr. Clay. That's just how it is.*

His father's family was short and muscular. Even when Lucius passed his father's height, he respected his daddy's strength. And when his physical strength waned, Lucius still respected the man who was a welder by trade and a mechanical jack-of-all-trades able to fix anything. He could diagnose a problem just by listening to the engine. He could repair cars and machines or tell you why not in half the time it took other mechanics who had regular clientele and better setups.

When things weren't happening in the shop, Henry Clay found welding work, a skill he mastered in the service during World War II. He was around the house more than Lucius's mother. Henry first met Faye Cooper when she worked at

The Hot Meal, a small diner run by the Sparks family. "Faye is short for Fayette, since you asked," Lucius's mother had told Henry, who continued flirting, "And what is that short for?" "Oh, I imagine it could be short for most anything, but my mama's daddy was partial to Lafayette, and my mama always thought it was a romantic name, so I got picked for it," Faye giggled.

Henry had returned from wartime factory service more skilled than when he left. A construction boom provided plenty of welding work for him back home in Texas. He was working on a big granary in Lovetts about ten miles away from Holmes, when he stopped off at The Hot Meal one night after work. Faye was a talkative nineteen-year-old with skin the color of freshly tilled soil just after a rain. She wore her hair pulled back and secured with a tortoise shell clip.

Henry, an eager twenty-three-year-old then, appreciated female beauty. He told his mother the girl "looked clean and sharp, and, oh, yes," he smiled, "pretty." Faye thought Henry a man of the world capable of opening up that world to her. Hoping to foster her favorable impression of him, Henry courted Faye, generously sharing what he knew of factory and nightlife in Gary, Indiana, and all the railway stops that lay between that place and Texas.

The War Department's reliance on his welding to help defeat the foreign enemy of America's freedom tangibly assured Henry of his worth in the eyes of his country. Whenever he thought about the war effort and his part in it, Henry was satisfied that he was like one of the integral pieces, which, when welded together with others, produced an even larger and stronger shield for American freedom overseas.

Henry made a friend during his time at the Indiana factory. Silas was nice, for a cracker. The two young men standing side by side on the factory's assembly line vowed to stand up as best man for each other, laughing about what their respective future brides' families and congregations would say, as they volleyed stereotypes back and forth, each volley more exaggerated than the last.

There was little to support the promises made by Henry and his white friend once they stepped outside the war. Riding the train together as far as Kansas City, they parted in embarrassed silence and unspoken agreement about the exigencies of postwar life and "getting on with it," his cracker friend Silas going further east before south and Henry continuing directly south to Texas.

He was picked up by his mother and aunt and brought back home to a party gathered in honor of his return. The spread of food on the Texas tables was something Henry had missed, working in the factory the last four years, protecting his country's freedom in Gary, Indiana, and coming into manhood. The celebration was more than a welcome home; for Henry, it marked his rite of passage as an American son.

ROUGH RETURNED TO THE TABLE holding a plate mounded with scrambled eggs and hash browns, and a second with cantaloupe and honeydew melon crescents. "Thought somebody might have nabbed you," teased Lucius. "You really gonna eat all that?"

"Not till I hit it with Heinz 57," Rough returned, reaching for the ketchup bottle. "Gonna need fortification in case I have to bust some Klan heads—then again, pinheads don't offer much resistance. I confess," said the paunchy agent, "I just like to eat."

Watching from the coffee stand, Pat timed her delivery of Lucius's meal to coincide with his friend's return from the buffet. "Enjoy," she said, as if presenting a special favorite meal cooked for a friend.

"Thank you, Pat," said Lucius, and after she left, as an aside to Rough, he shook his head, saying, "Can't beat southern hospitality."

"Yeah, let's see what kind of hospitality we have when the dorkboyz in *hoods* face off with boyz *in* the hood—you think the New Black Panthers will show again?"

"No idea," smiled Lucius, as he punctured and sopped up fried egg yolk with a chunk of pancake, "who's gonna be swingin' from red, white, and blue bunting at the Hunt County Courthouse."

BETWEEN TWO WEDDINGS, EACH WITH their own rehearsal, and the regular Sunday morning program at Holy Innocents', Lily saw her family only in snatches that weekend. In fact by Sunday night, she couldn't remember whether she'd seen Scott at any time in the last three days, and had to check with Rodney who verified her recollection as true; their youngest had spent the weekend with a friend, attending Oakland's Juneteenth Festival of the Lake all three days.

Lucius caught up with Lily the week following to report on the Greenville Klan rally, "lasting about one and a half hours too long" for the former Texan, now White House correspondent. "Both the regional and national directors of the fastest growing arm of the Klan spoke from the county courthouse steps—in plain view, flanked by Confederate-flag-waving geeks—with some lame recorded military march music in the background," jeered Lucius. "Fuckin' typical spectacle—publicly disavowing violence they secretly condone."

"What was the response?" asked Lily.

"There were only about three hundred spectators, a lot of antiracist protesters, Black and white. Some jackass supporters waving a Confederate flag, while protesters were burning every scrap of Klan propaganda crap they could get their hands on."

"Amazing," Lily scoffed. "Did the New Black Panthers make the party?"

"No, and I'm still not sure why not," said Lucius. "But they'll have another chance in a week—the *Texas* Knights of the Ku Klux Klan had to reschedule their little Klanklatch after the *Arkansas* morons preempted."

"Why all the way from Arkansas—the Texas group isn't orthodox enough, or what?"

"Harrison, Arkansas. Knights of the KKK's national headquarters. Big pricks from 'The Natural State' upstaged the little *Lone Star State* dicks."

"The *Natural* State?"

"Yeh, Arkansas's nickname."

"So, where is the roving reporter now?"

"Shrevepoht, Luuuziana, Revr'nd Lily," said Lucius. "Minimal damage compared to recent fires, less minimal when you're talkin' fifty members. And, of course, the huge loss in terms of Black Americans feeling safe is getting huger."

"Where to next?"

"I fly back to D.C. this weekend, hopefully to be on hand when the president affixes his signature to the Church Arson Prevention Act next week," said Lucius. "And I'm really anxious to get home."

"I bet," said Lily, hearing fatigue in his voice. "Have any pets missing your company at home?"

"No, I'm not a dog or cat kind of guy," said Lucius. "Won a goldfish once at a fair, but when I found it belly-up three days after I took it home, named it, fed it—the whole kid thing—I decided then and there I never wanted another pet depending on me. How 'bout you?"

"We have a dog that stays in the yard. Kids' dog, parents' responsibility," said Lily. "Personally, I'd rather be cleaning up after horses."

"How's your family?"

"Rodney's consumed by a tricky case, kids leave for Alabama in a few days to visit Rodney's mother and family in Birmingham."

"That's right, your soul man's from Bombingham . . ." Lucius mused, then let it go. "And, how are *you?*"

"Busy priest-ing. A couple of weddings, you know, the usual. Rodney and I hope to get away once they decide this drug lord's fate—sometime next month—I'm hoping it doesn't limp along till August and run into the start of the kid's school year."

"Those kid times seem so distant now," said Lucius. "You have a great thing goin' there in Oakland. It turned out good for you, Revr'nd Lily."

"Speaking of which, I gotta go maintain my *Revr'nd* credentials, sorry," said Lily, distracted by the time. "Gotta make some hospital visits—summer is such an illogical time for tragic illness. I think God screwed up on that one. So, anyway, thanks for the call. Good to hear from you, alive and well, and hoping for a safe return to your home in America's capital."

"Yeh, I'll call you with an update when I get back to my fair city on the Potomac—"

"Do," said Lily, not wanting to be rude, but worried about having enough time to eat before going to the hospital to see three critically ill parishioners. "Goodbye, Lucius."

Detecting her harried tone, Lucius kept it simple, "Goodbye, Lily," then hastened to add, "Take care of yourself and that beautiful family."

"Thanks, Lucius," replied Lily, struck by his thoughtfulness.

IT WAS THE SECOND IMPORTANT phone call Lily took that day. Midmorning, Lucius checked in to see whether she had heard the news about the president signing the legislation giving federal prosecutors further jurisdiction in burnings and other desecrations at America's houses of worship. The success of the Church Arson Prevention Act was good news, especially for Saint John's AME, the latest target. Neither, however, was the news of the day. Indeed, the president's signature on the US Civil Rights code amendment and the North Carolina congregation that, days earlier, suffered fifty thousand dollars of damage from Molotov cocktails thrown in and at the church, igniting the oil poured around its foundation, were both upstaged.

Terrorists bombing an American military complex in Saudi Arabia the week before meant that reporting immediately shifted from domestic to international terrorism and continued to remain with the nineteen killed and seventy-three injured in Dhahran and the two groups claiming responsibility.

Breaking-news advantage, Lucius suggested. But then, why was daily ink still being committed to the mustier ValuJet crash story? Lily wanted to know. The fickle media produced remittent coverage, making social ills appear to disappear, Lucius observed. And *definitive* reports like *USA Today*'s that hit the stands the prior weekend and the AP's, due out day after the next day's fireworks, would, Lucius feared, hammer away at any further need for media attention to church arsons.

Nobody wanted to hear how many unsolved burnings there still were, Lucius bemoaned. Much less that the total count didn't even include *all* cases of Black church desecrations by white vandals, most of which either got written off or investigated as petty teenaged pranks. Lucius noted that except for Black-on-Black, white-on-Black crime in America inspired the least investigative effort and the lightest punishment.

Lucius continued, criticizing current church arson prosecution for not doing a better job corroborating the link between the crime and the hate spawning it. "It's easy, once you have suspects in custody. I mean, god*damn*! Don't stop at the obvious—follow a whiff back to its goddamn source."

"Like an investigative journalist."

"Like somebody who knows—and cares about what they're doing."

"Why haven't you ever sought public office?"

"In your parlance, Revr'nd Lily—not my *calling*."

"Has anyone ever solicited your nomination?"

"Yeah, as a matter of fact . . . for Adventure Guides chief—when my son was in grade school."

No pastoral matters hurrying Lily, they chatted leisurely about holiday plans on separate coasts. Lily said she was looking forward to an extra-long weekend with Rodney, the kids being in the middle of their annual Alabama sojourn with Grandma Davis. "Will you be seeing your son?"

"Not till the leaves turn," sighed Lucius. "He's tramping around the continent, currently on a bike trip through Tuscany, I believe."

"Ah, youth. Would be nice to have that kind of freedom again . . . by the way, what's your son's name? I apologize . . . I don't think I asked before."

"Apology accepted—though I should probably shoulder some of the blame. I'm not always forthcoming with personal information," Lucius said, writing himself a note to check on the status of his ex's promised contribution to their son's law school expenses.

"Miles deserves a break. He worked hard at BU the past four-and-a-half years."

"Following in your footsteps?"

"Shoe size? Yes," Lucius answered with pride in his voice. "Interests, not exactly. BA, anthropology. After Europe—Hastings."

"So—Miles is his name?—in the fall, Miles and I will be neighbors across the Bay from each other."

"You *and* his grandparents—Claire's folks are still in Berkeley."

"Will it be difficult, I mean, with Miles so far away?"

"A plane ride's all," Lucius superficially brushed off Lily's question, hoping to derail any further delving into his relationship with his son. "I'm out on the West Coast periodically, for work."

"Are your parents still on the Gulf?"

"Your mind is a steel trap—how did you remember?"

"Important things get embedded," Lily stated, as if reciting a proverb. "I told you before, our encounter changed my life." Lucius hoped the silence on his end would go unnoticed, as he digested what Lily had just said. "Does Miles get to see your folks very often?"

"No. No, he never got to meet them," Lucius rued. "They both passed before he was born."

"Oh. I'm so sorry . . . my folks too. Never even met Rodney," said Lily, retrieving a dim memory. "How 'bout yours? Did they have a chance to be in-laws?"

"My father. But he was pretty messed up—traumatic head injury," Lucius replied as he felt the familiar father-love rise and ball in his throat. "You know, one of those invisible, in-your-head kind of disabilities that really was. Only back in the day, nobody knew how to treat it. They got to be in-laws with my sister. Twice, in fact," chuckled Lucius. "Girl was wild and beautiful. I guess she did a good thing, after all. Making our folks grandparents—my mother, especially—was a real good thing. . . . Hey! don't you have some prayin' to do before the holiday?"

"Sounds like you have a train to catch!"

"No, I just don't want to tie up the line, case your man or your parishioners need you."

"Actually both—in about an hour. I have the usual Wednesday-at-noon service, then my man's meetin' me at Le Cheval, kind of a Vietnamese, French-around-the-edges place downtown Oakland. Been there?"

"Not in this lifetime."

"Well, when you come to visit Miles, I'll take you."

"That would be nice," said Lucius, accepting her invitation. "Well, Lily, have a good one—they shoot guns off on the Fourth in Oakland?"

"Are you kidding?—they shoot guns off *every* day, in*clu*ding the fourth day of July!"

"Like we say in D.C., never leave home without your American Express inside a bulletproof vest."

"O-kay! Happy Fourth, Lucius—and thanks for the call. Really. Wow! I feel so blessed to have friends in high places—"

"Let's just . . . leave it at that," snuffled Lucius. "Later, Miss Lily. And, y'all make sure, now, those Oaktown gunslingers check their piece at the door."

LILY ASKED CHESTER, THE CHURCH sexton, whether he noticed the man who came into the chapel at the start of the service but left directly after Lily said the opening salutation. He said he hadn't seen anyone but the three who came forward, desiring priestly laying-on-of-hands: an Ethiopian refugee with her usual petition for her dead husband's repose and two men in shirt and tie who walked over from the Kaiser Building to pray for healing for their mutual colleague with a new cancer diagnosis.

And a fourth, old Mister Tweed who, despite perhaps needing healing ministrations for his bedridden wife and his own diabetic condition, disdained "showy faith," preferring rather to wait till after that part of the service to join the rest of his cohort at the altar rail for communion. Then together, except for Chester, who partook only once a year at the Easter vigil, in uplifted palms they received the holy food Lily dispensed. With raised hands, she guided the cup of holy drink to their lips.

Considering the small congregation and her lunch date with Rodney to follow, Lily shortened her homiletic remarks commemorating Saints Peter and Paul's martyrdom during Nero's first century persecution. Church tradition held that the two saints, though contentious in life, walked a common path of faith that ended for both in Rome with Paul's beheading and Peter's head-downward crucifixion.

In the sacristy before the service, Lily had ruminated backwards over American martyrs who died between the chapters of Juneteenth and Independence, as she vested in alb and cincture; the ankle-length white robe represented Roman street dress, and the belt, crocheted by arthritic altar guild hands, symbolized the whip used on Jesus by his torturers.

Stepping into the alb's opening, she stepped out of the linear measure of chronologic time and into the momentous focus of *kairotic* time—*220 years after slaveholding white American colonists sign a document declaring independence from foreign rule*, she thought, *this current American president signs another document empowering freedom from racist tyranny at home.*

"Sorry to interrupt—did you want to use the white linen or the multicolored?" Maura was the first Black parishioner inducted into Holy Innocents' old-guard altar guild. Shortly after Lily's arrival, the guild president came to her complaining about an aging membership unable to provide coverage. After her first meeting, the problem became obvious: an all-white altar guild in a multiracial, urban parish.

Lily was grateful the young, single professional Maura was not only partial to altar ministry, but also willing to put herself in nomination. Though it was within her prerogative as rector to appoint members to the guild, Lily wanted to ensure that Maura's dignity would not be compromised as the guild's good Christian women tested the waters of racial confluence.

"I think for today, despite it being martyrdom we're observing—let's use the cloth of many colors." *Martyrs wore skins of many colors*, thought Lily. *Some churches have wooden communion tables; this one has a cold stone altar.*

"Anything else, Mother Lily?" Lily knew that Maura used the clergy title as a "Father" parallel, nevertheless, Lily imposed her own interpretation. Knowing the address was honorific, coming from one whose roots were planted in Black church tradition, Lily felt doubly honored by the young woman's acknowledgement of her spiritual authority. "No, Maura, thank you. How's things with your fiancé?"

"I don't know," Maura laughed, shaking her head. "I think the man needs an overhaul."

"Dr. Stephen's not that old, is he?"

"*Shouldn't* be," Maura asserted, "but I don't know what it is with him. Says he's 'sooo tired' all the time. Doctor's hours aside, I'm a young woman. I want at least as much attention as his *office* girls get. Damn! Oh, sorry—"

"It's the old wrestling match between quality and quantity—but as far as my emotions go, I think it may be a bogus distinction!"

"You know that's right!" Maura cheered. "I really love him—I just think he might need to try some of his own medicine."

"Physician, heal thyself."

"Speaking of which, I won't be able to stay for the service today. I've gotta get some papers into the county before one p.m. today."

"The big project here in Adam's Point?"

"Yeah, the restoration's going really well. Just have to stay on top of it." Maura interned, then was hired on by the East Bay architectural firm McGill and Sons.

"I'll miss you, but I understand," Lily absolved. "I gotta get up to visit the site again."

"You won't *believe* how it's changed—the whole face of the house is restored to the original. Really beautiful."

Lily responded to Maura's excitement. "It must be satisfying work—restoration. Hope it continues to go smoothly. When's the grand opening?"

"It's already being marketed as 'Oakland's Christmas House,' so I'm hoping we'll meet all our deadlines and be able to cut the ribbon weekend after Thanksgiving."

"Well, I don't want to hold you up—go with my blessing!" said Lily, putting on her stole. "And, Maura. Thanks for all your help. I always look forward to midweek."

"Mutually," Maura beamed.

"Keep me posted on the restoration."

Maura snorted. "I know you mean house *and* fiancé!"

LILY GOT TO THE RESTAURANT and was seated at their favorite table before Rodney arrived. Le Cheval's owner, Mister Thieu, sang the praises of his chef's duck à l'orange special as he signaled a waiter to bring Lily her standing order: coffee, Vietnamese-style with sweetened condensed milk over ice. "I know what you like, Miss Priest Lily," was his standard remark upon scooping the tall glass off the server's tray and presenting the drink himself. Mister Thieu awaited her palate's approval, remaining at attention as Lily took a sip and pronounced the drink "God's nectar, Mister Thieu." *Mister God*, Lily mused. Concluding their ritual, the restaurateur nodded to his waiter and then to Lily, saying, "Victor will be with you as soon as Mister Rodney arrive."

"Thank you, Mister Thieu." Lily knew she would order the special but perused the menu just the same. A listing of new appetizers, including filo-wrapped pâté on a bed of greens, started a tug of war with her first selection. Her stomach now audibly growling, Lily checked her watch and wondered what was keeping her husband.

"Her Holiness, what're you doin' here?" Since settling the extortionist parishioner case following Lawrence's death, Keith had disappeared, with Lily's blessing.

"Whaddya mean—this is Rodney's and my hangout, man. C'mere and lemme make sure it's not a ghost I'm seeing." Lily got up and threw her arms around the younger man in mint resort wear.

"You like the color?"

"Skin *and* duds," said Lily, leaning back and admiring his whole presentation. "Tan's still fresh—you must've *just* swum ashore."

"Sunday. Too soon, unfortunately. Been back on the job twelve hours now," sighed Keith, slumping into the chair Lily pulled out. "Took Monday to decompress."

"And then some," Lily sympathized. "Whew—*this*'s been a season not worth repeating."

"I'd do it in an instant, if I could have my baby back for two," Keith returned, as Rodney, sneaking up behind Lily, landed a kiss on her cheek. "And who's this young stud makin' moves on my woman?" Rodney teased, drawing Keith into his bear hug. "How you doin', young man?"

Keith started nodding before spooning out words from inside his gut. "Okay . . . considering."

Rodney's brows bent over eyes creased in compassion, "Yeh, considering what you've been through, probably *just* okay, and no more. So, how'd the cruise work out?"

"You're lookin' at it," said Keith, raising his hands and flipping his wrists open. "Ta-daaaaa. Go ahead and finger the shirt, Rodney, I know you wanna finger my shirt."

"That's some nice cloth you got coverin' that tan hide o'yours."

Keith nodded again. "Yeah, the sun felt good," he said, lips closing behind the sentiment, then opening again, permitting further escape. "You know the cruise was all Lawrence's idea. For our tenth anniversary."

"Hence, the double-dark," declared Lily, as she reached out and firmly clasped his hand, her other hand gently stroking its sun-browned back.

Locking their grip more firmly, Keith toasted his partner. "Yeah, this extra tan's for you, Lawrence. All for you." Then, as if remembering a late appointment, Keith dropped her hand, saying, "Gotta run, you two lovebirds. Didn't mean to be interlopin' on your nooner."

"Not at all," said Rodney, "good to see you, Keith. Now you're back, you better come by for some'f the clergy woman's extra fine chili."

"Yeah," Lily concurred, "I just made a batch."

"Enough for an army?"

"The usual," laughed Lily. "How'd a rogue like you get my number?"

With a promise to follow up on their invitation, Keith left, leaving Lily to describe the special to Rodney as Victor made his approach to take their order.

THE INTENSE AFTERNOON SESSION LEFT Rodney sucking in air back in his chambers, after declaring the federal district court adjourned till after the Fourth of July. Bounced back into Rodney's jurisdiction the prior week, drug trafficker K.C. Mack's retrial had gained notoriety from the start, both in print as well as on TV's nightly news. The case was sent back when appellate justices determined that Judge Davis's now-retired predecessor had committed a "reversible error" by suppressing a forensic expert's testimony.

Remanded cases summoned extra pressure; the bench could make the same ruling, or not. Rodney, familiar with Mack's first trial, was impressed with the defendant's new counsel, a legally nimble attorney, to date an unknown to his ninth circuit courtroom.

Rodney welcomed the holiday break from the acute vigilance Mack's sharp young defense strategist exacted. In addition to catching up on much needed rest, he looked forward to using some of the long weekend for uninterrupted library time to bone up on more recent decisions, as well as reexamine past precedent.

Rodney picked up the phone and answered his clerk's buzz, "Yes, Phoebe."

"There's an Ethan Bierstadt to see you. Says he's an old acquaintance?"

Though he had less hair and some extra pounds, the male Rodney noticed sitting in the back of the courtroom during the proceeding's last half hour seemed vaguely familiar. Eerily familiar, as Rodney recalled the last, disturbing conversation with Ethan some twenty years ago.

Presuming he cleared the metal detectors, no other precautionary measures seemed warranted in the case of Lily's ex-fiancé. "Did he state his business?"

"Just that he was in the area and wanted to drop by to say hi. Sorry, should I ask him to—"

"Is he standing right there?"

"Yes," answered Phoebe, starting to get upset with herself for not being more professional in her handling of the stranger who came calling on her boss.

Checking the clock on his desk, a present from Hartwig on the Senate Judiciary Committee's approval of his appointment, he said curtly into the phone, "Tell him I only have seven minutes . . . if he'd like to schedule sometime next week when I could offer a more cordial reception—"

"Will do," said Phoebe, sighing relief that maybe she hadn't messed up after all.

Relieved not to have to be dealing with a present unknown from the past at that late hour, Rodney replaced the receiver in its cradle and began scooping papers together on his desk. As he reached for his briefcase, the phone buzzed again. "What now, Phoebe?"

"He says he only intends a brief hello. Says he'll only take up a minute of your time."

Consulting the desk clock again, Rodney relented, "Okay, then. Why don't you ask him to come in."

"I will, your Honor. And, sir, I told him Deputy's locking up at four on the nose. Is there anything else?"

"No. Thank you, Phoebe. If I don't see you before you leave, have a good holiday."

"Thank you, sir. You, too."

MARSHAL RUDY VICENTE WATCHED till the clock's hand reached twelve.

"Goodbye, Deputy, have a good one," Phoebe tossed over her back as she exited the courtroom. "See you after the fireworks."

"Judge's visitor, he still in with him?"

Phoebe stopped just outside the doorway and turned.

"Guess so. Unless he took him out the back way. Anyway, you'll be locking up—you can check to make sure everyone's out, right?"

"Goes with the job," Rudy mumbled. "I was just askin', 'cause I didn't see him leave. No problem, though—get outta here. Go have some fun!" Phoebe was already halfway down the hall. "You, too, Rudy," he answered himself, mimicking the young woman's chirpy voice, then grumbled, "Doesn't gimme the time of day."

Sliding a chained key into the slot and bolting the courtroom's heavy double doors, Rudy realized the start of his vacation. With a light step, Deputy Vicente proceeded to the front of the courtroom, whistling "I'm a Yankee Doodle Dandy." He rapped on the justice's door, calling, "Your Honor, you there?" Hearing no response, he knocked again. Still no answer, he turned the doorknob, but it was locked. "Guess he's already on vacation too," the deputy shrugged, finding it odd Judge Davis didn't say goodbye before he left. Especially before the long holiday weekend.

"Whatever," he said, as he walked around the bench and back down the center aisle to let himself out the front. Pulling out his key, Rudy remained bothered by the nonroutine lack of closure to his work week. He turned to retrace his steps, heavier now, to the chamber's door.

Unlocking and entering the darkened room, he saw a sagging figure collapsed against the desk front. Switching on the light, Rudy yanked out his radio and yelled for help. Half a face hung off the bone; unnaturally angled legs propped up the crumpled body. Macabre and lifeless, no movement remained save for blood streaming down the torso to form an ever-widening pool on the carpet beneath.

Within seconds, paramedics were on the scene, efficiently rolling Rodney's limp form onto a stretcher. As unnecessary as it seemed, out of dignity for the dead, they started an IV in a futile attempt to replace some of the fluids still draining from the judge's body carried by urgent ambulance to Highland Hospital.

THE SOCIAL WORKER DID NOT tell Lily that her husband was dead on arrival when he reached her at the church, still packing up by herself, Jules having left already. There had been a shooting, he said, then quickly asked if she had someone that could bring her to Oakland's main trauma center.

She continued, calmly, pulling together items needed for working at home over the much-anticipated holiday weekend: a writing pad with sermon notes and drawings, a dog-eared *Revised Standard Bible,* and, fingering its frayed colored marking ribbons, her *Book of Common Prayer.* Placing the stack of materials in her red leather case, Lily phoned upstairs to see whether Eleanor, the Senior Services Director, might still be in her office. The agency's message came on after three rings, giving the normal hours of operation said to resume the following Monday.

Though unreliable after the four-thirty onset of his own private sherry hour—which began even earlier during holidays—the church sexton was, at least theoretically, on the premises. Chester's voice slurred as he answered her call to his apartment, located off the back portion of the church roof. "Repeat that again, if you would, Reverend Vida," he said with his usual formality, now comical from drink.

Certain that his driving would be impaired, Lily wished the loyal but inebriated *maître d'église* an enjoyable Fourth. "Oh, quite," giggled Chester. "You, too, madam," confirming Lily's surmise that he would be happier serving tea to lord and lady of the manor on return from the hunt.

Forgetting the social worker's instruction, Lily took the van keys out of her purse, saying to herself it was silly spending any more time trying to find someone to drive her to Highland; she could drive herself. And besides, they would have told her to hurry if it were serious. The hospital had specified her husband was somehow involved . . . maybe that drug dealer being retried was shot, and Rodney, as the judge, had to accompany him to the emergency room.

Before she could resolve the content of her conversation with the hospital, Lily heard tapping on the church's side door glass. "Oh, Robert," Lily said, as she stepped out of her office and opened the door to one of the soup group's founding members. The father of three was now gainfully employed and the proud owner of a new, used car.

"Glad I caught you, Rev'n Vida. Jus' wanna drop off some ah my special sauce," said the tall man, sunlight reflecting off the diamond stud in his ear, "'cause I know y'all gon' be doin' your patriotic barbecue duty t'morrah."

"Come, c'mon in," Lily gestured. "Thanks, Robert—so . . . so nice of you. Hey, I'm in a little bit of a rush right now. Just got a call from Highland Hospital. Something about Rodney, or someone associated with Rodney being injured. . . . I, I was just, uh, on my way over there, uh—"

"You all right, Rev'n Vida? Look, I drive ya," Robert said, dangling his car keys. "Got gas, and in a clean car."

"Do you mind?"

"Fuh you?" laughed Robert. "Heah, what you need carried?" he asked, following her into her office. "Gimme that and you grab yoh pocke'book, theah—you need me to lock up?"

"Yeah, yeah I do," said Lily, hanging the purse by its strap on her left shoulder before digging for her office keys.

"These them?" Robert picked up the set of keys from her desk and threw a patient grin in Lily's direction. "Now go on out t'doh, and I be right behind, lockin' up." Lily watched the stoop of his large frame, as Robert fit each key in its hole. "Okay, we ready to roll."

As he opened the passenger door to his car parked at the curb, Robert said, "Been waitin' a long time to get you back fuh th'good you done me an' mah family—hop in, Rev'n Vida."

WHAT LILY DID AFTER COMING to Highland Hospital like a beggar for Rodney's life was lost in the fog of seeing her husband's hideously massacred body. Somehow, her sister Dee was at her side the next morning, and her children, accompanied by Rodney's sister, were returned to her from Alabama that afternoon. Lucius caught a plane from Washington that made its descent through a night sky, alit with Fourth of July fireworks.

Other family, more Rodney's than hers, followed closely on their heels, along with condolences that came from as near as across the Bay, and as far away as the White House. Between Jules and Lucius, each sent item got recorded and organized, pending Lily Vida's future response.

THE IMPOSSIBLE WAS ACCOMPLISHED at the hands of San Francisco's College of Mortuary Science students; their artistry restored Rodney's face, matching molding clay to his flesh and getting the two shades nearly the same.

Holy Innocents' choir braved to be glorious, scheduling extra rehearsals to "get it right" when, as per his will's instruction, they sang the blues at Rodney's burial service with the Rev. Hugh Lovelle officiating. Dubbing himself "nearly retired," her former mentor, now in his early seventies, looked as distinguished as in their earlier years working together in New York.

Lily was grateful when Hugh announced upon arrival that he would be staying through the second, maybe even third week of her and her children's new grief, filling in the gap of maternal grandfather during the sad and seething mourning for the father and husband never to be replaced.

IN THE WEEKS BETWEEN CAPTURE and arraignment, much debate ensued about the charge to be brought against Ethan, whether white-on-Black hate crime or, as Lily's ex-fiancé, a crime of passion. A citizen enraged over federal bench rulings was a third motive advanced for Rodney's murder.

Evidence from the killer himself decided how he would be tried, finally. Harder to argue, but more accurate, nevertheless, Ethan Bierstadt was arraigned in federal court on charges of violating US Civil Rights Code when he murdered Rodney Davis, his former fiancée's husband. Ethan's confiscated journal described in meticulous detail the plans he formulated and scrubbed before settling on the one he put into play July third. With his own handwriting, Ethan used racial epithets to label each sketch diagramming intended targets on *Lily's Negro's* body for the handcast *black bullets* he would shoot from his handcrafted *white* plastic gun.

TRUSTED MEMBERS OF HOLY INNOCENTS' and Lucius, taking a leave of absence from his D.C. desk, shielded Lily and her children from media jaws and incessant demands made on her to be present at political rallies, additional memorials, and community tributes.

"I HEAR THE *TRIB'S* LOOKIN' for a new editor," Lucius began.

"So I hear."

"Maynard's gonna be a tough act to follow. First major Black owner-publisher—man's a living legend, way he saved the paper—"

"Yeah, saved the paper, but not himself. . . ." Lily knew personally about the former editor's stress over keeping Oakland's daily financially viable without compromising its unique East Bay–mix perspective.

"Such a loss for us."

"You knew him, then?"

"His son's in the twins' class. Has been all through grade school . . . yeah, Bob and Nancy's only child," tsked Lily. "Another brokenhearted family—"

"Kids back in school?"

"Just."

"How's that for you?"

"Actually, they were ready—and if they weren't, *I* sure as hell was," declared Lily. "We all needed some normalizing routine—everything's so damned *ab*normal around here."

"What're you up to today?"

"Lake Merritt. My usual three-point-four miles. How 'bout you?—must be almost lunchtime at the White House."

"Wasn't invited, I think I'll just eat my bag lunch on the White House lawn," said Lucius, feigning disappointment.

"At two's a briefing on international terrorism, part two—follow-up to the conference the president called in July after the TWA bombing."

"Yeah, well, you'll have to catch me up—I lost a whole chapter there. Maybe an entire book."

"Put in a good word for me at the *Trib*," Lucius half-jested, "and I'll play as much catch-up ball with you as you want."

"How's Miles doing?"

"Hasn't broken the old man's bank yet—only called once, needing a *small* infusion," chortled Lucius. "Went over budget at the bookstore."

"Quit your whining," Lily scolded, "you know you like to be needed."

"*Me*. I like *me* needed, not my money."

"It's a male thing," Lily jeered. "Should be used to it by now. . . ." Her voice caught on an emotional snag, and she couldn't finish her taunt.

"It's okay, Lily. It's okay," Lucius consoled. "I'm a big hankie."

"You know, Rodney told me the same thing," Lily bawled into the phone, "when that sorry fucker Ethan disappeared on me. . . ."

"Yeh, well he's about to disappear again," Lucius said sharply. "Soon's they figure out how many life sentences to pile on his soon-to-be cock-sucking ass. Coward bastard."

"Irony is," Lily continued, crying and talking, "a better man—if Ethan *had* been a better man—Rodney and I would've never hooked up." Sobbing more, "Sorry . . . life sucks right now."

"It sucks that I'm, uh—" Lucius changed what he wanted to say, "that you're unavailable to go to lunch with me today."

Lily chuckled through a stuffed nose, "Hey, I could just about hop a plane today. If it weren't for the kids. . . ."

"How're they doing?"

"Scott has gone back to 'Wylie' and been acting out a little, you know, petty stuff. Zor' is no longer mute, and Dezzy's blue vocabulary has increased tenfold."

"Good for him," laughed Lucius. "Good for all of them. And you, Lily—*Vida*! I think your parents knew what they were doing with that name, grandmother's, right?"

"Yeah, a real *life*monger," Lily reflected. "Funny. *Vida's* so I'd keep something of *Lily* for myself—and Rodney."

"That tricky line, as you called it. You walk it well."

Lily started crying again. "Not always . . . but, I hope enough."

"Rodney's face when he looked at you told the whole story, Lily. The man was justifiably crazy in love with you."

"I miss him so much, I, uh, I'm lost," Lily wept. "Every day, I have to find my feet again . . . if it weren't for antidepressants, I really don't think I could do it."

"You're doin' just what you need to do for now, Lily. It's okay, it's okay," Lucius repeated.

HE WAS BACK; SHE WAS GONE. Wearing his customary Huck Finn color-coordinated T-shirt and fringed cutoffs, the "Oakland Greeter" was once again perched on the wall at the Twelfth Street end of Lake Merritt, saying, "Good morning, darlin" to Lily as she passed by. The woman making her stone bench bed in cocooned layers of sleeping bag and blanket at the other end of the lake, however, was gone. *Was she headed south for the winter like northern birds or New Yorker snowbirds?* Lily wondered.

Rounding her walk from Harrison to Grand, the spot was empty where she was used to seeing the wrapped form with a nose exposed or sometimes a pad of hair, as the only evidence of a human being. Often a fresh deli bag had been left, as an offering by one of Oakland's employed rushing to catch the bus, Lily imagined, but not in too much of a hurry to remember a city sister. On warm mornings, Lily mused, the chrysalis woman might have her breakfast in bed, alfresco.

This morning was cooler; Lily could smell September. Twisted tree branches ending in purple bur looked like gnarled fingers of a dowager who recently had her nails done. Sounds of summer playgroups had been vacuumed up by local schools. *Change of venue*, Lily thought. *It was that time of year for everyone, jubilant and suffering alike.*

Lily walked past their favorite sushi restaurant displaying plastic replicas of menu items in the window, past the old Korean men, sitting propped on canes on a bench advertising Albert Brown Mortuary, past the Sauers' toy/bookstore they had patronized for all their kids' birthdays and their kids' friends' birthdays.

When she reached her car parked in front of Brewberry's, Lily looked down at the fallen leaves lassoing her feet, then resolutely lifted her face to greet the wind's herald of a season ended, and a new season just begun.

———

ACKNOWLEDGMENTS

I'M GRATEFUL FOR THE VISION OF She Writes Press and its skilled shapers: Brooke Warner, Samantha Strom, Anne Durette, Elizabeth Kauffman, and Krissa Lagos.

For Vernyce Dannells, whose story editing and sensibilities improved my novel and whose ranging artistry and fierce compassion nurture all.

For St. Paul's Episcopal Church, School, and Towers, Oakland, California.

For *Friday Morning Writers*, whose writing and reading knits us together for life; the *fiction femmes*, whose author experience unpacks the publishing process; and for *Wellness City Citizens*, who know injustice but nonetheless, generously and bravely, choose life.

For Sisters: Marilyn Kehaulani Yee, Nancy LaRue Butts, Sharon Bernstein Perlmuter, Sandy Robertson Browning, and Jeanne Mason St. Ellen; for Karol Wahlberg Goldsmith, Jan Breidenbach Armstrong, Pam Gould Campbell, and Alieca Richie Hux; for Marilyn Horn, Sherry Campbell, Nancy Jensen-Case, and Kathy Brady; for Laura Combs, Bettye Kelly, Marie Eskandari, Kate Dare-Winters, Bertha Reilly, Jacquie Taylor, and Joan Blades; for Deidra Gray, Dr.

Cheryl Lew, and Dr. Georgiana Rodiger; for the Rev. Drs. Pamela Cooper-White and Rebecca Lyman and the Revs. Jeannette Myers, Katherine Lehman, Ruth Becker-Witt, Ellen Tanouye, Margie Patterson Latham, Ajuko Ueda, and Joyce Corbin Cunningham; for Elizabeth Fillpot, Diana Kittredge, Mary Kimball, and Nancy Barnes Wilson; for the *Firsts*: the Philadelphia Eleven and the Washington Four, the Rev. Dr. Pauli Murray and the Rev. Dr. Fran Toy, the Right Reverend Barbara Harris, and the Most Reverend Katharine Jefferts Schori and for former President of the Episcopal General Convention House of Deputies Bonnie Anderson.

For Brothers: Rabbi Bruce Benson and the Revs. Jim Boline, Fletcher Davis, Michael Wyatt, Donald Seaton, Boyd Lyon, and Shane Benjamin; for Tim Harrison, Stewart Herman, the Rt. Revs. Richard Chang and Chester Lovelle Talton, and the Most Reverend Michael Curry.

For Mothers: Alice B. Ray, Dee Barrett, Mozella Lambert McLaughlin, the Rev. Joyce Dodson Washington (Mrs. Booker T. Washington III), Vera Bouleware Hart, and Marian Gold Krugman.

For my cousins, especially David Trunnell, J. Hamilton and Carol Licht, and Caprice Spencer Rothe; and for my nieces and nephews: Hana Haber, the Agrens, Hamiltons, Hamilton-Bakers, Hilsabecks, O'Neills, Peckhams, Sullivans, Christophersons, and Pooleys.

For my parents and parents-in-law: Wava Trunnell Hamilton and James Hall Hamilton, and MaryAnne Walker Hilsabeck and Dr. John Richard Hilsabeck.

For my sister Elise, my brother Jim, my sister Heidi, and for my Hilsabeck siblings.

Most important, my gratitude and deepest love for David, Brent, Burr, and Sang Hee, who inspire new thought, keep me humble, and frame our life as family with constant love.

ABOUT THE AUTHOR

POLLY HAMILTON HILSABECK was in the second wave of women ordained priest in the Episcopal Church in 1985 in the Diocese of Los Angeles and currently lives with her husband in Durham, North Carolina.

Connect at: https://www.pollyhamiltonhilsabeck.com

Author photo © Cambria Storms

SELECTED TITLES FROM SHE WRITES PRESS

She Writes Press is an independent publishing
company founded to serve women writers everywhere.
Visit us at www.shewritespress.com.

Valeria Vose by Alice Bingham Gorman. $16.95, 978-1-63152-409-7. When privileged Southern woman Valeria Vose discovers her husband's infidelity through his lover's attempted suicide, she turns to an Episcopal priest for direction and solace—and spins into a clandestine, ill-fated love affair that forces her to confront all her preconceived values and expectations.

Boop and Eve's Road Trip by Mary Helen Sheriff. $16.95, 978-1-63152-763-0. When her best friend goes MIA, Eve gathers together the broken threads of her life and takes a road trip with her plucky grandma Boop in search of her—a journey through the South that shows both women they must face past mistakes if they want to find hope for the future.

Purple Lotus by Veena Rao. $16.95, 978-1-63152-761-6. Tara, an immigrant woman in the American South, is trapped in a loveless, abusive arranged marriage, until she discovers self-love—a powerful force that gives her the courage to find herself and to confront a cruel, victim-blaming, patriarchal culture.

Who Are You, Trudy Herman? by B. E. Beck. $16.95, 978-1-63152-377-9. After two years in a German-American Internment Camp in Texas, teenager Trudy Herman's family moves to Mississippi, where Trudy comes face-to-face with the ingrained discrimination—and has to decide whether to look the other way or become the person her beloved grandfather believed she could be.

The Wiregrass by Pam Webber. $16.95, 978-1-63152-943-6. A story about a summer of discontent, change, and dangerous mysteries in a small Southern Wiregrass town.

Beginning with Cannonballs by Jill McCroskey Coupe. $16.95, 978-1-63152-848-4. In segregated Knoxville, Tennessee, Hanna (Black) and Gail (white) share a crib as infants and remain close friends into their teenage years—but as they grow older, careers, marriage, and a tragic death further strain their already complicated friendship.